Bryan Appleyard

Richard Rogers

A biography

faber and faber

LONDON · BOSTON

First published in 1986 by
Faber & Faber Ltd
3 Queen Square London WC1N 3AU

Book design by Cooper Thirkell Ltd

Typeset by C R Barber (Highlands) Ltd
Fort William

Printed in Great Britain by
Butler and Tanner Ltd
Frome, Somerset

*British Library
Cataloguing in Publication Data*

Appleyard, Bryan
    Richard Rogers: architect
    1. Rogers, Richard, 1933-
    2. Architects –
    Great Britain – Biography
    720'.92'4   NA997.R6/

    ISBN 0-571-13976-0

*Library of Congress
Cataloging-in-Publication Data*

Appleyard, Brian
    Richard Rogers.
    1. Rogers, Richard George.
    2. Architects – England –
    Biography.   I. Title.
    NA997.R64A85 1986
    720'.92'4   [B]   85-31164

    ISBN 0-571-13976-0 (pbk.)

For Christena

Working in philosophy –
like working in architecture
in many respects – is really
more a working on oneself.
On one's own interpretation.
On one's way of seeing things.
(And what one expects of them.)
Ludwig Wittgenstein

I seem to be a verb.
R. Buckminster Fuller

Contents

Acknowledgements   *9*

Introduction   *11*

1   A better world . . .   *15*

2   . . . And how to build it   *59*

3   *'Ciao, vecchio!'*   *105*

4   Steel cuckoo   *159*

5   Dead albatross   *221*

6   Dat ain't building . . .   *235*

7   Dreams of function   *277*

8   A smiling public man   *325*

Notes   *349*

Index   *353*

Acknowledgements

I would like, first of all, to thank Richard and Ruth Rogers for the patience and candour with which they have retrieved the memories and provided the information which form the basis of this book.

9

In addition I would like to thank the following for their help in assembling this narrative: Laurie Abbott, Courtenay Blackmore, Michael Branch, Michael Davies, Norman Foster, Marco Goldschmied, Gordon Graham, Jan Hall, Anthony Hunt, Brian Pettifer, Peter Rice, Ab Rogers, Ben Rogers, Roo Rogers, Su Rogers, Dr and Mrs W.N. Rogers, Zad Rogers, Georgie Wolton and John Young.

I would also like to thank Tina Himsley for her help with the archives of Richard Rogers & Partners and Carol O'Kelly for her powers of organization.

Will Alsop provided me with invaluable architectural guidance and Nigel Andrew helped eradicate my literary solecisms. Finally I would like to thank John Bodley of Faber & Faber for his encouragement and advice.

Introduction

Architecture is the most unequivocal of all the arts. It imposes a quasi-permanent change on the fabric of the world. It uses real people and their real lives as 'material' to be processed by the artist. And its audience is there by obligation more often than by choice. In no other art is the imagination so frankly on trial.

This, perhaps, explains the partisan fury which often accompanies critical discussion of architecture. A great deal seems to be at stake and the artist appears to have been allowed to get away with so much. A difficult or bad novel, painting or piece of music only upsets or delights a tiny audience of volunteers; a similarly awkward building in the midst of a city assaults thousands daily.

The negative result of this is that architecture has both claimed and been blamed for too much. The pioneers of the modern movement said their art could change the world. Small wonder, then, that the inheritors of that claim should be blamed for a world that seemed to have been changed for the worse. In Britain the destruction of city centres, crudely insensitive housing developments and mindlessly constructed office blocks have all been brandished as refutations of the modernist rhetoric of the past. Architecture has retreated to a variety of fall-back positions – 'community architecture', 'post-modernism', 'brightening the place up a bit'.

But all that is to ignore the causes of the problem. The attempts of the first modernists to justify their art on a grand scale arose from an awareness that all justifications were in danger of vanishing. The stylistic carnival of the nineteenth century had run out of steam and new reasons had to be found why each and every design decision should be taken. There was not one modernist reason, there were dozens; but they all shared a ferocious, proselytizing demand for discipline. The vacuum of a godless, meaningless, truthless world threatened chaos; the only possible response was to invent new orders. This explains the moral rigour of the new architecture. To restrict its claims to the merely aesthetic would seem to compound the errors of the past – now design decisions were to be invested with values of truth, honesty and social advancement.

But these were just words. They could be applied to the buildings but the greatest could never be caught in this moral net. The finest work of Le Corbusier, Mies van der Rohe or Frank Lloyd Wright could not be explained by any ideology of pure forms, truth to materials or organic architecture. They were imaginative feats, exercises of creativity which treated the practical problems of architecture as helpful obstacles – just as a novelist might deal with time or a painter with space.

Unfortunately, once stripped of that level of creative power, the ideologies meandered on. Lesser architects took them up and the results are all around us. Modernism had not solved the problem, it had merely expressed it in the most beautiful terms that could be achieved. It meant that every subsequent architect ought to have been obliged to start from square one. Yet the ideologies implied that something had been achieved which could be passed on. There was assumed to be a modernist stylistic repertoire which could replace the classical or Gothic disciplines of the past. In fact there was nothing but freedom.

In a sense there was not even a problem. A great building may be born of a struggle to create a new cultural synthesis, but its completion will always imply a condition of rest, of the end of struggle. Problems in art, as in philosophy, are not solved, they are merely found to be no longer problems.

In this context the history of post-war British architecture becomes a vital and interesting period rather than a catalogue of disasters. Both in its theoretical work and in its experience of building, it can be seen to have been struggling with a legacy which could not simply have been ignored. It is pointless to pretend we live in the eighteenth or nineteenth centuries, even if the voices of the past frequently sound more real than those of the present. Architects are obliged to live in the shadows of great men who designed and built from nothing, inventing rationales which were, of necessity, meaningless but which helped them produce fine buildings. They are unlikely to help anybody else do the same, but the terms of the debate can be taken up by new generations who may wish to invent their own conditions of rest.

The work of Richard Rogers represents one of the finest flowerings of the British struggle to cope with the modernist inheritance. Once again the rationales of humanism, socialism and truth to materials are evoked to explain his works and, once again, they fall short. For his buildings are far from the simplifications of much of mainstream modernism – they are elaborate, busy concoctions which display and celebrate the thousands of design decisions involved. In this sense they expose the madness of a simplifying ideology, for the difficult mysteries of aesthetic choice are blatantly on display at every turn.

It is in acceptance of this complexity that this book takes the unusual course of combining three separate elements: a biography, a critique, and a defence of modern architecture. This would not seem so unusual if Rogers were a poet or a musician, but architects are more often dealt with either as professionals or technicians for the trade press or as fashion designers for the popular press. But to treat them as artists requires a degree of acceptance of complexity and contradiction which has seemed to be unpalatable both to the theorists and to the cataloguers of fashion.

Such an acceptance involves a balance of historical, personal and cultural factors. It may not finally explain any more than the ideologies did, but it will at least allow the architect's imagination its day in court.

1 A better world …

Richard George Rogers was born on 23 July 1933 at La Pratellina nursing home in Florence. The birth was late by several weeks. Two grandmothers from Trieste had been kept waiting at a nearby hotel while his mother had spent her days walking up and down the banks of the Arno in an attempt to accelerate the process. Post-natally the baby remained unable to grasp what was expected of him. He showed no desire to suck – neither his mother nor three wet-nurses succeeded in stimulating his appetite. A German nurse was engaged to try a more disciplined approach, but she too failed. Food was to continue to be a penance rather than a pleasure for Rogers until the age of fifteen; as a result he was to remain very thin throughout his childhood but he did grow precociously tall.

Italy had been under the complete control of Mussolini for eight years, although *Il Duce* had actually executed his semi-legal seizure of power in 1922. He had done so with the tacit consent of a large proportion of the liberal middle classes who felt that fascism might be a necessary temporary evil – an essential corrective for a disordered state. Left to their own devices, liberals had proved incapable of bringing the rural and urban elements of Italian society into any kind of balance. But, with the elections of 1924, the old liberals found themselves consigned to political oblivion and, from 1925, Mussolini assumed his dictatorial role as fascism attained the high point of its power in Italy.

Within this fragmented society, held together by a malign political will, the various elements of the old order began to glimpse their impending dissolution. One of these was the Anglo-Italian community, a strange legacy of the English fascination with Italy in the nineteenth century. The Rogers family were proud members of this beleaguered group. Rogers's paternal great-grandfather, William, had travelled from the north of England first to Paris, to train as a dentist, and then to Venice where he finally settled and established a practice. His surgery was in the building which now houses Harry's Bar at the end of the Calle Valleresso on the banks of the Grand Canal. Across the water was Longhena's church of Santa Maria della Salute and, beyond, Palladio's San Giorgio Maggiore. One of William's products still survives in the study of Rogers's father, William Nino. It is a small circular tin labelled 'Fragrant Tooth Powder – William N. Rogers – English Surgeon Dentist.'

The north-country dentist died young leaving 'nine or ten' children, two of whom married into the family of their mother, Eugenie Manni. One of these boys was to become the father of Ernesto Rogers, the architect, and the other of William Nino. The latter's father, Marcello, had always intended to take over the practice and was learning dentistry in Geneva at the time of his father's death. Nino, in fact, was born in Trieste and lived there for the first three years of his life. On William's death the lucrative practice, which Marcello was not ready to take over, immediately began to fold and debts to mount. The decline was halted for a time when Marcello finally set up in practice in Trieste in 1908. But he had inherited a more uncertain world and his family moved back to Switzerland at the start of the First World War, then to Nice, back to Trieste and at last to Florence in 1926.

Throughout, the family had retained its British nationality. Every Italian city in those days had its British colony and the passport represented a membership card, usually to the most select clique in town. Genuine expatriate Britons could still enjoy an astonishingly high standard of living – an army major could afford a *palazzo* – and the English style was admired and copied. So the Rogerses dwelt happily at the smart, privileged end of Italian society.

But Mussolini's confidence grew from 1925 onwards, opposed only by a disjointed agglomeration of liberals, communists and socialists. Such enclaves as the Anglo-Italian community were too fragile and too decorous for the new order of society. Perhaps in reaction to this threat, Nino's sympathies were with the left when he became a medical student in Florence in 1926, and he engaged in some mild subversion with all the confidence of one who felt his passport set him apart and endowed him with political, as well as social, privileges. In the event he did little more than pass letters around and his activities did not interfere with his social life in and around the Florentine English colony.

A friend since the age of thirteen in this milieu was Ermengarde Gairinger. Her Christian name sounds as strange to Italian ears as it does to English – she was named after the heroine of a Manzoni poem – and she is generally known in both countries as Dada. Her father had been a civil engineer and architect and latterly one of the directors of Assicurazione Generale, Italy's largest insurance company. It was also a Gairinger who was responsible for building the company's offices in the piazza della Signoria in Florence as a pastiche of a Renaissance *palazzo* – a project which, Rogers was to admit in a speech years later, resulted in the one bad building in that great square. An earlier Gairinger had combined the same professions with some pioneering social work during a cholera outbreak in Sicily. At home in Trieste the family was of some considerable importance and featured in huge murals depicting the various buildings and rebuildings of the port. One hill was dominated by the extravagant Villa Gairinger. They were, however, left with two other substantial country houses outside the town and an apartment.

Dada and Nino met again when they were eighteen and they finally married on 9 April 1932. Before the wedding Nino stipulated that his future wife must continue her education. Nino was nothing if not systematic, and indeed one of Rogers's earliest memories was the sight of his mother leaning over his father's shoulder helping him read a German medical textbook. It was an image of a husband and wife professionally as well as personally involved – an ideal that Rogers was to pursue throughout his own career.

But there were immediate problems. Mussolini's foreign

policy had been generating a series of crises and Nino had grown alarmed by Italy's increasingly risky international posturing. In contrast to this dangerous madness stood his dream of England as a haven of common sense and liberal virtues. Indeed his anglophilia knew no limits. He would always read an English rather than an Italian newspaper and he had a fondness for G.K. Chesterton's Father Brown stories. Even his systematically cultivated obsession with the Florentine Renaissance, which manifested itself in his encyclopaedic knowledge of the city's buildings and works of art, bore a close resemblance to the heartfelt enthusiasm of any English amateur. It was this dream that drove him to England soon after his marriage in order to investigate the possibilities of emigrating. His main worry was whether his Italian qualifications would be recognized in Britain by the General Medical Council. In the event there was no problem but another crisis in Italy threatened to prevent the export of any capital and he returned home. There Dada was resolutely refusing to indulge his anglophilia. Both she and her family thought Nino was over-reacting to the political climate. Their resistance, combined with the birth of Richard in the following year, led to the whole emigration issue being deferred.

Their first home was a flat in the via La Marmora with an enormous roof terrace which gave spectacular views over all of Florence as it encircled Brunelleschi's immense dome. (The legend of the young Rogers's clumsiness was to be born on this terrace when he dislodged a flower-pot which crashed to the pavement below, narrowly missing a passer-by who climbed the stairs to remonstrate with his parents.) Inside was a collection of wood and marble furniture designed by Nino's cousin Ernesto. Into this affluent and cultivated Florentine environment with connections via Dada in Trieste and via Ernesto in Milan, Richard Rogers was born. The question of England either as a haven or as a poor, grey substitute for the brightly coloured delights of the old Italy hung over the family. But, for the moment, life had returned to comparatively normal after Nino's expedition.

Nino settled down to his medical research work in Florence with the systematic diligence that was to characterize his whole career. Meanwhile his son settled into the role of the adored and only offspring of a large, wealthy upper-middle-class Italian family. His early years were divided between Florence and Trieste. It was a privileged world, but it was also a cultivated one. Dada had always been intrigued by anything new and she kept abreast of modern art with a rare open-mindedness. In later years she was always persuading her son to confront the difficult or incomprehensible in any cultural field humbly, on the basis that its significance would eventually become clear. She was also to inculcate a certain devotional curiosity about the future – her greatest wish remains to see the world in a hundred years' time. Yet there is a deep streak of pessimism in her nature which prompts her to remark frequently: 'I wish I was religious so that I could face both today and tomorrow more easily.'

Nino's cultural contribution was characteristically a little more rigorous. His research into the Renaissance, which resulted in a couple of published articles, centred on its political aspects, notably its guild-based social order and the professionalism of the government of Florence before the reign of the Medicis. His inclinations produced a curious mix of liberalism and authoritarianism, both uneasily blended with a Nietzschean belief in the primacy of individual will. 'My will is my God,' he would announce periodically and write on the endpapers of his books. He displayed considerably less patience than Dada with modern art and architecture as well as with the young Rogers. Appropriately enough for such a Spartan, determined individual, his passion was mountaineering and he went on numerous ambitious expeditions with a small, tight-knit group of friends. Among his circle was one known as Little Leo. Thirty years later Nino was to suggest that his son look up Little Leo on a trip to New York – he had become Leo Castelli, the leading art dealer in the heady world of post-Second-World-War American painting. Nino, too, was without religious faith, though the lack troubled him less than it did Dada.

It was an idyllic phase of servants, chauffeurs, doting relatives and lavish Christmases. Rogers was to remain sickly, although never to a serious degree. His continuing reluctance to eat led to furious rows, one of which prevented him going out to see Mussolini parade through Florence. But on the whole he seemed very happy. Dada, worried about his situation as an only child, cultivated friendships with other children and he displayed an early gregariousness. It was, above all, an Italian upbringing with its combination of effusive warmth and love and sudden outbreaks of firm discipline – a childhood of 'kisses and smacks', of 'discipline, love and food'.

Meanwhile, beautiful, extravagant Trieste provided him with an image of all that he should aspire to. There, Dada's family lived their splendid, aristocratic, cultivated existence in their houses in the hills surrounding the town. They seemed to incorporate all the grandeur of the Austro-Hungarian empire at its peak. From Ricardo Gairinger – Dada's father – Rogers took his Christian name, although Nino had ensured it was anglicized even on the birth certificate. But the boy was to remain somewhat perplexingly wayward to these *hautes bourgeois* and, in later years, they came to regard him as hopelessly out of control as his manners, education and army career all collapsed in disarray. He was, by common agreement, the family's black sheep.

However, those Italian days were numbered. By 1938 it had become clear to Nino that a choice had to be made if they were to stay in Italy – either he could take Italian citizenship and be called on to fight for the fascists or he could retain his passport and be interned. The pattern of the approaching conflict was now all too clear. Of course he would accept neither and once again travelled to England to make arrangements for emigration.

To his dismay he discovered that he was far from alone. The flood of the professional classes from the Continent meant that it was no longer a case simply of having one's qualifications recognized. Lists of immigrant doctors per-

21

Dada and Rogers, aged two

mitted to practise had been closed. Luckily Nino was able to call upon his original enquiry in 1932 and the promises made to him at that time were enough to allow him to be registered with the General Medical Council. His father, Marcello, was not to be so lucky. He arrived in England only to discover he had to re-train as a dentist at the age of sixty.

Also emigrating was Nino's brother, Giorgio, from whom Rogers had taken his middle name, again anglicized. Giorgio was a concert pianist whose career was blighted by crippling stage fright – an ailment shared, in less damaging form, by the rest of his family, all of whom found public speaking exceptionally difficult. Notices of performances at the Wigmore Hall were to be reasonably good but he finally succumbed to his nerves and became an academic.

The contrast between Giorgio and Nino could not have been greater. Giorgio was bisexual and devotedly artistic. He was an altogether frailer being to whom Nino's mountaineering and vaguely Nietzschean philosophies were anathema. He took an immense interest in the young Rogers, having no children of his own, and in later years encouraged his artistic aspirations. He provided a model of masculine sensitivity which was to do much to offset the stark polarity of an artistic mother and a no-nonsense careerist and austerely intellectual father.

Rogers attended some of Giorgio's concerts in London. And he grew closer to him, attracted by his somewhat softer, less rigorous approach to life than that propagated by Nino. But the connection weakened, until in the late 1970s, a couple of years before Giorgio's death, they rediscovered each other. Rogers saw him through his final illness.

By 1938 even Dada's opposition to the move to England had crumbled. Her family now accepted the impossibility of Nino and his relatives staying in Italy. It was, nevertheless, traumatic. Dada and her son arrived in England in October 1938 and discovered they had to live in a boarding-house in the strange no man's land between Bayswater and Notting Hill Gate. From marble furniture and views over Florence she had been consigned to one of the miles of anonymous stuccoed Victorian terraced houses that wander disconsolately northwards from Hyde Park. No money could be taken out of Italy legally so they had become penniless overnight. Nino had smuggled out £800, but with characteristic rigour, he refused to touch any of it, preferring to keep it intact as a cushion against the worst possible misfortunes. Thus their income derived solely from the locum work which he was doing in central London. He was also applying deliberately for all the lowest paid full-time jobs advertised, on the principle that those were the only ones for which he could reasonably hope to be in the running. From being an admirably English Italian, he had become a rather over-Italian Englishman. Knowing this, he expected few favours from a country drifting into war against the fascists, even if it was his beloved England.

But he did at least speak some English which was more than could be said for Dada and their son. The immediate remedy for Richard was to start at a local nursery school to which Nino walked him each morning painstakingly teaching him the English words for everything they passed on the way. Dada, meanwhile, had to cook – almost for the first time in her life – on the primitive stove provided in the digs. Her success was at first limited, but she proved resilient enough in the face of their new domestic situation. Heating turned out to be a constant problem and on the coldest nights they would fill their bath, which was housed in a cupboard, with hot water in an attempt to warm up their rooms.

Dada was less able to cope with the grim spectacle of immediately pre-war London. Initially impressed by the sight of Piccadilly Circus at night, she had grown miserable at the lack of any other visual interest. She took to walking down to Notting Hill and Holland Park in the hope of finding some view comparable to that from the via La Marmora or a sunset with some hint of Florence about it.

Their first English Christmas produced only a small lead submarine for Richard. Italy, with its annual tide of gifts, had

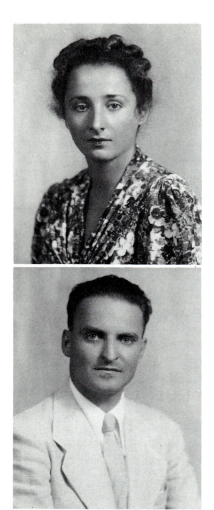

Above: Dada Rogers
Below: Nino Rogers

been incomprehensibly withdrawn from his life only to re-emerge occasionally in the ensuing months in the form of boxes of crystallized fruits which arrived intermittently until the war finally severed all communications with home. Luckily he was still young enough to treat this greyer, damper, colder world as a setting for new adventures rather than a land of purgatorial exile. He spent time in the cold spaces of air-raid shelters at Notting Hill and subsequently Surrey after they moved. Only later did Italy and the whole notion of 'abroad' become coloured with the tones of escape and liberation.

Nino's first full-time job was at a tuberculosis sanatorium at Milford near Godalming in Surrey. He was given a room at the clinic and Dada and Rogers moved in with a young couple in Godalming itself. Leaving London provided some visual relief for the sensitive Dada but this was offset by the enforced separation from her husband. The house was about an hour's walk from the clinic and, once her son was asleep, Dada used to hike across the fields to meet her husband.

They had found another nursery school, at which Rogers set the style for the rest of his academic career by persuading all the pupils to eat some berries which he assured them, everybody ate in Italy. They were poisonous and, though the dosages were too small to do any damage, the escapade produced a brief panic among his teachers.

But Dada was growing discontented with the lack of anything to fill her time. Nino's parents had managed to move in nearby and, with them available to babysit, she persuaded Nino to find her some kind of work at the sanatorium. He agreed that she could help the nurses on the condition that she did not handle infected bedding. She started work but this condition proved impossible to fulfil – she could hardly set herself apart from the nurses by turning down half the work-load. Soon she was clearing bloodstained sheets along with everybody else. She contracted TB; it was the final, depressing climax to Dada's first encounter with England.

For her cure she went home. This was still just possible in

March 1940 as Italy had not yet entered the war. Rogers, now nearly seven, had lost his homeland, his language and his mother in rapid succession.

Dada travelled to Milan on the Orient Express and was met by her family. She still remembers fondly the first sound of an Italian voice when the train made an overnight stop and the words *'Felice notte'* drifted up from the platform. She was sent to a sanatorium in northern Italy where the doctors insisted on complete rest for several months. Dada was alarmed at the length of time involved as Italy was clearly heading for war and she feared she would be unable to return to England which, for all its shortcomings, at least contained her husband and son. On dubious authority the doctors assured her all would be well and she was still there when Mussolini declared war on an already defeated France on 10 June 1940.

She finally left the sanatorium in October with no money but the 1,500 lire her father had surreptitiously thrust up her sleeve, and embarked on a prodigious journey which was to foreshadow the spectacular travels of her son after the war. Her first stop was Geneva where she stayed for some weeks with friends while making elaborate plans for the rest of her trip with the British consulate. From there she travelled through the South of France to Spain and finally to Portugal. She clutched the plates of her chest X-rays all the way to prove that she had genuinely been ill and that her intention was no more sinister than to return to her family. She made it back to England in November.

For Rogers it would have been a rapturous return except that, just as his mother was leaving Italy, he had embarked on the most traumatic phase of his early life. In September 1940 he became a boarder at Kingswood House School in Epsom. This was accommodated in a red-brick Victorian house set at an angle to the road on Epsom's West Hill. It stands on the brow of the hill and looks down to Epsom Common about a quarter of a mile away. The town centre is about the same distance in the other direction. He could have been a day boy, but his father's fears about TB infection as

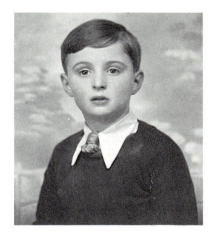

Rogers photographed
in about 1940

well as the absence of his mother prompted him to send Rogers away as a boarder for the time being. Meanwhile Nino had taken a job at Epsom District Hospital which, it was assumed, would need his services as a physician for war casualties more than Milford would need them for TB victims. The family moved to Epsom, first to hospital accommodation and later to a tiny flat in South Street, set in a small 1930s built parade above a pet shop and consisting of a bedroom, living-room and dining-room.

So Rogers was obliged to board at a school only a short walk from his home. He had been made aware of the sad social stigma that attached to TB in those days. It was a misfortune of which he could never speak, leaving him with the impression of something shameful to be concealed within his family. The tendency of the disease to be hereditary, as well as its highly infectious quality, could damage job prospects and generally produce all the reactions of the English middle class to any 'social disease'.

Kingswood was an ominously traditional English school, ill-equipped to deal with this faintly exotic boy who was struggling to cope with the combined pressures of the previous two years. He had been used to being controlled at home in the form of the usual see-saw of kisses and smacks but Kingswood was utterly incomprehensible to him from the first. Nothing had prepared him for the arbitrary discipline he was to face and his failure to adjust was to plague him for the rest of his childhood and youth. It produced in him a predictable anti-authoritarian bias, but one which he somehow had to unite with the need for control and rigour which he had inherited from Nino. For the moment, however, rules were simply random outrages applied at whim.

On his first night at Kingswood he constructed a bed for his teddy bear from school towels and the next day he was beaten for stealing them. He took to crying for entire nights to be comforted only by a sympathetic headmaster's wife who stroked his head for hours. The beatings continued and were combined with an appalling degree of alienation from his peers. He was not helped in this by being not only foreign but also Italian, a nationality which generated little sympathy in the children of the Epsom middle class. Indeed so alienated was he that they did not even bother with a nickname – his brother in later years was known in his schooldays as Spaggers, but that was after the end of the war.

There seemed, however, to be something more. Academically he was progressing alarmingly slowly. He could not keep up with his class in reading and writing and he was unable to learn anything by heart. A variety of explanations were put forward: they ranged from the difficult time he had endured, from the most sympathetic observers, to his bone idleness, from the least.

The pressure of school finally produced what appears to have been a kind of nervous breakdown. Rogers almost ceased to function. One day he was interrogated about the accusations of another boy that Rogers had been one of a number of bullies. Such was his state of mind by this stage that his short-term memory had vanished completely. His answer to the charges was simply that he could not remember what he had been doing half an hour before. He was found guilty and sentenced to the school's standard punishment for bullying – being obliged to fight the boxing champion. At that time it was a boy called Sears who duly battered Rogers around the ring.

At the culmination of this hallucinatory phase he found himself standing on the roof of the school one night trying to force himself to jump. He had despaired of surviving the anguish caused him by the place.

For the rest of his time at Kingswood – he was there until June 1946, although he ceased to be a boarder after the first eighteen months – he remained one of the school's most disastrous pupils. He barely began to read until the age of eleven and, almost alone among the middle-class pupils, he was assumed to be incapable of passing the common-entrance examination which would win him a place at a public school. In particular his inability to memorize left him out of step with the standard method of primary-school teaching of the day. His parents were baffled and upset – their son was not displaying the qualities which could reasonably be expected of a scion of the Gairingers and the Rogerses. At one point they went so far as to have his IQ tested at the Tavistock Clinic and were relieved to discover it was well above average.

Rogers's state of mind at the time, however, was best revealed when he answered yes to a psychiatrist at the Tavistock who asked him if he wanted to stay at Kingswood. He was afraid to say no because of the alternative horrors which might lie in store.

Both Dada and Nino shared an unshakable faith that there was nothing really wrong with the boy. They recognized the school's shortcomings but at the time there seemed to be no alternative. Besides, Nino was determined his son would master the English system. If anything, this made discipline at home tougher than at school. He was constantly obliged to take on extra academic work from special tutors in a desperate attempt to push him into catching up with the other boys. Also Nino provided no pocket money and thereby turned Rogers into a fairly daring thief, an occupation which added to his problems with the Kingswood authorities.

Relief and a degree of excitement were provided by occasional trips to London to visit Marcello and his wife, Lina. While Marcello had been fighting his way through dental school at the age of sixty, Lina had taken to making small cloth flowers which she sold to Dickins & Jones and any other department stores which would buy them. Giorgio was also in town and would play Chopin and Schubert to Rogers to shake him out of his frequent depressions.

London also provided the thrill of air-raids and the nightly dashes down to the shelters. The young Rogers would have hated to have missed the blitz.

In addition he developed the habit of walking off his depressions. This began when he was a boarder at Epsom: Nino would visit him at weekends and take him on walks over to Epsom Downs – after which he had to be forcibly dragged back to school. It was a habit that has continued throughout his life, most usefully as a means of ordering his thoughts at times of crisis.

Nowadays Rogers's educational problem would be diagnosed at once as dyslexia, a learning disability which can take a variety of forms. All his children suffer from it with varying levels of severity and his entire career has been a struggle with the massive disadvantages which it inflicts upon its victims. He can still memorize nothing unless it is connected to some practical end – he cannot even remember the Lord's Prayer, in spite of having recited it on almost every one of his school-days. His reading is fine though he becomes stumbling and awkward if asked to read aloud. His handwriting requires close familiarity before it is easily legible and the composition of formal, ordered prose in the smallest quantities can take him hours and dozens of rewrites. The English language has remained slightly alien territory to him, yet he lost his fluency in Italian during those first years in Surrey. He seems never to have had a mother tongue.

Kingswood aside, however, Rogers was beginning to find a role, for in spite of his difficulties he had retained the gregari-ousness and a certain social confidence conferred on him by his early years in Florence. He had also inherited his father's physical courage. At Kingswood this was enough to make him a success in the school Scouts. And, outside the inward-looking atmosphere of the school, his foreignness was attrac-tive, a mysterious exoticism which made him a desirable friend. One mother spotted him in the street, immediately introduced her somewhat lonely son to him and suggested they become friends. This was Michael Branch who, unlike the Kingswood bullies, was overwhelmed by Rogers, whose personality seemed to act like a magnet on the wilder misfit sons of the Epsom bourgeoisie. His courage, and the combin-ation of his height with sudden outbursts of furious temper – generally attributed to his Italian blood – gradually earned him enough respect to cancel out the victimized isolation he suffered at Kingswood. For Branch, an altogether frailer figure, he was a protective hero. Rogers responded to his new range of friends by developing fierce personal loyalties and playing to the hilt the part of the avenging angel. He was fearless and rash, devoid of the timid inhibition inherited by even the wildest of Epsom youth.

The Gang was formed around 'Roj'. It was not explicitly led by him, but he was unquestionably its central character. The core membership was about eight and the floating total came to eighteen or twenty including all the various associates. The complete failure of academic life to absorb him had left Rogers with a partly unengaged intelligence, a habitually outgoing character and a subversive courage, all waiting to be applied in other directions. He began to adopt the role of an outlaw around Epsom: making contact with locally stationed Canadian soldiers in order to collect cigarette cards with pictures of bombers and tanks; lurking in the vast cellars and service areas beneath Epsom Hospital – he was later to call these places 'my Italy'; and conducting extensive research into the town's sewers. This last project earned him yet another beating from his teachers who were terrified he would bring typhoid into the school. He had become like a character from Richmal Crompton's 'William' books – his favourite reading matter at the time – forever dirty and forever in trouble. He became an inveterate builder of camps and dens which he would decorate spectacularly with chandeliers stolen from the house then occupied by the Canadians. Fragments of these chandeliers came to be used as the Gang's currency.

One of the Gang's favourite games of that time was known as Free Falling. This involved several gang members climbing to the top of a tree. From there it was a race to reach the ground. Roj was the undisputed champion. He perfected his technique to the point where he could all but perform a single, uninterrupted fall to the earth. The only braking he required was a few featherlight touches on passing branches to slow his descent.

The Gang, with several changes of personnel, persisted

until Rogers started his National Service at the age of eighteen. During the Kingswood years and the rest of his schooldays it seems to have provided a world in which he found an identity resolutely denied him by the education system into which he had been thrown, for the problems of his life until then had made him independent but they had never dented his essential need of the company and partnership of others. An inner ring of six to eight friends, and later colleagues, has remained a necessity to him throughout his life. The world of the Gang was defined by childish subversion and adventure which thrilled at the nearby anarchy of the war – Rogers used to chase doodlebugs on his bike – in which he evolved an acute sense of 'real' justice in opposition to the arbitrary persecution he suffered at school. For, in spite of the academic problems, his mother's support and love still preserved a considerable degree of self-confidence, while his father provided the physical courage and belief in the virtues of self-help which carried him through. From the moment he came in contact with them, Branch was aware of the self-contained, self-sustaining nature of the Rogers household. They seemed, somehow, on a different plane.

But, although the Gang was to survive in one form or another, its style was to change when Rogers found his most enduring escape from unwanted discipline. He discovered girls and for no man can the discovery have come as a more undilutedly pleasant surprise.

In his last year at Kingswood he took up with Julie Tree, a sixteen-year-old local girl with black hair and startling green eyes. This was in 1946 and the family had once again been dislocated. Nino had been called up just before the end of the war to serve in the Royal Army Medical Corps in India and subsequently Manchester. Richard's only sibling, Peter, was born in 1946 and Julie helped out by providing a babysitting service for Dada. The new child had little noticeable effect on Rogers compared with the joyful turmoil induced by his discovery of Julie.

Dada and Nino's liberality was surprisingly extensive and,

even though Rogers was only thirteen, they had no objection to him taking girls home. It was better, argued Nino with characteristically tough pragmatism, than forcing them to go behind a hedge somewhere. In fact Rogers was initially too nervous about the whole thing but, by the age of fourteen he was Julie's lover. Such was Rogers's complete immersion in the phenomenon of Julie Tree that Branch felt Roj had been lost for ever.

Julie and Rogers would spend evenings together in the South Street dining-room, which he used as a bedroom, with the full blessing of his parents. The arrangement continued over the next two years in which he was entirely faithful to Julie. Indeed, such was his fidelity, that his uncle, Giorgio, was eventually to demand impatiently of him why he had not found other girlfriends. Subsequently he did and with them the evenings extended into whole nights once the family had moved into its first house. Rogers now believes this indulgence freed him from the whole set of traumas normally associated with adolescent sexuality and left him with a lifelong inability to understand dirty jokes. For his contemporaries at Epsom it contributed to the general sense of outrageousness in the Continental milieu from which he sprang.

But the new-found land of womankind and his improving social abilities had no impact on his academic career and by 1946 Rogers had been dismissed by his teachers as a more or less hopeless case. He left in June 1946 to go to a crammer in Sutton in a final bid to get through common entrance. Dada and Nino never despaired of the possibility of some kind of academic success and, in spite of the dissident life of the Gang, he was invariably known as a boy who laboured under a fierce regime of additional work. It was also accepted that, whatever the project in hand, he had to be home every night for dinner at eight – a time sacred in an Italian household. There mother and father would speak Italian but Rogers would answer in English. Nino had always been mistrustful of the idea of a bilingual child – he believed it caused confusion and a failure to progress far in either language. As a result Rogers's knowledge of Italian had, by now, more or less evaporated.

The crammer – known as Downs Lodge – was a curious institution with very few pupils and classes of only four or five boys. They were largely misfits and drop-outs from the school system as well as foreigners who, like Rogers, had simply failed to grasp what English education was all about. The idea was to provide a headlong rush at common entrance as well as a certain amount of non-academic stimulation.

For Rogers, at least, it worked. Possibly at first it was simply the relief of being released from Kingswood where every relationship had been tainted by his academic failures. But, in addition, he discovered to his amazement that he was not overwhelmingly disadvantaged. Others were even worse than himself and his main teacher – a defrocked priest – had the air of an outcast, a role which Rogers himself had grown accustomed to playing. This teacher was persuasively pragmatic – it doesn't matter, he would argue, how you hit the damn ball as long as it gets there. Rogers took to the notion that there was no stylistic absolute and discovered he could actually do things as long as he was left to his own devices to evolve his own rules and techniques. Sport became a liberation and at Downs Lodge he was made captain of everything. Miraculously he began to improve academically – his final report in December 1947 consisted of a series of delighted and startled comments about 'progress' and 'improvement'.

He was finally pushed through common entrance and started at St John's School, Leatherhead, in January 1948. St John's is a vast, rambling, dubiously Gothic pile on the Epsom Road. It is a Church of England school which then specialized in producing candidates for the priesthood and which had a fairly traditional idea of discipline, not dissimilar to that of Kingswood. Its hearty, healthy brew of sport, hard work and bracing spirituality broadly categorized the sort of artistic sensitivity that Rogers was absorbing from Dada as something to do with homosexuality. The Sutton crammer had been a great leap forward, but St John's nearly sent Rogers back to square one.

At first it was not too bad. His new confidence in alternative techniques meant that he achieved a sporting reputation. He could hit a ball further than any of his contemporaries and he was at one point school boxing champion, a qualification which was to come in handy in later life. He ran so well that he would often take both the first and last stages in relay races.

But the strange ritual of English public-school life with its enslavement and torture awoke once more Rogers's sense of injustice. He resisted the traditional initiation ceremonies of being kicked and pelted with books. His physical strength meant his resistance was successful, but it was to earn him almost a schoolful of enemies. Unconsciously he began to slip back into the role of outlaw and gradually the academic problems returned to plague him. Once more his teachers began to write him off. His first reports from St John's express cautious hopes for improvement mingled with a few reservations about his spelling and untidiness. But, by the Easter term of 1950, the headmaster was concluding simply: 'A very weak candidate, I fear.' Even in history, a subject in which he had initially been top of his class, he declined to 'still below average but he is doing his best' though even that report was untypically favourable. At one point the careers master was driven to advise his parents that the best that Rogers could achieve would be a job as a policeman in South Africa. Almost from the beginning everyone felt he had no chance of going to university. Once again, his life fell into three irrevocably separate parts: school, home, and the Gang with only the last two being remotely compatible.

During term-time he was separated from Michael Branch but he had developed the habit of writing him long, rambling narratives about the Gang's adventures in his absence. In December 1949 he wrote from St John's:

Here are some of the news from home. We have a gang meeting every Saturday usualy at Tabbys, I turn up at about 9.30 & go home at about 11. About a month ago Tabby Louis & me raided

Jenafor hous. We made a good job of it pulling up their tennis posts & net & winding it round their french windows. We found that the sundials came to peaces so we carried them into the middle of the tennis lawn piece by peace and built them up side down. Tabby put a minature bird on the steps of the french window, we let two of my firworks off in front of Robins and Jenafor's window. They didn't seem to make much difference. We unhooked the swing & made their garden couch look as though a wirlwind had hit it; the coushins were up side down, a small garden table on its' side etc. When we had climbed over the stone wall into their garden from the RAC it had half collapsed, and the garden was rather trodden underfoot as you can imagin. We had just finished our operations when the french window opened & out stepped Jenafor's father with his dog ... (illegible) ... the mother had seen us crossing ... (illegible). We were more or least in the open so we pelted like hell into a spiney, broke through some small trees which cut a corner of the garden off. Then the dog came out. Boy! Were we trapped the trees litrally cut off a corner of the garden & at the back of us was a 4 ft garden fence with 10 ft of wire netting stuck on top, at the front os us was the open lawn with the dog sniffing round and Dad not daring to come out was looking from the french windows right across the lawn at us. We prayed it would rain and hoped the dog would not find us. Louis suggest a rush but I was against it & I beleive Tabby agreed with me. Then it started to rain & the dog was called in, talk about relief.'

37

The same letter goes on to describe another escapade in which Tabby and Roj were discovered coming out of the back of an empty house: 'The owner gave chase & we had the greatest of difficulties in escaping from being brough to the police.'

At St John's this outlaw was to come into contact with the apotheosis of the entire system of arbitrary discipline which had so far succeeded only in grinding him down – the Army Cadet Corps. Physically Rogers was well suited to the curious rituals involved in this process, which supposedly hardened and prepared the boys for anything life might subsequently throw at them. Temperamentally, however, it was hopeless. He was outraged at the discipline and just fearless enough to be pushed into doing something about it. His Italian blood finally got the better of him and his relations with the Corps exploded when, in a fit of irritation with another boy, he declined to carry the bren-gun while on exercise. Under the authority of the captain, a chemistry master, some sort of court martial proceedings were instituted and the issue became a *cause célèbre* for the entire school. Rumours were flying that the Ministry of War was to be brought in, presumably inspired by similar over-reactions from authority in Terence Rattigan's play *The Winslow Boy*, which had recently been filmed. In the event a friendly housemaster put an end to the whole affair, but not before Rogers had been ostracized by the entire school and banned from games. In the midst of the despair of this period Rogers was reduced to cutting one of his wrists – though not in a potentially fatal spot – in order to avoid further contact with the military.

But the persecution continued – Rogers's combination of courage, cockiness and classroom incompetence apparently proving unpalatable to masters and boys alike. Once again he was flung into the boxing ring with an older boy. This time he was called Tonks and was Rogers's senior by four years. Once again, he was battered about the ring. Such rituals were much approved of by a new school governor – Field Marshal Montgomery. But this beating was too much even for Monty who told Rogers after the bout: 'You did your best, but you were not good enough.'

Meanwhile the housemaster who had extricated Rogers before was forced to come to the rescue again. The school prefects were about to administer *en masse* a beating to Rogers for running across a section of grass normally reserved only for their use. He had been a stage manager for the school play and, with the audience waiting in the auditorium, had felt justified in taking a short-cut across the lawn to pick up some forgotten equipment. The prefects disagreed and the next night he entered the dormitory to find them lined up with their canes. He leapt out of the first-floor window before they could make a move, the second occasion on which jumping to freedom had occurred to him. He had clearly developed an easy and almost affectionate relationship with great heights, an echo of Dada's fondness for views and the terrace in Florence, though this time it was only from the first floor and he was able to hide out until he could find his housemaster (who was able to overrule the prefects on the grounds that the beating had somehow been unconstitutional).

But the difference between jumping to his death and jumping to escape and live again was a significant one. By now Rogers was a seasoned survivor and the life of the Gang was flourishing. His social abilities were far in advance of anything that might be suggested by his performance at school and they were beginning to be combined with an innocently left-wing ideology derived from the debates he both heard and took part in with his parents. (This lent a certain idealism to the raids he led on Epsom Conservative Club dances with Michael Branch, although the real motive was an overwhelming ambition to prise the Tory girls away from the Tory men. Incredibly he usually succeeded, presumably owing to a certain sexual *savoir-faire* far in advance of his years.) At home he was accustomed to a running socio-political debate in Italian which he answered, as usual, in English.

Encouraged by Dada he was beginning to read voraciously. When they moved into South Street they had discovered complete sets of Dickens and Mark Twain bound in red, all of which he consumed. Books became an obsessive interest. (He seemed to devour them – occasionally over-enthusiastically as when he was punished for damaging school books.) And he found a curious affinity with Chaucer. It turned out to be one area of scholarship in which he was able to compete – he seemed to understand Middle English better than he did modern. It suggested a private language denied to others, parallel, in some ways, to the private vocabulary he had developed with the members of the Gang.

But the emphasis in the family debates, particularly from Nino, was always on a sense of social justice, of political awareness which, having been transplanted from the rich soil of opposition and dissent in Italy, had taken root in the thinner loam of post-war reconstruction in England. Nino's politics were, however, a good deal tougher than the prevailing version of British socialism. He had read Plato's *Republic* to Rogers at an early age to demonstrate the kind of hardened practicality which he advocated. The debates fed Rogers's own sense of burning injustice at his treatment at school and in the cadet corps and, to a degree, must have validated his attempts at subversion. When, for example, a ruling was made that no boy could see his girlfriend during term-time without permission from his housemaster – a ruling that included non-boarders like Rogers – he organized vast queues of boys outside the masters' studies to ask permission. The success of this particular project had the practical result of eliminating a potential barrier to his evenings with Julie Tree.

By now it was clear that Rogers had found a somewhat odd niche for himself in English life. He was conversationally adept and seemed more able to get on with parents than with children. He was mature and confident for his age, presumably in part because he had the rare qualification of a long-standing love affair to his credit. But in a wider sense he was also finding a public role he could adopt which would tie together the various elements of his life.

Part of this role was directly political arising from the family debates, but also from a curious friendship he formed with a member of the Labour cabinet of the day, James Chuter Ede. Chuter Ede lived in East Street, Epsom, and was the MP for South Shields. During the years of the war-time coalition he had been Parliamentary Secretary to the Board of Education and he became Home Secretary after the Labour victory in 1945, a post he held until October 1951. During that period he was to change his mind publicly and memorably on the subject of capital punishment. His wife, Lillian, (who died in 1948) had come under Nino's care. A strange, silent relationship was struck up between Rogers and, at first, the couple though later, the widower. Chuter Ede would take him out for the day in his sixteen-foot motor launch – the *Brown Duck* – which he kept moored at Hampton. Rogers would return home in the evening after these outings somewhat puzzled by his own behaviour – he had often spoken no more than five words during the entire day. For the childless Chuter Ede it was clearly his presence alone that was enough. He supplied Rogers with a steady stream of books on birds, animals and education.

But with Rogers's parents the Home Secretary did talk – usually about education, a shared obsession, and about the need for reform of the entire British system. It was a relationship that moved Rogers partly because of the sheer eminence of the man. But there was also the fact that he was a man in a position of immense authority who, nevertheless, showed every inclination radically to change the society in which he lived – the same English society which seemed to have been designed specifically to persecute the young Rogers. 'He was the most humble man I have ever known,' recalled Rogers.

A letter written by Rogers to Chuter Ede in December 1949 sounds like a dutiful note written at the insistence of his parents, but it does evoke the strange, calm formality of the relationship:

It was very kind of you to remember me and give me such a beautiful bird book. I am enjoying school much more now and I managed to get my colts colours on the last day before becoming a senior. School certificate is looming over the horizon and I don't like the look of it. We had four exams at the end of the term a sort of mock school certificate. I failed badly in Latin, not quite so badly in French and got a credit in English and history.

The improved spelling suggests Nino watched over this letter to the Home Secretary – it was, nevertheless, badly blotted.

So, in spite of the intellectual desert of his school life, the academic under-performer was subjected to heady levels of debate at home and, from Dada, to a fairly consistent cultural bombardment. She took him to London for contemporary music concerts, always reminding him that he should not be afraid of being baffled at first. He attended the Picasso and Matisse exhibition at the Victoria and Albert Museum in 1945, an event which symbolically reopened British doors to Continental culture after the war. It remained purely symbolic as the paintings drew as much fire as they ever did from an irate British public – Evelyn Waugh gravely assured readers of *The Times* that admirers of Picasso were not necessarily, in other respects, stupid, and Roger Marvell lugubriously explained to readers of the *New Statesman* that, 'The painful truth is that we live in an incomparably specialised age. . . .'[1]

In such a climate the Rogerses would have delighted in admiring Picasso and Matisse and all that they stood for – most obviously, vivid colours in a grey land, but also the outrageously new against the grimly disciplined old.

But the most important reinforcement of this burgeoning 'Continental' identity was the travelling. As soon as the war was over he began to travel to Italy every year – the first trip, in 1945, took three days because of the elaborate combination of trains and buses which was needed to journey through the wreckage of Europe. At first he was accompanied by Dada, who took him to see his grandparents in Trieste and, in Milan, Ernesto, who had by now become the conscience of modern Italian architecture. One trip included Nino, who showed him over his beloved Florence, explained the benefits of a state run not by a prince but by the intelligentsia and eulogized the cool, clear, balanced light of Brunelleschi's architecture and the wonders of Masaccio's frescoes. The flowing darknesses of Michelangelo were to continue to provide Rogers with problems into later life.

Once he was old enough, he travelled alone. His parents strictly declined to finance these expeditions, though Dada invariably provided vast food rations. But he earned enough money in the school holidays to get by and besides, he became a confident hitch-hiker, particularly fond of sleeping out at night and adept at surviving in the European countryside while virtually penniless. The technique on rainy nights was to break into convenient barns. Once he had made it to Trieste his grandfather could always be relied upon for a subsidy, even if the aristocratic Gairingers remained dismayed by the appearances of the black sheep.

His relations provided him with an impressive background

Rogers' paternal grandparents, Marcello and
Lina, in Venice

Grandfather,
Ricardo Gairinger

Maternal grandmother,
Carla Gairinger

– there were his wealthy grandparents and the hugely influential intellectual, Ernesto, with his architectural practice and his journalism. But the effect on Rogers at this stage was a rather general one. He was not influenced in his view of what he should do – he had no such view – nor did he feel he wanted to return permanently to Italy. For one thing what remained of his spoken Italian was far from good and, for another, the effort to be English, to find some way of fitting in, was not to be abandoned. Besides, Nino was as determinedly English as ever. Yet the sense that he came from an immensely gifted family accustomed to being at the heart of artistic and economic developments must have been reinforced if only subconsciously.

The travelling also gave him a European sensibility entirely lacking in his contemporaries. One effect of the war had been to sever completely Britain's cultural ties with Europe and the re-emergence of Continental phenomena like existentialism was observed with horrified fascination by the English intelligentsia. Yet, for the more sensitive, there was a suspicion that the loss of Europe might be a more serious matter than simply the removal of the need to cope with exotic philosophies.

'To imagine Europe – that is the hardest thing we have to do,' wrote V.S. Pritchett. 'The picture comes to us in fragments and to piece it together and above all hold it in the mind is like trying to hold a dissolving dream and to preserve it from the obstinate platitude of our waking life.'[2]

Dada's cultural education programme did not betray the same English uncertainty. It continued in Italy with concerts, opera and art galleries, but in Italy, unlike in London, they were not doing something different from everyone else. There they were living in a cultivated community which did such things as a matter of course. From the moment he returned Rogers felt at home in Italy – it provided him with a different world to set in his imagination against St John's, Epsom and the Gang. For him the dissolving dream was a rediscovered harmonious world in which his disorderly nature was tolerated, indeed admired – though not by the Gairingers.

He finished at St John's in June 1951, with a degree of order having been retrieved from the academic mess. He had assembled a reasonable handful of qualifications – though at a rather later age than most of his contemporaries – but it remained clear that any kind of further education was out of the question. The only hint of a possible career came from his family who felt that the ancestral profession of dentistry might prove less demanding than, for example, medicine. He even went so far as to visit the London School of Dentistry with Marcello. But he was told: 'You have no hope, Mr Rogers, you do not have even the beginnings of the necessary academic qualifications.'

By this stage Rogers's lack of prospects was beginning to be a serious embarrassment. Nino had become a consultant at St Helier Hospital, Carshalton, and the family fortunes were beginning to rise to something like their pre-war level. They had even bought their first house. Dada had originally insisted on something modern, but there was nothing available in the Surrey suburbs, so they settled for 130, Northey Avenue, Cheam, a typical piece of 1930s English housing with its wide, grand frontage and white cement-rendered walls. It was a huge leap up the suburban ladder for the family and, for Rogers, its size made it a useful meeting-place for his inner ring of friends. Nevertheless they needed an extension built and Ernesto was contacted in Milan to produce a design. He declined to take on such long-range work, but recommended instead an English architect who came up with a flat-roofed wing to the house with a suitably modernistic ribbon window to the front and a rather daring 'Scandinavian' – i.e. large – window to the rear. It all attracted a degree of local attention.

But Rogers's first direct experience of modern architecture did not 'take'. His second, however, seems to have kindled some small and incompletely recognized flame. This was his visit to the Festival of Britain whose centre was the strange cluster of buildings which sprang up on the South Bank of the

Thames in 1951.

The Festival had been planned for the centenary year of the great Crystal Palace exhibition six years after the end of the war. Those years had seen a combination of austerity and social innovation under a Labour government which was destined to prove unable to deliver enough immediate economic benefits to match its long-promised restructuring of society. Yet it had come to power by defeating Churchill, an apparently invincible war leader, and it did so because the euphoria and optimism arising from the war were different from that of 1918. This time it was not a case of a militarily powerful Britain claiming its rightful victory, it was a case of an unpleasant task successfully completed. Britain itself was felt to be deeply flawed and badly in need of radical change. There was a sense that the old ruling class had finally had its day – even high-ranking army officers had registered their postal votes for Labour.

'It was not a vote about queues or housing, but a vote of censure on Munich and Spain and Abyssinia,' wrote Cyril Connolly of the election,[3] adding: 'Talk of it as a vote against the religion of money and the millionaire hoodlums.'

With an empire in decline and a sure knowledge, among intellectuals at least, that militarily and economically Europe as a whole had been the real loser of the war, the sub-text of the Festival was that a new wholly modern, wholly egalitarian world was to be born. It became the first official adoption of modern architecture in Britain. There had been a few modern buildings before the Second World War but they had remained on the fringes of taste. During the war modern rebuilding plans were submitted to compete with staunch Beaux-Arts schemes[4] and they had some impact on the final solutions adopted, but it was not until the Festival that modernism was advertised as part of the whole utopian package.

All the buildings except the Royal Festival Hall were temporary so a certain tendency towards the fantastic was encouraged, with Powell & Moya's Skylon and Ralph Tubbs's

Dome of Discovery. But in the event, only the RFH, a product of the alternately demonic and inspired London County
Council architects' department, rose above the generally
worthy mediocrity of the buildings as a whole. The layout,
however, with its emphasis on the picturesque rather than the
rationalist traditions of modernist thinking, was a revelation.
It offered a loose informality of urban style which seemed
profoundly foreign to the working class who flocked there
from the rows of Victorian terraces.

It was that contrast between the dull, shabby cloth-capped
English and the shimmering futuristic Festival that perhaps
struck the deepest chord in Rogers. People could bounce their
radio messages off the moon at the Festival, but back at home
austerity was still biting and slums covered the nation. For
Rogers it symbolized the contrast between his pre-war dream
and post-war realization: a cultivated, informal, wealthy
Italy and the dark, poor, grey of England with its passion for
arbitrary discipline. In fact the Festival had come at a time
when both the social reforms of the post-war years had run
aground and ideas of modern architecture were beginning to
be seriously questioned. The aesthetic reconsiderations which
were to mark the 1950s and to define the whole of Rogers's
architectural education were already under way. The genial
conceits on the South Bank were soon to be rejected as
sentimental, effeminate and trivial – to be seen as a betrayal.[5]

For the moment, however, Rogers's only sure future was
National Service. Soon after leaving St John's, he decided to
take his mind off that prospect with one last trip before the
army removed all such possibilities for two years. He had a
lengthy list of Italian relatives to visit including Dario Bartolini, also dyslexic and also an architect, who was to become a
founder member of the avant-garde Archizoom practice; his
Aunt Lucia, known as Chichi; Eugenio Gairinger and his wife,
Lida, a psychoanalyst, who was later to fill him with enthusiasm for Greek architecture; and finally Carlo Bartolini,
an academic, and Dario's brother.

With a large member of the Gang – he was known as Big

John, weighed 16 stones and was 6 feet 3 inches tall – he hitch-hiked to Venice where they stayed at the youth hostel on the Lido. They had teamed up with some Dutch students and were making one of many trips on a *vaporetto* when Rogers's fat friend inadvertently trod on the toe of a Venetian butcher. A riot ensued in which Rogers dimly remembers a great deal of pushing and shoving and the distinct sense that he was escorting the opposing side off the boat to be picked up by the police who were waiting on the shore. In fact the reverse was the case and Rogers and his friends were arrested. The police, however, were reassuringly offhand. They persuaded Rogers to sign something which seemed entirely harmless and asked him to return the next day to pick up his passport. Happily convinced the entire incident was in the past, he did as he was told and was promptly arrested again and thrown into a cell on unspecifed charges with a collection of prostitutes and smugglers. An appearance before a magistrate did little to clear up the matter and he was led through the streets in manacles in a line of prisoners to be taken to an island in the lagoon where he was put in solitary confinement in a highly dangerous and squalid gaol. Within hours he began to feel he was going mad. There was nothing to read and he lost track of time. He remembers watching one man of eighty starving to death because he had no teeth and the guards would give him only hard bread to eat. His sole human contact was with an American murderer who came into his cell to remove the pot. This man had been imprisoned after he had picked up a couple of Italian girls, left them briefly to buy some food and returned to find them annexed by two Italian men. He had taken out a gun and opened fire. In prison he had calmed down a little and taken a university degree. He knew the system well enough eventually to persuade an examining magistrate to look into Rogers's case. It transpired that he was charged with knocking out the butcher's teeth and sexually assaulting his wife – the latter accusation at least, as Rogers pointed out, was hardly credible in the midst of a riot on a *vaporetto*. In true Italian fashion it turned out that the magistrate's father worked for Rogers's grandfather, bail was arranged and he was quietly advised to flee. He left the prison with a prostitute who took him around 'her' Venice and looked after him for a few days, until he left for Trieste, a city then subject to no national government. Ultimately a full pardon was organized.

Rogers had spent his eighteenth birthday in prison as a suitable climax to his youthful years of subversion. He entered the army in November 1951 in a reasonably optimistic frame of mind. The military, after all, seemed to offer possibilities for somebody possessed of physical courage and stamina as well as the hope of adventure. In the event he was rapidly disillusioned. The morning inspections where non-existent dust was discovered by the sergeants, the cleaning of floors with boot polish because of the refusal to give recruits the proper cleaning materials, the need to shake dying leaves off the trees in autumn in case any fell on a visiting general, and the relentless, institutionalized bullying filled him with rage. Nevertheless, his physical prowess and a certain stubborn pride kept him going. His initial period was taken up by a course designed to find officer material – there were many drop-outs but Rogers lasted to the end. One reason for his survival was that he realized that the sergeant – who had suggested the recruits come to him with their troubles – was the filter for officer material. Those who appealed to him vanished from the course. Rogers did not believe in asking anybody in authority for help.

So he stayed the course but he had been rumbled long before. He was identified as a potential anarchist rather than an officer and was marked down as a private for the duration. The remainder of his first year was given to menial tasks and a half-hearted attempt to train him as a clerk which foundered on his dyslexic inability to master a typewriter keyboard. A sympathetic and bored sergeant allowed him to cheat his way through a test which put him on record as being a competent typist, but he was exposed as soon as he was confronted with real work. The nadir of this phase was reached with employment in the kitchens which involved slaving in heat and darkness for twelve-hour shifts. This usually meant that it was dark when he started work and dark when he finished. Characteristically he hatched a plot with fellow conscripts to arrange cover for the weekends to allow them to leave the barracks. Equally characteristically, Rogers was caught the first time and Dada was obliged to give him up to the military policemen who called at Northey Avenue. He spent a few days in a cell, an experience to which he was beginning to grow accustomed and which was further to confirm his conviction formed in Venice – that prisoners were always to be preferred to guards.

But a benign spell seems to have been cast over 1953, Rogers's second year of National Service. Trieste was still the subject of a border dispute between Yugoslavia and Italy and the city was under British and American military rule, a fact that angered the increasingly radical Rogers. It was precisely the same state of affairs that had persisted after the First World War. Then, the dispute had been resolved in 1920 when the city had been incorporated into Italy. After the Second World War the British and Americans had forced the Yugoslavs out and imposed military rule until a political solution could be found. A degree of tension persisted in the city with occasional bombings and in 1953 a major incident was narrowly avoided when Italian troops mobilized as a gesture against Yugoslav claims. Finally, in 1954, a memorandum of agreement was signed and Italian claims were accepted. So the city, when Rogers arrived as part of the British garrison, still lacked a nationality but it retained an exciting, risky air.

In November 1952, soon after he had arrived in Trieste, he wrote to Michael Branch:

Congrats on swindling the medical bods, I am pleased to see I have brought you up with the right ideas. Just keep the old flag flying & you will get a long way in this rather stupidly honest world. Swindle, chisel and swindle again & never say die that's what's got me where I am now (a Private in the British army).

Rogers with Marta, his Yugoslavian love

Life as a private was hardly an onerous responsibility. The day generally began at six in the morning ending at one in the afternoon. His loathing of the whole organization remained, fed by the suicide of one soldier in the garrison purely as a result of the persistent bullying to which he had been subjected. Rogers had long before concluded that the army maintained itself in being solely by fear and he was determined to play no part in the procedure. Instead he developed his civilian life. For a start he had discovered a way out of the army camp via a sewer and in addition he possessed a full set of civilian clothes as well as, somewhat oddly for a private, a season ticket to the opera. There was also Marta, an extraordinarily beautiful blonde Yugoslav girl, who, although clearly devoted to him, did not succumb with the usual ease to his advances. Perhaps in an agony of sexual frustration he proposed to her although it came to nothing. Such was his involvement with her that one night she distracted him sufficiently to make him miss a major family dinner. This had been arranged especially in his honour by Dada, and Ernesto Rogers was among the guests.

Rogers described the life and his affair in a letter to Branch dated September 1953:

I am thoroughly enjoying this life. I am never bored, I have no real worries, I have no thinking to do or dicisions to take, I have been going out with a girl for nine months & I am quite fond of her though she is very tactless & collects boys by the dozen. Bar abuot two or three weeks I have managed to keep her in her place & things have been going amazingly sweetly the last couple of weeks. I could go on speaking about her for houres but it will be much easier to tell you verbally. She is a devil of girl & I have thoroughly enjoyed these last nine months. We have been midnight, or I had better say 3 am swimming, we have been up to . . . [illegible . . .] in the mountains on a beautiful lake miles from the nearest inhabitance except for our small hotel for a very pleasant weekend, we have spent a week in The Dolomite climbing around 9,000 ft up & down to Florence. we have skied and gone to concerts & operas, we have made love & we have had some glorious rows. She works next to me, on the same tablein the office or at leastshe works for our chief clerk left in March & since then this office has been soly Italian bar myself so I have no boss. During the summer months when I wasnt skipping off on leave I worked or at least turned up at the office from 7.30 am to 9am & perhaps from 12 to 1.30am. No one worked in the afternoons. The official houres being 7–1.30.

He goes on to explain that an allowance from his family doubles his pay – though that was only 25 shillings a week – and complains that he has not enough time to fit in all the sporting activities he would like. 'We have a marvellous libery as well as a good American libery. There is nobody in Trieste or probably in the British army who has such a terrific time as I ...'

He stayed, when he could, with members of his family in Trieste and, if he had any length of leave, he would travel to Milan to see Ernesto.

His cousin was a dramatic figure – a small, round-shouldered homosexual who was at the centre of an intellectual circle which had carried the torch of the modern movement in Italy before the war and relit it afterwards. Ernesto was born in Trieste in 1909 and graduated in architecture at Milan in 1932. Also in 1932, unusually for the Rogers family, he had renounced his British citizenship to allow him to join the fascist party, apparently in his enthusiasm for futurist architecture, a form whose aspirations could conceivably be met by Mussolini's social ambitions. In any case, at that stage membership of the party was widespread even among the liberal middle classes. He went into practice by founding the firm BBPR with Gianluigi Banfi, Ludovico Belgiojoso and Enrico Peressuti. In 1935 all four members joined CIAM – the Congrès Internationaux d'Architecture Moderne – as an affirmation of their commitment to the mainstream of the modern movement.

By 1938 the real significance of fascism became clear to Ernesto with Mussolini's adoption of German racial laws and he retired into anonymity. Banfi, his partner and a Jew, was later to die in a German concentration camp. In 1942 all the members of the practice started working actively against the fascists and, in 1943, Ernesto was obliged to flee to Switzerland where he was interned at Vevey until the end of hostilities. Mussolini had been overthrown and Italy was effectively a German-occupied territory, making his position impossible. His role during the war as a known opponent of the fascists meant he emerged in 1945 with considerably more authority than most of his contemporaries. The practice was reborn as BPR – without Banfi – and Ernesto became editor of *Domus* and later, in 1954, of *Casabella*, two Italian architecture and design magazines which, under his editorship, wielded immense influence and played central roles in establishing the status of Italian design today.

The practice built several blocks of flats in Milan and the Italian merchant navy pavilion at the Paris exhibition in 1937. But it was the Sun Treatment Centre at Legnano which fully established their name before the war. It was distinguished modernist work but, as with so many other practices, the style was modified by the Second World War. In 1946 their monument to the victims of the concentration camps was unveiled in Milan. It was a cubic-space frame on a cruciform base with strong overtones of De Stijl. It represented an assertion of the rationalist tradition and the specific opposition of that tradition to fascism. If Ernesto had once been enthralled by the drama and uninhibited assertion of futurism, he was now turning away from it in disgust. The gesture coming from a former fascist who had lost a partner to the Nazis carried immense weight in post-war Italy. The architectural conflict that lay behind the monument was to surface again in his young cousin's search for form.

The practice's later style moved further towards a sort of poetic contextualism which reached its climax with the Torre Velasca in Milan – an office and apartment building which seemed to hark back to the unique top-heavy form of Italian medieval towers.

Rogers's visits to Ernesto resulted in a few early experiments – he was given pencils and paper and told to design his ideal house. The results were always covered up in case any visitors to the studio should mistake them for the work of the practice. It was clear he had no aptitude for drawing and there was the continuing problem of his relative lack of educational qualifications. Nevertheless, it was in Ernesto's studio that Rogers decided he wished to be an architect.

In a letter to Branch dated September 1953 he wrote:

I am going to try to get into the AA school for Architecture London University but its the stiffest Architecture place in England to enter & the fees are colossal. Poor Dad. My main worry is that as you know I cannot draw for anything & you have to show them a portfolio of drawing etc which I cant produce by Aprile. I have spent a few day in Milan at my cousins Architectural office & I thoroughly enjoyed myself especially as his staff is very young. I suppose that if the worst comes to the worst I may get him to shove me into University for they are always trying to get him up for lectures as he is among the worlds four or five leading modern architects but I dont want to start that way if I can help it in fact I should prefer not to do architecture if I have to depend on his help for I shall only end up being weeded out later on.

As a start Ernesto had managed to arrange for a tutor to visit Rogers in Trieste to teach the rudiments of 'geometrical drawing'. But in the meantime his grandmother had suffered a stroke at a dinner party and died a few days later. Rogers's main task then became to play chess with his grandfather every night in an attempt to distract him from his grief – he had been showing every sign of breaking down under the strain. With that and the army his self-education programme had to wait.

His National Service finally ended in November 1953. He left the army a convinced pacifist with a hopeless record and a profound hatred for all forms of military discipline just as he had left school with minimal academic qualifications and a loathing of arbitrary rules. Yet he also left as a socially-gifted, reasonably well-read and highly-confident individual. And he knew what he wanted to do. Architecture seemed to offer the means to effect a resolution of the many conflicts of his early years. It was a resolution he had unconsciously begun to glimpse in his sense of a liberated, European liberalism which he nursed in defiance of the fragments of the isolated wartime

England he had so far experienced. His unofficial education from his parents, with their culture and their politics, as well as from Ernesto, with his modernist convictions of the social importance of architecture, had filled him with a radical and largely impractical view of what his chosen profession would involve.

So, for the twenty-year-old Rogers returning to Cheam in the autumn of 1953, the world which included the army, Kingswood, St John's and the Venetian police needed to be changed to one more adapted to the needs of James Chuter Ede, Julie Tree, Dada Rogers, Michael Branch, Marta, the Gang and a certain defrocked priest. And he was going to build it.

2 ... And how to build it

The beginning of Rogers's architectural education coincided with the first skirmishes of the long and still continuing war over the future direction of modern architecture. Like most students, however, he managed to remain some years behind contemporary developments while being blissfully convinced that he was in the vanguard of progressive thought. For him the one unquestionable obligation on the prospective architect was the absorption of the ideology, aesthetics and history of mainstream modernism. This was reasonable enough for, although the modernist consensus was in the process of being thoroughly undermined, the work of the masters and the broad history of the movement had retained their inviolable significance. Sullivan, Wright, Le Corbusier, Gropius and Mies stood unchallenged; it was what came next which was beginning to cause problems.

But first it is a question of grasping the main threads of modernism in architecture as they were being handed down to the generation of students which Rogers was about to join. From the perspective of an opportunistic survivor and hater of authority in Epsom in late 1953 its most notable feature was the scale of its claims. Giants bestrode the first half of the century demanding that a new world should be constructed upon the corrupted fragments of the old – a world for Rogers rather than his persecutors.

'I was not the only one then sick of hypocrisy and hungry for reality,' wrote Frank Lloyd Wright.[1]

'Architecture or Revolution. Revolution can be avoided,' wrote Le Corbusier.[2]

'The evolution of structure marches with the elimination of ornament from useful objects,' wrote Adolf Loos.[3]

The faithful modernists never lost this sense of urgency and epic scale, nor the conviction that only architecture stood between the world and chaos. Maxwell Fry, one of the most unwavering of English disciples who was to work with Le Corbusier at Chandigarh in India, wrote in 1969: 'The one great end of our time is to find a form in which we may successfully survive. The alternative can be none other than disintegration.' And, to identify the precise nature of the problem, he described the English Victorian terraced house, exemplar of the ruins that were to be swept away: 'There it is, as unlovable as it is possible for a man-made thing to be; and this loveless foundling, begot in greed and sin, of parents unknown is reproduced in rigid lines of street after street disappearing into the smoke-obscured light of a day that knows no season, in undifferentiated and godless boredom.'[4]

The potent rhetoric of the movement with its violent contrasts and visionary posture was all that any student in the 1950s, discontented with the apparent littleness of England, could require. For Rogers, after twenty years of irreconcilable demands, it was a heaven-sent synthesis.

The history he was to learn was the highly deterministic version of the recent past promoted by Sigfried Giedion[5] and later, more sensitively, by Nikolaus Pevsner.[6] This took the view that the forms of modern architecture were the only truthful forms of the age. In this interpretation, the history of previous styles was a legible, directed narrative whose climax was the final, mature flowering of modernism. To dissent from this position was to be guilty of a kind of immorality. This is to simplify somewhat their historicist[7] critical position which had been developed from the writings of Hegel and Burckhardt, but in essence it was the simplified form in which modernism was absorbed by students of the day. Its grand historical imperatives neatly echoed the injunctions of the artists, whose work the critical posture was designed to explain.

Giedion's determinism, in particular, provided the critical discipline of a single linear development of the modern movement. At the same time he provided sweeping parallels with developments in other arts and in the sciences – most dubiously with Einstein's thought which provided him with his under-researched interest in space–time. Its attraction was that it disposed of many of the complications which arise from a closer study of the period – did away with the contradictions inherent in any attempt to construct an intellectual history from the evidence of an artistic one.

But in reality contradiction is woven into the fabric of modern architecture. From its beginnings its practitioners and theorists have striven to unite a variety of conflicting impulses and ideals. Frequently the stridency of their rhetoric has arisen from a need to disguise the insecurity of their position. Le Corbusier's *Towards a New Architecture*, for example, derives much of its power from the struggle between aesthetics on the one hand and sociology and politics on the other. Its clarion call is all the more effective because of the mystery of the unresolved meaning at the centre of the book. In the case of Le Corbusier it was this conflict which was to prove the inspiration of his greatest work, rather than any accident of his historical destiny.

Modernism in architecture was more or less contemporaneous with modernism in other art forms although, inevitably because of the time required for acceptance, designing and constructing buildings, its principal manifestations occur rather later. Mainstream history says that buildings first became definably modern with the work of Louis Sullivan and his pupil Frank Lloyd Wright in the United States in the 1890s. These developments were then matched by the work of Adolf Loos in Austria, Auguste Perret and Tony Garnier in France and by Peter Behrens and the Deutscher Werkbund founded in 1907. New construction techniques provided one impetus for this first wave – steel frames had allowed buildings to rise higher than was previously possible with load-bearing masonry – while Perret and Garnier had begun to explore the apparently limitless flexibility offered by reinforced concrete.

But there was also the impulse to provide new types and forms of buildings specifically for a new world. Nineteenth-

century industrialization had been wrapped in a variety of
architectural disguises and this electicism had tended to reduce the role of the architect to that of exterior decorator. He
could offer neo-Gothic, neo-classical, neo-Romanesque and,
latterly, arts and crafts revivalism and art nouveau as the
surface dressing of any plan. This does not, of course, amount
to an aesthetic condemnation – the juxtaposing of the brilliant technologically determined glass roof over the platforms
of St Pancras station with its fantastic Gothic hotel frontage
produces an effect only possible because of Victorian stylistic
concerns. Nevertheless, the revulsion against this development produced a tangled mass of rhetoric in which it was
established that a building, above all, had to be 'honest'. The
point was that an applied style, with its repertoire of meanings and symbolism derived from another, unindustrialized
age, constituted a lie. This familiar confusion of moral and
aesthetic values gave rise to some of the most spectacular
claims of the modern movement in which aesthetic preferences were elevated to the status of new commandments for
the new world. It was also to make the modern movement an
easy target for ridicule as its utopian aspirations crumbled
over the next three decades.

The rejection of electicism demanded a new single-
mindedness of approach which was obliged to be true to the
dominant forces of the age – industrialization and the machine. These could no longer be clad in off-the-shelf styles;
new forms had to be discovered which would capture and
express their essence. Le Corbusier found them in American
grain elevators and ocean liners[8] and concluded that during
the débâcle of the nineteenth century, the engineers had
usurped the true role of the architect. But always the classical
artist in him battled against his polemic, rendering his pro-
nouncements thrilling yet ambiguous. The same struggle was
discernible in Gropius, who spoke in his 1919 Bauhaus pro-
clamation of the virtues of handicrafts, but who, by 1920, was
uncompromisingly devoted to the machine age aesthetic.[9]
Perret and Garnier more cautiously aimed to unite the old

and the new by using reinforced concrete in an attenuated classical context. But the most unambiguous converts of them all were the Italian futurists who flung themselves headlong into the age of the machine. For them that included accepting the machine's historically short life as a pattern for the way the past was simply to be tossed aside with each succeeding mechanical epoch.

In fact the visionary savagery of the more extreme machine cults left behind little in the way of built memorials. For one thing they ran headlong into that supremely futurist event the First World War and, for another, the inherent instability of the systems they were proposing hardly suggested finished buildings. (I shall deal with the specific impact of their legacy on Rogers in Chapter 4.) But the machine/industrial aesthetic survived as a mainspring of modernism to find its highest expression in the best work of the Bauhaus.

Meanwhile, the struggles of Le Corbusier with himself and his architecture made ever more tenuous the connection with the industrial forms which had influenced his earlier thought and he was to suffer from his much-misunderstood statement that a house was a 'machine for living in'. Far from being an inexpressive, inhuman motto it was intended to be a statement of the minimum that a house should offer. Le Corbusier's meditations on the differences between and the mutual functions of the fine arts and the useful crafts remain his least recognized contribution. Wright, embittered by the way the Europeans seemed to have stolen the show after his first brilliant innovations, developed along his own unique path until descending into his last, fantastic and uncontrolled inventions.

The major late arrival on the scene was Mies van der Rohe, a former pupil of Berlage, the Dutch champion of Wright, and the last director of the Bauhaus before it was closed by the Nazis on 10 August 1933. There was something chilly, ascetic and intolerably artistic about Mies after the warm splendours of the earlier modernists.

'If you meet twin sisters,' he is reported to have said in response to an attempt to remove the tag 'art' from architecture, 'who are equally intelligent, healthy and wealthy, and both can bear children, but one is ugly, the other beautiful, which one would you marry?'

Mies brought a supremely precise and sure sensibility to the use of modern industrial materials. In truth to materials and rigorously rational planning lay the only possible architectural imperatives for the new, godless age. The tautness of his steely pessimism set him apart from the mainstream but the sheer quality of his building made him unavoidable.

And Mies had most clearly identified the problem at the heart of modernism – that once there was no Truth, the artist lacked any rationale which would justify one set of choices against any other. His answer was to construct an artificial 'morality', a new classicism with austere demands for purity and precision. But it was only one man's solution and it was ultimately inimitable. For the sound and fury of the nineteenth century had only succeeded in drowning the noise of the emptying of the reservoir of transmissible sense which had kept the stylistic extravaganza afloat. Modernism was an attempt to find a new source and the search was conducted by a generation of geniuses who believed they would succeed by an effort of artistic will. Its legacy to the students of the 1950s was an ill-defined visionary quality, a certain freedom arising from the belief in innovation and radical solutions, a firm linkage of aesthetic and moral values and a portfolio of unquestionably great buildings – many of those by Mies yet to be built – against which they had to pit themselves.

Modernism gave another much more damaging legacy in the flood of mediocre buildings which were later to drown many of Britain's city centres. The first British response to modernism had involved the whole package of bigotry evoked by words like 'foreign', 'intellectual' and, in its lowest form, 'Jewish'. As early as 1928 Evelyn Waugh had created Professor Otto Friedrich Silenus:

The only perfect building must be the factory, because that is built to house machines, not men. I do not think it is possible for domestic architecture to be beautiful but I am doing my best . . . Man is never beautiful, he is never happy except when he becomes the channel for the distribution of mechanical forces.[10]

Unfortunately much British modernism played into the hands of such potent enemies. The problem was that amiable, well-meaning architects were trying to produce an amiable, well-meaning British modernism by watering down the un-palatable aspects of the foreign masters. But this also pointed to a deeper problem. For modernism had not produced a style which could simply be drawn upon by lesser practitioners, as had classical or Gothic architecture. Instead it had produced too much freedom – almost anything could be attempted and then dressed incongruously in Corbusian concrete or Miesian steel. Such freedom could constitute a breathtaking release in the hands of the masters – in the hands of their followers it could easily become a new imprisonment.

It was a daunting inheritance but, for Rogers, it all made perfect sense as he began to absorb the details at Epsom College of Art, where he had gone to take a 'foundation course' before going to the Architectural Association. He had chosen the AA on the advice of Ernesto, passed the exam and was due to start there in the autumn of 1954. This gave him two preparatory terms at Epsom in which he chose to study life-drawing and photography. The first was logical enough and the second was simply because he was interested and had the dim suspicion that it might be useful later on.

The course itself, however, was almost beside the point. The work was undemanding and, in any case, Rogers's draw-ing still failed to show much promise. The real point was that he had an aim in life – to be an architect – and his definition of what that aim entailed had the widest possible cultural con-text in the best modernist tradition. He launched himself on a furious programme of cultural and architectural self-education, a process that centred on heated debates in the

local coffee bar primarily with two other students, Brian
Taylor and Georgie Cheeseman.

Brian took Rogers's breath away and provided him with a
model of the artist as antisocial outsider, a useful hint as to
how his own aberrations might be classified. Working class
and waywardly brilliant, he immediately informed Rogers
that he would never be an architect as he was too hopelessly
middle class. He painted superbly and was an expert on
everything, being notably well informed about insects. He
was a consummate storyteller and when short of money he
worked as a night-watchman. Rogers's parents were entran-
ced by him and Dada, in particular, was delighted to find her
son at last moving among the sort of inspired people she most
admired.

Georgie was another matter, although her effect on Rogers
was to be infinitely more profound. She was the daughter of a
wealthy Lloyd's underwriter from East Horsley and considerably more easygoing than Brian Taylor. She was cheerful, quick-witted and devoted to Wagner. Periodically she
gave both Rogers and Taylor driving lessons and generally
provided a sobering, sceptical influence on their debates.
They would occasionally be joined by her younger sister,
Wendy.

Rogers's certainty about his future made him something of
a rarity among the vaguely artistic types who had made their
way to Epsom. Unless they were studying bookbinding or
anything irreversibly career-directed, their futures tended to
be undetermined. He also sounded slightly different – the
remnants of his accent were still just detectable in, for
example, his over-emphatic pronunciation of the g at the end
of good morning. And he looked different – he wore 'Continental' shoes with very thick soles and prominent stitching
around the sides as well as a shirt and jacket in contrast to the
standard duffel coats and sweaters of the other students. He
always carried books under his arm and generally exuded an
air of being not quite English – possibly American or French,
those being the only two nationalities the average Epsom

Rogers on the fringes of 1950s Bohemia

student of the day could imagine with any degree of clarity. His spectacular feats of hitch-hiking reinforced the impression that he was a rather daring and exotic character.

Among students in those days such an appeal was validated intellectually by the growing influence of existentialism. The forms of this which had developed during the Second World War had been disdainfully rejected by many of the established British intelligentsia as soon as the works of Sartre and Camus began reappearing in the late 1940s. A.J. Ayer, in particular, had displayed the frosty impatience felt by his generation in *Horizon*.[11] But to the students it offered a sort of subversive egotism which fitted well with the growing but ill-defined atmosphere of discontent. In that context hitch-hiking and foreignness seemed like the appropriate existential activities.

The college – a domestic Edwardian building – had an informal atmosphere which allowed Rogers to relax after the long years of strict schools and the army. It was like a large house rather than an institution and was sufficiently small for everyone to know everyone else. In such an environment his confidence – always encouraged by Dada and never entirely destroyed by his education – blossomed and expanded to include his new intellectual interests.

In line with his general air of foreignness, the intellectual traditions in which he immersed himself were consistently non-British, apart from a passing fascination with vorticism, a suitably radical and polemical movement. He placed himself in the mainstream of the pre-beatnik avant-garde of the time. Sartre and Camus were required reading, as were Salinger, Steinbeck, Miller, O'Neill, Dos Passos, Dostoevsky, Joyce, Orwell, Huxley, Eliot, Hemingway, Apollinaire and even Plato, to whom he had been introduced by Nino. In the evenings he even took a night-school course in philosophy, a subject then under the benign shadow of Bertrand Russell, whose *History of Western Philosophy*, a luminous exposition of enlightened liberal atheism, had been published in 1946. Meanwhile, Nino had returned from his army work in India with much talk about and enthusiasm for the work of Gandhi and Nehru to add to this rich, humanist stew.

The corpus of modernist architecture fitted effortlessly into this collection. The CIAM was the one true church and Giedion's *Space, Time and Architecture*, determinist, grandiloquent and relentlessly moralizing, was its Bible. 'No other building,' wrote Giedion of Berlage's Amsterdam Stock Exchange, 'accords so well with the demand that lay behind the movement in architecture at that time – the demand for morality.'[12]

The CIAM had been founded in 1928 by Hélène de Mandrot. She had asked Giedion to organize a meeting of modern architects at her home near Geneva. Le Corbusier, Stam, Rietveld, El Lissitzky and Berlage attended and Karl Moser became its first president. Subsequent meetings codified the aspirations of the modern movement and its authority ensured that it survived the war. But after the 1956 conference in Dubrovnik, it collapsed in disarray, primarily because of the intellectual assault launched against it by the same English theoreticians who were to dominate Rogers's years at the AA.

Dada and Nino were delighted with their son's sudden and wildly enthusiastic immersion in modern culture. Instead of being the rather directionless leader of a gang of misfits and dissidents, he was now at the faintly glamorous centre of young artistic life in Epsom. But their disciplinary fads remained. Notably, they were not interested in providing nonessential financial support. As Rogers was already planning another epic holiday before going to the AA, this meant he had to raise money by giving swimming lessons at Epsom baths. A somewhat frenetic pattern of socializing and work was established.

But for all the intellectual stimulation provided by Giedion and the others, it was Georgie who had become the centre of his life. He fell helplessly in love with her in a way that dwarfed the cosy, affectionate relationship with Julie Tree. Where Julie had been a reassuring element in his life, Georgie

Georgie Cheeseman

became its entire *raison d'être*. In part it was her intellectual
confidence and sceptical gaiety which attracted him, but she
also presented to Rogers the image of someone completely at
home in her world, sure of her position and lacking the fever-
ish uncertainty that had marked his life until then.
Significantly, Michael Branch was to comment that both
Georgie and her sister, Wendy, exuded the same air of being
on another plane to the rest of the world that he had detected
in Nino and Dada. The sisters seemed to have avoided the
usual traumas of youth.

Rogers's relationship with Georgie was to set the pattern
for the sexual partnerships of the rest of his life. He wanted
her not only in his bed but by his side at every possible
moment – helping him as Dada had once been seen tenderly
translating Nino's German textbooks. He involved her in
every aspect of his activities and leaned heavily on her to help
him overcome his continuing academic and practical
difficulties. She was drawn into the Rogers family to discover
that for Dada and Nino she represented to them the ideal girl
for their son. Years later it was Georgie who was to warn
Rogers's second wife, Ruth, not to marry him as he would
expect her to look after him every minute of the day, just as
Dada had cared for Nino. Georgie was to be the first person in
Rogers's life in whom he discovered himself.

But ironically she also provided the one occasion when the
increasingly legendary Rogers charm failed to work. Her
father in his 'Tudorbethan' mansion at East Horsley – Rogers
described it as 'the ugliest house in Surrey' – was dismayed at
the arty types with whom his daughters seemed to be spending their time. He developed a deep dislike for Rogers in
particular and was horrified when he realized the boy planned
to take Georgie on his next hare-brained summer holiday.
Cheeseman called Rogers up to his office and threatened to
sue him if he went ahead with the plan. The joint holiday idea
had to be dropped.

So, having completed his minimal academic preparation
for the AA at Epsom, he set off on holiday alone. The trip took

him through Spain, France and North Africa – where lack of food and an uncontrollable stomach disorder had rendered him almost too weak and helpless to take in the architecture of Tangier with its obvious foreshadowing of the hard, white phase of the modern movement. (He does, however, dimly remember trying to do some drawings of the peasants' mud architecture.) On the way down he smuggled a girl disguised as a man into a Paris brothel and later teamed up with another girl in Bordeaux whom he met again on the way back through Spain. In true Hemingway/existential style he ran with the bulls at Pamplona and, in true Rogers style, spent a night in prison in San Sebastian, having been caught swimming naked with the girl. From Spain he travelled through southern France and on to Florence and Naples. Finally he reached Trieste where he received the usual family subsidies.

The real importance of this journey was that it was the first time he had consciously set out to study architecture. He took with him Giedion as his modern guide and Rudolf Wittkower's *Architectural Principles in the Age of Humanism* for the Renaissance. Wittkower was then the most influential critic attempting to establish the relationship between the modern movement and classicism. In addition, there was Pevsner's *An Outline of European Architecture* with its ringing conviction of the centrality of the art: 'Thus architecture is the most comprehensive of all visual arts and has a right to claim superiority over the others.'[13] For Italian painting he studied the writing of Eric Newton. By the time he returned to England to start at the AA he felt, at last, reasonably well educated and firmly convinced that he had grasped the central elements of modern architecture and its essential rightness. It was a sensation exactly paralleled by that felt by James Stirling – whose path was repeatedly to cross Rogers's in years to come – when he left the Liverpool University School of Architecture in 1950 'with a deep conviction of the moral rightness of the new architecture'.[14]

The Architectural Association is a curious organization situated then as now in some Bloomsbury-Georgian terraced houses in Bedford Square, a couple of minutes' walk from Tottenham Court Road. It is a private school with a carefully nurtured international reputation for radical architectural thought and a prodigious capacity for the rapid assimilation and rejection or acceptance of new ideas. It repeatedly produces the most extreme, speculative and often unbuilt architects of each generation and its students are invariably exposed to the view that good building is, by its nature, innovative. Its characteristic methods are distinctly cerebral rather than practical, although the individuality of its teachers makes any such generalizations dangerous. For Rogers, however, its argumentative and artistic rather than practical and professional approach must have seemed ideal.

Rogers's first-year teacher was Robert Furneaux Jordan, an architectural historian who wrote detective stories under the name Robert Player. Born in 1905 he began teaching in 1934 and had been Principal of the AA from 1948 to 1951 during which time he transformed it into the first fully modern architectural school in the country. Much to Rogers's taste, Jordan carefully cultivated a European – as opposed to little England – perspective. He invited Ernesto and his partner, Peressuti, to lecture at the Association.

When Rogers arrived, the AA was still unique in Britain in its devotion to the new architecture and, as London had not yet been despoiled by third-rate modernism, the importance and stature of the movement was not seriously being called into question. As he was to discover later, however, its postwar incarnation was eventually to be defined as a betrayal. Jordan's approach was broadly sociological and his interpretations of history tended to follow a conventionally left-wing line which took the modern movement primarily as a form of social engineering. But, best of all from Rogers's point of view, Jordan's teaching style was relaxed and informal, the only educational atmosphere in which Rogers could function.

Yet, even at the AA, a degree of basic competence was required and Rogers's drawing remained a serious problem. He would stand in front of the most expensive buff-coloured paper and then proceed to attack it directly in ink. He did not, as even the best draughtsmen do, start with a light pencil sketch. The results were usually incomprehensible.

But the AA system allowed him to struggle along for a time. This involves 'juries' who sit in judgement on students' schemes and offer comments and discussion. The idea is to provide something of the climate of an architectural practice and to give the student as wide a range of reactions as possible rather than simply an anonymous mark. From his reading and with his social confidence, Rogers could talk his way through juries without drawings and occasionally convince them that he had a degree of talent, however fugitive.

Judged alongside other students, however, he was clearly trailing badly. He retained his foreignness and oddity value but among sophisticated contemporaries like Eldred Evans – who was to win a competition for Lincoln town centre while still a student – he scarcely represented a promising prospect. But help was on the way in his second year when Georgie joined the AA and immediately began to provide a lifeline to some sort of respectability by helping him with his drawings. At one jury James Gowan, later to become the partner of James Stirling, challenged Rogers about some unusually lucid drawings: 'Come on, Richard, are these yours or Georgie's?'

Such amiable tolerance was not to be expected from Michael Pattrick, the second-year tutor. Even in his obituary Pattrick was described as 'forbidding ... a forthright and battling champion ... little time for frivolities.'[15] Rogers clearly counted as a frivolity and inevitably it was Pattrick who spotted from his office Rogers and Georgie across the courtyard exchanging exam papers. 'How', one sympathetic but frustrated tutor asked Dada and Nino, 'can we be expected to make an architect out of a man who cannot make two lines meet?' Pattrick's advice was to forget all about architecture and try furniture design.

But Pattrick's rigorously traditional and disciplined approach to the craft was at odds with the mood of the age. With another teacher, Hugh Morris, Rogers and his friends were concentrating more on the conceptual basis of the modern movement. He attended meetings of an odd little communist cell run by Morris which focused attention on the demands of the modern movement for architecture to lead social change. With the backing of this kind of certainty, his technical shortcomings began to seem like less of a handicap. 'A very good effort,' wrote Morris of one of his projects, 'which should encourage you to overcome your diffidence about your ability to draw when you really try, as much as it has encouraged the jury in the belief that once you have increased your ability to draw you will be able to produce excellent work.' With the aid of sympathetic tutors like Morris, a feeling was now developing at the AA that beneath the strange combination of bad drawing and cultural *savoir-faire*, Rogers appeared to have an unusual talent. And as would happen in later years, those who knew him best began to detect what he was trying to express in his drawings.

Socially he maintained his 'gang', a circle of intimates among whom, although he was not a dominant figure, he invariably stood out. He seemed to be the only one who did not smoke, the idea never appears to have crossed his mind, and his clothes remained noticeably smarter and more cosmopolitan than those of his peers. He drank beer, a habit he had acquired in the army, but it was the age of coffee bars and coffee was more suited to Rogers's Italian manners. His reading was maintained at a ferocious rate and his range of reference in conversation was intimidating. Nino had always told him never to read trash under any circumstances for fear of contamination, so his choice of material was exclusively serious.

But behind his style was Dada. Her habits of aesthetic appreciation had been passed on intact to her son. In an entirely unEnglish way visual judgement and commentary formed part of her everyday life. It was a habit that rendered Rogers even more exotic to the less cultivated public-school graduates at the AA. 'His confidence seemed surprising in view of his work at the time,' commented one contemporary at the AA, 'until you met Dada.' Even his bedroom at Cheam contributed to the effect. It was dark green with Japanese prints. The other students, from their 'Tudorbethan' houses, assumed it must be the only room of its kind in England; a single, sacred shrine dedicated to the mysteries of Continental art. The room measured only 9 feet by 12 but it was a regular venue for late-night discussions which continued the Epsom themes of Continental philosophy, left-wing politics and fierce aesthetic conviction. 'We knew for a fact,' recalls Georgie, 'that if something was ugly, it was evil.' But a more English dimension was being added to the disquiet. Something appeared to be afoot in the land – there was a mood of generalized discontent and vague excitement which seemed to indicate that London might not be quite the backwater they had assumed.

The 1950s were now under way. It was not merely a question of duffel coats, jazz and coffee bars – a more radical reassessment of culture was happening which was to attain its most popular manifestation in literature but which emerged earlier and more lastingly in the visual arts. It centred on the Institute of Contemporary Arts and, most notably in terms of personalities, on Richard Hamilton and Alison and Peter Smithson. Hamilton was not an architect but he had been inspired by another Giedion book *Mechanization Takes Command* published in 1948 which dealt with the relationships between nature and technology. From there he was to move on to an obsession with machinery, both in the real world and in science fiction, and with the iconography of consumer advertising which was to result in the creation of pop art.

In 1953 at the ICA the Smithsons along with Nigel Henderson and Eduardo Paolozzi staged the 'Parallel of Life and Art' exhibition, which included scraps of paper and magazine images, and in 1956 Hamilton joined up with the Smithsons and others for the explicitly 'pop' 'This is Tomorrow' exhibition at the Whitechapel Gallery. Although gallery-based, this group was intimately linked with developing architectural thought, partly because of the presence of the critic Reyner Banham who was to trace the origins of the New Brutalism from those early days at the ICA,[16] but mainly because of the formidable Smithsons. Rogers was to encounter Peter Smithson in his final two years at the AA and it was to be a considerable shock.

Peter Smithson had married Alison Gill in 1949 and they had set up an architectural practice together. Immediately they placed themselves in the intellectual vanguard of the battle to defeat the softened modernism which had sprung up since the second world war and was generally identified as Swedish, or labelled as the New Empiricism or the New Humanism. This battle of styles was fought out within the London County Council where the harder line Stalinists[17] were defending the programmed 'Swedishness' of Roehampton's Alton East housing estate and insisting that all houses of four storeys or less were, by definition, domestic and thus must have pitched roofs. 'Let's face it,' commented James Stirling acidly on the supposed intellectual heredity of this movement, 'William Morris was a Swede.'

The Smithsons' school at Hunstanton appeared in 1954 – it had been designed much earlier but delayed by the post-war steel shortage. Superficially, this was a classically hard-edged Miesian building which in itself would have been enough of a statement of the Smithsons' loathing of picturesque English-Festival-style compromise. But there was nothing Miesian about the brutally exposed services and the sheer frankness of the entire fabric – the corners, for example, displayed none of Mies's careful sculpting; they were, simply, corners.

Then, with their scheme for mass housing in London's Golden Lane in 1952, they veered in the direction of Le Corbusier whose *unite d'habitation* was then nearing completion in Marseilles. But they took the master's interior shopping street and placed it on the outside as a 'street deck', an idea that was to attain its apotheosis with Jack Lynn and Ivor Smith's gigantic housing scheme at Park Hill, Sheffield.

For Banham this was the birth of the New Brutalism – 'a

sustained polemic on style'[18] which was to constitute the first and last undermining of the CIAM consensus. Not that the Smithsons were attacking modernism itself. 'We believed New Brutalism to be the direct line development of the Modern Movement,' they wrote in 1973[19] in their characteristically disordered prose. But, amid this excitement, it was difficult to see how the obsession with advertising and technology fitted in. There was nothing expressly technological about any of the Smithsons' schemes – unless one counts the naked services in the interior of Hunstanton – and it seemed once again that architecture was only paying lip service to its perceived obligations to the machine age. Instead, Moroccan and Japanese architecture were called on for antecedents (Japan was fashionable having been seen in colour for the first time in Britain in 1954 with the release of the Japanese film *Gates of Hell*) and pop art and the 'overlaid imagery' of American advertising were left to the galleries.

Also involved in the ICA scene in those days was James Stirling whose reputation grew steadily throughout the 1950s until the Leicester University engineering buildings of 1963 established him internationally. In 1955 he created with his flats at Ham Common, Richmond, a highly English version of Le Corbusier's Parisian Maisons Jaoul. Ernesto, at one point, asked Rogers to send him back a report on this project for one of his magazines. If the Smithsons were the theoretical heroes of the hour, then Stirling was the practical master – all were engaged in the struggle simply to find out what to do next without actually overturning the achievements of the giants.

But students have too many other problems ever to succeed in being absolutely contemporary, and Rogers was only narrowly managing to scrape through his third-year intermediate exams at the AA while Stirling was building housing at Preston and the Smithsons were plotting the overthrow of the CIAM. His success in passing at all startled his tutors, but tasted like ashes to him as Georgie had ended their relationship. She could no longer accept the intensity of his demands and his dependence on her. Not only had Rogers lost his draughtswoman, he had also been deprived of someone who seemed to have overcome the contradictions of his upbringing. He was devastated in spite of the consolation of Georgie's younger sister, Wendy, who became his next girlfriend and who attempted to set him back on his feet. It was in this condition – and accompanied by Wendy – that he met a party of students in Milan during the summer holiday of 1957 who had travelled from England on their scooters.

Depressed as he was, he still seemed to them a spectacular figure. He was dressed in immaculately pressed jeans, white shirt, a blue V-necked pullover and a Jaeger slimline bow tie, a fashion presumably derived from Le Corbusier. Indeed he was going through a Le Corbusier phase. He had met Charlotte Perriand, the furniture designer and associate of the great man, and she had shown an overwhelmed Rogers around the master's awe-inspiring monastery at La Tourette. Thus attired, he represented everything that the English students, who had been until then impressed with their own cosmopolitan daring, knew they were not. Su Brumwell, then just a sixth former who had fallen in with some AA students, could not take her eyes off him. He took the students out for dinner: 'He always seemed to have funny money in Italy,' Su observed later.

She met him again at a bonfire-night party later that same year at a cottage in Lewes, Sussex. They stayed the night at the cottage and then travelled back to Cheam on Su's Lambretta – Rogers had already developed the habit, which still continues, of talking people into giving him lifts. Su was smitten by Dada and Nino but, more importantly, Rogers was overwhelmed by her father and mother when they met soon afterwards at the Brumwell home near Dorking.

Su was the adopted daughter of Marcus Brumwell, whose father had died before his birth could be registered. His mother had remarried and stepfather and stepson had never seen eye to eye. He went to Rugby but there was insufficient money to send him to university and he found employment instead in a clerical post. But his childhood had left him with a stubborn, rebellious streak which emerged in a fierce letter to the managing director of Stuart's advertising agency, one of whose campaigns had offended Brumwell's embryonic left-wing principles. Stuart Menzies offered him a job on the strength of the letter and five years later, on his retirement, passed the job of managing director to him which Brumwell held until his own retirement.

The job itself was not enough for him, however; he was depressed by what he took to be the immorality of advertising and felt he needed more ideologically appropriate challenges in his life. He met his future wife, Rene, playing tennis at a club in Dulwich where the couple also met Ben Nicholson, the artist, who seemed instantly to provide Brumwell with a whole programme of aspirations. He had no artistic background of his own but he became deeply involved with Nicholson's paintings and started buying them. In those days before the Second World War, of course, they were not expensive. Nicholson drew this new and enlightened patron into the group of artists, subsequently known by the name of the Cornish town where they settled – St Ives. They represented English modernism, a movement dogged by its own awareness of the achievements of the great European masters, but growing in confidence. Apart from their art they were united by the between-wars political consensus – humanist socialism formed in opposition to Franco and Hitler but on the brink of disillusionment and reconsideration at the time of the Stalin–Hitler pact. They were toppled over that brink during the Hungarian uprising of 1956.

They were also united by a utopian sense of the centrality of art; it was the harmonizing principle of the humanist world as well as the inspirer and reflector of social change. In this they were reinforced by the presence of Naum Gabo, the Russian sculptor. Gabo had co-authored with Antoine Pevsner the *Realistic Manifesto* published in Moscow in 1920 and often known as the Constructivist Manifesto. In the optimistic turmoil of Russia at the time it called for entirely new forms of art to deal with entirely new forms of life. Cubism

and futurism were bourgeois forms, out of touch with contemporary reality.

'Space and time,' [wrote Gabo and Pevsner], are reborn to us today.
Space and time are the only forms on which life is built and hence art
must be constructed . . . The plumb line in our hand, eyes as precise
as a ruler, in a spirit as taut as a compass . . . we construct our work
as the universe constructs its own, as the engineer constructs his
bridges . . .

Today is the deed
We will account for it tomorrow
The past we are leaving behind us as carrion
The future we leave to the fortune-tellers
We take the present day.[20]

But, even in 1920, the Soviet authorities regarded it as a
dubious document and it became clear that Gabo's own revo-
lutionary aspirations were at odds with those of the Party. He
moved to England and subsequently to America where he
died in 1977. (It was in Gabo's house in America that Rogers
worked on his first commissions.)

Meanwhile, another great modernist, Piet Mondrian, was
also living in England and borrowing money from Brumwell
to pay the rent. Just before the war Mondrian had been ready
to leave for America. But he had little hope of paying back the
£37 10 shillings he owed. Instead he gave Brumwell a painting. This hung in the Dorking home until Brumwell sold it for
£18,000 to help pay for a house built by Rogers and his first
practice – Team 4 – some years later in Creek Vean, Cornwall.
(The painting was later to be sold for $1 million.)

Immediately after the war Brumwell founded the Design
Research Unit which was involved in the building of the
Festival of Britain's Dome of Discovery and which was later
to rescue Rogers from his first major professional crisis when
his partnership with Norman Foster broke up. Brumwell was
also closely associated with the Labour Party as chairman of
its science and arts committee. He was a key protagonist in
the post-war dream of socialist reconstruction.

The Brumwell connection was destined to be lasting and

important. Its immediate impact on Rogers was to place him in the novel position of being on good terms with his lover's parents. (The experience of Mr Cheeseman had accustomed him to the belief that his affairs were to be conducted against steady parental opposition.) Rogers found himself provided first, with a new woman around whom he could organize his life and secondly, with an extraordinary range of contacts among the middle-aged artistic world of the time. It was a world which shared the pre-war optimism of the architectural modernists. It was most obviously exemplified by Herbert Read, another of Brumwell's friends. Read, born in 1893, had been a tireless propagandist for modern art in almost all its manifestations. His aesthetics were based on notions of organic form and his politics on a kind of amiable anarchy. The Read view was simply that modern art was all it claimed to be – that Utopia could be aesthetically generated. The connection was later to provide Rogers with a secretary, Read's daughter, Sophie, and an opportunity to review a rather saner account of modern architecture than that of Giedion – Leonardo Benevolo's *History of Modern Architecture* – for one of Read's publications. Rogers grew to know Read well, staying with him in London and Yorkshire, where he joined him for long walks over the Dales. Later Rogers was to do some drawings for a conversion of Read's London flat but the project came to nothing.

The Brumwell connection also provided him with the Hut. This was a 20-foot by 10-foot wooden shed in the grounds of the Brumwells' house – known as Deer Leap – at Westcott just outside Dorking. It was an absolutely standard garden shed which in later years Rogers improved with a bright green floor and a single, huge window overlooking the North Downs. It became a regular retreat at times of difficulty and, in effect, a second home. It remained in the family after the Brumwells sold Deer Leap in 1964 and for a time there were plans for Rogers to build a more permanent structure in the form of his Zip-Up house. But these came to nothing and the land and the Hut were finally sold off some time after the

Above: Su Brumwell and Rogers
Centre: Marcus Brumwell
Below: Rene Brumwell and Rogers

break-up of his marriage to Su.

In 1958, however, there were more immediate problems. Opposition to nuclear weapons was growing and in February, Bertrand Russell, Canon Collins, Michael Foot and others had formed the Campaign for Nuclear Disarmament. In the first week of April the first Aldermaston march left Trafalgar Square – Su and Rogers were among the crowd.

'Young women students, untidily but sensibly dressed in jeans, duffel coats and heavy shoes, marched by, all smiles, with a horror notice held in one hand and a young man, sometimes bearded, held even more tightly by the other,' reported *The Times*.[21] In fact the somewhat derisive tone of the press reports – which included the charge that the marchers were 'a communist rabble' – persuaded Su and Rogers to change their plans. The original idea had been to march for only the first day. But, incensed by the Establishment's scorn, they marched on to Aldermaston and joined the subsequent annual marches.

By this time Rogers was in the process of completing his last six terms at the AA, but taking three years to do so. Pattrick was still dismissive of his abilities and wrote irately in reply to a letter from Rogers asking for some form of guidance:

I have discussed your career with one or two members of staff, and from what I have heard, it does not seem that you have taken much initiative yourself. I do not think the A.A. is in any way 'vague' about your future. As you know, we were extremely surprised when you were passed by the Intermediate examiners, and in the latter part of your third year we had doubts as to whether you should go on at all.

If you wish to return to the School next term, you may do so, but I must emphasise that it will be on a probationary basis. If you cannot keep up with the remainder of your unit you may not be able to continue in the School.

The real issue is this: you have some ability in design, but although you are now twenty-four, you seem to be completely incapable of organising your time or acquiring any understanding of the practical side of an architect's work.

Rogers had spent some time working with architectural practices to gain experience, but seemed to make little headway. He worked with Bill Howell, who had just left the London County Council, and was vaguely involved with Howell's and Amis's house at 80 to 90 South Hill Park in Hampstead. Howell's reputation among architects at the time was immense. With the LCC he had built the second phase of the Roehampton Lane housing development. This time the anti-Swedes had won and Howell was able to put up hard, clean, concrete slabs based on Le Corbusier's Marseilles *unite*. Roehampton as a whole was, even then, beginning to be recognized as one of the few, the very few, undiluted triumphs of 1950s British architecture. But, even with such a modernist hero, Rogers was hopelessly at sea. The role of the junior in an architect's office involves precisely the tasks he was least qualified to do – drawing and tea-making. He did, however, spend a more congenial and relaxing time with Stirling Craig, the third-year tutor at the AA, and his wife, at Stevenage. As an architectural influence Craig's careful, vernacular houses were of little interest to Rogers, but after the taxing rigours of Pattrick his approach provided a breathing space and helped restore his confidence.

It may have been instrumental in the sudden turn-around in his academic fortunes, for when he returned to the AA something finally seemed to click. His ever-widening cultural range was beginning to pay off and his own peculiar form of architectural communication was beginning to be understood. A report dated July 1958 signed by Pattrick and John Killick, the fourth-year tutor, grudgingly concedes a little more than usual: 'He has a genuine interest in and a feeling for architecture, but sorely lacks the intellectual equipment to translate these feelings into sound building.'

Su was also being drawn into architecture. In 1958 and 1959 she and Rogers went on holidays to Italy, Greece and Paris, and he discovered that she liked nothing better than to spend her time looking at buildings. Her father had overruled her instincts, however, and insisted that she went to the

London School of Economics to study sociology – the most ideologically acceptable course he could think of. But she loathed her three years at the LSE, made few friends and spent most of her time in the Rogers circle. With increasing success at the AA and somebody who was, in effect, a willing apprentice as well as a formidably organized companion, Rogers's prospects were improving rapidly.

At the AA he was quickly becoming a somewhat curious star. His new tutors included Alan Colquhoun, another graduate of the ICA sessions, John Killick, now in partnership with Howell, and Peter Smithson – an awesome trio of intellectuals from whom Rogers gradually began to realize the ambiguities rather than merely the virtues of modernism. Colquhoun was the most cerebral of the three and he would later mount the single most wounding assault on the Pompidou Centre. He was also to go into partnership with Su's second husband, John Miller. Killick started in practice with Howell in 1959, taking with him an acute sense of the need for some unifying rationale for modern architecture. His conclusion was becoming increasingly widespread at the time: 'Our authority today sounds perhaps mundane and uninspiring . . . it consists of what can only be summed up in that rather flat word – the programme.'[22] This remark of Killick's was actually a reference to a theoretical debate which had been started by John Summerson with a lecture at the Royal Institute of British Architects in May 1957 entitled 'The Case for a Theory of Modern Architecture'. Summerson was addressing the key problem of modernism – its rationale, the reason why any one thing should be designed in any one particular way. His answer was the programme.

'The source of unity in modern architecture is in the social sphere, in other words in the architect's programme,' he said.[23] This was a carefully constructed response to the wilder speculations of Giedion whose parallels with nuclear physics he dismissed as 'phantasms of the Zeitgeist'. Banham and Smithson in the audience were not satisfied – the programme, they pointed out, does not generate actual forms. But the slyly perceptive Summerson knew that he was touching on the problem at the heart of late modernism – its lack of a communicable rationale once the masters had departed. The idea of the programme provided a framework which, like the concept of mimesis in aesthetics, is difficult to destroy. It was to become an idea which would be modified in Rogers's work into the stylistic realization of 'process'.

But it was Peter Smithson who was the dominant figure at the AA at the time and with whom Rogers was finally to establish a rapport which won him the fifth-year prize. Smithson said from the first that Rogers was 'a funny guy' and he has been uncertain to this day in what sense he meant 'funny'.

Perhaps it was Rogers's discussion-based approach which appealed to the perpetually theorizing Smithson. In any case by this time the cracks in the modernist consensus were obvious even to the most out of touch student. The CIAM was breaking up and at midnight on 28 January 1957 MARS – the Modern Architectural Research group – was dissolved. MARS had, in effect, been a British version of the CIAM. It had been founded before the Second World War and had carried the modernist flag with its reconstruction scheme for London published between 1939 and 1945 in opposition to a Beaux-Arts scheme from the Royal Academy. But by 1957 there were too many variants of modernism for them to be held together by one organization. Both the CIAM and MARS represented the determination of the pre-war modern movement to organize itself, partly as a combative device but also to suggest a degree of cohesion and unified direction.

Rogers, however, had not yet grasped the ruthlessness of the new British position. Perhaps under the influence of the soft pre-war modernists with whom he was mixing, his own student style was drifting towards a mild romanticism. He felt the shock of how far out of step he had become when he submitted a fourth-year essay to Smithson on the current work of Ernesto, which by then had attained its mature contextualist style. The essay spoke warmly of this new, softened modernism, but it was anathema to Smithson who dismissed it all as romantic nonsense and demanded that the essay be rewritten. Similarly, a housing scheme by Rogers for Richmond Park, which displayed the same romantic tendencies and which derived in part from the neo-liberty revival in Italy, received the same response. It even had bow windows, a feature unlikely to inspire much sympathy from the Smithson who had designed Golden Lane. Rogers saw the writing on the wall – Ernesto, the architectural hero of his youth, was now beside the point as far as his new teachers were concerned. The softer mood of Italy had crashed into the rough concrete and visionary posturing of England.

Nevertheless, Rogers and Smithson came to some kind of accommodation and it was Rogers's scheme for a school for difficult children in Wales, constructed from local materials predominantly wood, that won him the fifth-year prize. He left the AA as an academic success for the first time in his life. His final report, signed by Smithson and a presumably startled Pattrick, says: 'An excellent year's work for Rogers, who at last can bring work to fruition. This student brings to the A.A. a capacity for worrying about the effect the building will have on people and a concern for shape on the inside, which has been an asset to his year.'

Yet he was also in stylistic confusion. The revelation of the level of intellectual complexity that was now infesting modern architecture did nothing to suggest a way of erecting buildings. Rogers had absorbed rather than assimilated the debates and was capable of making wide-ranging references rather than convincing syntheses. There were many hints in what he had absorbed of the elements of his own mature style – not least in Stirling's Leicester University drawings that were then beginning to emerge with all their constructivist overtones – but for the time being he still had a considerable body of the modernist repertoire to exorcise.

However, one building completed in 1932 came to his notice in 1959 and was to have the most far-reaching and unequivocal influence of anything he encountered during this period. It was a building which already had an underground,

cultish following – encouraged by Stirling – and Herbert
Read asked Rogers to write about it after his return from
Paris with Su.

In 1928 the father of Madame Dalsace, the wife of a
Parisian doctor, had bought an eighteenth-century townhouse in rue St Guillaume. Pierre Chareau and his partner
Bernard Bijvoet were engaged to rebuild on the site. Their
first problem was the lady in the top-floor flat. She refused to
be moved. Chareau's solution was to underpin the upper floor
with steel and to demolish the rest except for the staircase. He
then constructed on three floors one of the most extraordinary houses in the world – the Maison de Verre. It was a
technological leap in the dark: the walls were entirely constructed from translucent glass lenses at a time when French
glass manufacturers were specifically refusing to give guarantees to their products when used as building materials. External steel ladders doubled as lighting gantries which provided illumination from outside. Inside, the house represented a breathtakingly thorough exploitation of mass-produced
materials with mobile book racks and storage systems, five
different types of skeletal staircase, pivoting closets and service ducts to free the walls of any necessity to carry wires and
pipes. The plan was relentlessly 'transformable' with mobile
screens and closing sheets of glass at the bottom of the staircases. Everything was mobile, specially designed and representative of a determination to produce a technologically
defined environment. Materials were taken to the limit – one
library ladder is supported solely by an extraordinarily thin
steel tube.[24]

Rogers absorbed all this in wonderment but without any
sense that he could actually do anything with it. It was to lie
dormant for eight years in his imagination.

With Rogers's course complete, Su still had a year to go at
the LSE. She was living at a flat in the house of the designer
Henrion in Pond Street, Hampstead, and Rogers was spending most weekdays there, going home at weekends. It was the
beginning of a connection between Rogers and Hampstead

Marcus, Rogers and Su at the wedding

which was to last precisely twenty-six years. Dada was not happy with this arrangement; she felt that he should live at home all the time and she was beginning to miss the crowded life he brought into the house at Cheam. But neither the Rogerses nor the Brumwells were entirely happy with the solution – Su and Rogers were married on 27 August 1960, a move which was felt to be somewhat unnecessary. Certainly, the Rogerses adored Su and the Brumwells adored Rogers but they were living happily together and Su, at least, was still young enough to put off any such serious decisions.

The wedding took place at a registry office in Reigate and the reception, complete with marquee, was at the Brumwell home. For their honeymoon they flew to the South of France and stayed overnight with Georgie at a house she had rented – Rogers had already established his lifelong ability to stay on excellent and even intimate terms with former girlfriends. From there they set out on a six-day voyage in miserable conditions on a slow boat to Israel. For two months they toured Israel, Syria and Lebanon; they were enthralled by the desert and the great Graeco-Roman ruins which punctuated its vastness. They returned to England for Su to start her third year at the LSE and for Rogers to take up a job with the Middlesex County Council's architects' department under Whitfield Lewis.

In terms of the work this period was to be almost completely baffling. Rogers produced his own unique drawings which were duly passed up through the hierarchy and then vanished. For a while he wondered what became of them until he realized they were simply passed from one desk to another and then finally deposited in a large chest, never to be seen again. After his breakthrough year at the AA, he was obliged to revert to his usual role of living his life almost entirely outside whatever he happened to be doing full time. It is worth noting, however, that Nino says he was told by a senior staff member at Middlesex that Rogers was the finest junior they had ever employed. Lewis, in the reference he gave Rogers on his departure from Middlesex, said: 'I would rate this student in the top 5 per cent of my 300 (approximately) employees in relation to his ability.'

Towards the end of the academic year Rogers and Su decided to try and live abroad for a while and they began to look around for scholarship opportunities. Su's parents were against this idea for the characteristically English reason that Rogers was now of an age where he ought to be earning a living rather than extending his education. Dada and Nino took the Continental view that you cannot have enough education and were in favour of the plan. Rogers, siding as usual with Continentals, put in for the *Prix de Rome* with a design for a monastery but lost, perhaps consoling himself with the memory of Le Corbusier's remark that the prize, along with the Villa dei Medici, was 'the cancer of French architecture'.[25] In any case, Rogers and Su were both far more interested in the United States.

First, Rogers armed himself with a series of references which could, at last, be glowing.

He has travelled widely on the Continent, [wrote John Killick] and has the tastes and sophistication usual in a cultivated young man, who knows Europe well. His primary interests are in the visual arts. His choice of personal belongings and the decoration of his home indicate a man of discrimination and taste. He likes swimming and ski-ing, in fact sport where a personal rather than a team role is played. He is married. I have known him well for the last five years.

Rogers and Killick had grown to know each other during late-night drinking sessions at Killick's flat. These sessions had taken on an increasingly desperate air as Killick had a fatal illness and he was to die soon after giving this reference.

Alan Colquhoun wrote: 'The impression I gained, and which has grown stronger the longer I have known him, is of a man of unusual integrity and sincerity, who brings his problems before him, a freshness of approach unaffected by received ideas or fashionable attitudes.' Finally, there was even a brief endorsement from James Stirling: 'He is one of the best students out of the AA in recent years.'

Rogers and Su applied to five American universities and took up the only one that offered them both a place – Yale. Philadelphia had offered Rogers a better scholarship and the opportunity to study under Louis Kahn – but it had to be Yale. Su was to study urban planning and Rogers architecture. Rogers was also awarded a Fulbright scholarship. He was obliged to turn up at the reception, where all the Fulbright scholars were to meet, with one leg in plaster owing to a snapped Achilles tendon resulting from a skiing accident. That plaster is the one thing that Norman Foster was to recall of that, their first, meeting.

They sailed from Southampton on the Queen Elizabeth in the autumn of 1961. Rogers looked down from the deck at little England. The ship was the biggest thing in town and it was being waved off by men with bicycles who wore cloth caps. Arriving in New York, the ship was the smallest thing in Manhattan and the streets were alive with traffic. It was another new world. Yet again he was to feel that there was something wrong, something inadequate about England. Confronted with the America of the future or the Italy of the past, its scale seemed petty . . . parochial.

While still on the boat, Rogers and Su were startled to hear themselves addressed over the Tannoy as they edged into the harbour. A representative of the local paper in New Haven, Connecticut, the home of Yale University, had come aboard from the pilot boat. He had been sent to write a piece about the young couple coming over to study and he was to entertain them in New York. America was turning out to be everything that Rogers had dreamed of – even as welcoming as Italy.

The local newspaper report in the *Register Magazine*, New Haven, dated 5 November 1961, was headed: 'Yale Students From Britain: Their First Look at U.S.' A front-page picture spread shows them landing at New York, peering from the top of the Empire State Building, walking through the Union Carbide Building on Park Avenue, staring baffled at an automat and reclining on the lawn at Yale before the Harkness

Tower. Only in the last picture does Su's face appear, the photographer having mysteriously caught her turning away on every other occasion. Inside, Rogers is allowed to speak at length about architecture in a vast two-page spread of interview and more pictures of both of them, looking awkward yet faintly insolent, both in tight, white trousers. 'On the whole,' Rogers says, 'the country is fantastically beautiful, but the use we make of it [architecturally] is pretty poor. Buildings should complement the natural resources, such as trees, rivers and seas, rather than be in conflict with them.' The final picture shows them with Mrs Miriam Gabo, the wife of Naum.

Their first lodgings were at the Gabos' house about twenty miles from New Haven. They commuted daily to the university in one of Gabo's cars. Both came to regard the Gabos as their second parents. Unfortunately they had arrived five days late; neither had been too concerned about this after the easygoing atmospheres of the LSE and the AA but at Yale it nearly resulted in their expulsion.

The architecture school especially would stand no such nonsense. It was run by the ferocious Paul Rudolph. He worked his students as hard as he worked himself – as a practising architect he had run through 180 commissions in the years between 1952 and 1960 and he had never had a partner. Stylistically he was obsessed, although with different results, with the same problems that the Smithsons had been attacking in London. In 1960 he wrote: 'Action has outstripped theory. The last decade has thrown a glaring light on the omission, thinness, paucity of ideas, the naïveté with regard to symbol, the lack of creativeness and expressiveness and architectural philosophy as it developed during the 1920s.'[26] In 1969 he was to complete the interdenominational chapel at Tuskegee Institute in Alabama with its contorted, expressionist plan – it was miles away from anything towards which the Smithsons and Stirling had been moving.

To Rogers he simply barked that he was five days late and had exactly ten days to finish his first project or he was out. The effect of Rudolph's regime was to make students feel they

Su and Rogers on 42nd Street in New York. This
photograph was taken for the Yale local newspaper

never had enough time to finish projects. This served the educational function of accustoming them to working under pressure but produced a persistent sense of frustration. It also came as a shock after the ruminations of the AA. There, the agony was likely to be intellectual, at Yale it was practical. Rogers, for example, was dismayed by one conversation with Rudolph about how deep a sunken car park next to a building should be. Rogers argued from the standard AA position that its depth should be determined by the functional require- ments of the circulation of cars and pedestrians. But it became apparent that Rudolph's argument was based on his feeling that car roofs looked pretty from above *en masse*. The correct position, therefore, could be determined by discover- ing at what level pedestrians would be given the best view. This was a world away from Peter Smithson on urban structuring.

But the real benefit of working at Yale was the whole American environment. There were architectural giants around, all of them struggling with the seemingly inescapable problem of what to do next. Louis Kahn was promoting a new, more poetic synthesis from the elements of modernism. Eero Saarinen had evolved a wholly personal expressive style which seemed to re-create itself with every project. He was also to inspire new uses of industrial materials which were to surface in Rogers's work a few years later. Serge Chermayeff arrived at Yale in Rogers's final semester and contributed his views on urban space and an analysis of community and privacy. 'I have observed with some pleasure,' wrote Cher- mayeff, 'that the mythical beast "international style" did not rise from the ashes of World War Two.'[27] It was Chermayeff whose influence was to prove the most lasting – his analysis of the uses of space was to emerge repeatedly in Rogers's work.

In addition, there were the rest of the British. That year was known as the English year at Yale and an American–British split developed, summarized in two pos- ters – one, from the Americans, said: DO MORE, the other from the British said: THINK MORE. Rogers joined up with

Norman Foster who, though two years younger, was on the same course. Foster came from a working-class Manchester background and had studied architecture at Manchester University. In every respect he was Rogers's opposite – a brilliant draughtsman whose education had accustomed him to the hard, practical slog of finishing projects on time with accurate drawings and precise details. To him Yale was easy-going by comparison – but he was impressed by the way the school was open day and night. Rogers, by contrast, was horrified at the workload and spoke dismissively of the level of intellectual debate at Yale. But he was affected by the critic Vincent Scully who taught architectural history: his grand cultural generalizations appealed to the widely read Rogers, even if the purely visual emphasis of his history was as strange as Rudolph's fascination with car roofs.

Foster and Rogers teamed up on several projects, notably on one scheme for science laboratories at Yale. Rudolph's brief for the project displayed a characteristic despair at the failings of modernism and a resulting lack of poetry: 'This is an urban problem. It is also the problem of the architect, as planners and developers have failed to rebuild our cities. They are obsessed with numbers (people, money, acreage, units, cars, roads, etc.) and forget life itself and the spirit of man.'

The Rogers and Foster solution was a low central spine of car parking, lecture halls and restaurants from which, at right angles, the new science departments stepped downwards to meet the existing university buildings. There was a certain rationalist, AA quality about the plan but the landscaping and 'poetic' service towers were strictly American. Most obviously the whole project was inspired by the visionary work of Louis Kahn. Philip Johnson, one of the judges of the project, was not entirely impressed. He stared at the balsawood model and then proceeded to crush the service towers in his fist muttering: 'Have to do something about these.'

Nevertheless, Rogers and Foster found they liked working together and Foster's slick perspective drawings were providing picturesque realizations of Rogers's sophisticated but ill-expressed ideas.

James Stirling was also teaching briefly at Yale and grew to know Foster, Rogers and Su. This small English collective would travel down to New York at weekends. Stirling would buy them bullshots and whisky sours at the Four Seasons, silently stealing the attractive ashtrays as he did so. The management responded by coolly including six ashtrays on his bill. Eldred Evans, the meticulous designer and draughtswoman from the AA, also joined the group. Once more she humbled Rogers with her stunning drawings and intellectual sureness. Of all the students of his generation she seemed to him unquestionably the most talented.

There was one final Yale influence, the importance of which was not recognized at the time, and it came from the West Coast. Foster, Rogers and Su met Craig Ellwood, a Californian architect, who introduced them to the whole post-war history of the West Coast avant-garde. Among the works of their formidable tutors, these odd, *ad hoc* steel constructions must have seemed peripheral – but their inspiration was available when Foster and Rogers found they needed it five years later.

Commuting from the Gabo house was proving demanding, however, and at the end of their first semester Su and Rogers moved into a house in New Haven in which they lived rent free on condition they provided companionship and a 'babysitting' service for the old lady with whom they shared the house. Problems immediately ensued as she was forced to buy air purifiers to destroy the smell of the garlic they used in their cooking. At Christmas she travelled to Miami leaving them free to throw an enormous party which was unfortunately discovered by the maid. Rogers solved the problem by threatening to expose her failure to turn up every day if she mentioned a word about the scenes of debauchery that she had discovered.

Later came a two-week journey with an American student, Carl Abbott, around the buildings of Frank Lloyd Wright. In

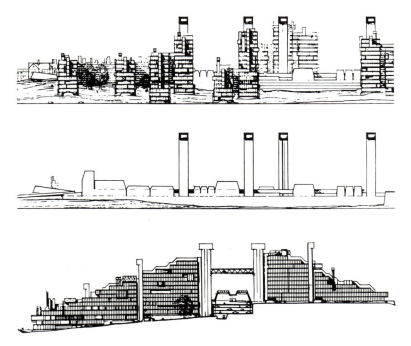

The Foster/Rogers 1961 scheme for the campus at Yale

100

Norman Foster, Rogers and Carl Abbott at Yale

the car were Foster, Abbott, Su and Rogers. The men took it in turns to be Su's 'husband' while the other two hid in the back. By this method they could get away with just one double room at motels. They managed to take in 90 per cent of Wright's buildings and most of the work of Mies van der Rohe.

The revelation of Wright's work turned Rogers's mind to aspects of the modern movement which he had not previously taken seriously. Giedion fatally underplays Wright in his history and, besides, his buildings gain more than most from being experienced in the flesh rather than from photographs. The immediate impact was to produce in Rogers an ambition to build houses with the same mysterious yet revelatory ground plans, and a similar relationship with the landscape.

As it happened, there were two distinct possibilities that he might actually achieve this. One came from his old friend, Michael Branch, to whom he had been sending drawings from Yale and the other was for Marcus Brumwell. Brumwell had already commissioned Ernst Freud to design him a house in Cornwall and had sent Rogers some of the drawings. Rogers's response had been scathing. Both projects remained, for the moment, remote possibilities.

At the end of the Yale year Rogers and Su decided to head for California. Su's course was actually of two years' duration but she had decided that life was too short to stay at New Haven much longer. They had precisely $35 between them and a temperamental Renault Dauphine which caught fire at regular intervals. They would, they decided, find work wherever the car finally broke down for good.

Amazingly, it kept going. They made it to Kansas where they were put up for a night by some cousins of Su's who gave them another $10, and a few days later, after living entirely on baked beans and surviving several fires in the Renault, they arrived in San Francisco where they immediately landed on their feet. They stayed at a youth hostel where the woman in charge loaned them money and soon afterwards they both found jobs – Su at the Federal Housing Authority and Rogers with Skidmore, Owings and Merrill, the architectural practice which, more than any other, laid claim to the possession of the Holy Grail of American modernism. They found a flat in Montezuma Heights and began what Su later described as 'the golden period of my life'.

Professionally, however, Rogers's experience was predictably disappointing. He had been taken on as a draughtsman and failed as usual. They tried him at modelmaking but he was little better at that. Yet he was absorbing what amounted to a new mood at SOM. He was working under Charlie Bassett who had formerly been Saarinen's right-hand man and who had something of his master's flexibility of approach. This was in contrast to the rigorously modernistic style which had characterized SOM's work up to that point. They had, after all, produced Gordon Bunshaft's Lever House in New York, one of the most influential glass boxes of them all. A building with which Rogers was minimally involved for Texas Gas did strike home with its freer use of steel and glass while the SOM office itself stuck in his mind. Its service core was separated out from the rest of the building. He recalls clearly looking down the side of this core from his desk and seeing the faithful Dauphine in the car park, on fire as usual.

During this stay in California Rogers also visited houses by Rudolf Schindler, a highly influential Austrian artist who had worked in America for Frank Lloyd Wright. He had died in 1953 leaving as his masterpiece the Lovell Beach House at La Jolla in California. At Yale Rogers had written an essay on Schindler for Vincent Scully, so he arrived at a neighbouring house by the architect feeling happily convinced he knew all there was to know about the man. He was admitted by a lady who allowed him to wander round, lecturing her on the immense architectural significance of her home. As he was leaving the lady suddenly remarked: 'Mr Rogers, let me give you a piece of advice. Take a year off. Get some perspective. Stop working. Just think.' Startled, he asked her who she was. 'Mrs Schindler,' she replied.

The Rogerses would have stayed in America for another year

but towards the end of 1962 the real possibility began to emerge that they might actually be able to build the Brumwell house. They left their jobs and took the Dauphine for one last American tour. This time they went south, travelling at night through Arizona to prevent the car overheating. They covered Mexico – sleeping under the car at night – and then started back towards the East Coast. Su had to stop on the way and borrow a typewriter from a garage to type her last housing-authority report. Finally, they made it to New York and sailed home in time for Christmas, this time on the liner United States. Southampton must have looked even smaller.

They moved back into the flat in Pond Street and contacted Georgie and her sister Wendy, who had now qualified as an architect at London University's Bartlett School. Georgie was now married to David Wolton, a publisher and hop merchant. Wendy was living in a flat round the corner from the Rogerses in Hampstead Hill Gardens, half of which they all began converting into an office. Foster returned from America later in 1963 to find he was a partner in a practice which was to be called Team 4 Architects. But barely two weeks after the nameplate went on the door Georgie left. The frenzied, competitive mood in the office had proved too much for her frame of mind. She was perhaps too sceptical for the wild idealism of Foster and Rogers. They kept the name, however, and Georgie agreed to remain on the letterhead for the time being – they needed her as she was the only one who possessed the necessary RIBA qualification which allows architects actually to set up in practice. Su became, in effect, an apprentice to the team and they started work, their heads full of Wright, Le Corbusier, Stirling and a whole range of less conventional ideas which they barely even knew they possessed.

3 'Ciao, vecchio!'

A comparison between the offices of Foster Associates and Richard Rogers & Partners reveals illuminating differences between the personal styles of the two men, twenty-two years after they first went into practice together.

Norman Foster has turned the ground floor of a Victorian classical building in Great Portland Street, just behind the Royal Institute of British Architects, into a cool, grey and white temple consecrated to his architectural repertoire. From the street, only the automatic doors and the plate glass windows, made blank by the use of wide, perforated Venetian blinds, are visible. From inside passers-by can be watched as if through gauze, evoking the mood of a 1950s black-and-white French film. Beyond the doors you ascend a shallow ramp to the level of the grey, slightly raised flooring to be confronted by a receptionist seated at a desk of immense technical sophistication. As you cross the dramatic space between door and desk the floor 'rings' slightly, drawing your attention to the void beneath your feet. To the right are models of a Buckminster Fuller geodesic dome and of his Dymaxion car. In the middle distance architects are at work. Filing cabinets and plan chests are meticulously aligned. The tables at which discussions are held are slightly lower than usual, making the manipulation of large drawings and documents simpler, but creating an unease in visitors who find rather more of their bodies exposed while seated than is customary.

Richard Rogers's offices are also in Victorian buildings, but these are classical warehouses beside the Thames, just downstream of Hammersmith Bridge. In 1985 the firm was waiting to move into another part of the complex but, for the moment, he and his staff were housed in an L-shaped block facing partly on to a courtyard and partly on to the river with

Harrod's Furniture Depository on the opposite bank. The metal window frames are in bright blue and the interiors a mixture of bright red, bright yellow and a sharp but pale blue. Metal shelving carries overflowing files and various catering facilities seem in a constant state of flux. Against the stippled white walls lean drawings and samples of building materials.

As soon as you enter you are among architects and their characteristic clutter. The site is spectacular, with views over a wide sweep of the Thames. A central square in the midst of the warehouses has been landscaped by Georgie Wolton and the block of flats, designed by Rogers on another part of the site, has been landscaped by Michael Branch. The site is being developed with a view to allowing the staff of Richard Rogers & Partners to bring their children in during the day.

For all their popular presentation in the press as being somehow indissolubly linked by their mutual fascination with High Tech, the two men are worlds apart. Foster is a focus of control, intensity and long, carefully defined, highly qualified monologues which proceed through, rather than in response to, the demands of others. Rogers seems agonized by detail and organization, constantly switching attention to and from those around him and talking unpredictably, sometimes inaudibly and with little inhibition. But, to this day, each represents for the other one of a handful of people in the world who can genuinely produce excitement in any discussion of architecture.

It was the same in 1963. But at the respective ages of thirty for Rogers and twenty-eight for Foster, perhaps the differences were less defined. And in any case they must have been overwhelmed by their one key similarity – an uncontrollable ambition to be great architects. Furthermore, in Hampstead in those days they were still fresh from Yale and they shared a determination to bring the intensity of their experience of America to little England. Unimpressed by most of what had been built in Britain, they wanted to bring the qualities of Kahn, Saarinen, Mies and, most of all, Wright to the house style of Team 4.

Initially, however, there was a problem of organization. Foster, on arrival, misunderstood the status quo – he did not realize that Georgie and Wendy were architects. He had been under the illusion that he and Rogers were to set up in practice together with, perhaps, Su, and had no idea that a former girlfriend and her sister were to be involved. On top of that Georgie's sudden departure provided them with the problem of being dependent on an inactive partner if they were to work at all. In an attempt to overcome this obstacle Rogers and Foster went through a process of befriending other fully qualified architects. They invited them to dinner and carefully stimulated envy with lavish and exciting descriptions of the freewheeling creativity and relaxed working conditions at Team 4. Finally, they would offer a partnership with a hammy show of reluctance. Each time, the same thing happened – the prospective partner went away enthusiastic, investigated his future firm in more detail and immediately pulled out.

Perhaps if they had gone to examine the Team 4 office they would have pulled out sooner. The outer room of Wendy's flat had been turned into the drawing-office, forcing her to create a bedsit for herself in the remaining room. Given Foster's and Rogers's habit of working long hours and the fact that both had become accustomed to having access to their work at all hours of day and night, privacy was at a premium. This problem grew more acute when Foster moved in with Wendy, having overcome his first doubts about this strange woman who was threatening to dam his creative flow.

But it worked after a fashion until the one occasion when the office's appearance became wholly unacceptable. This was when Ken Bland, the head architect with the development company Wates, visited them to discuss a possible housing scheme in Coulsdon, Surrey. Rogers and Foster persuaded one of their assistants, Frank Peacock, to make a large wooden box in two halves which could be placed over the bed. Glossy magazines were then scattered over its surface. Peacock's carpentry was so good that it gave a convinc-

Norman Foster and Wendy Cheeseman

ing representation of a suitably architectural-looking conference table, the join being invisible. An Eames chair, one of the first in London, was placed nearby. Bland turned out to be a dangerously large man who ignored the chair and sat on the box causing it to bow perilously and revealing to everyone in the room but Bland a tangle of bedclothes. Bland didn't notice but, on the other hand, Coulsdon was never built.

In spite of the surroundings Team 4 formed the careers of both Foster and Rogers, allowing them to work through a complex repertoire of influences and finally, just before its dissolution, to complete a critically acclaimed building which was to lay the foundations for both their future developments. In style the team's radicalism and informal office life were all that could have been expected of a young, mid-1960s practice in Hampstead and they earned themselves a steady cult following. The lifestyle was entirely a product of Rogers's thoughts on how work should be organized and was derived from the latest thinking at the AA. Students from the association frequently applied, usually in vain, to spend their year in practice with them. In the event they were never to grow large enough to take on more than three faithfuls who were to stay with them on and off for the next twenty years.

John Young jumped the queue of AA applicants, having been told he stood no chance of getting the job, by wandering in with his drawings of a ziggurat of prefabricated houses and persuading Rogers to take him on. Young was a public-school product who had disturbed his teachers with arty pretensions, His father, an art teacher, had indulged him but insisted he study architecture at the Bartlett School while his own teacher had recommended the AA, an altogether more fashionable alternative which Young finally chose. During his third year he developed an interest in prefabricated housing which was the foundation for the design he brought to the Team 4 offices. He had seen a picture of the team in an architectural magazine peering together out of the window of Wendy's flat in the sort of album-cover pose usually adopted by one of the pop groups of the time. When he arrived,

Peacock was already there. Peacock had been with Rogers at the AA and had displayed the kind of practical talent which Rogers himself knew he lacked. Peacock was invariably the one man in the office who seemed to know every detail of every project. He was a carpenter who could build most of the things he designed – like the Bland-deceiving bed-box.

One evening Laurie Abbott turned up unannounced. He had decided that Team 4 were the only people worth working for on the basis of some published drawings for three houses in Murray Mews, Camden Town. He had been attending an architectural school at Walthamstow which had failed to capture the extraordinary Abbott imagination. The Team 4 offices were open one night but apparently uninhabited when Abbott wandered in with his girlfriend. He placed her on a high stool, made coffee and studied the Team's work for an hour or so before Rogers appeared at about 10 p.m. He was shown Abbott's plans for a Sin Palace in Leicester Square and he hired him. It proved a wise decision in more ways than one: Abbott's primary interest was not architecture but cars, so as well as producing drawings of extraordinary brilliance and precision, he serviced the white Mini Traveller belonging to Rogers and Su which was used as the office car. With the secretary, Sally Appleby, that was the total permanent staff of Team 4.

But there was one other important personality – Anthony Hunt, the structural engineer. Wendy had known him as a result of some small-scale domestic conversions she had done prior to Team 4. He subsequently met Rogers and Su at a dinner in Earls Court held by the architect Neave Brown whom Roger had known at Middlesex. Hunt had a range of experience from working at Conrans and the engineering practice Samuely before setting up on his own. Most importantly, he was used to working with reasonably adventurous architects and was prepared to take the kind of innovative steps with both materials and structure that Team 4 was to require.

Some weeks after the dinner they called him in to help with perhaps the smallest job he had ever seriously been asked to consider. Su's parents had bought land in Cornwall near Feock around an inlet known as Creek Vean. It was here that the Ernst Freud plans, on which Rogers had poured so much scorn while at Yale, had been sited. But now Team 4 had been given the job which involved a massive conversion of the small Victorian house on the site and, while he was waiting for it to be completed, constructing a small retreat for Brumwell himself. This was to be a simple concrete structure emerging from the earth like a granite outcrop to present a glazed front to the sea. Inside were seating, a worktop, storage units and a small kitchen. Originally, engineering had been considered unnecessary, but Team 4 felt slightly nervous about the concrete reinforcing and ensuring that the retreat would not simply slither off its granite footings. Hunt obliged and was subsequently asked to look at the conversion plans for the house. These proved so extensive and the Victorian House so badly built that Hunt concluded it would be cheaper to knock the whole thing down and start again. Brumwell agreed and drawings began to emerge by the hundred from Hampstead for what was then known as the Cot House and subsequently as Creek Vean. In Brumwell the team had found a client who was, first of all, family, secondly, indulgent of the artistic ambitions of the young and thirdly, because of both of the above, able to be bullied by the combined forces of Foster and Rogers.

Meanwhile, it had become clear that the house for Michael Branch was never going to be built. There was, however, some further work from relatives in the form of a house conversion for Wendy's mother and the three small houses in Murray Mews – one of the clients for these houses was Dr Owen Franklin, the stepson of Gabo whom they had met at the sculptor's house in America, and who remains the family doctor of the Rogerses. The members of the practice had also bought four plots for £2,000 each in Camden Square in the hope one day of trying their hands at property speculation with a development of small houses. The sites became testbeds for every idea Rogers ever had from Frank Lloyd Wright villas to zip-up houses but none was ever built and the sites were sold off in 1972.

There was thus enough work to provide at least an air of activity. The office style, in those days, was in any case so frenetic that the actual quantity of work bore little relation to the total energy expended. Drawings were produced by the hundred covering every detail and every option for every detail. Foster was almost invariably responsible for the final drawings which were actually shown to clients. Rogers would frequently arrive in the office at six and leave at two in the morning. Once he remarked to Su that, although he accepted the impossibility of ever having a whole weekend off, he did think perhaps he would like one day. Christmas and Easter holidays were reserved solely for sleeping – at one family dinner at the Brumwells' Rogers managed to slump unconscious into the soup. Both Foster and Rogers continued into professional life the youthful competitive fire of their Yale days. They were driving each other ever harder, though to what end may have been unclear.

The problem was that they were trying to maintain this style now that they had to cope with real bricks and mortar. In the case of Creek Vean an indulgent relative produced a degree of toleration for their practical shortcomings; in the case of Murray Mews they had no such protection. The three houses had the major disadvantage, as far as planning was concerned, that they were all to be different, painstakingly tailored to the needs of each client. But the worst problem was the contractor whose sole positive attribute was that he was cheap. He had appeared on the scene with the aid of a mysterious intermediary called Fingers who taught Rogers his first important lesson in building management: it is very difficult to sack a bad builder because nobody else will undertake to make good his botched work. Fingers was to be the first of a long line of experts whom Rogers would habitually call on in the belief that here, finally, was the man who would solve all their problems. None of them ever did.

The experience also taught Young about the power of architects. He was contacted by the contractor to produce a plan for the placing of some very expensive tiles in the bathroom of the Franklin house. The tiler was due the next day. Loyal to the traditions of the practice, Young worked all night, laboriously mapping out the tiles in the configuration which would require the minimum cutting. He appeared the next morning with an elaborate scheme which folded out to reveal each wall. The tiler was profusely grateful. Young left, pleased with himself, to return that evening and discover that the tiler had completely ignored the plans – he had, however, luckily proved to be one of the few competent workers on the site.

But everything else went wrong. From the beginning water penetrated the houses seemingly at will and the sunken living-room of the central house – number seventeen – remained entirely flooded for long periods of the building process provoking lugubrious and embittered jokes about indoor swimming-pools. A cast-iron chimneystack descended from a ceiling to miss the centre of a fireplace by 9 inches and one increasingly enraged client revealed to a horrified Rogers that what he had taken to be a damp-proof course was, in fact, newspaper painted black. The worst moment came when the same client who, unfortunately for the team, knew something about building, stood with Rogers by his house's main drain which ran along the ceiling of the garage, told the contractor to flush the toilet and was instantly inundated with water from a junction that nobody had bothered to complete. Such problems generated new problems: they lengthened the building period to the point where the clients' changing requirements became significant elements of the design process. Dr Franklin, for example, was married during the construction process and altered his order from a bachelor townhouse to a family home. The process was beginning to convince Rogers either that he should give up the profession or that architecture ought really to be making more positive attempts to come to terms with change and to be finding some way of incorporating it into buildings.

In the midst of this the Rogers's first baby, Ben, was born. The couple had decided that their student days were over and now was the time to start a family. Rogers has, in any case, always seemed happier when the logistics of infant life are added to his burdens. Ben was two weeks late and even then took two days to be born: Su went into hospital on Sunday evening and gave birth at 2 p.m. the following Wednesday with Rogers present as he was at the births of all his children. At 5 p.m. Rogers returned to the hospital carrying a type-writer and asked Su to type an important document. He still could not master a keyboard, in spite of the army's best efforts, and certainly could not conceive of the possibility of his wife not being available to help him out. Luckily she had recovered well from the birth and Su did his typing – it was a piece of journalism, an article on kitchen conversions for *Homes and Gardens*.

By now they had moved from Pond Street into a house belonging to Betty Ventris in North End, Hampstead. Mrs Ventris was the widow of Michael Ventris, an architect who happened to make his name by deciphering the Linear B Mycenean script, and the house had been designed by him. His widow subsequently married another architect, John Killick, Rogers's former tutor, who had also died. Rogers had visited the house when it had been inhabited respectively by Ventris and Killick. The idea now was that Mrs Ventris should travel the world for a year leaving Rogers, Su and Ben to look after the house. In the event she did not go. The Rogerses were reduced to living in one small bedroom while the atmosphere worsened in the crowded house, although Su had taken on additional duties such as cleaning and cooking for dinner parties instead of paying rent. It seemed like a replay of the uncomfortable living arrangements at Yale. After one year of this domestic depression in North End with Su pregnant again and Ben fifteen months old, they left the house and returned to Henrion's and then, a year later, into the flat in Belsize Grove which Rogers was to occupy with one brief break until October 1985. Initially they shared it with students, one of whom was Mark Sutcliffe who was later to become a partner of Norman Foster.

The point was that the fury of the Bohemian life and work of the office inevitably put organizational pressure on the domestic arrangements and, attractive as that might be to AA students wishing to join, it was beginning to look less so to a man with two children. Also, Foster was not quite relaxed about the curious *mélange* of home and work which characterized everyone else's style at the time. He took exception, for example, to a large Afghan hound which started appearing around the place. This belonged to his secretary, Sophie Read, Herbert Read's daughter. Furthermore, the appalling practical problems of Creek Vean and Murray Mews were weighing heavily on Rogers. He had not had the solid background in building and design procedures which Foster had acquired at Manchester, nor did he have the sort of personality which could ride out the problems. The low point came after a particularly awful day at Murray Mews when he trudged in the darkness up to Hampstead Heath, flung his head into his hands, sobbed and vowed to give up architecture. It was a moment that echoed his thoughts of suicide on the roof of Kingswood House. Just as he had then felt himself confronted by a system and logic which he could never hope to understand, so on the Heath he felt he could never hope to find any way of mastering the whole process of completing a building.

But the Murray Mews houses were finally handed over and, in spite of some evident shortcomings in the finish, can now be seen to have represented an ingenious and entirely worthy architectural début. Spatially the houses represent an impressive solution to the problems of the site and the use of greenhouse glass sloping at 45 degrees to illuminate both floors, as well as placing the bedrooms along a gallery, suggests a high degree of confidence and an obvious debt to Stirling. In spite of all the pressure, Foster and Rogers had displayed an extraordinary reluctance to compromise on any of their ideas. Sure enough the houses were tailored to the clients but the architects stood their ground on what they took to be critical design elements. They refused, for example, to have windows on the wall fronting on to the street. In the case of the Williams house – number nineteen – the client won to the extent of having a few bricks removed and glazing placed behind, but that was as far as they would go.

Overall, Murray Mews amounted to a competent synthesis of a large number of ideas about housing which were in the air at the time, and this quality means that the homes are still visited today by students studying the use of small sites. The Williamses, in particular, have grown so accustomed to this that they start unrolling the original plans the moment the front-door bell rings unexpectedly. They also have a cartoon by an AA student showing a possible extension to their house – the Centre Pompidou on the roof – and Norman Foster's famous helicopter parked outside in the Mews.

Creek Vean was another matter. It produced a comparable level of practical difficulty but the end result provided the first sign that Team 4 were on the way to doing something entirely their own. The partners were helped by the fact that this time the contractor, although prone to taking unpredictable days off, was conscientious and interested in the work. In addition the site allowed all the freedom that Murray Mews had denied them. Yet at first the practical problems of freedom were as bad as those of imprisonment. Foster and Rogers felt it allowed them to change their minds about everything. They ran through something like fifty different designs for the house.

Laurie Abbott started on the drawings and, much to Frank Peacock's amusement, he worked with meticulous care. The standard architect's pen was not good enough for Abbott who had adapted it to produce even finer lines. He carried with him a small steel file to sharpen his nibs the moment they showed signs of blunting. This meant that if the ink flow was blocked for any reason the nib would simply slice through the paper. Peacock's method was to produce beautiful drawings in pencil for, as he pointed out to Abbott, the bosses were bound to change their minds. Abbott did not listen and continued to produce his exquisite drawings. In the event minds were changed so often that by the time the day arrived for him to travel down to the site, the only drawing he could take with any confidence was a rough sketch of the found- ations. Even this proved inaccurate because Rogers changed the angle at which the two wings of the house met so new foundations had to be dug and the old ones abandoned.

The job was planned to take six months but finally spanned three years. The house was to be built in the most expensive concrete blocks on the market and had been designed with a multitude of complicated angles. Thus one man had to be employed full time on site for eighteen months cutting the blocks with a specially designed tool as if they were so many lumps of cheese. Glazing was again a major factor but this time Abbott came up with the material neoprene to fill the joints instead of the greenhouse system used at Murray Mews. Neoprene is an expensive but remarkably adaptable synthe- tic rubber and its use here represented one of the practice's first experiments with relatively recent technology to solve a problem. The potential for its use had been demonstrated in an impressive building of 1960 – the Cummins Engineering Factory in Darlington by the American practice, Kevin Roche, John Dinkeloo and Associates, an offshoot of the original Saarinen practice. There neoprene gaskets had framed the full height of the vertical glazing. But Creek Vean's almost horizontal glazing made more extreme de- mands on the material.

Aesthetically, the house clearly owed a great deal to Frank Lloyd Wright with its careful following of the terrain and its placing below the summit of a hill – Wright was a believer in buildings being related to hills as eyebrows are to heads. There was also the spatial freedom and the way the house reveals itself during the process of walking through it. Unlike Wright's houses, however, it displayed a somewhat assertive, brutal air partly because of its material – the defence for which was that there was a tradition of concrete block building in Cornwall – and partly because of the uncompromising lines of the plan. These had arisen from the need to house Brumwell's substantial art collection which the team had accommodated in a long, corridor-like gallery and a small picture store. There was also the need to exploit the views: the rooms are arranged in fan patterns so that the plan seems to reach towards the sea and up the river valley. And, finally, a degree of flexibility was built into the house: the plan allowed for additional rooms to be added along the house's main axis.

From the beginning the local authority had been under the impression that the concrete exterior would be rendered, something almost unthinkable in the late modern climate of the day when the flat, white stucco of the 1930s had been rejected in favour of something harder, more Smithsonian. It was never rendered and the house remains without proper planning permission to this day.

But the most notable first impression of the house arises from one of the very last decisions taken by Rogers and Foster. Having produced his austere piece of hillside sculpture and having pushed Hunt as far as he dared go with the thinness of the roof deck, he decided to bury the whole thing under a mass of vegetation. The first problem here was that the idea had not been allowed for in the design. Rogers brought in none other than his old friend Michael Branch, now a landscape architect, to sort out the problem. Branch discovered only 11 inches depth was available for planting on the roof. So he was obliged to work out a drainage system using roof tiles under the soil. The scheme worked for a year until the plants began to die off for no apparent reason. Eventually Branch worked out that they were being warmed throughout the year by the heating ducts which Rogers had designed into the structure. They were thus allowed no dormant period. He replanted them and the roof garden has since flourished.

In retrospect the impulse to bury the house in planting may

be seen as springing from the 'organic' inspiration of Wright. It represents a rather literal interpretation of the idea which Wright had summarized in the phrase 'a thing loving to the ground' and in the aspiration 'it will be a companion to the horizon'.[1] In fact the almost supine relationship to the landscape implied by these formulae is neither a feature of Wright's Jacobs House of 1937, of which he was speaking, nor 119 of Creek Vean. Both display a conscious imposition of form on the landscape which can be described as 'natural' only in a certain cultural context. In a revivalist architectural context 'natural' might be taken to mean only those houses which fitted obviously into the received vernacular. In England that would have meant tile-hung walls and small, functionally located windows. But, whatever the rationale, the effect is to break down the rigour of Creek Vean's geometry and to provide a distinctly mysterious aspect to the house as it emerges from the cliff in sections defined solely by the particular condition of the vegetation at the time. There is thus an indeterminacy about the appearance which contrasts with the finality of the blank wall on the road side. For the planting is not disciplined but rough, forcing its way through the steps and right up against the house. It seems actively to conflict with the fabric – tough, natural change at war with tough, artificial permanence. Equally important for the future was the fact that Laurie Abbott's neoprene never leaked.

The house was a complete critical success, receiving an award from the RIBA for a work of outstanding quality in 1969 – it was the first private house to do so. It had been expensive – £30,000 – and the sale of one Mondrian had not raised enough to fund such extravagance, another picture had also to be disposed of. As a project it had been hopelessly badly organized, but then the Brumwells must have known they were indulging young and inexperienced architects and were prepared to accept the chaos.

Apart from the enormous advantage of being spoiled by the client, the commission had conferred another huge benefit in that it allowed Foster and Rogers to begin their careers in a

The Brumwell house at Creek Vean. © *Brecht-Einzig*

Creek Vean. © *Brecht-Einzig*

The Michael Jaffé house

very unEnglish way. Fairly large set-piece houses are the kind of projects with which Australian or American architects commonly launch an *oeuvre*, but in Britain there are a few such commissions. Radical architects are seldom offered that kind of opportunity and are consequently obliged either to sell their radicalism to commercial clients or to capitulate.

Domestic work continued to provide all Team 4's work. A house for Michael Jaffe was built in Radlett, Hertfordshire. This did not receive anything like the same attention as Creek Vean but it did represent a significant stylistic development. Certainly it shared its ground-hugging quality but its plan is harder, more rationalist than Creek Vean with the house being fitted into parallel walls which simply follow the downward movement of the sloping site. This greater formality suggested a move away from Wright and towards a more idealistic conception of space in contrast to the empiricism of the Cornwall house. It achieved a rather non-architectural fame in that its interior was used for some of the scenes of 'ultra-violence' in the film *A Clockwork Orange*. But Stanley Kubrick, the director, was not interested in the outside so he cheated by implying that the house had a traditional exterior. More appropriately, it inspired the interest and approval of James Stirling.

Meanwhile, Marcus Brumwell had been persuaded to buy land on the far side of the Creek and the team had produced a plan for a picturesque cascade of waterside housing descending to the beach. Planning permission was not forthcoming and the scheme was abandoned after a public inquiry, the first of many in Rogers's career.

Finally, Wates, in an experimental mood, had commissioned them to produce a housing scheme for Coulsdon. This represented, in some ways, Team 4's first 'real' job. Whereas all the other work had arisen through friends and relatives, this was a genuine commission. It arose from a letter written by John Donat, the son of the actor Robert Donat, to Neil Wates after they had lunched at the Savile Club with Henrion, the designer who was also the Rogerses' landlord. The letter suggested a way of 'narrowing the gap between the Wates image and what is actually being built'. This would involve giving three young architectural teams an open brief for a housing scheme on a Wates site. The teams suggested by Donat were: Ahrends, Burton & Koralek, Team 4 and Evans & Gailey – the practice formed by Eldred Evans.

124   Innovation in this sort of private housing had been encouraged in the late 1950s and early 1960s by some brilliantly landscaped Span schemes by Eric Lyons in Blackheath. Team 4 followed Lyons in his use of materials but were less keen on his straightforwardly picturesque approach to landscape. Instead they preferred a characteristically more aggressive solution and one which owed a great deal to the teaching of Chermayeff at Yale on the separation of private, semi-private and public spaces. The site was 69 acres in Coulsdon which the team divided up with woodland into ten separate fields. These were joined by pedestrian routes and the whole was surrounded by a road which fed car parks in each field. This produced a highly distinctive 'rationalist' look to the scheme with the car parks sunk below the level of the houses and access to them via railway-type platforms – a borrowing from Le Corbusier. It was a scheme that leaned heavily on Chermayeff's analysis of the need for a hierarchy of spaces divided by 'locks' which reinforced those spaces and signalled movement from one to the other. To this day Rogers feels it was one of his best unbuilt schemes. It foundered when the momentum within Wates finally petered out. There were prolonged rows about contractual arrangements which soured the atmosphere in the office and produced Team 4's worst crisis. The whole scheme was finally abandoned after the team's break-up.

Rogers's second son, Zad, was born in November 1964. The children's names – abbreviated versions of those of Old Testament characters – were the choice of both parents, though neither were religious. But the fact that they are all single syllables arises clearly enough from Rogers's lifelong desire to reduce things to their essentials whether they be words or roof

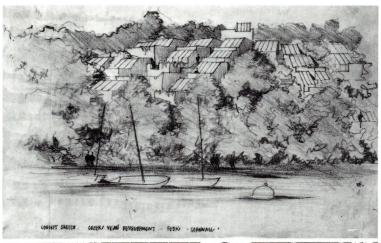

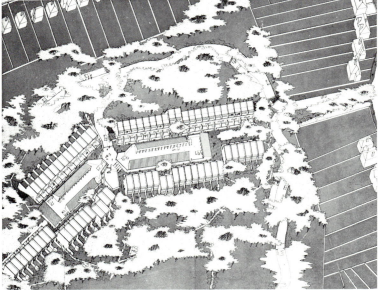

Above: Norman Foster drawing of the housing scheme
for Creek Vean
Below: Housing scheme for Wates at Coulsdon

decks. Rogers had always looked forward to having a family while Su displayed considerable ingenuity in arranging their family life while working steadily at the practice as administrator and architectural apprentice. There was one major hitch when Ben, sleeping in his pram outside the office, vanished. Luckily he had only been taken by a policewoman to the local station. She had assumed he had been abandoned. Ben went to nursery school as soon as possible and the Rogerses felt they could now stretch to employing some help at Belsize Grove. A lady was taken on, and some complex arrangements made with Frank Peacock's family, which all produced a reasonably steady routine allowing Rogers and Su to work together more or less full time. In addition Jan Hall, a sixteen-year-old teacher at Ben's nursery school, had become fond enough of Ben to offer to take him out on Saturdays. Su agreed and hired her for additional babysitting. With a few breaks Jan, who has become a close friend of the family, has remained part of the Rogerses' lives ever since, providing a splendidly reliable nanny-housekeeping service. Nevertheless, with Foster and Wendy having reconciled their differences to the extent of marrying, the blending of home and business life had introduced a potentially subversive polarity to the life of the practice.

Now, though, Team 4 were on the brink of their major success – a building in which both Foster and Rogers were to discover most of the elements that would compose the originality of their mature styles. And the primary element was steel. But the Reliance Controls factory in Swindon did not spring quite as fully formed from nowhere as is sometimes suggested. There had been a project for a school in Sutton, Surrey, which had come to nothing at a fairly early stage. Even so, it was clear that it had been intended as a predominantly steel building. The inspiration had been the Smithsons' Hunstanton School and references to that building are clear enough in the completed Reliance factory.

But, if the Smithsons provided an English precursor, it was the Americans who provided the real inspiration. First of all, there was Wright again who had spoken of 'this new resource of tenuity – a quality of steel – this quality of *pull* in a building ... was definitely lacking in all ancient architecture because steel had not been born into building'.[2] Wright's peculiarly American romanticism had softened the edges of new technology by presenting it as a form of simplicity and this was taken up by a generation of Californian architects who were brought together by the magazine *Arts and Architecture* under John Entenza. He commissioned a series of 'case study houses' which had been published in this country in Esther McCoy's book *Modern Californian Homes* in 1962.[3] The central work of this series was Charles and Ray Eames's house and studio in Pacific Pallisades.

Born in 1907, Charles Eames had worked in Eliel Saarinen's office before joining with Eero Saarinen in 1940 to enter the Organic Design In Home Furnishings competition run by the New York Museum of Modern Art. Their entry consisted of moulded plywood chairs which have ever since remained some of the most distinctive products of modern design. The Eames house was built with his wife, Ray Kaiser, in 1949. It sprang from his experience of the production of furniture both in war and peacetime. From that he derived an awareness of industrial processes and products which allowed him to construct a house off-the-shelf using standard, widely available parts. The result was cheerful, *ad hoc* and cheap. It suggested a casualness and open transformability in its architecture that seemed to break away from the agonizing of the past. Or, in the case of Rogers, from all the damp-proof courses, sawn blocks and disintegrating drains. In addition the method of building from catalogues of industrial parts suited John Young perfectly. Not only was there his fascination with prefabrication, there was also his consuming interest in industrial technology which made him a walking catalogue in his own right.

But there was more than just Eames in the McCoy book. There were also Craig Ellwood and Raphael Soriano who were producing impersonal steel pavilions that offered simple, endless flexibility within their rigidly rectangular plans. The designs said: Do what you like in here, we are just the architects. In the mid-1960s such an approach had obviously found its natural era. The prevailing mood of informality and anti-authoritarianism found an architectural expression in a form that declined to offer even the most basic degree of regimentation. On the one hand the buildings were off-the-shelf, implying they could be available to everybody rather than simply those with special expertise or access to particular materials. On the other, they were easily transformable, changeable for changing needs, and were, as a result, appealing to a generation which valued above all the possibilities of a condition of constant becoming. The rather contorted romanticism of Wright which had found a kind innocence in steel was thus simplified – these *ad hoc* homes were 'natural' purely because they were made with the materials most easily to hand. Where once brick had been the obvious material, now it was industrial steel.

But, initially at least, the ideology behind the American houses hardly mattered, it was the method that Team 4 needed. For the partners had startled themselves by talking their way into the Reliance job. There had been a shortlist of three, all recommended to the head of Reliance, Peter Parker, by James Stirling. The brief was to produce 30,000 square feet of light industrial space within ten months of the first meeting – this was to be simply expandable to 110,000 square feet. Since they had absolutely no relevant experience and no time to go through their usual process of laborious trial and error and bewildering changes of direction, the off-the-shelf method or 'building on the phone' represented at first a pragmatic rather than an ideological decision.

The beauty and efficiency of the end-product was, under the circumstances, astonishing; though it was perhaps a certain inexperienced naïvety in the approach that actually pulled them through. They produced a simple rectangle to incorporate offices and work-space. It was clad in profiled steel decking which was used both for roof and walls. The steel structure was external to these walls and braced with slender steel members joined in a wide, flat X-shape. The rectangular plan, derived from the California houses, unquestionably had a deliberate ideological rationale. It allowed the factory to be among the first to adopt a strictly egalitarian view of the workforce by offering no evident hierarchy of functions. There was one entrance for all and one canteen. Certainly, there was a manager's office, but externally it was unsigned. Meanwhile the steel structure and decking was the obvious answer to the need for speed and cheapness, and in the use of the decking to the limit of its performances for a vertical wall span of 12 feet, they were, with the help of Hunt, breaking new ground. Finally, one wall of the factory was glazed. This was the side which could either face into a courtyard as the complex was expanded or be unplugged to run into a new, joined unit. The success of the whole as far as the company was concerned can be measured by the final cost of £4 per square foot of which only 7s. 6d. was attributable to superstructure.

Had the building simply been an efficient solution, that might well have been that. What made it an architectural success was the degree of freedom of aesthetic manoeuvre which Rogers and Foster had created for themselves within the straitjacket of the brief. The building's final appearance was a clean horizontal with the one vertical accent of the black water-tower unashamedly lifted from Hunstanton School. Within this conception the detailing is evidently chosen for reasons other than the merely functional. The diagonal bracing, for example, appears on all four walls. In strictly engineering terms this is unnecessary – it need only appear on two – but both Rogers and Foster demanded it should run right round the building. In addition the flat X-junction at the centre of the bracing is just one of many possibilities Anthony Hunt was able to offer. Hunt recalls that Foster made the final decision at the last possible moment over a lunch at which he had simply offered a range of options drawn on paper napkins.

The quick simplicity of steel and glass came as a revelation after the struggles with the 'wet trades' of brick and concrete. The team had still pushed the schedule to the limit – working drawings were sent down on overnight trains to Swindon to be available for work to be done the next day – but somehow the materials had responded as if alive to their taut and

ferociously concentrated procedures. They had also responded to the team's insistent desire to reduce the elements of structure to the minimum. Hunt had already experienced this need in Rogers who had reduced the thickness of the roof on Creek Vean as far as the engineer would allow. With Reliance, Hunt says, everything was simply 'stressed to the limits'. Aesthetically, Rogers and Foster had discovered that steel expresses this kind of rigour with a directness denied to wet-trades buildings. The steel structure and its bracing do more than simply express structure, they also express its movements actual and potential. This was the 'pull', the 'tenuity' of which Wright had spoken.

Suddenly they found themselves with a whole new expressive repertoire that had remained relatively unexplored within the mainstream of the modern movement. It also caught the prevailing political mood of the time. The open, indeterminate spaces of Reliance appealed to Rogers's left-wing instincts at a local level and, at a global level they suggested the kind of efficiency and freedom in the use of resources which was being demanded by Buckminster Fuller as mankind's only possible salvation. Fuller's conviction that materials and design technology would increasingly offer people 'more with less' represented the post-war version of the more sociologically based utopias of the pre-war modernists. It placed imperatives of lightness and flexibility upon architects and provided a visionary and apocalyptic rationale for every step of the design process. It offered, in other words, one way of filling the void felt consciously or unconsciously beneath every decision.

But it is images that strike deepest into architects' imaginations and last longest – and that was the real point of

130

Reliance. It had provided Rogers and Foster with the imagery of naked technology and engineering. They were to use it in radically different ways – the immense trouble they took in slotting the services into Reliance simply made Rogers impatient, whereas Foster was to develop from it an obsession, visible in his later buildings, with the flawlessly complete skin. Foster, for example, was always pleased with the way the fluorescent light tubes fitted into the corrugations of Reliance's decking. Rogers, in contrast, thought this made the lights more difficult to change and was to move towards a more expansive and more easily changeable style. But neither of them has yet abandoned the inspiration it provided. Having worked through the sculptural and spatial repertoire of the moderns they had now discovered a form in which they could at last produce something entirely their own.

131

Reliance won the Architectural Design Award in 1966 and the *Financial Times* award for the most outstanding work of industrial architecture in 1967.

In essence, [wrote the *FT* award assessors] it is an unpretentious structure for the manufacture of electronic components, designed for flexibility and expansion and built quickly and cheaply on a typical industrial estate plot not very different from hundreds up and down the country; and yet on entering it the visitor is immediately aware, even if he has not noticed it from outside (for it is consistent both externally and internally) that he is in a distinguished building. Its uncompromising simplicity and unity of general conception and detailed design create an atmosphere that is not only pervasive but notably comfortable to be in. It is refreshing to find something so beautifully direct that it looks like a lost vernacular.[4]

Among those assessors there had been a flash of deeper insight than is normally required for such competitions. 'A lost vernacular' evokes a lost paradise, a prelapsarian condition of innocence in which the world is once again pristine and complete. And that is the real dream of visionary wholeness which lies behind the work of Buckminster Fuller. In him the American dream of elemental union with the things of the earth was taken from its rural context to be placed in a technological one – an extrapolation of the half-realized thoughts of Wright. In the process the explicit mysticism became implicit, disguised by the need to appear feasible. The simple sense and legibility of Reliance had made it seem, even to the assessors, innocent of the long, sophisticated debates on design. There seemed to be no architectural straining after effect. For Foster and Rogers the visionary tone was modulated into a rather cooler ideological rationale which would only have explained the elements of the building, not why it worked as architecture. But that hardly mattered – for they had been born again in steel and nothing can match the fervour of converts.

Windows were later inserted – by a management less sensitive to the building's seminal nature – into the profiled steel walls, ruining the whole feel of the building. They also revealed the extent to which Reliance, although constructed on the best Californian principles of *ad hoc* architecture, was in reality a very smooth, finished building. The flexibility was highly controlled by a classical sensibility.

But in spite of its public success, Reliance produced virtually no new work. There was just one ill-fated project – a development in Derby for a company called Fletcher and Stuart. This was designed to be a curving wall of offices and works clad in black, anodized aluminium on an old railway site. But only the first phase was completed and it was generally felt to be a considerable let-down after Creek Vean and Reliance. The company did, however, let the architects take away some old wooden moulds of giant cog wheels that had been lying around the place. They still stand around the homes of Young and Rogers, mournful memorials to Team 4's least satisfying job.

Following a pattern that would be repeated on a grander scale ten years later, great success for Rogers was thus followed by massive depression. Lack of work was putting intolerable strains on a practice whose internal problems had already become critical. It was now clear that Foster and

Rogers were two powerful personalities who had burnt out their capacity for co-operation. Where once their differences seemed complementary, they now seemed contradictory and had inevitably been heightened by the fact that both their wives were working in the practice. There were quarrels over whether Su should be made a full partner – both Wendy and Foster resisted this on the ground that she was not a trained architect.

Once it became clear that the split was approaching it was Rogers who was afflicted with the greatest degree of insecurity. In practical terms he was the most threatened – neither Su nor Rogers had ever expected or received much in the way of parental subsidy. But the impending break-up was provoking a deeper crisis of confidence within Rogers. In Foster he had found a personality who, in practical terms, made up for his own deficiencies as a working architect – in particular his draughtsmanship – and in psychological terms provided him with an equal who could help him realize his ideas through the barrier of his own difficulties of communication. Rogers had begun to feel that he could only function in partnership with somebody as gifted as Foster. This sense of professional and personal incompleteness found its obvious correlative in the childhood conflict between inside and outside school. It was to form the foundations of his most crushing adult depressions. Invariably its primary manifestation is in the conviction that he will never be able to build again – that the brute matter of the world cannot be bent to his will any more than can its language. It is a conviction that is generally accompanied by the consideration that he can fall back on teaching. During the days of Team 4 both he and Foster had effectively subsidized the firm by occasional teaching work – Rogers was making around £900 a year from the Regent Street Polytechnic at the time of the break-up. But it did not represent a living wage and besides, whatever the condition of his confidence, he knew it represented a distraction from what he ought to be doing. He therefore began searching for a way out of his depression.

His first step was to return to his contacts among the middle-aged English modernists by visiting Sir Leslie Martin, one of the central figures in the post-war British mainstream and an architectural godfather to the succeeding generation. With Gabo and Nicholson, Martin had edited *Circle: an international survey of constructive art* which had been published in 1937 and captured precisely the benign optimism associated with the modern visual arts at the time. 'A new cultural unity is slowly emerging out of the fundamental changes which are taking place in our present-day civilization;' began the editorial, 'but it is unfortunately true that each new evidence of creative activity arouses a special opposition, and this is particularly evident in the field of art.'[5]

Martin studied Rogers's portfolio and told him simply that he believed he had no need to worry, he would make it. He recommended that Rogers look for work among the local authorities who were, in those heady days of the late 1960s, still substantial builders. Ideologically both Rogers and Su were keen on this idea. But after Camden and Lambeth had yielded nothing, rescue came yet again in the form of a Marcus Brumwell connection.

Brumwell had founded the Design Research Unit, a design practice which, after a reasonably distinguished past including work for the Festival of Britain, was facing a less certain future amid the fierce competition of the explosively expanding design industry in the late 1960s. Since 1945 it had been run by Misha Black, an architect, who, in 1933 had founded the Artists' International Association, a left-wing pressure group, and, in 1938, had co-ordinated the important MARS group exhibition of modern architecture. In 1939 he had been responsible for the design of the Kardomah chain of restaurants and for the interiors of London buses. He had overseen DRU's successful phase but was now aware that it was in danger of falling behind. Specifically he was concerned about the standards of its architectural team. His solution was to employ Rogers and Su as a practice under the umbrella of DRU. They would be paid a salary – for Rogers this added another £900 to his teaching income – and any fees earned would go to DRU. Yet they would remain an independent operation known as Richard & Su Rogers. Rogers had wanted to preserve anonymity in the name, a condition he insisted on at Team 4, but Martin had advised strongly against this.

Their first job was to write a report on DRU itself. The memory of that still makes Rogers wince – the report tore the whole organization apart and, in effect, ensured that he could never be anything but a resented outsider within DRU. Such youthful indiscretion was, during the mid-1960s, a trademark of Rogers. He had developed a habit of producing shocking statements of one kind or another. Once, because a young radical was required as a contrast to Hugh Casson, he had been asked to co-sponsor Peter Sheppard as president of RIBA. His speech called on the Institute to sell its building and attacked the entire profession in the language of Herbert Marcuse, a thinker in whom Rogers had immersed himself.

In June 1967, Rogers and Foster called their tiny staff together in the Hampstead office and told them the work had dried up. Foster was to stay on with Wendy at Hampstead Hill Gardens to finish the last detailing of the Derby building. Rogers was to leave for DRU, taking with him whatever vestiges of hope were left for the Wates scheme at Coulsdon. John Young was to remain with Foster for the moment, although he had to return to the AA for the autumn term. He went back, but Rogers managed to negotiate a deal with the school which allowed him later to work with Richard & Su Rogers. He was to complete his fourth year and to abandon his fifth year leaving him free to work full time with Rogers as he has done ever since.

Young's first extra-curricular experience turned out to be the site supervision of a house at Ulting, Essex, for Humphrey Spender, a teacher at the Royal College of Art and a brother of the poet, Stephen Spender, and his wife. This was Rogers's first job without Foster and at first it seemed obvious that he should follow the direction suggested by Reliance Controls. But, as he stared at the empty Essex field which he

Reliance Controls

was to fill, he was overcome with doubt. He could easily have designed a traditional wet-trades house with brick arches and an altogether familiar look for the Home Counties middle class. It was a moment of perfect equilibrium – he could have chosen either brick or steel. He does not know what finally made him choose steel. But the important thing is that he does not say it was ideology – it was an aesthetic choice like any other.

Yet it was one that he went to some lengths to rationalize. In July 1969 Rogers was to produce two manifestos explaining both the practical and ideological bases for the move away from the 'wet trades' and from traditional architecture. The first is called 'Education' and begins with an attack on universities which are described as 'closed authoritarian institutions, operated primarily for the benefit of those running the institutions'. A breezy *non sequitur* follows: 'Technology offers the possibility of a society without want, where, for the first time, work and learning need only be done for pleasure, and the age-old capitalist morality of earning one's keep, the backbone of the existing power structure, would be eliminated.' An architect, in this context, should be 'a problem solver in the field of environment'. But, instead: 'At the end of every year there are the same soul-destroying static images; at best some more tastefully done than others.'

The piece closes:

The way to justify the need for architects is not by creating a closed shop as propagated by the RIBA and most of the schools it controls, but by throwing the profession open to all those who are interested so that architecture becomes a truly multi-disciplinary activity. Only when all answers become the outcome of necessity, expediency and economy, will the architect and student be in a position to question whether an object is needed at all, and to suggest to the client a complete reconsideration of any problem.

The second manifesto was considerably less theoretical and outlined the entire rationale for changing from one type of building to another. As such, it is worth quoting in full:

Our first buildings were tailor-made to suit the client's specific programme, constructed of traditional materials using standard contractual procedure. However pleasing these buildings were they had serious organizational problems which led us to radically changing our approach. These problems were:

1 Both large and small buildings took at least three years to build so that by the time the client moved in his needs had changed; married, divorced, children, income increase, etc.

2 It was impossible to keep on good terms with the other two competing parties over such a long period, i.e. the builder and the client.

3 At a time when Britain alone needs 400,000 houses per year we needed four architects to produce four houses a year.

4 It was impossible to control workmanship as most of the work was done on an open site by semi-skilled labourers and quickly covered by other materials.

5 The number of different materials and trades made it impossible to supervise the construction.

6 The materials were mainly highly absorbent, likely to move and were never the same twice.

7 The cost of condemning bad work or making changes to parts already built were prohibitive.

8 The architect ended up doing the contractor's job and organizing the site, the subcontractors, the suppliers as well as doing some of the actual building in a desperate attempt to keep control of standards, time and cost.

After four years of practice it was apparent that we had to change our approach or go out of business. Since about 1966 our buildings have been:

1 General purpose as against tailor-made so that basically the same shell can cater for different requirements, different sites, different clients.

2 Allow for maximum flexibility for future growth and change.

3 Erected in a minimum amount of time.

4 Have a high environmental standard.

5 Need minimum maintenance.

6 Constructed of the minimum number of prefabricated standard components.

7 Have dry joints of a yes/no variety.

8 Use maximum spans with minimum internal structure to eliminate internal obstructions and to give flexibility to partitioning. These partitions are easily moved by the client.

The Rogers house at Wimbledon by Richard and Su Rogers.
Dada's pottery is visible on the kitchen counter and her studio –
now John Young's home – is across the courtyard

9 Services are in ducts for ease of access.
10 Roofs are built first to give shelter.
11 The main contractor is replaced by the site architect, who deals with specialist subcontractors, often not from the building trade.

The Spender house cost a mere £12,300 and work on the site lasted from July 1968 to January 1969. Perversely, despite the alluring simplicity of steel construction, everything went wrong as the client constantly demanded changes and improvements – indeed a correspondence about this house between Young and Spender continues to this day. Whatever the material, the client still had awesome power. But the house was relatively successful in spite of the slight awkwardness owing to the way the external steel frame penetrated the cladding. Much more successful was the next commission which was for a house in Wimbledon for Rogers's own parents. Cheam was now too large and, after twenty years, Dada and Nino were ready for a change. Once again Rogers's imagination was freed by a family commission and the problems of a private house.

Nino proved a demanding client, specifying that, as they were growing old, the house should be easily used by somebody in a wheelchair and be reasonably flexible to accommodate changing needs as time passed. In a fortunate echo of the brief Eames set himself in California there was to be a separate studio for Dada's new hobby – pottery. Dada's pots were to become Rogers's most precious possessions.

But it all slotted beautifully into the design processes suggested by the case-study houses and Rogers deliberately planned the construction of the house with the possibility of mass production in mind, an entirely different design consideration from the fine-art basis of Creek Vean. Both the Spender house and the Rogers house were described as prototypes and were presented as steps along the way to an entirely over-the-counter house which could be wholly self-built. The Rogers version represented the cleaner architectural solution. A bright yellow steel frame outlines the glazed walls at front and rear. Thus far the impression is of a mainstream modernist glass house. But down the sides – neither of which needs fenestration because of the way the house fills the site – aluminium sandwich panels joined by neoprene gaskets provide the walls. The panels were derived from the technology of American refrigerated trucks and they contributed an extraordinarily high degree of insulation as well as being relatively easy to cut.

Inside, Rogers was able to develop the theme of flexible space further than ever before. Hunt had engineered a clear span for the steel framework running the width rather than the depth of the house which provided both uninterrupted glazing and a complete absence of structure inside. Rogers used this space to produce a kitchen formed simply by a fully serviced counter running parallel to the side wall and bedrooms and a study divided from the living-room by sliding panels. In front of the house is an identically constructed but smaller pavilion intended as the studio. It is inhabited today by John Young.

Perhaps the greatest success of the house is seen in the use made of the site. Both house and studio emerge from a mass of dense planting and are almost completely concealed from the road by an earth mound. They are thus discovered as quiet pavilions, entirely at home amid the trees. The house fills the site width but for an access path to the back garden and sets a rhythm of similarity and contrast with the smaller studio. The Rogers and Spender houses were subsequently chosen to represent British architecture at the Paris Biennale in 1969.

Sensitive site considerations were not, however, Su's and Rogers's primary concern at the time. Both the houses had clearly only been half-way down the road of radical use of materials about which they were now dreaming. They spoke enthusiastically about the possibility of buying a house in bits from Marks & Spencer and, apart from the laying of the foundation, eliminating the need for a builder completely – a belated revenge on the Murray Mews contractor.

The opportunity to see how far they could go was provided by the entirely theoretical Dupont House which was to win the second prize in the 'House of the Future' competition. The first prize went to a relatively uninteresting entrant so the Rogerses received all the publicity.

Called by the practice 'Zip-up No. 1', this used the same sandwich panels as the Rogers house but this time with higher density foam which allowed them to span 30 feet and thus made further structural support unnecessary. From that point the house was simply put together in modules which could be added to as they were required. From a hardware dealer you could even buy a special tool which would allow you to put windows, doors, cat-flaps or letter-boxes into the walls at will. The energy efficiency was prodigious – one 3 kilowatt fire was enough to heat the whole house. In the design process John Young had come into his element. His earlier fascination with prefabrication became a fascination with zip-ups and with the investigation of alternative technology from outside the building industry. It was the beginning of his lasting role as the man who finds practical and detailed ways of enhancing Rogers's ideas and as his invaluable and permanent ally. He is also a spectacular and original designer in his own right.

The Spender and Rogers houses had been successful but they had been lonely struggles. Building still seemed an agonizing process, mainly because of the endless problems of small, private houses. With the Zip-Up Rogers finally recovered from the loss of confidence he had suffered during the break-up with Foster. It was entirely new and involved technology in a more satisfying and relaxed way. The tautness of Reliance had been replaced by a technological freedom, an improvisatory quality that did away with the need to slot pieces together to form a smooth 'perfect' skin.

A factory for Universal Oil Products in Ashford, Kent, would have provided a larger-scale test for the new-materials theme but the deal fell through. DRU, however, had moved into new offices in Aybrook Street near Marylebone High Street and Rogers and Su were asked to carry out a conversion and extension as well as redesigning the interiors and the

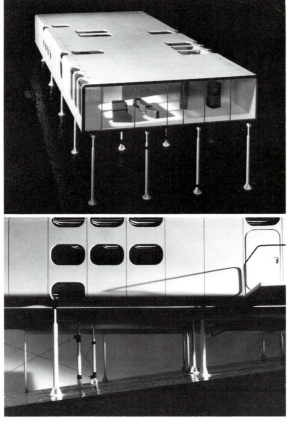

The Zip-up House. © *Brecht-Einzig*

furniture. Their early 'concept montage' showed the roof of a green Volkswagen Beetle projecting from the top floor of the old building. This was to be the largest job of the practice and resulted in the extraordinary 'yellow submarine' roof that still dominates Aybrook Street, although the scheme as a whole has been badly spoilt.

It was a pleasant enough job but its real value was that it put them in touch with Renzo Piano. Piano had written to Rogers, expressing admiration for his work and pointing out the similarities in the directions they were both pursuing. He had a practice in Genoa, a wife and family, but he was possessed of a dream of England precisely parallel to the one which had brought Nino here in the first place. To Piano thirty years later the country still symbolized a haven of peaceful creativity far from the political storms of Italy. Additionally he had found the professional options in Italy distinctly limited – he could either be an *architetto di salotto*, a cocktail party architect, or a developer's architect and neither appealed to him. He travelled to London to meet Rogers and Su and subsequently advised on the Aybrook Street conversion. Piano was the son of a builder and had immense knowledge of all industrial building processes. On a series of long walks around London Rogers discovered that they could talk together about architecture in precisely the absorbed, animated, mutually understanding way in which he had spoken with Foster.

Some years later the new partnership was to receive a letter from a company in Finland called Piano Waltenberg. 'We would like to know,' it began, 'if it is possible for you to sell us second-hand pianos. If it is please send us some information about the instruments, prices, quality, the time of delivery and so on.'

By this time the practice had established itself as a virtuoso performer with radical materials of the kind that other, more traditional practices tended to avoid. It had become the architectural exponent of much of the 'alternative' creativity that was taking place at the time in other fields. A new

Zad. Ben and Ab Rogers at Creek Vean

stylistic repertoire was developing but it was remaining within domestic and partly theoretical confines. The considerations were primarily technological and practical and based upon a Fulleresque ideal of a world saved by the efficiency of new materials and design. Work, however, was scarce. Apart from Aybrook Street there was only a long-term and highly speculative town-centre development in Cambridge. This scheme, known as the Kite, was to rumble on for ten years producing a trickle of fee income but no end product beyond a hangover of bitterness in Rogers about the behaviour of rival practices. It began in 1969 and was taken over immediately by Marco Goldschmied who had been employed on Young's recommendation, although he could not have been a more different character. Where Young was interested in design, technology and materials, Goldschmied was interested in management and strategy. They had been contemporaries at the AA and Goldschmied had arrived at Aybrook Street after first applying unsuccessfully to Foster. Soon after his arrival it became clear that he had brought in one talent the practice clearly lacked – the ability to produce weighty, strategic essays which would impress potential clients like the Cambridge developers. Pierre Botschi also joined the firm at this time – he brought a particularly Swiss precision to the practice.

A new team was forming which, with Piano's arrival in mid-1970, seemed to promise a new creative phase. But the lack of work continued and deeper personal problems had by now emerged to overwhelm Rogers. His third child, Ab, had been born in July 1968. By that time, however, unknown to Su, the break-up of their marriage had become inevitable. Rogers had conducted surreptitious affairs for some years, but his meeting with Ruth Elias was to mark the beginning of something entirely different, something that was to provide him with a means of liberating himself and a resolution of the traumas of his childhood and youth.

Ruth had grown up in upstate New York. Her early years were spent in a small town called Woodburn until the family moved, when she was aged fourteen, to Woodstock. Her father was a doctor specializing in cancer who had decided he wanted nothing more to do with New York City soon after the Second World War. It was a decision that was to create a rebellious hankering after city life in his daughter, although she did not rebel against her parents' left-wing politics. After

an education at public high school and on a ranch in Colorado, she went to Benington girls' college in Vermont. But she was not happy there and took two terms off to stay with friends in London. She arrived in a gloomy Muswell Hill in the autumn of 1967 and was given a list of eight people she might like to contact while in London. The only ones she rang were the Woltons, the parents of David who had married Georgie. Georgie was there and she invited Ruth round to her house where she met Su and Rogers.

They did not meet again for another year in which Ruth mixed in the highly politicized world of young London in the late 1960s. She worked with the campaign against the Vietnam war by assisting draft-resisters. To stave off demands from her parents that she continue her education she enrolled at the London College of Printing at Elephant and Castle to study typography and graphic design.

Among her friends at the time was one who shared a flat with Su's brother, Joe, and it was at a party there that she ran into Rogers for the second time. He invited her to lunch at the AA.

It soon became clear that this was not just to be another phase for Ruth any more than it was just another clandestine affair for Rogers. With fateful momentum it all became very serious, very rapidly. The intensity startled them both. They began to see each other every day, even if only for five minutes and separation became agony. They developed an almost complete inability to say goodbye or to hang up the phone which has lasted to this day. During that period they never saw a film together, never watched television and never read a newspaper – time was too precious. Ruth started writing notes covering the details of every meeting – something she had never done before – she recognized the importance of the affair from the start.

At Christmas Ruth stayed with friends in Scotland and Rogers travelled down to Cornwall. Soon afterwards he had to go to Ireland to look into a possible housing job. They were still relatively new to each other and Ruth had said only that she might come with him. Rogers stood outside the Aer Lingus terminal in Knightsbridge, immediately opposite the Brompton Oratory, half convincing himself that she would not come, but she did. On a later trip to Ireland they were accompanied by John Young, a close friend of Su, who was profoundly upset by the revelation of the affair.

More trips together were organized using Rogers's ability to take on lecturing jobs around the country. Ruth would appear at the back of the hall and often be mistaken by the students for Su. She wore mini-skirts and invariably startling colours, pink tights, yellow boots and a blue skirt, which looked remarkably like the pinks and yellows of the Zip-up House. 'Which came first,' asked one student, 'your colours or your wife?' After one of these lectures – at Liverpool – they were driving north in a rented car. Rogers began to overtake a lorry only to find, half-way round, that he did not have enough power. Another lorry was hurtling down towards him. He assumed they were both finished but he attempted to tuck himself in as closely as possible under the lorry he was over-taking. Somehow he misjudged the manoeuvre – the car bounced off the lorry, slewed across the road and came to a halt hanging over the edge of a cliff as the oncoming lorry roared past.

In March, Ruth tried to finish the whole thing at a meeting in Parliament Square. She told Rogers it was no good and said he should go back to his family. Rogers plagued her on the telephone, even attempting to persuade her by the bizarre means of boasting about a car – a Jaguar – a client had lent him. The separation only lasted two days. At Easter Ruth went to Spain by herself, a holiday which wounded Rogers. In the summer she went home and he went with his family to Vernazza, a village near Genoa in Italy where they met up with Piano and where Rogers goes into retreat every year. Ruth had developed the habit of writing to him via Young at the office; now she wrote to the post office at a neighbouring village which meant Rogers had to take a two-hour walk to pick up the letters. On Ruth's return to London she took a flat in Warrington Crescent. It projected high above the neighbouring rooftops, giving Rogers the kind of view he loved.

Up to this point Su had suspected nothing, but Jan Hall had begun to notice a slow transformation in the routine of life at Belsize Grove. The comings and goings changed disturbingly until, one babysitting night, a strange American woman appeared at the door and told her she could go home. The affair was to be made public.

For a man brought up within the tight discipline and effusive affection of a close Italian family, the decision to leave Su and their three children represented the almost unthinkable. Indeed it was his background that made Su blindly confident of the stability of their marriage until so late in the day. When he finally admitted to this affair which had got 'out of hand', his first request to Su was: 'Don't tell my mother'.

Ruth was the antithesis of Su: where Su was disciplined, organized and seemed to have a life of children and work which existed almost independently of Rogers, Ruth was riotous, immensely energetic and capable from the first of making him the focus of her life. Superficially she represented a sudden eruption of young life in the world of a thirty-six-year-old man who was facing a future with nothing more than a few fragments of work, who was persistently insecure about his own capabilities. There were, however, others who could have fulfilled that role – the only difference this time was that he had fallen hopelessly in love with Ruth and had detected something in her which answered his every need.

In spite of Rogers's demands for secrecy Dada had guessed what was going on and she confronted Su a few days later. Su told her everything and Dada went away upset.

At Christmas 1969 Ruth's parents came over and she told

them the whole story. The man she loved, she explained, was fifteen years older than her, he earned £1,000 a year, he was married and he had three children. They were appalled.

But the separation was to be conducted in an almost breathtakingly civilized manner. It took place over a year in order to minimize the shock to the children. Rogers knew it was pointless to challenge Su's right to their sons so he simply spent fewer and fewer nights at Belsize Grove until, by mid-1970, he had left completely. He did so having been dogged by the sense throughout that all he needed was somebody to appear, beat him over the head and tell him that what he really wanted to do was to stay with his family. Perhaps detecting this element in his mental condition, Su persuaded him to visit a psychiatrist, in the hope that the crises in his life would be revealed to be disordered rather than inevitable. But the visits were fruitless.

Civilized as it all was and in spite of his new love, 1970 was a dreadful year for Rogers. His family life had folded around him and, although the practice had remained intact with Su still working in it, the flow of new work had dried up completely. In desperation he decided to take up a teaching post in the United States for three months from the autumn. The idea was to take the pressure off the situation at home and to give Rogers himself a degree of breathing space. This proved misguided. Cornell University was then at the centre of an architectural debate though not in any spectacularly creative sense. Two figures dominated the school: Colin Rowe, a massively influential Englishman who had been James Stirling's first and most important mentor at Liverpool and Oswald Ungers, the professor of architecture who had a practice in Ithaca. From the beginning it was made clear that Rogers was not expected to speak to Rowe, such was the level of animosity between the two sides.

It was a trip in which Ruth introduced Rogers to her world. She took him to New York and its galleries and they visited her parents who were then living at Providence, Rhode Island. (Fred Elias asked Rogers privately if he was convinced he was doing the right thing. He was not worried about Ruth, she was giving up nothing, it was Rogers who was taking the big step.)

It was towards the end of the three months that Rogers received a letter from Misha Black telling him of DRU's decision to end their relationship. It seemed like the last straw. There had always been resentment within the organization directed at these apparently privileged outsiders, particularly after they had been awarded work by DRU itself at Aybrook Street and after their damaging report on its activities. With no fee income to speak of flowing from the arrangement, Black could no longer provide a justification for continuing with Rogers. They were allowed to continue to use the offices as conventional tenants but the future now looked bleaker than ever.

After visiting Ruth's parents the couple returned to London. The practice was in the same hopeless condition as when they had left so they were obliged to look for the cheapest accommodation they could find. In the event they exceeded their rent limit of £10 per week by £1 and settled in a tiny flat in Park Hill Road not far from Belsize Grove where Su was now living with the three children and John Miller, another architect. Jan immediately began to help them out by going round to tidy the flat after a day's work for Su. Ruth would talk to her at length before she could tidy anything and, when she did start work, she played Bob Dylan and the Beatles at full volume on the record player. Jan began to like her in spite of the legacy of their first suspicious encounter. For Rogers the return to London had come as a relief – both the office and his family had seemed to survive without him. The cataclysm he had feared seemed not to have occurred. For Ruth, however, it was a difficult period. Rogers spent his evenings at Belsize Grove with the children and she began to feel that the whole position had reversed. Now she was the one being left behind. Soon afterwards her state of mind improved when she got a job as a graphic designer at Penguin Books under David Pelham and the financial pressures began to ease.

152

In January 1971 Piano & Rogers entered the competition for a museum in Glasgow for housing the Burrell Collection. They threw themselves into the task believing they were the perfect practice for the job. They produced a rectangular glass envelope with a steel structure holding the services. It failed even to be placed in the competition. But it had been an important project. The translucent, skeletal structure dug into the hillside with its mobile floor and rectangular plan foreshadowed the design that was to win a much bigger competition in a few months' time. The Burrell was finally completed in 1983 in the form of a substantially quieter and more conventional building by Barry Gasson.

At the same time they worked on a curious project for an American foundation to produce a standardized hospital which could be planted anywhere in the world but specifically for use in under-developed countries. It was commissioned by the extraordinary Dr Lalla Iveson. Again nothing came of it, although the project still crops up from time to time. But Piano and Rogers had discovered a way of working together and a style which seemed to emerge naturally from the partnership. Piano had brought a sophisticated awareness of building and manufacturing processes to the practice which allowed Rogers to develop his sense of the possible expressive powers and beauty of steel. The hospital provided 'clean' spaces sandwiched between two service floors. It was all balanced on four oil-rig-type legs and topped by four spindly cranes to manoeuvre service elements.

In the spring of 1971 Ruth and Rogers went to Rome (Rogers's first visit to the city since his student days) and then skiing in Zermatt. They were penniless to the point of being unable to buy a meal in the hotel and they lived on salami. Rogers snapped his Achilles tendon for the second time. (On the previous occasion, he had met Foster while he had his leg in plaster just prior to going to Yale. On this occasion too, the accident was to be an omen for future momentous events.)

All the work with Piano had so far been rather theoretical

as had been, on the face of it, a curious episode in 1969 involving Chelsea Football Club. There had been plans for a massive redevelopment of the ground, and the design and marketing company of Wolff Ollins had approached Rogers to join them in producing a submission. Richard Attenborough, then connected with Chelsea, had been responsible for choosing the team. There had even been talk that they might take over the partnership. Rogers's scheme was to build a massive umbrella over the whole stadium but Wolff Ollins seemed more interested in the straightforward marketing aspects and the project fizzled out. It had, however, brought them into contact with an engineer called Ted Happold from the partnership of Ove Arup. Arups were then still relatively fresh from the ambiguous triumph of the Sydney Opera House. It was ambiguous because, although the building was clearly a masterpiece, its construction had been a nightmare of politics and financial losses. Undaunted by that experience, Happold wanted to go for another major international job and early in 1971, he contacted Rogers again. He wanted Arups and Piano & Rogers to enter a competition for a building in Paris. Rogers was immediately violently opposed and he produced a long memo explaining why. Piano was in favour on the basis that, since they had no work, they had nothing to lose. There are several versions as to what finally decided them to enter. Certainly there was a meeting at Belsize Grove. (Rogers and Ruth had by then moved back there as Su and John Miller had moved out.) Happold had Piano on his side and apparently Su and Rogers against him. At some point Su rose to go and pick up the children and, as she was leaving, announced that she had changed her mind and they should enter. Rogers was outvoted but he still resisted. They immediately ran into difficulties finding an assistant to help with the competition drawings – Arups had by now financed the project to the tune of £300. After two phone calls to old colleagues by Piano had drawn blanks, Rogers said that the next one must agree or the whole thing be called off. Gianfranco Franchini agreed at once and pre-

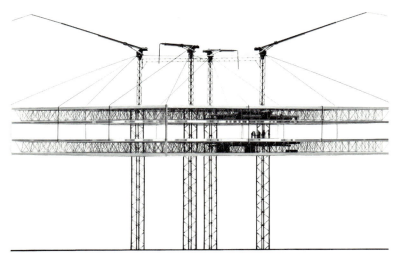

The model of the Aram Hospital

pared to move to London from Genoa.

Fate then proceeded to collude with Rogers in convincing everybody that the whole thing was a ghastly, ill-judged mistake. The rules of the competition stipulated that entries be posted no later than 15 June. With a couple of hours to go before midnight, Goldschmied was despatched with the complete entry to the twenty-four-hour post office at Trafalgar Square. The man at the counter refused to accept them on the grounds that the tube was too long. Goldschmied grovelled on the floor, unpacking the drawings and cutting them down, noticing as he did so that representatives of two other English architectural practices were busily doing precisely the same thing. Finally, he posted them only to have them turn up back at their offices thirty-six hours later with a message that there was insufficient postage.

Goldschmied, feeling personally responsible, tore round to the post office and demanded they give him a backdated postmark on the basis that he had been misled. A violent row led to the compromise that he could have a smudged postmark. A week later they received a phone call from France saying their entry had not been received. Ruth rang Rogers in desperation. He was in Portsmouth teaching. 'Forget it, sweetie,' he said philosophically, 'it's a loser.' A subsequent phone call revealed that all the English entries had accidentally been locked in an office but had now been recovered.

Soon afterwards, early on a Friday morning in the middle of July, Su was sitting alone in the Aybrook Street office. There was nothing to do and it was the custom for people to wander in at a fairly leisurely pace throughout the day. The phone rang, it was a reporter from *Le Figaro*. Rogers appeared soon afterwards and they both agreed that, in so far as they could work out what the reporter had been saying, it must have been a hoax. The phone then rang again. It was Piano from Genoa.

'*Ciao, vecchio* . . .' he began – he was marginally younger than Rogers and insisted on calling him 'Old Man' – 'are you sitting down?'

Then, at about ten-thirty, John Young appeared on the off chance that there might be something to do. He saw the two partners of a recently broken marriage dancing around the office. He assumed that, at best, someone had paid some fees. But Su simply turned to him and said: 'Guess what, we've won the Pompidou Centre.'

4 Steel cuckoo

The Centre National d'Art et de Culture Georges Pompidou was born of a conception so precisely French that the ap- pointment of an Anglo-Italian architectural practice to build it seems perverse. It represents the latest flowering of that form of royal, imperial or presidential patronage which periodically feels the need to endow Paris with yet further glories. The city, as the embodiment of all that is French, must from time to time receive cultural tributes, usually with the name of the provider of the political impetus prominently displayed. In an egalitarian age the president was to have some trouble with this last requirement as many, inspired by the example of Rogers, persisted in calling the building 'Beaubourg'. But nowadays Pompidou Centre is the name that has stuck.

So the building is the product of *la gloire*, that curious combination of personal and national vainglory which the French have always found an entirely acceptable justification. In Britain any project of comparable single-mindedness would either be destroyed or held up for years by a system innately mistrustful of such visionary self-glorification. In France it took just nine years from conception to opening ceremony. Even that, however, was not quick enough for its initiator – Pompidou died on 2 April 1974.

The reasons Rogers had brandished at Piano, Happold and eventually Su for not wishing to be involved with such a scheme arose directly from this background. He loathed the idea of a cultural monument and its association with one man. To participate would seem to represent a volte-face in the direction his work had been taking towards an increasingly available, serviceable and reticent architecture. Everything about this project reeked of the grand gesture, the wasteful flamboyance, the bad faith which opposed the Fullerian virtues of efficiency and flexibility. Furthermore, he mistrusted the very word culture with its élitist overtones, and this mistrust was compounded by the obvious centralizing tendencies within the very idea of a national arts centre. The ideological opposition was strengthened by more practical considerations such as the suspicion about the organiz-

ation of the competition within the British profession, and an apparent certainty that the whole thing was, in reality, a forum of architectural ideas rather than a serious building project. Besides, nobody could conceive of the possibility that any nation but France could win.

But Rogers and almost everybody else had misread the situation. For a start Pompidou was in no doubt that his centre was to be built. Large teams of planners had been at work for months defining requirements and establishing chains of command for the project. It was the president's pet, something that would outlast the memory of any political triumph and, over the years it was that which was to become the decisive element. It forced the job through obstacles that would easily have overwhelmed a scheme conceived by a committee or department. It also resulted in the important early decision to separate the Centre from existing bureaucracies like the Ministry of Culture. Finally, this personal quality allowed government money to be found for a building that might otherwise have been regarded as dangerously radical: if its success could be attributed to Pompidou, so could its failure, so greater risks were justified.

The other element of the general background which was to have a significant impact on the design process was its Parisian site. The first firm decision that anything should be built there at all was taken in 1968 when it was announced that a library was to be erected on the Beaubourg Plateau. This followed much discussion about the future of Les Halles nearby. Indeed at one stage Rogers visited the president to try and persuade him not to demolish Les Halles – he did not want the whole area to be changed. The markets were to be moved out to the suburb of Rungis, a move that precisely paralleled the movement out to Nine Elms of London's Covent Garden. The debate about Les Halles had drawn attention to the problems of the whole Marais district, which included the Beaubourg Plateau. Beaubourg itself had been cleared in the 1930s of its slum housing in response to the problems created by large-scale prostitution and the highest levels of tuberculosis in the country. The site had been left empty and latterly had provided a truck park for Les Halles. By 1969 Pompidou had succeeded de Gaulle and adopted the library scheme. But he added to this the idea of combining it with a museum of modern art to replace the inadequate existing facilities at the Palais de Chaillot. Pompidou's monument was to be in the heart of old Paris, and it was that urban context which was to play a key role in the design process and which was to inspire some of the most furious opposition to its style.

On the positive side, it was these elements which had made way for the appointment of foreign architects. Pompidou wanted the best in the world and the glorification of Paris required the same, whatever nationality was to provide the inspiration. The result was that the competition was neither rigged in favour of the French nor was it an excuse for a festival of outrageous architectural ideas.

Finally, although it was an age of big projects – the West had not yet had its confidence shattered by the oil crisis – it was also an age of the kind of political uncertainty which makes such projects risky. Student unrest in the late 1960s had been serious elsewhere in the world, but nowhere had it come as close to mobilizing a revolution as it did in May 1968 in Paris. The insurrection petered out eventually, but it had been too effective for either the French government or middle-class society to feel confidently victorious. It had been, perhaps, the most traumatic period for French society since the war.

Rogers's doubts had partly arisen from the central role France had played in the wars with the students and from her formidable reputation for winning at almost any cost. The image of the French riot police had been a consistent element in the left's hate-iconography in the late 1960s. Indeed, the police presence was still overwhelming in Paris in 1971 – none of the Piano & Rogers team had ever seen so many armed police on the streets.

Pompidou had decided from the first that the Ministry of Culture was not to run the project. He wanted to ensure that both in conception and execution, it would not be restrained by existing thinking on arts centres. He set up a team to produce a brief which emerged in July 1970 and was accepted by the president, apart from a few reservations about the number of parking spaces and toilets. As well as specifying square footage and so on, the brief had added an industrial design centre, the general notion of an information centre and placed considerable emphasis on making the place active all day. The idea was to avoid the deadness which can afflict palaces of the performing arts during the day. Somewhat airily, it also emphasized flexibility – though the compilers had no idea of the gargantuan scale on which Piano & Rogers were to interpret that word. The brief as a whole could have defined almost any building from a temple to a tent. The one thing that Sebastian Loste and François Lombard, the heads of the team, did know was that it would be massive. They had specified 1 million square feet, making it the size of Harrods.

With the acceptance of the brief, the first task was completed. Lombard became head of the *programmation* team which was to work alongside the architects throughout. Loste stayed with the project until its third year, acting as liaison with government and generally exuding all the mystique of the French civil service. It was only then, after Rogers had struggled manfully to speak to him in faltering French, that he revealed that he had been educated at Cambridge and spoke perfect English.

A project manager was needed and with this appointment Pompidou was to execute the one stroke of managerial genius which would ensure that his Centre would be completed. He ignored all pressure either to hand over the job to the Ministry of Culture or to appoint somebody young and experienced in the role of artistic management. Lombard had supported the latter course. Instead he chose Robert Bordaz, a huge, elderly, white-haired *conseiller d'état* who had organized the French evacuation after Dienbienphu in Indo-China, run the French broadcasting company and even administered the Cannes Film Festival. A formidably authoritarian figure, Bordaz inspired fear, resentment and a certain fatherly affection. He spoke no English and was to be known throughout as Monsieur Le President behind his back and Monsieur Bordaz to his face, almost never Robert. Only Ruth was to succeed in breaking through this exterior and, throughout, she was alone in addressing him by his Christian name. Bordaz watched them all unceasingly. If, during building, Rogers ever slipped off to London illicitly, he would receive a telegram from Bordaz telling him that, unless he was back on site within forty-eight hours, there would be no further work for him. With the memories still fresh of the arbitrary and insensitive discipline of his schooldays, it was a regime which Rogers found unpleasantly evocative. But nobody now denies that but for Bordaz, either lorries would still be parking on the Beaubourg Plateau or a fatally compromised arts centre would be failing to attract the crowds.

Once Bordaz was in control the administration began to click into place and the competition was launched. The jury contained one French architect, Aillaud, who was largely unknown, Michel Laclotte, head curator of the department of paintings at the Louvre, the writer Gaetan Picon, Jorn Utzon, the Danish designer of the Sydney Opera House who was later to drop out because of illness to be replaced by Herman Liebaers, director of the Royal Library of Belgium, Sir Frank Francis from the British Museum, Philip Johnson, the virtuoso American architect who had worked alongside Mies van der Rohe on the Seagram Building in New York and who has since been responsible for an extraordinary variety of post-modern improvisation, Oscar Niemeyer, the main architect of Brasilia, Jean Prouvé, a French engineer specializing in innovative building methods and consequently a logical ally for Piano & Rogers and Willi Sandberg, a Dutch museum curator who had been immensely influential in contemporary thinking about museum and gallery design. It was a jury that defied analysis. Rogers felt strongly that Johnson would tilt the balance against them; the Yale teacher who had once squashed his balsawood service towers had already moved too far into post-modernism to accept their style. He had met Sandberg through Gabo.

Architectural competitions are highly unpredictable endeavours especially when they involve large public buildings which are likely to arouse popular feelings. So much depends not only on the jury but also on the brief and the client, that there can be no simple way of ensuring that the best – by any definition – entry will win or that, even if it does, it will be built in the competition-winning form. In addition the complexities of national or local interest may be put above mere architectural quality, making a degree of political analysis a necessary part of every entrant's preparation. (The competition for a design for an extension to London's National Gallery, which Rogers was to enter, demonstrates how badly wrong things can go. In that case a winner was chosen even though the design was deemed inappropriate by a divided jury which had been working from an inadequate brief. The design was duly modified and then rejected before the entire brief was changed by an endowment to the gallery.) The central problem with competitions is that they involve the production of a brief which the architects are expected to fulfil. Since a large element of any architect's work is supposed to be the precise definition of a brief, in a competition he is, as it were, being brought in too late and without the possibility of any relationship with the client.

Nevertheless, there were 681 entries from around the world for the Beaubourg competition. They were judged blind in the sense that no member of the jury knew which architects were responsible for which entry during the judging process. In the case of one entry the jury was convinced throughout that its playful references to the past indicated the hand of Robert Venturi beyond any doubt – in fact they were wrong.

As for the winner, one rumour suggested that Johnson had indicated to Lombard ten days before the announcement of the winner that Piano and Rogers were streets ahead of all the rest, but there was no doubt that nobody had the faintest idea of who had come up with the scheme. Indeed the revelation of the name Piano & Rogers produced looks of alarmed ignorance from the jury members when it was announced. The looks turned to smiles of relief when Ove Arup & Partners were announced as engineers. At least there was some substance behind this wild proposal.

Back in London, once the qualms about entering had been overcome, the preparation period for the entry had been relatively brief. The form of a glass envelope with a double-layered external steel structure had already been evolved for Burrell and the team determined to work along the same lines. After that the overall shape wavered somewhat – Piano at one point coming up with a vast, inverted pyramid – but finally settled on the hard, rationalist rectangle. The concept of flexibility prompted them to adopt the idea of the maximum possible span to provide uninterrupted floor space. This was about 150 feet, which would have filled about one-third of the site. The team then decided on a piazza in the front of the building so that the structure itself would be pushed right up against the rue de Renard, reinforcing its line and movement towards Notre Dame. They managed that much in London, but then progress seemed to slow and Rogers travelled to Genoa with Piano and Franchini and finally back to London where the scheme was completed. The engineering input at this stage was limited although Arups had come up with the idea, as part of the search for flexibility, of movable floors which was included in the submission. Nobody had any clear idea whether this was feasible, but it could always be worked out in the unlikely event of them winning. Also, there were external video screens hung from the structure. These were intended to cover parts of the building with images of movement and change which could be constantly updated. On to the competition drawings, true to the spirit of the age, were glued photographs of Vietnamese girl soldiers to illustrate how the screens might look. Giant lettering was included reading: 'Animated Movies Production for the . . .', 'Computer Technique of . . .' and, filling one bay, 'Caroline, go to Kansas City immediately your friend Linda has been busted,' to demonstrate that all sorts of information could be acquired from the Centre Pompidou. These screens were later to be removed from the design by order of Giscard d'Estaing, officially on grounds of cost, although Rogers was told by the president that he was concerned about their use for political agitation. The fixings designed to hold them up, however, are available on the finished building should there ever be a change of heart. The moving floors on the scale initially planned did not survive either. They were later modified to become moving mezzanines and, again, the finished building could accommodate them. Only one was finally installed.

In planning terms, the scheme showed some familiar pre-occupations. The segregation of pedestrians and cars was achieved, both by using the building as a wall between the piazza and the road and by sinking the whole site about 12 feet below ground level. It was raised on Corbusian *piloti* which allowed both movement and sightlines through the building. Conceptually they had adapted the brief to their own preoccupations.

We recommend, [began the written part of their competition entry] that the Plateau Beaubourg is developed as a 'Live Centre of Information' covering Paris and beyond. Locally it is a meeting place for the people. This centre of constantly changing information is a cross between an information-orientated, computerized Times Square and the British Museum with the stress on two-way participation between people and activities/exhibits. The Plateau Beaubourg information centre will be linked up with information

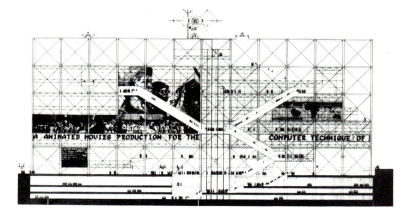

Drawing of the piazza elevation from the competition entry

Concept

We recommend that the Centre Beaubourg is developed as a 'Live Centre of Information covering Paris and beyond. Locally it is a meeting place for the people.'

The Plateau Beaubourg information centre will be linked up with information dispersal and collection centres, throughout France and beyond; for example, university centres, town halls, etc.

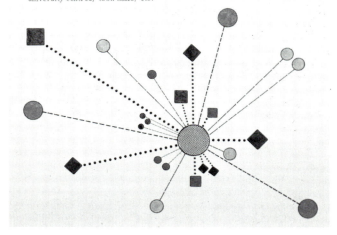

The first page of the Pompidou Centre competition entry

dispersal and collection centres, throughout France and beyond; for example, university centres, town halls, etc.

Design processes, thus summarized, can seem deceptively lacking in context. Most of those broad, early decisions survived the building programme remarkably intact and, once understood, provide a significant part of the experience of the finished building. The piazza, the external services and the steel structure can all be explained and understood in terms of the uses of the site and can be employed to describe the overall effect. But they fall far short either of explaining why the building is the way it is or of grasping its total impact. Architects' procedures may seem to respond to the brief and their own predilections as if there was no yesterday, only tomorrow, and as if a building, unlike anything else in the world, could be wholly new. But in fact they lean over their drawing boards with heads full of images which, from time to time, they may attempt to codify into an ideology but which, in reality, defy waking reason as thoroughly as do dreams. Yet they have the ancestry of the past and it was Rogers's past which, thanks to the crucial intervention of Renzo Piano, crystallized into a style and form for the Pompidou Centre. For it was Piano's fascination with detail, industrial technique and the process of building which was to act as a catalyst in bringing together Rogers's own obsessions – developed over the years of his career which now suddenly seemed to have been revealed as a prologue. It is now necessary to examine some important aspects of the common past which Piano, Rogers and every other architect in the world shared.

The relationship of modern architecture to technology, upon which I touched earlier, is a much misunderstood subject. This is partly because most of the early history of the modern movement was written with a good deal of disingenuous hindsight and on the basis of a relentlessly deterministic view of history. This resulted in the construction of an argument along the following lines: Modernism is an inevitable and correct response to the spirit of the age. The dominance of the machine and technology are the primary characteristics of our age so there is an indissoluble link between modern architecture and the machine. Le Corbusier had said the genius of the engineer had usurped the role of the architect: Mies had turned the I-beam, a supremely industrial product, into a new Doric order of architecture and Walter Gropius had, after his initial hesitation, come down on the side of an industrial as opposed to a craft-based aesthetic. In spite of all that, however, there is evidently no simple relationship between the key modernist masterpieces and the machine. Le Corbusier's built forms were, from the beginning, highly sculptural and entirely devoid of the repeatability and rawness characteristic of proudly industrially based products. He had, in any case, developed complex and subtle lines of thought which separated the utilitarian from the beautiful in response to the essentially fine-art-based nature of his personality. Mies's obsession with the all-encompassing grid and with repeated elements perhaps comes closer, but his fastidious insistence on the quality of his materials and finish combined with the extraordinary abstraction of his approach hardly suggests an affinity with the realities of technology and industry. With the Bauhaus the affinity becomes perceptible, although not on any large scale. For, accepting the large elements of straightforward aesthetic decision involved, Breuer's furniture and the other domestic products which emerged under Moholy-Nagy's rigorously rationalist direction can be seen to be formed from an aesthetic in genuine reaction to the experience of the machine. In addition the very organization of the Bauhaus had been an attempt to respond to the age of industry by bringing together several disciplines under one factory-like roof.

But, on the whole, it is clear that an attempt to fit the products of the great age of modern architecture into an ideology simply labelled the machine aesthetic makes little sense. The primary works ranged from highly sculptural buildings capable of analysis entirely in terms of the classical canons of architecture to cool exercises like Mies's Barcelona

Pavilion whose innovations lay essentially in the articulation of space. In the latter case it might be argued that the absolutely impersonal geometry of the final effect could be related to a wider degree of alienation arising from a mechanized society, a phenomenon Mies himself, in his weaker moments, was apt to embrace as an aesthetic. But artistic impersonality has deeper roots than that and it would be artificial in the extreme to attempt to relate such a work to one aspect of the society in which it was produced.

But there was a secondary tradition which, as it were, had taken the masters at their word and attempted to produce a language derived from the same sense of the machine. To a large extent this was a language of the nineteenth century and it sprang in many respects from an unselfconscious tradition. It arose from the engineer's need to innovate structurally in order to cater for the needs of the rapidly industrializing world. In the case of conventional buildings this was not yet necessary. Hotels, offices, block of flats or government buildings were built on an unprecedented scale and, to some extent, demanded new forms of the architect. But the functional demands of the buildings were easily sheathed in the borrowed styles which were to produce the eclectic carnival of the nineteenth century. Industrialization was creating wholly new demands in other areas: in bridge-building, railway stations and factories. Here, stylistic requirements could be incorporated but only in counterpoint to the functional demands of the structure – it would clearly be impossible to clad Brunel's Clifton suspension bridge in Gothic stonework, although, as I have mentioned, St Pancras station could, with complete confidence, simply place Gothic and ironwork side by side. The new forms involved required lightness and large spans, qualities found only in iron and later steel. In the case of wide roof spans, glass was the material at hand for filling in the spaces between the structural members.

Architects who from the earliest days had felt pangs of guilt at the arbitrary eclecticism they had been obliged to pursue[1] gradually absorbed and exploited these new materials. Victor

Baltard, under the instructions of the great rebuilder of Paris, Baron Haussmann, had exceeded anything he did either before or after with the iron and glasswork of Les Halles in 1853 while Henri Labrouste had adapted iron to the principles of the Beaux-Arts tradition – most notably at the Bibliothèque Nationale. But with London's Crystal Palace in 1851 the beginnings of an entirely new form of beauty were glimpsed. A competition had been launched in 1850 for a designer of what was to be a temporary building. The winner, Horeau, a Frenchman, was picked from the 245 entries but, as is so often the way with competitions, he did not get the job because his design, along with those of everyone else, was regarded as impractical since all the specially made parts would have to be thrown away after use. Joseph Paxton, a conservatory builder, rushed in opportunistically with a scheme which involved complete prefabrication and a system of supports which doubled as drains from the guttering on the roof. It used simple repetitive elements to cover 18 acres of Hyde Park including some large trees. Paxton's impetuosity had resulted in a gamble on the ability of the glass, iron and wood trades to meet his demands. It was not a question of their technical ability, it was a question of quantity. The building simply consisted of the most elementary devices for dealing with condensation, dust and rainwater derived from Paxton's experience with greenhouses, but its size raised serious questions about the availability of the necessary quantities of such products. It was, in this sense, an entirely innocent design in that decisions were taken wholly practically with the aim of fulfilling the brief as cheaply and simply as possible using available technology. What Paxton had not allowed for was the aesthetic impact. The immense size of the whole combined with the small scale of the repeated elements to produce an effect of infinite and indefinable space. Visitors were overwhelmed by the quality of light. It was an entirely new form of architectural experience: 'In contemplating the first great building which was not of solid masonry spectators were not slow to realize that here the standards by which architecture had hitherto been judged no longer held good,' wrote E.L. Bucher.[2]

The materials were suddenly endowed with a meaning far beyond the satisfaction of a well-resolved engineering problem. It was a meaning that stood for newness and innovation unencumbered by the inconography of the past. The pressure on Paxton had forced him to produce a building whose simplicity and comparative lack of decoration proved to be one of its most potent devices.

Iron and glass become the standard materials of the great patriotic and commercial exhibitions of the latter half of the nineteenth century. They attained their apotheosis with the Galerie des Machines built by Dutert for the Paris exhibition of 1889. This was about 1,400 feet long and 350 feet wide and its immense space was enclosed with chilling and elemental simplicity by glazing stretched over vast, three-hinged iron arches. These curved sharply inwards just above their bases and thus visually destroyed the traditional distinction between load and support which had been the foundation of classical architecture. The three hinges allowed movement in the arches to compensate for expansion or contraction due to changes in temperature or slight inaccuracies in erection. But, aesthetically, their presence also communicated the sense of great forces held in tension. This tautness combined with the Crystal Palace effect of infinite space to provide an almost emotionally crushing effect on visitors. The building was demolished in 1910 but the Eiffel Tower, built for the same exhibition, survived to tell at least part of the story.

The overpowering rhetoric of these buildings sprang from a confident materialism which was content crudely to stagger and disorientate its audiences. They were virtuoso displays of an agnostic faith which defied enclosure in the mere concept of art. There was, it is true, a certain English pastoral quality about the Crystal Palace: 'The curious association of an unmistakable grandeur with a certain gentleness was never again to be achieved,' wrote Giedion.[3] But the adoption of the same materials for the great exhibition pavilions demonstrated that it was the possibilities of the bombastic effects of scale at the service of grand national or commercial gestures which was the real attraction.

In any case, it was reinforced concrete which was to provide the technological base for the mainstream of modern architecture. Steel-frame buildings were to provide the basis of the Chicago school of Sullivan and his contemporaries, but the peculiar and fascinating 'tenuity' of the material played no part in their aesthetic. Mies retained a fidelity to steel's beauty, but in his own fiercely controlled way which refused to become intoxicated by the expressive repertoire of the material. Besides, American fire regulations said structural steel members had to be encased in concrete, so the I-beams that soar up his Seagram Building are the purest ornament.

The implications of this trend, however, were not confined to the quality of finish provided by the materials. Le Corbusier's opening doctrine 'the plan is the generator'[4] found a natural expression in concrete, a material whose nature was fluid and almost infinitely variable – ready to respond to the poetry of his plans. Clearly the effects produced by the use of concrete were markedly different from those produced by steel. Certainly, it could be made to span large distances and improving technology was allowing it to take on some of the engineered delicacy and daring of the early experiments with iron, as in the bridges of the Swiss engineer, Robert Maillart. But its real attraction for the modern movement lay in its sculptural qualities, combined with the potential it offered for a smooth, featureless finish with which they could express their 'pure forms'.

In the hands of Le Corbusier this was one thing, in the hands of lesser artists quite another. The heroic grandeur of his forms descended rapidly into thuggishness in the work of his imitators and the creative self-confidence with which he moulded concrete declined into arrogance. The same sharp deterioration can be seen in the followers of Mies's uncompromising steel and glass boxes. Gordon Bunshaft's Lever House with its block-on-a-podium form may have suggested a degree of improvisation upon the themes of the master but only in the hands of Mies did the forms maintain their peculiar tautness and finish. In the years after the Second World War steel and glass boxes were to fill city skylines. Occasionally the results were elegant but usually disastrous. The buildings were what Michael Graves has called 'one-liners'[5] and only when that line was very good indeed did they warrant a second look.

I have already spoken about the routes out of this impasse which were being formulated at the time Rogers began his architectural education in 1953. Although they were ways which questioned the prevailing modernist code, they did not deviate from the core of its tradition. Furthermore, they lacked a stylistic repertoire, a shortcoming which would not have been so painful had the modernist ideology not attached such moral overtones to the whole issue of style. In the initial phase of reaction against nineteenth-century eclecticism this may have made a certain temporary sense, but the ferocity of the reaction had continued long after it had outlived its usefulness. The result was that the suppression of the idea of style simultaneously suppressed the idea of variation making imitation almost honourable. This, in turn, suited the platonic background of certain forms of modernism which dictated that the search was on for ideal building forms which, once found, would obviously be repeated.

It may have made some administrative sense for the average architectural practice but artistically it was a hopeless state of affairs. The very freedom of the modern movement formed the bars of its post-war cage. And the recognition that it *was* a cage resulted, during the freedom-obsessed 1960s, in more precise attempts to escape being devised than the vague, cerebral rhetoric of the 1950s.

Most potently there was Robert Venturi, who laid the foundations for what has become known as post-modernism. He produced a highly specific analysis of the damage to the architectural repertoire which had been inflicted by some of the over-simplifications of modernism. Venturi's effectiveness arose from the accuracy and practicality of his thought. He spotted, for example, that, in their pursuit of pure forms and their rejection of decoration, modern architects were creating untouchable buildings – 'The introduction of one foreign element casts into doubt the entire edifice of some modern buildings. Our buildings must survive the cigarette machine.'[6] In attempting to produce a modern urban environment the architects were forgetting one of the key attributes of the city – its messy changeability. As buildings had become more pure, street life had become less so. It was ironic that an architecture so proud of its title 'modern' should seem to be standing aloof from the forms of life that were most characteristically contemporary.

But the legacy of Venturi's reaction has been the return to a somewhat insipid eclecticism, wan attempts to 'brighten the place up'. A more interesting response – and the one most relevant to the Pompidou Centre – was the rediscovery of the partly forgotten, although by now well documented, roots of modernism. Among these roots were the fabrications of Dutert and Paxton. These buildings have habitually been fitted into the tradition but without comment on the enormous differences between their forms and the forms of the tradition that was to dominate later buildings. In part this was because the buildings were regarded as temporary and, indeed, the iron and steel used does pose enormous problems of maintenance. But, deeper than this, lies the sense in which their whole aesthetic was at odds with the mainstream. Steel structures make tension apparent at every point. In doing so they evoke movement rather than stasis: the three hinges of Dutert's arches express overwhelmingly the sense in which the building is 'live'. Furthermore, they were used as simple spatial enclosures, producing the vast rectangular areas which were filled with appropriate activities in arrangements which could be entirely changed without the need for further architectural modification.

In contrast, most modernist buildings were highly planned, highly determined. The architect dictates how the space will be used after prolonged analysis of the client's needs. The importance of this process was such that, when combined with other elements such as the site and context to become the programme, it was elevated by Sir John Summerson to the level of the entire theoretical basis of modern architecture.

But behind these and every other aspect of the modern movement lay the awareness that new demands were being made of architecture. Not only was there the question of mass housing and the whole range of theories about the way people would live with new technology, there was also the necessity for buildings to fulfil wholly new functions – cinemas, new types of industrial buildings, larger-scale office blocks in-corporating new technology and so on. Le Corbusier later intended to fit these into new architectural forms as an alter-native to revolution. But elsewhere a real revolution had occurred – in Russia – and the initial effect was actually far more radical than anything envisaged by the theories of the West. It was there that constructivism was born. Architects and artists on the one hand tried to respond to a feeling that entirely new artistic forms could be created in the new revo-lutionary environment and, on the other, to the apparently limitless requirements for new types of building for a new society.

But the brief creative flowering was to be suppressed all too quickly by the real political forces of the revolution. The truth was, of course, that revolutionaries in the real world cannot be bothered with the anxious ambitions of artists. It had, nevertheless, been long enough for Lissitzsky, Malevich, Tatlin and Gabo to formulate an aggressive programme for new art of all kinds. Its somewhat nebulous theorizing is perhaps less important than its general atmosphere of hard, visionary shapes rising from the confused wreckage of the old order. The shapes, where clear, exposed their naked struc-tures to the world, revelled in their mechanisms and took on the black, red and white colourings of the new apocalyptic simplicity. These were artists who were attempting to do what they believed their society was doing – starting from scratch, abandoning the past and constructing a new, wholly independent, wholly self-consistent reality.

This sense of a ruthless leap into the future was shared by the parallel movement in Italy – futurism, which was founded upon the glorification of the machine and of movement. But,

unlike the same tendencies in the mainstream, this was in the context of an anti-rational cult. The futurists' love of machinery sprang not from awe at its functionalism and the cool reasoning of its construction and design. Rather, it was an enthralled *frisson* derived from its inhuman speed, its deafening noise, its unnatural odours. Similarly, they did not feel any fine-art pull towards permanence. For them, transience was all. The decay of machinery in use was a correlative of the decay of the human body. Machines could be superseded by newer, better machines. The new age needed no ground of certainty except mechanized intoxication.

But this was a programme for poets and painters rather than architects. It was a mood rather than a movement and it suggested immense pent-up energy lacking a means of expression. Yet, in the extraordinary case of Antonio Sant'Elia, it came close. He died during the First World War and no buildings which are known to be his survive, but his 'Citta Nuova' exhibition in Milan in 1914 showed forms of architecture arising from the same crises as the modern movement but driven to far stranger, wilder resolutions. His forms seem irrational, huge, and only held back from the brink of pure fantasy by their clear uses – railway stations and hotels, for example. The *Messaggio* accompanying the exhibition is worth quoting at length, such is the clarity of Sant'Elia's definition of the difficulties.

The problem of modern architecture is not a problem of rearranging its lines; not a question of finding new mouldings, new architraves for doors and windows; nor of replacing columns, pilasters and corbels with caryatids, hornets and frogs; not a question of leaving a façade bare brick or facing it with stone or plaster; in a word, it has nothing to do with defining formalistic differences between the new buildings and the old ones. But to raise the new-built structure on a sane plan, gleaning every benefit of science and technology, settling nobly every requirement of our habits and our spirits, rejecting all that is heavy, grotesque and unsympathetic to us (tradition, style, aesthetics and proportion), establishing new forms, new lines, new reasons for existence, solely out of the special conditions of modern living, and its projection as aesthetic value in our sensibilities.

Such an architecture cannot be subject to any law of historical continuity. It must be as new as our state of mind is new, and the contingencies of our moment in history.

The art of building has been able to evolve through time and pass from style to style while maintaining the general character of architecture unchanged, because in history there have been numerous changes of taste brought on by shifts of religious conviction or the successions of political regimes, but few occasioned by profound changes in our conditions of life, changes that discard or overhaul the old conditions, as have the discovery of natural laws, the perfection of technical methods, the rational and scientific use of materials.

In modern life the process of consequential stylistic developments comes to a halt. Architecture, exhausted by tradition, begins again, forcibly, from the beginning.

Calculations of the resistance of materials, the use of reinforced concrete and iron, exclude 'Architecture' as understood in the classical and traditional sense. Modern structural methods and our scientific concepts absolutely do not lend themselves to the disciplines of the historical styles, and are the chief cause of the grotesque aspect of modish constructions where we see the lightness and proud slenderness of girders, the slightness of reinforced concrete, bent to the heavy curve of the arch, aping the solidity of marble.

The formidable antithesis between the modern world and the old is determined by everything that was not there to begin with. Into our lives have entered elements whose very possibility the ancients could not have suspected; material contingencies have crystallized, spiritual attitudes have arisen, with thousand-fold repercussions: first, the formation of a new ideal of beauty, embryonic still and obscure, but already stirring the masses with its fascination. We have lost the sense of the monumental, the massive, the static and we have enriched our sensibilities with a taste for the light and the practical. We no longer feel ourselves to be the men of the cathedrals and ancient moot halls, but men of the Grand Hotels, railway stations, giant roads, colossal harbours, covered markets, glittering arcades, reconstruction areas and salutary slum clearances.

We must invent and rebuild *ex novo* our modern city life like an immense and tumultuous shipyard, active, mobile and everywhere dynamic, and the modern building like a gigantic machine. Lifts must no longer hide away like solitary worms in the stairwells, but the stairs – now useless – must be abolished and the lifts must swarm up the façades like serpents of glass and iron. The house of cement, iron and glass, without carved or painted ornament, rich only in the inherent beauty of its lines and modelling, extraordinarily brutish in its mechanical simplicity, as big as need dictates, and not merely as zoning rulers permit, must rise from the brink of a tumultuous abyss; the street which, itself, will no longer lie like a doormat at the level of the thresholds, but plunge storeys deep into the earth, gathering up the traffic of the metropolis connected for necessary transfers to metal cat-walks and high-speed conveyor belts.[7]

180

But such incautious faith in the future and in technology was to die, like Sant'Elia, in the First World War, an entirely futurist, modernist and technological event to be replaced by the more elaborate and sophisticated justifications of the mainstream. The importance of Sant'Elia was that he seemed to incorporate with such intensity so much of the intellectual and historical milieu of modern architecture. In spite of his futurist context, he was not, as the quotation shows, as simply anti-rational as some of his fellows and his vision had hardened into almost realizable buildings. The suprematist note was perhaps to become too quickly unpalatable in view of its political associations. But this was by no means a simple matter – a good liberal like Ernesto Rogers was, for example, to join the fascist party because of his delight in futurism. And Sant'Elia had defined a form of architecture possessed of a certain flamboyant generosity with his external lifts and his celebration of mechanics. Such energy found its natural home in the idea of the avant-garde along with movements like Dadaism which seemed determined to dance on the grave of Western civilization. The mainstream, in contrast, tended to view itself as a purifier of the culture with its emphasis on ideal forms and elemental classical standards.

It is with the avant-garde that the Maison de Verre, which

Rogers had visited with Su, rightly belongs and its status as a cult building in the 1950s was a minor but significant part of the preparation for the efflorescence of the architectural avant-garde in the dionysiac years of the 1960s. As we have seen, the dissenting moderns in the 1950s were not abandoning the tradition; primarily they were reacting to its picturesque dilution in the post-war years. But there were those in the 1960s who were happy to go further and rediscover the realms of the futurists, the constructivists and even Dutert and Paxton. This new wave was to take the idea of the moving, changing city and the discontinuous, existential creatures who inhabited it to its logical conclusion. The Bad Faith of permanent monuments arrayed in their pseudo-permanent styles was to be overthrown in favour of the ethic of indeterminacy.

Archigram, a group centred on the AA, broke away from the Smithsonian debate to produce a vast range of fantastic projects including plug-in and walking cities. To the Smithsons it was Mickey Mouse architecture and it certainly remains an almost entirely theoretical exercise. But its importance lay in its populist technophilia. It was no mistake that the images of Archigram bore close resemblance to the images of science fiction which had played such a large part in the genesis of pop art in the 1950s. Richard Hamilton wrote of those images:

The new union of man and machine ... liberates a deeper, more fearsome human impulse. This new affiliation, evoking much that is heroic and much that is terrible, is with us, not only in the sky, but in every street where a boy joins magically with his motor-bicycle, his face whipped by the wind and stiffened by a passion for which we have no name. Like the machinery of motion, it is with us for all foreseeable time. It creates, as we watch, its own myth, the poetry is needed: man has no other means of assimilating disruptive experience to the balanced fabric of thought and feeling.[8]

Ten years later the iconography of the myth was reinforced for Archigram by the imagery of real, rather than cartoon, space travel. And it was all viewed through further layers of

technology in the form of television and the movies. Everything had changed. Through the 1950s new materials were
appearing everywhere. Technology was being democratized
down to the level of nylon rather than tin washing-up bowls.
The associations of the word ceased being merely large scale
and industrial and became intimate and domestic.

So the daily experience of people was being changed, indeed
it was becoming attuned to change itself. A nylon washing-up
bowl was disposable; possessions as a whole were becoming
transitory rather than enduring and the imagery of advertising was to celebrate the possibilities of continual change. The
imagery of art and architecture was obliged to be just as
radically new. Where futurism and constructivism had found
a fine-art correlative in Marcel Duchamp's wily and knowing
celebrations of the machine, Archigram found its correlative
in Warhol, Lichtenstein and Hamilton, the celebrators of the
new iconography of the joyful union of men and machines.

The contribution of Cedric Price was more cerebral with its
emphasis on indeterminacy at every stage of the design process. His thought was derived primarily from the philosophy
of science of Karl Popper who stressed the provisional, hypo-
thetical nature of all knowledge. For Price this meant that
every decision and procedure was to be questioned and sub-
verted by wider questions. Will Alsop, a former associate of
Price, has recalled that typically architectural schools of the
time would find themselves with student projects that went
curiously wrong under the mysterious influence of this new
thinking. For example, a project would be set that required a
design for a swimming-pool in, say, Hammersmith. Back
would come a finished project arguing that Hammersmith did
not require a swimming-pool as there was already one in
Fulham and so here, instead, was a design for a bus to take the
people of Hammersmith to the pool in Fulham.

But when Price did design, he did so in a spectacularly
indeterminate version of the constructivist mode. His Fun
Palace project of 1965 for Joan Littlewood – a woman whose
theatre and politics may have been said to have influenced

Rogers as much as any architect – involved a single permanent architectural element which was the system for moving
different things in and out of the area in which the public was
to disport itself. Everything moved, everything was in steel
and everything could be changed. The movement involved
was evocative of the system of transportation for people
within the Galerie des Machines. It was not a building as such,
rather an ever-changing, completely transformable system.
Price's view of all buildings was, in any case, that they should
last only as long as they fulfilled their function and then they
should be knocked down or, in the case of the Fun Palace or
the Inter-Action Centre in Kentish Town which was actually
built, taken apart with a spanner.

For all their seeming eccentricity, however, the importance
of Archigram and Price should not be underestimated. They
represented a profound and genuine reassessment of the modern movement in the light of experience and of emerging
technologies. They were re-conceiving architecture from the
ground up, having discarded much of the burden of ideology
which had become attached to modernism. In Price's lateral
design thinking can be seen the perception of architecture as
pure programme – an activity which may or may not result in
a designed building. And Archigram aimed to liberate the art
into real, teeming experience of urban life as thoroughly as
pop art had been felt to liberate painting and sculpture into
the world of 'real' imagery.

It was this somewhat anarchic and impractical revival of
the avant-garde in the 1960s which provided some of the
design impetus behind the Pompidou Centre. But it would be
entirely wrong simply to see the building as a product of that
environment, even of an environment that takes in all the
other technology-based architectural movements around the
world – like, for example, the Japanese Metabolists. It makes
more sense to see Archigram and Price as contemporaneous
expressions of the same imaginative re-surfacing of the alternative modernism that occurred at that time. Besides, its
emergence in Piano and Rogers was of a notably sterner and

The team that won the Beaubourg competition. *Back row from left:* Marco Goldschmied, Su Rogers, John Young, Renzo Piano. *Front row from left:* Sally Appleby, Peter Flack, Rogers, Jan Kaplicky. Gianni Franchini is missing from this picture

more rigorous kind than anything to be found in the Archigram archives and it is worth noting that Peter Cook, the leading Archigram figure, was to criticize the building for being 'too consistent',[9] for Piano and Rogers's strong rationalizing tendencies pushed the building in the direction of a distinctly harder-edged celebration of structure and indeterminacy. The central, rectangular block, for example, remains behind all the external services and steel skeleton as a solid feature. And the overall uncompromising plan owed more to the Galerie des Machines than to the curving, organic forms of Archigram.

From this tradition the Pompidou Centre entered with its taut, live, lucid structure, its huge structural span, its poeticizing of technology, its populist air, its sense of movement and change, its celebration of function in the complex, rhythmic distribution of services across the façades and its obvious openness to extension and addition. Furthermore, it was to be a building which could tolerate any amount of urban mess – cigarette machines could be attached to every single member without destroying its sense.

The tradition provided the images and memories that were at hand when Rogers reluctantly and Piano enthusiastically sat down to imagine the Centre. And, to their amazement, they were to face the one challenge that so seldom confronts the architectural avant-garde – they were going to have to build it.

Rogers travelled to Wimbledon after they heard the news of their victory. He found his mother at the foot of the garden. 'Mum,' he said, 'I've won Beaubourg.' Dada cried with pleasure.

Back at Aybrook Street, once they had begun to believe it, the news that they had won produced panic in the office. They had been invited to a party on the Seine that same evening and frantic phone calls were being made to find passports and to cope with children. In anticipation of future problems, there was also some difficulty in establishing who was to pay for the plane tickets. Finally John Young, his girlfriend

Angela Linney, Rogers and Ruth made it on to the plane that evening. On landing in Paris, it immediately became clear to them that the affair was likely to be a little more formal than the Architectural Association's carnivals on which they had modelled their expectations. They were met by a government driver in a black Citroën limousine and taken to a hotel where they were given half an hour to prepare themselves. (This was more than enough time as they all lacked a change of clothes and in any case had not thought one necessary.) Then – the girls in mini-skirts, the men in jeans and T-shirts – they were taken to a riverside quay by the Eiffel Tower. They were late and the party was well under way on the *bateau mouche* as they pulled up alongside. They were, of course, wildly underdressed – everybody else was in formal evening attire. Nevertheless to cries of, '*Vivent les Anglais!*' they were each put at the head of a table and celebrated like visiting royalty. The guests consisted of government officials and jury members among others. Rogers and Young stared about themselves wide-eyed. That morning they had been making their desultory way to Aybrook Street, all but workless and entirely unknown, that night they were being toasted by Philip Johnson and Oscar Niemeyer, and all the while being quietly assessed by Robert Bordaz.

The next day Su turned up with John Miller as did Piano from Genoa. The car also appeared – it was a white Mini Traveller, registration number EYO 60C, whose main characteristic, as one client had pointed out, was that it had moss growing in the windows. Inside were Goldschmied and his wife, Andrea, Sally Appleby and her husband, and Peter Flack, an architect. They had travelled overnight arriving at the hotel at 4 a.m. to discover that it operated a face-saving service which involved washing and pressing shirts and returning them in Cellophane complete with a cardboard bow tie within three hours. Franchini also arrived as did Arup's men, Ted Happold and Peter Rice. At this stage, Rice was the only person in the team who believed the building would go up. He had quietly assessed the background, considered the

A model built during the development of the design

logic of the French position and decided he had a real job on his hands. For everybody else it was still highly questionable but they had 250,000 francs prize money and a wild weekend in Paris before they needed to think too much about it.

Su, however, was already thinking deeply. The slow and remarkably low-key break-up of her marriage was now over.

Throughout, everyone had retained an astonishing degree of calm. During the establishment of the two separate homes – the children with Su and Miller and Rogers with Ruth – their professional relationship had continued on an even keel as demonstrated both in Su's contribution to the management of and thinking behind the Pompidou Centre. As far as the world was concerned they had arrived at an entirely viable working equilibrium.

But from the moment she had taken the first phone call, Su had begun to realize it was not as easy as that. She went to Paris as a member of an architectural practice which had just won one of the most important commissions of its generation, yet also with the burden of the knowledge that she could have nothing to do with it. The emotional strain of working at high intensity for an indefinite period of time with Rogers both in London and Paris would be too great. Ruth, she saw, was the woman in his life now, in all aspects of his life, and on the following Monday she announced she was leaving the practice. She returned to London with Miller. Rogers asked Marco Goldschmied to take over her administrative responsibilities.

A year later Rogers received the following sad note from Creek Vean:

Thank you for your nice letter, and I am glad that one of my bank guarantees is now off my shoulders.

I hear you have another big job in London (?) but no more details – many congratulations – I should like to know more some time. I would like to come and see your work some day as you suggest and to meet Piano.

As you know I greatly admire your outstanding talent and shall always be thrilled by and proud of your, I hope, worldwide activities.

I remain of course very sad that our own main link was broken, though we are still permanently connected by your three lovely children. Rene and I are glad to have helped you and still think of you as a very nice person and extremely brilliant and we must try not to cry too long over irrevocably, alas, spilt milk. Good Luck.

Marcus.

Rogers and Piano, meanwhile, were trying to establish priorities and the sort of immediate problems they faced. Firstly, the question of the likelihood of the building going up was sharpened by some considerable hostility at a press conference. Secondly, there were contractual worries – French architects work on substantially lower percentages than English and, consequently, their work tends to represent a smaller proportion of the finished product. From the first it looked as though Piano & Rogers were expected to work for half the usual English rates. Thirdly, there were huge organizational problems involved in setting up offices and hiring staff and controlling over 1,000 workmen. Fourthly, there were the massive structural unknowns hanging over the building and fifthly, there was the tricky question of French involvement. Idle talk had already made it pretty clear that the French profession was determined to take over as much of the project as possible. During that weekend the jury member, Prouvé, provided one essential piece of advice which would prevent that happening – do not, he said, be tempted to team up with a French practice nor, indeed, get too involved with the French system as a whole. This would, under normal circumstances, be quite customary on a large overseas job; but with the amount of prestige and envy attached to this one there would be the danger of Piano & Rogers losing control and credit. There was also the deeper point that their style required the whole building process to be present in the finished building – to lose control of the process would have been to lose control of everything.

All these problems, as the partners had realized amid the revelry, depended for their solutions on the degree of authority they would be able to impose. On the face of it this was unlikely to be much as they were an unknown firm with an eccentric design and precious little experience. For all the tolerance they were shown of their informal appearance, they hardly looked the types to take on the French architectural profession, building industry and civil service.

Yet, although they did not realize it at the time, their ultimate authority was to be endorsed after the first meeting with their patron – the president. The team which met him on the one and only occasion throughout the entire project was: Rogers, Piano, Franchini, Happold and Young. Apart from Happold, who was wearing a reasonably respectable 'engineer's suit', they were dressed in much the same style as when they had boarded the *bateau mouche*. Pompidou addressed them from behind an enormous desk. Impeccably dressed and wearing a pair of shoes, the quality of whose shine struck all of those present, he spoke grandiloquently of the vital importance to the nation of their project. It was the rhetoric of *la gloire*. As the speech progressed the winning entry was wheeled into the office on large display boards. When Pompidou finally looked again at the plans he faltered, clearly unnerved. They left soon afterwards, unsure of the significance of the meeting, though Rogers had retained sufficient presence of mind to collect the president's autographed photograph for his children.

Later that day they met Bordaz and, recovering from the somewhat equivocal presidential audience, they had drawn up a list of demands covering almost every aspect of their work. To their amazement Bordaz agreed to every point except the details of contracts. They had been given all the authority they could have wished for. It became clear later that Bordaz had spoken to Pompidou. The presidential decision was that the scheme and the team were fine and that they were to be backed to the hilt. It was a commission Bordaz was to guard jealously long after the death of his master.

But, even with Bordaz, the problems involved were immense. The first year of the project was to put appalling strain on everybody simply because of design problems. When the additional hurdles of personal and office logistics were added

190

together with the continuing uncertainty about the future of the building – compounded by the French insistence on paying as they went along rather than coming to a long-term agreement – it was a period of intense, unrelievable pressure.

Ruth, as a precaution, had kept her job at Penguin so the couple commuted between London and Paris. Penguin and her boss, David Pelham, proved extraordinarily liberal in allowing her time off. Rogers would stay in France every other week, usually in hotels, and travel back exhausted to London at the weekends. Money problems continued so hotels were necessarily cheap and rooms usually shared, giving Rogers the opportunity to boast in later years: 'I have slept with all my partners'.

The long-term intention had always been, however, that Ruth should work alongside Rogers and, by June 1972, the prospects for the building had improved sufficiently for Ruth to give up the Penguin job. Life had become all but intolerable in any case. For Rogers, hopelessly dependent on Ruth as he had always been on his women, Paris was becoming a nightmare. He needed Ruth, so she arrived in the summer of 1972 aiming to work as much as possible in the office. She found, with the help of her sister, Susan, who was studying painting in Paris at the time, a tiny flat at the top of five flights of stairs in the Marais district not far from the large hole in the ground that had once been the Plateau Beaubourg. Jan Hall and her husband were flown over from London, told to put up some shelves and paint the whole flat white and Rogers and Ruth settled down to a more sustainable lifestyle. The flat became the regular venue for daily lunches and wide-ranging debates with Rogers, Ruth and Piano. Piano has always refused to discuss work over food, so the ritual became an oasis of calm in the middle of the day. Ruth also discovered a talent for cookery.

Life in Paris became an idyll for the couple. They were away from London and all the local resonances of the recent past but, unlike the period at Cornell, this time they felt secure. They formed a circle of new friends, watched movies incessantly at the hundreds of tiny Paris cinemas and explored France. They often took the night train to the South for holidays. In the evenings at the flat Ruth would play chess with Rogers to calm him down after a day's fighting to build the Pompidou Centre. Ruth's sister, Susan, became a major part of their lives – she seemed able to reduce Rogers to helpless laughter at will – and her brother, Michael, visited them from his home in California.

Amid this new-found security, Rogers once more attempted to convince Ruth that she should become an architect. In London he had tried to persuade her to go to the AA and in Paris he badgered her to apply to, of all places, the École des Beaux Arts. She won a place but did not take it up.

By 1973 the money situation had begun to improve and in November Rogers and Ruth travelled to her parents' home in Long Island where they were married on the twelfth. The ceremony was in the living-room of the local justice of the peace. Just before the wedding, Fred Elias formed his hand into a gun and placed it at Rogers's head, 'You don't have to do this, you know,' he said. Philip Johnson sent a chocolate mousse cake from the Four Seasons restaurant in New York from which James Stirling had once stolen the ashtrays.

But in Paris they remained in the tiny flat until after the birth of their first child, Roo, in January 1975. During her pregnancy Ruth had been under the care of a Dr Vellay whose consulting rooms were in the Maison de Verre. The doctor had been baffled when the father came to the surgery to listen to his baby in the womb, for the man had appeared to be more interested in the structural detail of the building. Roo was born in Vellay's clinic in the Bois de Boulogne. There they were thoughtful enough to provide a bed for the father and Rogers stayed over a long weekend, doing nothing but playing with Roo and being brought champagne by their friends. Late on the Monday he reluctantly returned to work on the leviathan in the Marais.

With Roo to look after and, to their delight, Ben coming over to stay with them, Ruth now started looking seriously

Rogers and Roo in Dr Vellay's clinic

The apartment in Place des Vosges

for a bigger flat. At first they borrowed Piano's apartment which he had never used properly because of problems in moving his family back and forth from Genoa. Then, in the summer, Ruth, despairing of ever finding somewhere suitable, was walking across the place des Vosges when she saw empty windows. She discovered from the *concierge* that a flat was available. They took it at once and moved in during the summer of 1976. They were joined by Judy Bing, an architect who became their closest friend outside the job during this period. She had just separated from her husband, Bud Marschner, another close friend of the Rogerses. As the building opened in January 1977 it may have seemed rather late in the day, but they lived in the flat periodically for some months after the opening ceremony.

In terms of Rogers's home life, the middle phase of the construction of the Pompidou Centre represented a happy time, a recovery from the traumas of the two years immediately preceding the competition. Professionally, it was a baptism by fire into the mysteries of large buildings. Speed had been demanded by the client right from the original competition brief, which seemed to suggest that the building should be completed by 1975. In fact Arups had known full well from the beginning that this would have been impossible, even with a finished and fully detailed design from day one. With the perpetually evolving organism that was emerging in strange fragments from 'the architectural hippies', as the Parisians had christened the Piano & Rogers team, it was unthinkable. And professional accommodation was not as easily found as domestic. The 'hippies' were to find themselves shunted from office to office all over Paris. For a time they worked in an inflatable tent they had designed for themselves by the Seine, and Piano, much struck by the huge Seine barges which appealed to his industrial imagination, had even bought one and produced plans for turning it into a floating office. At one stage more architects were working on this scheme than on the Pompidou Centre. But an engineering consultation revealed that the barge would instantly have capsized. The last home was to be the Centre itself, once they had built enough of it to keep the rain out.

One of the principal difficulties was that the competition entry, although clear in some respects, was hopelessly inchoate in others. Moving floors, for example, had been specified, but nobody had actually worked out how to construct them. As a result, working from the hard rectangle of the entry scheme the first designing year produced some wild improvisations which reflected, as much as anything else, the massive influx of keen young talent into the offices in the first year.

Soon after the victory weekend, Rogers had called in Laurie Abbott, the nomadic designer who had first appeared in Team 4's offices with his Leicester Square Sin Palace scheme. This was to be a crucial and inspired move. Of all the personalities who have worked with Rogers over the years, Abbott is the most extraordinary and possibly the most brilliant. His drawings are stunning, either in their detailed depiction of engineering detail or in their general views of buildings. His near-exhaustive grasp of engineering products and their performance permeates his conversation and his work. He is a born freelance. Periodically he has been on Rogers's staff but he prefers to work alone. The call from Rogers asking him to join the permanent Paris staff came, however, when his second child had just been born and he had been in the process of applying for unemployment benefit. He had reputedly applied for ninety jobs without finding a single architectural firm which could understand him enough to employ him. He had married the small doll-like girl he had placed on a high stool while riffling through the contents of Team 4's office. Abbott thought about Rogers's offer for fifteen seconds and then started, with no success whatsoever, to teach himself French.

Abbott arrived to find himself thrown into a chaotic office in which at least four languages were perpetually being spoken and in which young architects, excited and overwhelmed by the possibility that such an avant-garde structure might actually be built, were struggling to find a role. It was

Roo, Rogers and Ruth. *Barbara Cheresh*

The Beaubourg team in the hole excavated for the building

the style neither of Piano nor Rogers to lay down hierarchies, people were simply expected to find something to do. From this chaos Abbott emerged as a central figure, tying the project together with his ability to hold vast quantities of detail in his head and to understand, throughout, the relationship of the parts to the whole. Since his primary means of communication is through drawing and design, he seemed to be able to sail through the language difficulties. In particular, he developed an affinity with a team of Japanese who had been taken on – they were disciplined and precise in a way Abbott appreciated. This all worked particularly well since after the first few months Young and Goldschmied had returned home to look after the London office. Young and Abbott, in many ways, overlap in their roles as Rogers's inspired designers and masters of detail. They would in effect have turned into rivals on the job.

Young's role in London was to keep the practice alive just as Piano had his home team in Genoa. In company terms it was a grotesque situation – this one vast job in Paris being serviced by these two tiny practices in London and Genoa. 'Beaubourg,' Young was to say years later, 'was like a cuckoo growing bigger and bigger while being fed by these two desperate little parents in Italy and England.'

In addition a group of old Architectural Association contacts were taken on: Tony Dugdale, with whom Rogers had lectured at Cornell, Alan Stanton, Michael Davies and Chris Dawson. All had been in the United States and the latter three had worked in a practice known as Chrysalis. Stanton had also worked in Norman Foster's office. This practice had been moving into the super-refined sphere of post-Archigram thinking with an interest in the almost immaterial aspects of buildings such as thermal barriers and light. The idea was that even more than simply being moving structures, buildings should be a dynamic fabric, responsive to everything that happens. This had resulted in a fascination with, among other things, inflatables about which Davies had had preliminary meetings with Rogers and Young in 1968. Chrysalis, operating in the California of the late 1960s, had strayed into some strange areas, a few of which involved testing structures and environments by living in them for days in the middle of the desert. But there were visa problems in the States and the Pompidou Centre sounded too good to miss.

Alan Stanton was to take on one especially critical role: he was made team leader of 'non-programmed' work on the Centre. The idea was that he should explore areas not in the brief. Most importantly, this would involve making all the different elements of the Centre interact, to produce the 'overlapping activities' which, Rogers is convinced, explain the success of any public space.

From amid this chaos of conflicting and obsessed voices speaking in Japanese, Italian, French and English, a new building started to emerge. It was shaped like a blancmange which sloped downwards at the ends in a series of terraces. It had a suspiciously Archigramesque feel to it and, for a long time, it was the front-runner until doubts began to emerge. Finally the juror, Sandberg, turned up and, with a stroke of quite brilliant insight, commented that the team was drifting and rapidly losing the qualities of the original design. He came at the right moment and suddenly everyone was back with the rectangle.

But at the same time the building was running into the first of its many problems with fire regulations. Structural steel has always been regarded as a fire hazard because it may buckle causing a complete collapse before the building can be evacuated. Thus regulations in most advanced countries insist that steel framework be encased in concrete or asbestos. In the case of the Pompidou Centre this would have resulted in a denial of the whole nature of the building, so the primary columns of the building were to be filled with water and there was to be a complex system of fire barriers. In the event of fire the columns would become huge kettles with water boiling off the top. But that was not enough for the original scheme was too high. In the central areas of Paris building height is restricted to keep everything within range of firemen's lad-

One of the huge 48-metre trusses arriving at the
Beaubourg by night

ders. So the building had to be squashed down to 130 feet – a requirement which resulted in the removal of the Corbusian open space beneath the building and, more importantly, the removal of service floors between each storey. The only other solution available had been to increase the depth of the building. That, however, would have damaged the entire planning conception and might have required internal support. And from the beginning the uninterrupted interior space had been one of the unchallengeable dogmas behind the design.

The whole thing was rapidly becoming an engineering nightmare. Arups were having even worse problems than the architects with their contracts and with establishing themselves in France, and on top of that they were having to find answers to the structural puzzles they were being set by Piano & Rogers. All the time this vast hole was being dug without anybody having a clear idea of what was to go in it. Arups had been struggling with various teams in Paris with Peter Rice monitoring progress from London but, by the end of the first year, it was clear that the process was not working. Rice was sent to Paris full time.

Peter Rice makes an improbable engineer, indeed he admits to never having liked the subject very much but was trapped at university by the discovery that he was very good at it. His real interests are in Irish literature and cinema and he thinks in unexpectedly broad terms. Born in Eire, he studied in Northern Ireland and then joined Arups because it seemed to be a relatively relaxed organization which would tolerate his habit of refusing to wear an 'engineer's suit'. He worked for four years in London from 1958 before moving to Sydney for three years as a key engineer on the Opera House, an extraordinary job for a man still in his twenties. Subsequently he worked in the United States with Frei Otto before coming back to London in time to meet Rogers and discuss with him the possibility of covering Chelsea Football Club with a large umbrella. Later, his was the page and a half of engineering in the seven-page written competition submission for the Pompidou Centre.

The gerberettes under construction

Views of the finished building

206

Views of the finished building

View of the finished building

The external escalator in use. *Martin Charles*

Interior of the finished building

Rice received the news that they had won almost at the same moment that his youngest daughter, Nemone, was born. Even so he was the calmest man in Paris on that critical weekend. He knew the building would be built and Sydney had taught him that you play such projects long. In this case, for example, he knew they had to make time for themselves. He detected, almost from the start, that there was a belief within the ranks of the French that the design process had been completed with the competition entry and the only additional work that was needed was some touching up here and there and a spot of styling. Nothing, of course, could have been further from the truth. The architects knew what they wanted but they needed the engineers to tell them how to do it and, in a unique building like the Pompidou Centre, that requires as much time as you can make for yourself.

In this context, Rice – along with two other engineers, Lennart Grut and Tom Barker – was the best possible partner for Piano and Rogers. First, because his thinking was strategic: he defined problems in all areas, not just engineering, more clearly than anybody else. Secondly, because he was sensitive to what they were trying to do: he did not, for example, try to talk them out of the 150-foot span in spite of the huge problems it created in the design of the steel trusses – these had to be deep enough to stop them deflecting with the load but not so deep that they took too much of the vertical height of the building. He accepted this requirement having realized that, sensible or not, it was essential to the building – without it most of the structural excitement and drama would have been lost.

But it was the mysteries of gerberettes and of cast steel which was to be his most lasting contribution to the building. In 1971 in Tokyo he had seen steel castings as they had been used by Kenzo Tange, the most celebrated of the Japanese Metabolists. He had realized that this offered a way of using steel that completely denied its familiar industrial connotations. Exposed steel is usually seen in its mass-produced forms such as I-beams and flanges. Using castings meant any form required could be produced. It is significant that it was Rogers who most immediately seized on the possibilities of this idea. Piano's inspiration arose more directly from the iconography of industry and had clearly conceived the structure as having an overall industrial feel. But Rogers detected that giving the steel a sculptural quality would set up an aesthetic tension within the building rather than simply exaggerating its constructivist overtones.

Having alighted on the idea of castings Rice then applied it to the most complex of all the engineering problems – the double external steel skeleton. This was needed to provide an external enclosure for the services and it also reflected Rogers's desire to produce a layered building in which the surface is replete with interest and incident. It represented a return to the more elaborate surfaces of the Gothic and classical styles. As a means of achieving this the double skeleton had appealed to him ever since he had seen a picture of Buckminster Fuller's Dymaxion car at the Chicago World Fair of 1934. It was not so much the car as the building behind with its vertical trusses creating a semi-interior, semi-exterior, space which seemed to offer precisely the layered effect he was after.

But there was no structural rationale for the outer skeleton. The mighty trusses could rest securely on the inner row of columns leaving the remainder of the steelwork almost as decoration, a hopelessly flabby state of affairs in such a building. Rice's answer was the gerberette, a little known engineering device invented by a German named Gerber in the nineteenth century. In essence, it is a see-saw. On the inner end rests the floor truss. It then pivots on the main column, placing it in a state of compression. The upward movement of the outer end is then contained by the outermost steel elements which are thus in a state of tension. The shape of the gerberettes was determined by computer and they were to be made in cast steel. They chose the most sculptured solution. It was with that solution that the entire steel structure fell into place and attained a logic and balance which continued

Renzo Piano and Rogers

into the final lucidity of the whole composition. Piano was later to say that the one way in which the entire building could have been improved was the removal of the interior, leaving the steelwork as one vast, empty sculpture.

By early 1973 the whole scheme was beginning to come together and Piano & Rogers were ready to call in tenders for the steelwork. Arups' quantity surveyors had estimated the cost of the steel at one quarter of the whole budget but the tenders came back 60 per cent higher than those estimates. This was to be the first of two major threats to the whole enterprise. The figures were so far out that they seemed to imply either that there had been a fundamental miscalculation somewhere or that they were the victims of a cartel of French steel producers. Bordaz, suspecting the latter, declared all the tenders invalid.

Rogers was convinced they were being victimized by the steelmakers and proceeded to leak an alternative scheme for an all-concrete Pompidou Centre. In later years, older architects were to ask him why he hadn't assumed it would happen in the first place, but he was still relatively inexperienced. As a result, he charged at the problem head-on, ablaze with all the outraged sense of 'natural justice' born in him during his persecution at Kingswood and St John's.

A concrete Pompidou Centre had never seriously been considered, but he was hoping to panic the steelmen with the possibility that the job would slip out of their hands altogether. There was a stand-off while each side tried to call the other's bluff. But meanwhile Arups were secretly negotiating with Krupp in Germany and Nippon Steel in Japan. Some months later Krupp came up with the right deal. It was passed confidentially on to the Établissement Publique – the client body – and, mysteriously, a French steel company came up with a tender 1 per cent lower than Krupp within an hour. It was a move that revealed both a leaky French civil service and the extent of collusion on the earlier offers.

The lower French tender was in an envelope in an outer office waiting for Bordaz. It was a critical moment. Throughout the project the French had felt inadequately involved and this tender was a desperate bid to ensure that another huge part of the building did not go abroad. Bordaz knew full well what was in the envelope, but he ignored it as he stalked into the office. 'I have,' he announced, 'no time to read this letter.' He went in and accepted the Krupp tender.

One year after that crisis another potentially fatal threat arose with the death of Pompidou. The timing could not have been worse. The building had not yet started to rise above ground and all that was visible were the five basement levels filling one vast hole. Within weeks the steelwork would be ready to provide a massive public relations boost as it soared over the Marais but the new president, Giscard d'Estaing, called in the project along with Les Halles.

Politically as well as structurally, the timing was bad. Not only had Pompidou, the initiator, gone, but also Giscard could hardly be expected to show much enthusiasm for a project glorifying the name of his predecessor. Furthermore, he had some useful excuses to hand. The sheer foreignness of the building, increased by the outcome of the steel negotiations, had caused bitterness in the French architectural profession who were fully aware that they had been frozen out from the beginning. Periodically, attacks were mounted and no less than seven lawsuits had to be fended off. Mostly these claimed simply that the building was a public nuisance, although one succeeded in stopping work for over a fortnight because of a quibble over site boundaries. Straightforward critical attacks were commonplace and the team consoled themselves with the fact that they were almost identical to the attacks launched on the Eiffel Tower.

Yet the mere existence of the animosity combined with the scale and cost of the project relative to the rest of the French arts budget made it appear a perfect candidate for cutting once Pompidou was out of the way. Even Bordaz assumed the worst when Giscard called it in. Immediately Arups produced an elaborate report proving that 80 per cent of the total cost of the project was already committed, so cancellation would be all but pointless. It seemed to work. Word came from the president's office that Les Halles would be cut . . . but not the Pompidou Centre. Then came the bad news: the building was to be lowered by one floor, all the services were to be removed from the exterior and the budget of IRCAM – the Institut de Recherche et de Coordination Acoustique Musique – was to

be cut by one third. IRCAM was the experimental music centre which was to be Paris's bait for luring Pierre Boulez back to France. It had become an integral part of the whole design.

The demands would have destroyed the project by the back door but luckily by now most of them were completely impractical. They were finally negotiated to manageable proportions. Cleaning and maintenance systems were removed from the roof and the service lift was made to stop one floor short of the top. All these multiplied maintenance problems in later years but, for the moment, they seemed to satisfy Giscard.

IRCAM's cut, however, went ahead. It was a bitter blow for Michael Davies. At the start of the project IRCAM had simply been a notional part of the brief which had been allocated 4,500 square feet of space. But Pompidou's determination to bring Boulez back to France knew no bounds. Boulez had left for America in early 1960s in disgust at French resistance to modern music. (In fact it had been Bordaz, as head of French broadcasting, who had pioneered the transmission of modern music.) Davies was detailed to be the team leader of IRCAM and to co-operate with Boulez. It rapidly became apparent that 4,500 square feet was inadequate bait for such a big fish. From the start of the meetings in 1974 the brief began to explode and it became increasingly clear that IRCAM could not be accommodated in the main building. It was agreed that an old school building at one end of the site should be removed and IRCAM should be buried under the resulting additional area of piazza. The decision to build it underground and in concrete was partly to minimize the noises of the city and provide the highest possible acoustic

At a press conference for IRCAM. *From left:*
Pierre Boulez, Robert Bordaz, Rogers and Piano

performance, and partly as a planning consideration to open up a vista to the Gothic church at the end of the piazza. The original plan was for a gasometer-type building which would rise and fall in the piazza to change the acoustic properties of the interior. This ran into resistance as it would have changed the character of the whole square so all the necessary mobility was designed into a completely underground building. By this time the project was up to 55,000 square feet but the Giscard cut reduced it once again. The hole, which had already been dug, had to be partly filled in and massive redesigning carried out. Finally, six months after the completion of the main building, Boulez was given his IRCAM.

Within weeks of the Giscard crisis Krupp's steel began to roll upwards. The arrival of the Germans with their beautifully aligned rows of bright blue huts transformed the ramshackle site created by the Algerian construction workers, while the steel itself finally began to give everyone a clear sense of what they had designed. Within a year virtually all the major design decisions had been taken and all that was left was a two-year race through thousands upon thousands of details. Laurie Abbott and his team, enclosed in monk-like seclusion, had turned out a total of 25,000 drawings by the end of the project and, as time grew shorter, they became ever more impatient at the prospect of any second thoughts from Piano or Rogers.

Two years before completion Rogers realized there was little left for him to do on the building. Piano's excellent French and political and technical expertise kept him busy but his partner was now beginning to feel at a loose end. Still, he wrote in one of his notebooks, there should be no trouble finding work after Beaubourg. One year later he was to write that Beaubourg itself might make it impossible to find any work ever again. He had entered a long depressive cycle exacerbated once again by the likelihood that he was about to lose his partner. Relations with Piano had been deteriorating since the end of 1975. It was all very familiar: just as the partnership with Foster had burned out so, on this one massive job, all the possibilities of co-operation with Piano seemed to have been exhausted.

As the end approached Rogers's gloom deepened. There had been work at the London office but it had been completed. This had freed John Young to return to Paris for the final year to take charge of the furniture design for the Centre – the subject of another row with the French authorities – but it held out no hope for the future. Rogers was tired and in despair – even Nino, normally to be relied upon to take the toughest line, was concerned.

Finally, the experience of the Pompidou Centre itself seemed to have turned sour. The last few days were a frenzy of activity. The piazza was cobbled within forty-eight hours of the official opening and hundreds of workmen were drafted in to finish the building. The opening-night party was a disaster. The catering was non-existent and 5,000 people were left stumbling about wondering what they were supposed to be doing. The architects stood, lost in the crowd, and listened in dismay as Giscard delivered an entirely political address without once mentioning their efforts. They left in disgust for dinner at the Café Curieux, a restaurant they often frequented but which, oddly enough, the Rogerses had never liked.

.

5   Dead albatross

'*Ça va faire crier*,' President Pompidou had predicted, and he was right. His Centre had risen from the ground amid an unending barrage of abuse and outrage. On the one hand there was the Geste Architecturale – the protesting group of French architects – with its rhetoric about the defacing of Paris, while, on the other, there was a steady stream of popular derision – the Pompidoleum, it was called, a distillery, a cultural supermarket, ugly.

The popular abuse, however, was to evaporate in the face of the Centre's undeniable success. First, it had been completed on time and within the $100 million budget. And, secondly, there were 6 million visitors in the first year, making it easily the biggest attraction in Paris. The French newspapers capitulated in the face of overwhelming numbers. In the United States the press was consistently friendlier.

The astonishing building that houses the Center [wrote Hilton Kramer in *The New York Times*[1]] – the object, of course, of the most concentrated abuse – is one of the most breathtaking architectural accomplishments of recent times, and certainly the most radical modernist building ever to be erected in Paris. Even in New York, which is so much richer than Paris in examples of fine modern architecture, the design of the Center would cause a considerable stir. It simply does not look like anything one has ever seen before, and is therefore especially frightening to people who cannot bear the idea of something really new in the art of building.

And Kramer went on to attack the charges that the building was inappropriate: 'It neither towers above the other buildings in the old Beaubourg quarter nor violates their scale in any way. Large as the building is, its scale is indeed remarkably discreet. Visually the building is bold, but it nonetheless takes a friendly attitude toward its immediate urban environment.'

'The building,' wrote Mark Stevens in *Newsweek* a year later[2], 'celebrates, instead, process over form and declares that technology – as symbolized by the architecture – may be a toy for casual pleasure.'

But Rogers was too exhausted to allow the building's evident popular success to snap him out of his depression.

Besides, the specialist architectural commentaries were proving less enthusiastic and something about their tone seemed to suggest a distinct change in the climate. Most hurtful of all was a lengthy attack by his old tutor, Alan Colquhoun, which appeared in *Architectural Design*[3]. It was an important critique because of the position it adopted rather than because of any specific points it raises.

Colquhoun's essay began with an accusation against Claude Mollard, a chief administrator of the Centre, alleging that he was indulging in 'double-talk' when he had spoken of the 'still latent' aspirations of the French people which had met the tastes and preoccupations of a president in the completed Pompidou Centre. The confusion in Mollard's position is rightly identified – is culture to be taught as the conservatives might say, or is it innate as the liberals might claim? But this is no more than the confused politics of state patronage of the arts. Mollard's real mistake, as far as an architectural critic was concerned, was that he then went on to justify the design of the building as 'functional', an expression of the avant-garde tradition of the Bauhaus and the *Neue Sachlichkeit* of the 1920s. Within such great modernist experiments can be found the model for the sort of cultural fusions which can be expected from the Centre. The claim appears to be that the 'functionalist' design of the Centre is somehow more truly modern than any of the alternatives whereas, as Colquhoun, again rightly, points out, it is simply one particular type of the modern that had been chosen.

The simplicity and clarity of the scheme is then praised, but Colquhoun's real doubts begin when he looks into the implications of this. For him the building is a supermarket of culture in which the architecture imposes nothing. He compares this to Mies's sense of buildings as ideal and unchanging as opposed to their uses which are not. Also mentioned are the great nineteenth-century exhibition halls and the Eames house. The attack then comes to the point.

This attitude assumes that architecture has no further task other than to perfect its own technology. It turns the problem of architecture as a representation of social values into a purely aesthetic one, since it assumes that the purpose of architecture is merely to accommodate any form of activity which may be required and has no positive attitude toward these activities. It creates institutions, while pretending that no institutionalization is necessary.

Clearly the 'innocence' that began with Wright and re-emerged in Fuller and the California houses was being called into question. Architects could no longer play such wide-eyed games and, interestingly, the Pompidou Centre was repeatedly to be attacked as a 'naïve' building.

After analysing the ideas of 'transparency', 'flexibility' and 'function' as embodied in the building and criticizing certain solutions chosen by the architects, Colquhoun goes on to say that the Centre 'presents an image of total mechanization but makes no connection between this image and the other possible images of our culture'. He sees all the problems as arising from two decisions: making the building a 'well-serviced shed' and using mechanical support systems for its symbolism. The first results in an over-schematic interpretation of the brief and the second, an over-idealization of process without direction.

He concludes: 'Both decisions presuppose that "culture" is an absolute which cannot be mediated by any final form and that its achievement must be indefinitely postponed. If this were true, all language, not only that of architecture, would be impossible.'

I have summarized this article at length because it demonstrates the kind of confusion into which academic architectural criticism habitually descends. Its main problem is its determination to see the building as an argument, an arrangements of words, a determination most obviously revealed by the way it starts from the easy target of Mollard's political trimming and develops it into an architectural critique. It is an approach that owes much to semiotics, but in a highly simplified form. The straight linkage between a purely pragmatic political confusion and a confusion in the building itself is one which the seasoned semiologist would have been at pains to disguise. Roland Barthes, for example, in his essay *The New Citroën*[4], which is comparable in its relation of design decisions to cultural generalizations, avoids the danger of appearing to make hopelessly glib connections, both by the subtlety of his thought and by the rhapsodic tone which recognizes the intensity of the experience he is describing. Colquhoun's jaded tone, in contrast, suggests somebody talking to an over-sophisticated audience which knows all the jokes in advance. His final two sentences do not follow from the preceding argument and the idea of 'achieving' culture is incomprehensible.

Nevertheless, it was a painful attack, partly because it came from an old teacher and friend and partly because it correctly identified confusions in the preconceptions of the Centre. Inevitably any easily understandable rationale for the building would have to lean heavily on those preconceptions – of culture, of usage, of interpretation – and Colquhoun's primary achievement was to establish what unreliable supports they made. But the building, like any building, would be judged as architecture precisely by the extent to which it transcended such categories and justifications. 'Architecture is a *gesture*,' wrote Wittgenstein. 'Not every purposive movement of the human body is a gesture. And no more is every building designed for a purpose architecture.'[5] In other words there is a distinction between the verbal play around the 'significance' of a building and its realization.

But Colquhoun also revealed that the climate in 1977, when Rogers emerged from the effort of building the Centre, was very different from that in 1971 when he began. Colquhoun's arguments laid a new stress on the significance of the past, on symbolism and on plurality. All can be seen as being in the Venturi tradition – reactions against the excesses and failings of modernism – although with a characteristically English cerebral twist. For the truth was that by 1977, the world had become post-modern, a style which allowed either outright condemnations of modernism as a whole or claims that modernism simply needed developing a little. The new stress was on historical context and interpretation – it was no accident that the critic Charles Jencks, one of the founders of the idea of the post-modern, rang Rogers to announce he had discovered the pattern behind the organization of the Centre's services, notably its great, vertical air-conditioning ducts. They were, he said, based on the rhythms of the columns in the Louvre. Such enthusiasm for exegesis was rapidly replacing the sociological programmes and utopian claims of the theorists of the 1950s. Clearly this has had its beneficial effects but it has also had the disastrous consequence of producing chic, fashion-conscious building, a contrived frivolity in the face of the grand claims of the past. In addition it accompanied a general economic retreat after the oil crisis in 1973 which, in itself, tended to make the ambitious projects of the past look dated.

So, for architectural critics if not for the public in 1977, the building could easily be identified as a huge fragment of an immediate past which was being left behind. A mistakenly close identification of its style with the 1960s extravagances of Archigram added to the overall implication that it was somehow 'dated'. Similarly, as the wild pluralism of the post-modern was to penetrate the popular consciousness, the building tended to find itself glossily portrayed among dozens of other contenders as one of many possible alternatives, all equally interesting, equally viable, from which the fashion-conscious architect or consumer could choose.

For the moment, then, it tends not to be widely acknowledged as the masterpiece it unquestionably is, for compromised as it may be by capricious fire regulations and political contingencies the finished building exudes a rare thoroughness, consistency and beauty. True, it can be seen as no more than a massive, rectangular, heavily serviced shed. But what other shape was logically demanded by the brief? The 'culture' that was to go inside was too polyglot, too incoherent to suggest one smooth hierarchy of functions for every space. The contradictions inherent in the very conception were not to be resolved glibly by two men who were, after all, only architects. Instead they chose simply to provide space, enclosed by a structure whose meaning lay in its own making. Every part is legible, revealed and revealing, providing always by its repetition and exposure a sense of place within the building and within the city.

And yet the revelation is not merely of industrialized parts and processes. Instead there is a contradiction – for all the raw muscularity of the finish, many parts are sculpted, primarily in cast steel, to provide an odd, organic tenderness. The gerberettes project like great bones and evoke a sense of delicate equipoise while the whole, as you come to understand its construction, seems to quiver between the forces of tension and compression. And it is perhaps in that fragility and apparent mobility that the real popular success of the building lies. It seems to lure people, fascinated by its curious frankness, into touching and entering its fabric. Inside, they find massive open spaces which, like those of a church, suggest awe and the possibility of participation in something larger than oneself, but which, unlike those of a church, do not define the awe or prescribe the participation. The idea of process had been discovered to fill part of the void beneath the feet of modern architecture but large, echoing spaces remained.

It was not, however, enough to produce any new work. Young and Goldschmied had overseen the completion of several projects while the Parisian cuckoo had been growing. The first had been the factory for Universal Oil Products, a commission which had originally fallen through during the time of the partnership, Richard & Su Rogers. This was finally erected at Tadworth in Surrey in 1974. It is a somewhat bland green box whose main innovation is the use of glass-reinforced cement panels to clad the entire structure. This skin is penetrated infrequently by round-cornered 'bus' type windows. It represents a remarkably closed form in view of the developing style of the practice. Its interior steelwork did, however, win an industry award. And, more importantly, the building attracted the attention of the American architect Kevin Roche, who commented that he wished architects in the United States could come up with buildings that simple.

The other completed project run by the London office was phase one of the Patscentre in Melbourn, Cambridgeshire. This was to establish a lasting and important relationship with Gordon Edge of PA Technology, probably Rogers's most sympathetic client. It ran until 1976 with phases two and three being finished in 1982 and 1984 respectively. This was a complex of offices, laboratories, workshops and drawing offices for PA International Management Consultants on a sloping 6-acre site ten miles south of Cambridge. The result was an expandable single-storey, smooth glass box raised on square-sectioned concrete columns to provide access and services. Its site has been heavily landscaped with undulating mounds alternately revealing and concealing the spaces and equipment beneath the slim line of the glass façade. The main entrance is ingeniously placed at the lower level so that visitors wind their way to the door through the mounds and thus, even when they have arrived, the main block has preserved its somewhat ethereal quality. Fishtail-shaped ducts feed air-conditioning into the lower edge of the glass in the only immediately apparent concession to the rawness of Paris. The effect is elegant if somehow incomplete and strangely domestic, probably because of the elaborate counterpoint with the landscaping. It won Rogers another *Financial Times* award in 1976. The co-operation with Patscentre was to result in a small, separate unit called Rogers Patscentre which conducted research into materials and designed a few buildings, though they were never built.

There was also a housing scheme at Basildon. This was

completed in two parts in 1971 and 1975. The fact that the firm took on the task in the first place reflects the precariousness of its position in 1971 pre-Pompidou. Both phases of the Basildon scheme were for ridiculously cheap, small houses using predetermined elements that were entirely dictated by the developer. The houses are, for the practice, best forgotten as are the appalling industrial relations on the site which at one stage involved flying in non-union labour by helicopter to the dismay of the radical but penniless architects. The shade of Chermayeff once again hovered over the organization of the houses but little more can be said.

More distinguished was a competition for Millbank Riverside Housing at Pimlico in London. This was a development for the Crown Estates and with its riverside site and urban context seemed to be a natural for the practice. The firm produced an airy, open scheme with high-level river walks which hung just below the apartments to allow privacy – a classic juxtaposition of private and public spaces. It was a clean and convincing scheme, but the jury did not think so and a strange, contorted development was chosen which did nothing to open up the river frontage.

So, by 1977, all the work seemed to be over and Rogers had nothing in which to involve himself. The practice continued to be called Piano & Rogers but in reality, both partners knew they would never build together again. In Paris a new design partnership sprang up called Piano & Rice which, with the help of Laurie Abbott, was to design an experimental car for Fiat. But in London there was only the promise of idleness and a rerun of all the insecurity Rogers had suffered at the time of the break-up with Foster.

It was at this point – unsurprisingly – that Rogers and Foster started discussing the possibility of joining forces once more. Foster had, by this time, completed the Willis Faber headquarters at Ipswich with its smooth, glass, reflective curtain walling following precisely the lines of the site, and the similarly polished IBM offices at Portsmouth. (In 1978 he would complete the Sainsbury Centre for Visual Arts at the

Patscentre in Melbourn near Cambridge

University of East Anglia. The buildings were to be immensely successful but none had much in common with the Pompidou Centre.) Foster had developed an entirely different aspect of the success of Reliance Controls – although he had always been a great admirer of the Centre. For him the fascination arose from the creation of meticulously finished skins and structures evoking the hard, clean edges of mainstream modernism in contrast to the *ad hoc*, unfinished mode which Rogers had now discovered. Yet they still found much to talk about and, before Pompidou was finished, they became involved in serious negotiations.

The talks lasted on and off until the autumn of 1977. Both discovered, to their delight, that all the bitterness of the previous break-up now seemed to have vanished so, superficially at least, there seemed to be no obstacles to a merger. Problems, however, immediately started to surface. Not only had their architectural styles diverged, they had also evolved entirely different approaches. Foster had become a one-man operation. He ran Foster Associates explicitly as a way of realizing his ideas. Rogers, in contrast, worked through people: what, if he and Foster were to become partners again, was to happen to Goldschmied and Young? The final meeting took place in a holiday lodge in upper New York State – a venue recommended by Kevin Roche. Rogers was teaching in the United States at the time. It rained continually and fog had closed in for the weekend leaving them unable to see the view which, they had been assured, was magnificent. There wasn't even anything to drink. In a couple of damp, miserable days they decided they were wasting each other's time.

Rogers returned to the new London offices – in a Victorian warehouse which used to be a depository for Whiteley's department store on the Avon Trading Estate in West London – to try and work out what to do next. In its idleness the whole practice became embroiled in ideological debates about its function in the world. For a period it seemed they would move out to the country and become a kind of architectural commune, never numbering more than twelve. Rogers began to convince himself that he was incapable of building anything ever again, that at the age of forty-four he would be obliged to retire, a one-building man.

Ruth realized he was suffering from extreme exhaustion and jointly they decided they must ease the strain by doing something entirely different before they could hope to make any sane decisions. In the autumn they travelled to Hollywood where they rented a small house in the hills while Rogers taught at the University of California at Los Angeles. Roo went with them and they established a peaceful life of lunching on the campus and then going down to the beach once work was over. They spent more time with Michael Elias – a man Rogers regards as one of the most generous he has ever met – and gradually the recovery from Paris got under way.

But both Ruth and Rogers were nagged by the insecurity at home and Rogers very nearly succumbed when the university offered him a permanent professorship with the opportunity of running a small practice in Los Angeles at the same time. Ruth was against the idea on the principle that he should be spending as much time as possible designing buildings; but, with London remaining quiet, it was beginning to look as though there would simply be no more chances. The Pompidou Centre seemed to be hanging around his neck like an albatross – huge and apparently irrelevant to the kind of clients who were around in the late 1970s.

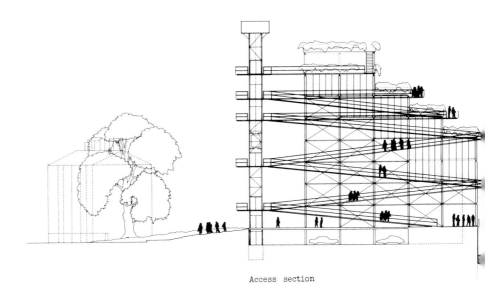

Access section

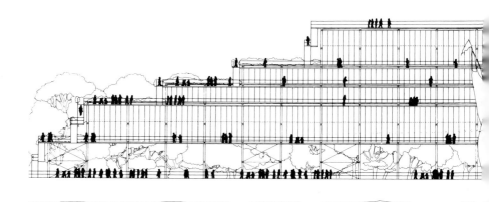

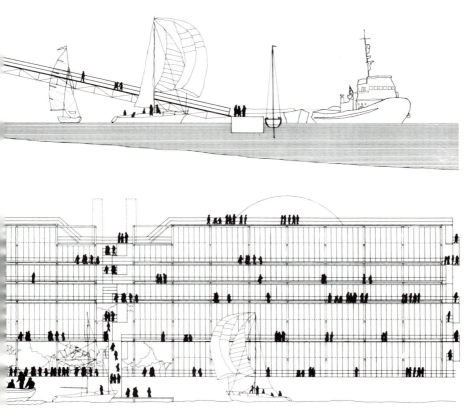

Two drawings of the Millbank Riverside housing scheme

6   Dat ain't building…

Meanwhile a peculiar problem had arisen in the City of London. Discreet enquiries had been made at the RIBA by a very large potential client who was keen to follow the correct procedures. In late 1977 the Institute rang the Rogers office and asked for some samples of the practice's work – brochures, drawings, photographs – they were told a major City client was interested. The samples were routinely dispatched. Nobody paid any particular attention – enquiries at architects' offices usually lead nowhere.

Besides, a mood of gloomy fatalism had spread through the office. Rogers was thinking seriously about returning to the States to settle permanently, Goldschmied was about to start working part-time and Young, having completed a book about glass-reinforced cement, was looking into the possibility of taking up mini-cab driving.

Piano & Rogers had been one of about forty practices to send in material, none of them had been told the identity of the client. There was nothing unusual in this. Work comes to architects in a variety of ways and discreet soundings within the profession happen all the time. In fact this client was Lloyd's of London to whom the need for an architect represented something of an embarrassment, for the old insurance market was in the process of outgrowing its third building in this century. Up to 1928 it had been housed in the Royal Exchange across the road from the Bank of England; it then moved to Leadenhall Street to a new building designed by Sir Edwin Cooper. Within twenty years this was also proving too cramped and, in 1958, the market moved next door into another new building designed this time by Terence Heysham, who had taken over Sir Edwin's practice. Wendy Cheeseman had, for a time, worked in Heysham's practice. Again, it took less than two decades for the new space to prove inadequate and, in 1977, the committee of Lloyd's made its first enquiries at the RIBA about how to find an architect to solve their problem; either by extending or by building anew, in such a way that they would not be obliged to abandon the result within twenty years.

After those initial approaches Gordon Graham, then president of the RIBA, decided to intervene by having a couple of lunches with Ian Findlay, deputy chairman of Lloyd's. It became clear that the Lloyd's problem was not simply a case of finding a bigger building, it was a case of finding an architect who could create room for them immediately and who could produce a building of extraordinary flexibility. An added complication was the unknown impact of new technology on the market. This could mean that, although the space required would certainly expand in the near future, in the mid-term it could contract again as electronics reduced the demand for actual market floor space.

In other words Lloyd's had a complex logistical problem, only one part of which was what the new building might look like. This suggested that a wide-open architectural competition – which Graham would normally have favoured – would be a waste of time. Lloyd's was in no position to provide a brief that made any sense; it was, in effect, open to suggestions of almost any kind. Graham came up with an alternative: if Lloyd's was prepared to put up £100,000 it could finance submissions from a shortlist of practices. If the shortlist was, say, six, all except the winner could be given £10,000 and the remaining money would cover the cost of the whole exercise. Furthermore, because of the peculiar nature of the problem, it would be specified that the practices would not be required to produce a building – merely their own analyses and possible strategies. Findlay agreed and the RIBA began to contact a wide range of architects.

The final shortlist could not have revealed the influences of its compilers more clearly. Foster Associates and Piano & Rogers were there because of Graham's enthusiasm. Indeed, such had been his conviction that these two represented the

best of British architecture that, after the shortlist was announced, he had taken Rogers and Foster to lunch at the
Reform Club in the hope of persuading them to go back into
partnership together – he then learned of the recently failed
negotiations and the foggy weekend in upper New York
State. Arup Associates, the architectural practice within Ove
Arup & Partners, also received Graham's backing but, more
importantly, they were shortlisted because they were already
in the process of finishing the administrative headquarters for
Lloyd's on the banks of the Medway at Chatham. That building, with its sweeping landscape of pitched roofs, was to be
finished in 1978 and to win three architectural awards over
the next three years. In addition Lloyd's had insisted that
overseas practices be represented particularly from countries
where the business of the market was strong. This was not
simply marketing public relations; Lloyd's also felt that modern British commercial building had been poor in comparison
with Canada and the United States. The committee itself
came up with Serete from France, of whom Graham had
never even heard, while he produced I. M. Pei, the immensely
successful Chinese-American, and Webb Zarafa Menkes
Housden from Canada.

These six were to be briefed on 8 November 1977. Rogers –
aware not only that the client was rather different from the
experimentally inclined French government of 1971 but also
that times had changed – bought a grey Yves St Laurent suit
for the occasion and borrowed a tie from Kirk Varnadoe, a
friend from the Paris days. The suit was fine, but the tie
turned out to be identical to the one worn by six other men in
the meeting room. In spite of these efforts to conform, Rogers
was pessimistic about the Lloyd's project, even after the
competition had been won. He felt the institution stood for
everything he was against – the old school tie, the English
Establishment – and, over it all, hung the ghost of the first
Lloyd's man he had met. That was Mr Cheeseman, the father
of Georgie and Wendy, who had once threatened to sue
Rogers over a holiday.

The briefing was a model of professionalism, even though it involved careful explanation from Lloyd's of why they could not, in fact, provide a brief as such. The uncertainty of the whole project was explained and the point repeatedly laboured that the idea was *not* to produce a building design. The architects were given three months.

On their return Serete were the first to be eliminated. They came back with a range of elaborate drawings complete with alternative window treatments from which they asked the committee to choose their favourites. There appeared to have been a breakdown in communication. Webb Zarafa and Foster went next, the latter because the committee took the view that he was simply too much of a loner who would carry the entire project inside his own head. 'What happens,' asked one member, 'if his helicopter crashes?' Pei produced a beautiful schematic model which came apart like a Chinese puzzle to reveal the workings of its interior. But Lloyd's felt he was too busy in the United States, where he had become one of the most sought-after architects in the country. He would not, therefore, personally be particularly close to their building, in spite of the immense size of the project. This left Rogers and Arups, the latter still being the favourite. The committee was split down the middle and both firms were asked to resubmit.

The Rogers team had performed spectacularly well at the first interview. The submission, although badly typed and rushed out at the last minute, had stuck closely to the demands of the brief. So closely, in fact, that it produced alternatives for every step of the process from what to do about the chairman's washroom on day one to the different completion dates for the new building. It provided twenty-four scenarios, one of which involved taking the old Cooper building apart like an orange and rebuilding in segments, an option that would have made working conditions impossible. There was also a daunting mass of mathematical material and a submission from Rogers himself about the fabric and history of the City and the need for the building to give something back to the street in the form of a constantly changing perfor-

Rogers about to leave Belsize Grove for the first
Lloyd's interview in the Yves St Laurent suit.
Roo is in the foreground

mance of its daily functions. But its main messages had been: Lloyd's does not yet know what it wants and neither do we until we have discussed the problem more deeply, and, secondly, Lloyd's has an immediate problem of space irrespective of the final solution.

Much of the credit for the clarity of the strategy must go to Peter Rice who, still playing it long in the way he recommends to all engineers and architects, had identified the space problems that would arise in the gap between commissioning and completing a building. Rogers was employing Arups again as engineers, a fact that was to cause some confusion in the Lloyd's committee who had not realized the level of autonomy which operated in the different parts of Ove Arup's empire.

For the second interview Rogers decided to vary the approach with more of the team talking and also brought in Renzo Piano and Jack Zunz, chairman of Ove Arup, whose presence produced further confusion about who precisely Arups were. Bringing in Piano was aimed at heading off suggestions, which were in fact correct, that the Piano & Rogers team was breaking up. Lloyd's had been unhappy with this indication of a degree of instability. But Rogers, having reached the last two, was now fighting with every weapon at his disposal to win the job and he was quite happy to use what Goldschmied calls 'Italian' methods. He spoke at length on the possible solutions, doodling as he did so and talking himself into a doughnut shape around a central atrium with external service towers to free the interior space. Again, he offered Lloyd's his twenty-four separate scenarios from building bridges between the Heysham and Cooper buildings to complete demolition. With the Cooper building being Grade II listed as a building of architectural importance by the Department of the Environment, the latter option might have proved impossible. John Young was too overwhelmed by the importance of the job to the practice to find the nerve to speak at all. This left Rice and Goldschmied to fill in the rest of the submission. Piano was the only member of the team who seemed convinced they had won.

At one point during this process Goldschmied met Ian Findlay in the washroom. 'If we picked you, would we get a building that looked like the Pompidou Centre?' Findlay asked. 'No,' replied Goldschmied hurriedly.

Arup Associates' second presentation was a repeat of the first. They had been, it transpired, over-confident.

After the interviews the redevelopment committee, chaired by Sir Peter Green, and Gordon Graham went into a session from which they swore they would emerge with a winner. Arups had the advantage of being a known quantity while Rogers had the disadvantage of being the co-architect of the Pompidou Centre. Time and again Lloyd's people were to ask if their building was to have brightly coloured pipes plastered over its exterior. Graham said he had no idea what Rogers would design but he was convinced it would not be another Pompidou Centre. In the end Rogers's presentation had the edge and seemed to suggest a massive range of skills at his disposal – from his own ideas of town planning to Goldschmied's mathematics and Young's materials and tech- nology. In addition, the argument was even put that, since Arups were the engineers, by choosing Rogers Lloyd's would be buying the best of both worlds. This was a massive misin- terpretation of the Arups set-up but it all helped the Rogers cause and all useful misconceptions were being encouraged. Everybody in the Rogers practice felt they were fighting for their professional lives.

On 22 April 1978 Courtenay Blackmore, head of administra- tion at Lloyd's rang the Rogers office to be put through to John Young. Young apologized that Rogers was in the Uni- ted States – he was teaching briefly at Yale – and then asked, pointedly and with ill-disguised tremor in his voice: 'Is there any way *I* can help?' Blackmore insisted he must speak to Rogers and Young agreed to tell Rogers the next time he telephoned. Rogers finally called Blackmore from Ruth's parents' house in Long Island, their traditional retreat in times of stress, uncertainty and crisis.

The routes to Rogers's two major buildings could not have been more different. The Pompidou Centre had been a speculative shot in the dark. He rushed into the task with the one overriding objective of putting the building up on time. Its budget was barely adequate. The result was a highly improvised structure in which individual design decisions emerged from a chaos of unknowns; somehow the parts were related to the whole, though nobody knew quite how. In the event it worked because the building fed upon the improvisation, taking its quality from its own ability to absorb any amount of variation and change. And although the finished building was to be significantly different from the competition entry, it was clear that the overall pattern was fixed from the moment Rogers and Piano reached agreement in the spring of 1971.

Lloyd's, in contrast, was to be a much more leisurely affair. The process of the competition itself had led Rogers through the early stages of design. He had stressed – and the committee had accepted the point – that they should not rush on to the site, as he wanted to allow the maximum time for thought rather than be confronted with the exhausting onslaught of a contractor in full swing, demanding decisions before he was ready to take them. The budget, although not specified in the early days because nobody yet knew what was going to be done, was clearly not going to be the constant worry it had been at Beaubourg. In this sense one aspect of the style was set simply by the process of preparation: this was to be a bespoke project, finely tuned to the demands of the client. Its air would be considered and complete, in contrast to the wildly *ad hoc* mood of the Pompidou Centre.

In view of all that it is perhaps startling how much the two buildings have in common – the layering of the exterior, the exposed services and the sculpted, exposed structure. But this mutual consistency does reveal the extent to which Rogers felt he had found his form. The careful process of meetings and debate about the building might suggest that he was simply one part of a decision-making team. Yet in reality if he had not been there, the building would have been entirely different. A vast range of people were responsible for specific design ideas, but it was Rogers who chose each one from a host of competing options.

His first move was to provide new space for Lloyd's to pull them through the building period and take some of the pressure off the schedule. Lloyd's business consists of underwriters sitting at their 'boxes' on the market floor. They are then approached by brokers who are looking for the best insurance rates for buildings, shipping, satellites or whatever. Growth of 10 per cent a year in the total business conducted means actual physical expansion of about the same amount on the market floor. Using existing methods there is no way of avoiding this simple additional consumption of space. In 1978 they were already at the limits of the capacity of their old building.

The two big uncertainties were the future of the world economy as a whole and Lloyd's part in it. A continuance of the economic order would guarantee the need for insurance but the 1970s had produced considerable doubts about the possibilities of any such continuance. Furthermore, Lloyd's itself was being challenged by overseas competition, specifically from the United States. In the event Lloyd's decided it had no choice but to assume its own continuing success. This proved correct but only just. The years of building were to see the institution repeatedly battered by scandals which badly damaged its public image as a gentlemanly, self-regulating institution. In some ways the building itself was to become one of the few things of which Lloyd's could be unconditionally proud in those long years.

Rogers's solution for the immediate space problems was to put temporary buildings on the roof and to convert the underground car park into underwriting space. Meanwhile, Lloyd's rented some additional office space in another building.

He was now confronted by several unknowns: Could the Cooper building be demolished? What effect would electronics have on the size of the marketing floor? Assuming there was to be a new building, could it be in steel?

In the case of the Cooper building, Rogers and Lloyd's had, perhaps, arrived just in time. Conservation as a movement had not yet developed the momentum that was to give it such power in the 1980s. Certainly there was profound revulsion about much that had been built since the war, but this had not yet matured into its later form of the obsessive defence of anything old against anything new. There was, however, a correspondence in the *Financial Times* between Gordon Graham and Marcus Binney of the conservation group SAVE Britain's Heritage about the merits of the Cooper building once it had become clear that Lloyd's would almost certainly want to demolish it. And Clive Aslet wrote in *Country Life* that it was 'one of the last great classical monuments in England' and described Cooper as 'a bastion of human values against the first waves of Continental modernism'.[1] The latter remark was to anticipate the form of the major anti-modernist attacks with its attempt to snatch back the ideology of humanism. It was a term that was to become an essential underwriter of stylistic preferences in the same way that 'Christian' had underwritten Pugin's love of 'pointed' or Gothic architecture.

But the arguments for demolition were strengthened by the fact that Lloyd's old building was, in fact, poor Cooper. Two better examples of his work were both within five minutes' walking distance: the old Port of London Authority building of 1912, which massively dominates Trinity Square by Tower Bridge, and the old National Provincial Bank headquarters of 1932. Thus demolition was largely unopposed and it was clear that in those benignly tolerant days many of the conservationists accepted that Rogers would probably produce something better than Cooper.

Binney wrote to Rogers in July 1979 after he had seen the exhibition illustrating the scheme. 'Personally,' he wrote, 'I found your designs both novel and exciting and light years ahead of the kind of developer's architecture we have seen recently – and are still seeing.' He went on to express a worry that the 'planning gain' Lloyd's had won with the designs in terms of lettable floor space might set a bad precedent in the City. The need for an expanding or contracting market floor within the building meant that its total area relative to the area of the plot was significantly higher than the ratio normally allowed – Binney was worried that other developers would use this as a way of prising better plot ratios out of the City authorities. And he went on to warn against economies later in the project which might damage the final appearance of the building:

In this respect I am sure you could not wish for a better or more enlightened client than Lloyd's but given the fact that much of the architectural adventurousness and appeal of your elevations depends on constructionally complicated and daring devices any simplification or modification could have a drastic effect on the interest and quality of the building at least externally. I hope therefore you will not mind if in writing to the City architect I stress the great importance of abiding by the detailed plans submitted, except for any modifications you deem necessary on design grounds.

Binney had also pleaded for the preservation of certain elements of Cooper's building – either to be sold off or incorporated into the new building. In fact Rogers was to preserve Cooper's grand entrance as an element in his completed design.

The question of the expansion or contraction of the market floor, however, was clearly not one that was easily to be resolved. Computers were moving into the insurance business but their precise impact, if any, on the basic form of Lloyd's business was unknown. Obviously, any solution would have to allow for all possibilities by providing space that could be used as a market floor or as ordinary offices, and by providing sufficient floor depth to admit all the requirements of any future computers. It was a more precise version of the 'flexibility' that had been blandly built into the Pompidou competition brief.

Finally, there was the question of steel. The material had,

by now, become almost second nature to Rogers. The discovery of its openness to improvisation, its sense of tautness and movement and its expression of the structure and processes of a building in Reliance Controls was not something he could lightly discard. And yet it was clear from the start that Lloyd's could not have a steel structure. The latitude they had been given by the Parisian authorities was not available in London and, in any case, the tightness of the site would have ruled out a similar system. Fire regulations said that structural steel had to be encased in concrete and, in such a densely occupied building as Lloyd's, there could be no question of any variation.

It took just over a year to produce a design – the scheme was made public on 1 June 1979. Throughout that time there had been monthly meetings with the Lloyd's redevelopment committee, yet when the model was unveiled some were still shaken at the sight of what they had commissioned. Rogers had stuck to his doughnut idea with the central atrium to tie together different levels of the market floor and to illuminate the interiors. He had also stuck to his original feeling that the building should fill the irregular rectangular site. His belief was that such crowded building was in the nature of the City of London and would preserve as much of its ancient 'grain' as possible. He was strengthened in this view by Gollins, Melvin and Ward's Commercial Union building immediately opposite which was completed in 1969. It faces on to a plaza which is several feet below pavement level and open on two sides. Down the left runs GMW's P & O building, a good example of the standard 1960s block-on-a-podium style derived from Bunshaft's Lever House, while in the centre of the side furthest from Lloyd's is the CU tower. This is unquestionably the finest office building of its kind in Britain – beautifully detailed and immaculately placed. It is a good 'one-liner', understandable at a glance but still worthy of contemplation. Yet Rogers felt its airy spaces detracted from that part of the City by over-simplifying the street pattern and denying the elements of surprise and variety at pavement level. The east-

Above: Alan Stanton's early drawing of Lloyd's
Below: Lloyd's under construction

ern end of the City is significantly different from the western. Road are narrower and pavements tend to be more crowded. It is dominated by the related shipping and insurance businesses. This suggested Rogers's building should be a centre in the way that the Bank of England was in the west. It was also to be an elaborate performance intended as a rebuke to the reductive style of the CU.

At first, therefore, his design had followed exactly the irregular boundaries of the site producing a curious amoeba-like doughnut. Little thought was given at that stage to the finish but there seemed to be no reason why it should be other than simply a smooth glass wall. It was evocative of Foster's Willis Faber building in Ipswich which was, coincidentally, an office block for the insurance brokers who had occupied Cooper's Trinity Square building after the Port of London Authority. However, it was clear that service towers were necessary to provide the massive weight of air-conditioning equipment required as well as escape staircases to empty the building in case of fire. In addition the unusually high density of occupation on the market floor meant that Lloyd's would need more toilets than any other building in London and Rogers wanted to prevent these from interfering with the flexibility of the interior by moving them into the service towers. (Toilets are an enemy of flexibility as they are so heavily and statically serviced. They remain one of the few services in the Pompidou Centre which he regards as badly placed.) The towers were to go on the exterior of the dough-nut. If placed around the interior, they would block views and interrupt the span of the market floor.

It gradually became clear to everyone that the central block should be a regular rectangle. Some have attributed this to Laurie Abbott, who had again appeared on the Rogers team. Characteristically, he is reputed suddenly to have decided that the design needed 'some rigour', to have thrown out the amoeba and drawn his rectangle. Around this were dotted the service towers, partly filling the complex shapes left on the site and partly leaving them available as semi-public, semi-private spaces. The design now fell into place. On the one hand the hard rectangle with its elaborate service towers provided a layered and complex external spectacle while on the other, the regular shape of the block would allow him to match the consistency of Pompidou with his structure. Rogers found, with some relief, that once again he was working with a highly rationalized plan. This gave him the repeatable and consistent forms which would make the building comprehensible to its users.

Throughout this phase the central block was intended to be a complete box, surrounding the atrium up to roof level. Rogers had argued strongly that in terms both of the use of space and retention of energy, either this or a sphere – a shape never seriously considered – was easily the most efficient shape. It turned out, however, to be impossible. Rights of 'ancient lights' to the rear of the building meant he could not confront Lime Street and Leadenhall Market with a single vertical. The box had to be stepped down in a series of terraces to allow light through to neighbouring buildings, a complex geometrical problem. This must represent one of the most fortuitous difficulties any architect ever faced. First, it made the rear elevation considerably more interesting; secondly, it provided a more complex and sympathetic relationship with the other buildings; thirdly, it led the view more naturally up to the atrium from Sir Horace Jones's Leadenhall Market of 1881 – the two have an obvious affinity, both having glazed barrel vaults – and finally, it opened up the southern end of the atrium to create the south window, an extraordinary ecclesiastical effect which had never, until that point, entered Rogers's head.

Lloyd's was following all this with a certain sceptical interest and Courtenay Blackmore and Peter Green went with Rogers to give an explanatory presentation to the Royal Fine Art Commission. This strange, largely powerless body can exert purely persuasive pressure on developers and planners to improve their schemes. Its stamp of approval is no more than helpful but it gives an air of respectability, precisely what Lloyd's wanted. In the event Lloyd's was staggered by the effusiveness of the response.

> The commission wished to compliment Lloyd's, [wrote the RFAC's secretary] on what they regard as a most enlightened piece of architectural patronage. They regret the loss of the great corridor leading from the monumental entrance to 'The Room' and also of the impressive, solid, almost Roman frontage to Leadenhall Street and the old Royal Mail Steamship Company façade. They nevertheless felt the concept to be such a brilliant one that these losses are justified in order to achieve what should be one of the most remarkable buildings of the decade. They were therefore pleased to give their building the strongest support.[2]

On top of that, press response was extraordinarily favourable – 'Lloyd's leads the architectural revival' was the headline on a *Financial Times* piece by Colin Amery[3], and the client suddenly began to feel pleased with itself. Blackmore, now the main liaison between the architects and Lloyd's, was overwhelmed by the success of the whole exercise. Blackmore had, at the competition stage, originally backed Arups but on being defeated, had put his weight behind Rogers. After winning the competition, it was to his house in Blackheath that Rogers and Ruth went to dinner on the day they returned from the United States. He was to become the main supporter and campaigner for every design decision Rogers made to the very end of the project. He was also to fight the hardest against Rogers's insistence that the roofs be flat. Lloyd's had suffered continuous problems with the flat roofs on Heysham's buildings and was determined never to make the same mistake again. Arups had made sloping roofs the most obvious feature of the building at Chatham but nothing would induce Rogers to do something similar. The compromise they reached was that the roofs should slope at the precise angle laid down by the Ministry of Agriculture for dairy floors – the reasoning was that such an angle must be the optimum for causing every conceivable consistency of muck to run off eventually. For Rogers, this solution had the significant attraction that it was completely undetectable.

By now the firm was known as Richard Rogers & Partners. The connections with Piano had finally been severed, although he was still technically a consultant on the Lloyd's project. Rogers had finally lost his co-architect, but it now meant little. The continuing success of Lloyd's had convinced him that he could build on a large scale as the sole top man. He had discovered he did not need a tough equal, he could manage with the people he had created himself to fill the gaps in his own competence. With Goldschmied as manager and strategist, Young in charge of design, materials and detail and Michael Davies increasingly adopting a boffin-like research role, he seemed to have produced a system geared entirely to designing buildings that were distinctively those of Richard Rogers. There was some disquiet within Lloyd's that one of its early fears had been realized, but soothing noises were emitted and proved adequate.

In November 1979 another competition was launched to find a management contractor, and in June 1980 Bovis was chosen. The Bovis director who was to run the job, Brian Pettifer, first met Rogers at a lunch with Blackmore at the Carlton Club. Rogers was late and arrived in a light fawn corduroy suit, open-necked shirt and what Pettifer took to be cheap training shoes, although he realized later he had been quite wrong – they were expensive training shoes. The contractors' competition was to be a good deal more fraught than the architects' – the job was to become the biggest private sector construction project in Britain and everybody was after it. Pettifer even went to Paris to inspect Beaubourg. He emerged from the Métro with his wife, Sheila, who stared aghast and asked: 'Is the City ready for this?'

Demolition of the Cooper building went on through 1980 and Bovis arrived on site with the first sub-contractor to start digging the necessary hole and laying the foundations. Relations between Bovis and Rogers had started well once the contractors had become used to his infinitely flexible way of approaching every problem. This had also thrown Lloyd's initially. Once the competition was over he had been expected to appear at some stage with a final design which he would insist on building in every detail but this never seemed to happen. Even the public version issued in June 1979 was presented as provisional. Pettifer, similarly, had been used to architects who simply ordered a building. Rogers, in contrast, would constantly discuss ideas in terms of the actual process of building them. He would modify his design as he discovered more about construction techniques. It was, of course, a habit derived from the Pompidou Centre where instant modification had been essential at every stage. But it also arose from Rogers's now fully developed method of working through alternatives until they matched some apparently pre-existing model in his imagination. That model, however, may only seem to exist. It is just as likely to have emerged in the process of decision. For him the very presence of Pettifer, Blackmore and Rice was somehow built into and expressed in Lloyd's.

With the arrival of the winter of 1980, however, the relationship was to be badly strained, for, after the breezy optimism of the competition and design process, the first site experiences raised fears in Rogers that the project was to be as exhausting and hair-raising as the Pompidou Centre. The three main teams – architects, engineers and contractors – seemed to be badly out of step. Arups, in particular, were some way behind in producing the structural solutions for the design. This is said to be an occupational hazard of working with Rice, whose brilliant strategies are frequently followed by prolonged agonizing about the engineering. Furthermore, a certain reluctance among sub-contractors to come forward to tender for the various tasks was beginning to convince Rogers that the Bovis contract was too heavily loaded in the company's favour. This mounting irritation and uncertainty came to a head when the excavation and foundation-laying suddenly fell months behind.

Rogers lost his temper and exploded at one of the quarterly strategy meetings. Blackmore was appalled, took him aside and told him it was no way for a gentleman to behave. Rogers had, for the moment, slipped out of the Yves St Laurent mask and back into that of architectural hippy. In fact Bovis had been struggling with extraordinary problems. The weather had been dreadful and the foundations of the Cooper building were radically different from those specified in the archive drawings. Huge, unexpected chunks of concrete had to be broken up and the retaining wall along Leadenhall Street had proved to be hopelessly inadequate. In fact it had hardly been a retaining wall at all. The building seemed to be booby-trapped. Attempts to shore up the wall had simply caused the whole thing to move. Rogers became convinced that the five-year programme was about to double and he was about to lose his reputation gained at Beaubourg for being on time.

But, quite suddenly, it all seemed to come together. The foundations were eventually finished and Arups had swung into action. By 1981, they were back on schedule in some areas and had found ways of saving sufficient time in others.

The main problem above ground was the concrete. Once it had become clear that the authorities would not tolerate an all-steel building, Rogers and John Young had started to look for some way of producing a form of concrete that would provide him with the same degree of tension and expressive energy. Lloyd's from the beginning had resisted the idea of an excessively 'concretey' building and had developed a specific prejudice against the 'elephant grey' material which had been the primary medium of the Brutalists. At a testing site owned by Bovis in Fulham various finishes were tried from permanent steel shuttering to a dye which gave the concrete blue veins. The first was too expensive and the second would have given the 270-foot-high columns the appearance of gigantic Stilton cheeses. In any case, Rogers and Young wanted neither. Rogers had spoken to Lloyd's at length about high quality concrete finishes but his words had fallen on deaf ears. To the Lloyd's committee, concrete was concrete. He finally made his point by producing the mix he wanted at the Fulham site and taking them to see it. It was still elephant grey

254

Aspects of the completed Lloyd's.
Illustrated London News

but it was smoother and denser than the coarse, pitted material they had visualized.

The finish, however, was only half the problem. Rogers's structure demanded two rectangles of primary concrete columns – the inner ring of eight running around the atrium and the outer ring of twenty around the outside of the central block. From these tall, slender columns a precast bracket and yoke assembly was to support inverted U-shaped beams which, in turn, were to support the concrete grid beneath the floor slab. Around the atrium they would be free standing, around the external structure they would be joined by six diagonal bracing elements. These were necessary as the structure had no internal stabilizing forms such as concrete lift shafts and cross walls. On the south side, where the building steps downwards, the concrete floors around the atrium gave way to a light lattice steel structure. The atrium steelwork was joined to the concrete by steel casting. It was a structure which allowed concrete to express the building's dynamic forces without falling into the heavy, oppressive inertia usually associated with the material. It was to produce what many have called a steel building in concrete.

But quality control was everything. Rogers and Young wanted all the beams and columns to be as consistent as possible. *In situ* concrete is poured on site into moulds. For consistency each mould was to be poured in one operation. Workmen taking a teabreak after filling half a mould cause lines to form along the junction because of different drying rates. In the case of the beams they would not allow a slight taper downwards, which is normal practice to make pouring easier. They wanted the edges as clean and sharp as possible and the section of the beams to be absolutely rectilinear. Only the massive junctions which joined columns to beams were to be prefabricated. Achieving this without producing beams pitted with 'blow holes' was to provide an enduring problem for the builders.

This method of using concrete avoids the weathering effects which have, over the years, given the material such a bad name. In the South Bank arts complex, for example, the flat surfaces of the buildings have become streaked and dirty, an effect which detracts from, or even destroys, the sculptural impact of the architecture. At Lloyd's, the complex articulation of the concrete itself together with the complex play of light and shade across the surface of the building incorporates the effects of the weather into the rhythm of the façades.

Young's obsessive pursuit of a uniform quality for the concrete was accepted by Bovis up to a point. It was, after all, a bespoke flagship building. But in the case of the service towers he met resistance. Pettifer pointed out that using *in situ* concrete for them would result in their construction lagging behind that of the main block. This could prove disastrous: lacing services through from the towers required them to go up at the same rate to avoid hopeless confusion and botching at a later stage. The sheer complexity of the wiring and ducting was such that it could not be planned entirely in advance, it had to be done as they went along. Young agreed on condition that Bovis would strive to match the concrete finishes and, with much sandblasting, they succeeded.

The first problem, however, was finding a contractor who was physically capable of achieving those standards. Bovis assembled a shortlist and asked each company to produce its own idea of how the work might be done. They were all offered details of Bovis's own research but were told they were at liberty to ignore it if they wished. The cheapest tender by £2 million came from a company called Gleeson, the smallest on the shortlist and the only one prepared to accept Bovis's research findings. For Rogers the arrival of Gleeson on site was to parallel exactly the arrival of Krupp at Beaubourg. Gleeson was to pour 32 miles of concrete beams and only 23 feet had to be redone because of imperfections. The columns rose, smooth and unpitted by blow holes.

Meanwhile, Sir Peter Green, the chairman of the redevelopment committee, had gone on a business trip to the United States. Sir Peter had become chairman of Lloyd's and was throughout the chairman of the redevelopment committee and the new building's most powerful champion – the Lloyd's equivalent of Bordaz. With him he took elaborate drawings of it. He showed them to developers over there who were impressed and asked its square footage. 'Oh, 600,000,' replied Sir Peter, still pleased with himself. He was then asked how long it was taking to build. 'Five years.' They were horrified. 'Over here we put up 600,000 square feet in eighteen months.'

Sir Peter returned to London and demanded to know why his building was taking so long. Representatives from Lloyd's, Bovis and John Young went out to America to find an answer. Young, of course, knew in advance. Speculative office blocks in American cities are simply thrown up with standard floor plans and basic curtain walling. There are seldom any floors below ground. Architects are minimally involved; occasionally the builder will let them loose on the foyer. Completion is counted as the date on which the ground floor is occupied.

One New York contractor agreed to meet them, studied their drawings for a moment and then announced: 'Dat ain't building, dat's fuckin' architecture!' He added that they would be lucky to get it up in five years.

Green and Lloyd's were satisfied but the trip had set a precedent for further reassurance jaunts to America. The next was to study external lifts. Rogers had specified that these should run up and down the service towers providing the occupants with a developing view comparable to that from the escalator at the Pompidou Centre. Passers-by would be treated to the spectacle of brokers and underwriters steadily rising and falling throughout the day. Lloyd's suspected there would be problems of corrosion and leakage and sent Blackmore and Young to find comparable lift systems in America. This proved difficult because although they could find external lifts in the south, they wanted examples in a demanding, northern climate. Their trip ended at the St Francis hotel in San Francisco where lifts rise thirty-two storeys to give a view over the Pacific. These were finally

found by Rogers who sent a postcard to Blackmore saying
simply: 'Eureka! I've found the lift.' A storm was blowing
rain horizontally into the building when they went to investigate. Young and Blackmore happily rose and fell for an hour,
yanking at the doors to try and make them leak and studying
the steelwork in the lift structures.

Bit by bit Rogers managed to force through his decisions
by an elaborate process of providing alternatives and then
convincing the committee they had only one choice. In determining the colour of the big round lighting elements – the first
details to be designed by Eva Jiricna – that fit into the
concrete ceilings, for example, he knew his own preference for
black would be met with dismay by the committee. By providing an immense range of alternatives he was able to keep
discussion going long enough to persuade them he was right.
He was, however, to lose on one point connected with these
elements. In the restaurant he filled in the corners formed by
the round dish in the square box. He intended simply to
provide a different effect in that one room. The committee,
however, demanded the same treatment throughout – they
had been disturbed by the sight of ducts and wires visible
between the dish and the concrete.

Nevertheless, it was a process that was producing a building of a consistency that defied its committee origins. But
Rogers was also having to take changes in the brief into
account. At one stage Lloyd's asked for another series of
meeting rooms. Luckily the spaces left on the site allowed
Rogers simply to plug a tower of these into the back of the
building. Air-conditioning demands kept increasing, making
the boxes at the tops of the service towers larger and larger.
This resulted in a significant change in the shape of the service
towers: the originals were far too slender to support the loads
of the new air-conditioning requirements and they grew stur-
dier as the design progressed. And finally there was the Falk-
lands War. This produced a scare among the fire authorities
that the aluminium in the warships had been the primary
cause of casualties – they thought it had melted and dripped

on those beneath. Lloyd's was told it could not use aluminium cladding anywhere on the building in case a fire caused it to drip lethally on to the pavements. Rogers offered mild steel or stainless steel instead, with the proviso that the former would cause maintenance problems. The committee took a deep breath and spent another million pounds on stainless. Blackmore, meanwhile, was fighting off complaints and threatened lawsuits from the aluminium industry because of an ill-judged public announcement of the issue. Aluminium, it turned out, had not been at fault but by then the stainless steel was going in.

As the job progressed John Young became the main job architect and indeed the hero of the whole project. Many of the key design decisions had been taken, but luckily Rogers found other work to occupy his mind so he was not afflicted by another depression to match that of the last two years of the Pompidou Centre. From then on, Lloyd's became Young's building. He worked solidly eighty hours a week on the project until its completion. Rogers grew used to visiting his parents in Wimbledon and seeing, in the small studio where once Dada had done her pottery, the spectacle of Young at 2 a.m. on a Monday morning struggling with his strategies for the coming week. Young is overwhelmingly responsible for the sheer quality of Lloyds.

But on the question of the interiors, Rogers was suddenly dragged back into the centre stage of the building's politics. He had taken on Eva Jiricna to run the team handling the interior design of the building. She is a brilliant but complex character, whose Czech accent and monotonous delivery makes her less than ideal for the sort of formal meetings which Lloyd's preferred. But there was no problem until the question arose of the decoration of the top two floors which would house the chairman's suite and the Lloyd's administrative offices. Part of this had already been determined – the committee room was to be a perfect reconstruction by John Harris of an Adam room from Bowood House in Wiltshire. This had been incompletely reconstructed in the Heysham building but now enough room was available for it. Rogers had set it as a free-standing 'jewel casket' projecting through two floors and surrounded by a single corridor. But by 1984, the political situation within Lloyd's had changed and the earlier determination to preserve the consistency of the building had evaporated. New personalities had emerged around the new chairman, Peter Miller, and the interiors were challenged. Clearly, new men felt they had to put their stamp on the building.

The first problem emerged over the Captain's Room, the primary dining-room within the building. To head this off Rogers, Jiricna and Young had a mock-up of their final design made up and a full meal served in the bizarre setting of a partitioned-off section in the middle of a building site. The meal was a success and the Jiricna design was adopted for the Captain's Room. The resistance continued, however, with the view gaining ground within Lloyd's that this new building was all very well but the eleventh and twelfth floors should, perhaps, have a more traditional appearance. Rogers was asked to produce a list of possible alternative interior designers. To his horror he found himself researching the strange, faintly sleazy *demi-monde* of fashionable decorators. He produced the list and proceeded to a presentation of Jiricna's scheme. The victory over the Captain's Room had given him too much confidence, however. The committee was clearly against him. By now they had even queried the colour scheme in the Adam room which had made use of painstaking research into Adam's original employment of colour. Some members of the committee were beginning to think all white would be more tasteful, an idea that would have made the massive expense of re-creating the room in the first place completely ludicrous.

Enraged, Rogers produced a long memo outlining the philosophy of interior design. It began by explaining how the whole building worked and how each part was devised to fit into a design hierarchy which expressed its role within the building. Frank Lloyd Wright was evoked to justify the idea of design consistency between a building and its contents and then, with an obvious eye on the new 'tasteful' types with whom he was having to contend, he proceeded to attack the whole idea of taste.

Taste is the enemy of aesthetics, [he wrote] whether it is found in art or architecture. It is abstract, at best elegant and fashionable, it is always ephemeral for it is not rooted in philosophy or even in true craftmanship being purely a product of the senses. As such it can always be challenged and is always being superceded for how can one judge whose taste is best? Yours, mine or someone else's? Good design on the other hand talks to us across the ages.

He went on to stress the comprehensibility of the new Lloyd's.

The new Lloyd's is a place where even a small boy can understand and catch the excitement of what Lloyd's and the City are about. From a distance he will glimpse the towers and the atrium marking the skyline; as he approaches, the building will gradually unfold; past the London plane tree on the north elevation, up the ramp, or stairs, into the glass lifts from which he will view London. Then across the glass bridge which offers him an unusual glimpse of the exterior of the building. As he enters he will see the low horizontality of the main floors, which then explode against the verticality of the great central atrium, the highest single volume interior space in Britain. Facing them, the viewer will see the great south window with London beyond and, easily visible below and above him, will be clearly exposed the nature and workings of Lloyd's, legible much in the same manner as the building is legible.

He comments on the specific ideas:

Around the Adam Room is a promenade full of orange trees and sculptures, with seats to relax and enjoy the view. The names of eminent Lloyd's personalities will be beautifully lettered on the external walls. The walk round the glazed promenade opens up a variety of vistas from the great atrium to the distant Thames and back to the generous waiting space with its formal staircase leading to the 12th floor. Here again the mood subtly changes, not dramatically for the space flows constantly, but with the constraints of the existing grammar of the building. A change more like the change of movement within a concerto.

Top left clockwise: Marco Goldschmied, John Young,
Michael Davies, Laurie Abbott

The rhetoric was understandable. The new Lloyd's people were looking among the twilight world of glossy magazines for an interior designer to replace Rogers's friend, a woman who is unquestionably among the most gifted designers in the world. Rogers was also attempting to educate a new generation of Lloyd's administrators who had not been involved in the building from the beginning, hence the long prologue explaining both the philosophy and efficiency of the building. He had even brought in Gordon Graham in his attempt to convince Lloyd's. But Jiricna's designs were rejected and a French company brought in, to Rogers's bitter dismay.

Similar problems emerged over a long standing attempt, partly orchestrated by Ruth, to persuade Lloyd's to invest systematically in modern art. It already possessed some poor pictures of the opening of the Heysham building but the idea now was to forge a link with the Whitechapel Art Gallery near by. Again this ran into problems with the new personalities and, by 1985, it seemed to have collapsed. One late triumph, however, was the agreement by Lloyd's to pay $100,000 for a 7-by-5-foot painting by the American artist Jim Dine, of the exterior of the new building.

Finally it had been agreed that there should be some form of exterior decoration. Rogers had been against sculpture on the basis that the overwhelming scale and detail of the Leadenhall Street façade would be too much for any artist to cope with. A clock had been suggested and Ruth took it on herself to approach Jean Tinguely. Tinguely is a Swiss-born sculptor who specializes in the production of fantastic machines capable of constant movement and change. He represents, perhaps, the underside of the machine cult with his subversive use of the silliness of mechanical movement rather than its excitement. His 'meta-mechanics' seemed in suitably playful contrast to the forbidding nature of the façade and offered a usefully distancing note from the usual automatic linking between Rogers's style and machinery.

Ruth's task was not easy. Tinguely habitually answers the phone with the first name that comes into his head and will stick with his adopted personality, denying the existence of anybody called Tinguely, throughout the phone call. With the help of Pontus Hultén, who was running the gallery at the Pompidou Centre, he was told Ruth's approach was coming and eventually, after several calls, did agree that it was indeed he, Tinguely, speaking. He pondered the commission for a moment and then said he would take it under one condition – the clock must never tell the right time. Rogers tried to sell the idea to Lloyd's but not entirely to his surprise, it was rejected. The brilliant and whimsical sculptor, Barry Flanagan, was finally chosen to design the clock.

It is apparent that all the clashes over the décor and the art arose primarily because of changes within Lloyd's. There were now fewer people in positions of power who were excited by the process of being led by the Rogers team in the way that Blackmore was. But the clashes also reflected changes in taste. Conservation as an issue was to gather momentum during the 1980s and this fed through into a widespread retreat both from the aggressively modern and from the sort of holistic and somewhat visionary arguments for consistency that Rogers had been putting forward. Certainly there had always been the predictable objections – as the scaffolding came off the building in 1985 letters appeared in newspapers protesting about this 'oil refinery' and Lloyd's members rang Blackmore to express rage at the continuing presence of the bright blue cranes on top of the service towers – they had assumed they were temporary features which would be removed once the builders left. But there was a more positive argument in favour of quieter, more instantly recognizable alternatives to the sort of sharp urban contrasts which provided a large part of the conceptual background for Lloyd's.

This had even surfaced in a challenge to the building from the City authorities. The planning permission granted to the building allowed Rogers to add drawings as long as they were approved by the City. As the service towers changed shape the news came out that the City wanted to put the whole issue back to its committee as the building had changed substantially from its original design. The move raised memories of the Pompidou Centre but it was a challenge that was to fizzle out. Rogers and Goldschmied produced figures that proved that only 2 per cent of the building surface had been altered – these were somewhat 'Italian' because they took the most generous view possible of what constituted surface area – and some political pressure was exerted within the City. In addition, Goldschmied put up a brilliant fight against the City's case. But the real clincher came when Lloyd's pointed out that they would be obliged to sue the authorities if there was any delay. A possible damages claim running at something like 1 million pounds a day was clearly not to be contemplated and the case was quietly dropped. But it was a warning of things to come.

In 1985 Rogers wrote of Lloyd's:

Our intention in the design of the new Lloyd's building has been to create a more articulated, layered building by the manipulation of plan, section and elevation which would link and weave together both the over-simplified twentieth-century blocks and the richer, more varied architecture of the past.

Approaches to buildings in cities are often along narrow streets, so they can be seen obliquely. Lloyd's is designed to be approached on the diagonal and viewed in parts. As the viewer approaches the building, the form gradually unfolds, the overlapping elements of its façade opening up to reveal spaces related to the pedestrian scale, spaces that are sheltered from the passing vehicles. Contrast is thereby created by the juxtaposition in depth of different layers and elements. First, there are the six strong, vertical, ever-changing articulated towers; then the free-standing, more rigid but clearly legible structural framework. Behind this are the translucent glass walls while, finally, in the centre, rises the glazed atrium.

The building pivots around the highest tower which marks the principal entrance opposite the Commercial Union Plaza and is on an axis with the Bank of England. The towers and building decrease in height as they meet the lower, Victorian Leadenhall Market.

The towers also serve to anchor the building and define the lines of the street, giving scale, grain, shadow and interest to the building mass. A tension is thereby established both between the different parts of the building and between the building and its immediate neighbours. The tall, serrated towers and the rounded atrium form are designed to enrich the skyline, placing the building in its urban environment amongst the spires, domes and towers of the past.

These techniques enable the viewer to participate in the dialogue between the different parts, between surface and depth, between tension and compression, horizontal and vertical, solid and void, and so his interest is revived and the form and meaning become easily legible.[4]

Elsewhere in the same piece he comments: 'The recognition of history as a principal constituent of the programme and an ultimate model of legitimacy is a radical addition to the theories of the Modern Movement.' A footnote to that remark refers to articles dating from 1955 in *Casabella Continuità* by Ernesto Rogers.

The evocation of Ernesto's later commitment to contextualism is significant. Ernesto had moved from futurism through the mainstream to a romantic sensitivity to site and history – a fairly clear development from youth, through middle age to elderly tolerance. Rogers's early attempt to jump straight to the final stage while at the Architectural Association had met with the derision of Smithson. This later attempt, however, represents a rather more considered and complex development.

For a start, Rogers's recruitment of the idea of history is in direct and deliberate contrast to the form in which the idea emerges in post- or anti-modernism. He is specifically not embracing the idea of modern imitation of or direct reference to past styles. The former has produced a rash of neo-Georgian of greater or lesser respectability and the latter has produced a wave of heavy-handed visual jokes. In addition, there is the line adopted by the practice of Quinlan Terry, which maintains that the classical style was handed down by God and its most precisely defined canons offer all the possibilities of variation any architect could wish for.

It is evident that these attitudes have been adopted on the rebound from modernism and this, to an extent, explains the polemical form of their justifications. Equally this has produced a polemical posture among some modernist apologists.

But Rogers is not simply trying to steer a middle course – his sympathies are unequivocally with the moderns. What he is aiming to do with the emphasis of his remarks on Lloyd's and with the whole tenor of his public stance at the moment is to define as 'modern' that which is simply the latest point in a historical process rather than only that which apocalyptically embraces the unquestionably new.

The significance of this in relation to Lloyd's is that it provides a sophisticated rationale which lays stress on the exterior, on its relation to the City as a whole, on its planning and on its performing role both as a symbol and theatrical event. All these elements may have been present in the thinking behind the Pompidou Centre but they have emerged far more explicitly as Lloyd's has neared completion. The first and most obvious reason is that Lloyd's is a private building. After some debate within Lloyd's, a public viewing gallery on the fourth floor was agreed upon, but primarily it was always to be a private, secure institution. Its interior, therefore, is of more interest to the client and Rogers's co-professionals who have studied it in detail in the architectural press, than to his wider public. Furthermore, this privacy encourages a more detailed explanation. The Pompidou Centre, because the public was able to 'play' with it at will, produced its rationale in the very process of being widely used, and in that process its design was to be justified. But Lloyd's will primarily be an external experience for the public. They will be aware of it as part of the City, as a passing event on the street, and so it must find its acceptance as a building among other buildings, a symbol among other symbols.

But there is a deeper level to this new historical emphasis in Rogers's thought. It is another way of attempting to explain himself to himself. Lloyd's, as I have said, has much in common with the Pompidou Centre and yet there was every opportunity for it to be entirely different. Part of Rogers's explanation is that it is as difficult to change one's architectural style as it is to change one's handwriting. The way he is able to work through a design process is with the aid of the knowledge that his style is based upon a celebration of exposed structure and services. 'Where does our language come into this?' is a characteristic question of his when leaning over a junior's drawing board. Such faith in a specific repertoire may coincide with functional explanations – like the ease provided by the style in the changing of service elements – but, in essence, his buildings are thus because Rogers wishes them to be thus and design processes must be finite.

Yet all that begs the question of *why* he wishes them to be so. The first answer is that it arises from the sense of liberation he experienced on discovering the delight of building with steel and off-the-shelf industrial products at Reliance Controls. Form and content seemed to come together as never before. Lloyd's may, in contrast, be an entirely customized, crafted building, but it retains in the dramatic concrete junctions and in the forms of the steelwork the elemental, almost juvenile thrill of seeing how things fit together.

Foster, however, derived a very different direction from the inspiration of Reliance Controls – a smoother, more visibly controlled, more classical direction. Rogers moved towards the Gothic, not disciplining his elements into patterns or symmetries but allowing them to express both their presence and their operation by the functional and purposive distribution. He is, as Peter Buchanan has said, 'not constrained by protocol'.[5] Rogers's direction clearly represents more of a contrast with the prevailing modernist view of 'good design' which places an emphasis on smoothness and simplicity in reaction to the mounting complications of Victorian eclecticism. And in this sense it can be seen as a conscious reaction against the increasing lack of expression and variation within the different straitjackets of mainstream modernism. Those straitjackets had become the equivalents of the Victorian classical or Gothic stylistic sheaths and, as such, were guilty of the same crimes of 'dishonesty'. When those crimes had first been identified at the turn of the century by Loos and others the mechanized aspects of buildings had hardly been developed – nowadays true modernist honesty would demand the frank expression of those aspects which have become almost as large an element as structure. The paradox is, of course, that, in being expressed, they become decoration, the ornament against which Loos had fulminated.

270   Thus far the exterior of Lloyd's may be seen as both a reaction against modernism and a recovery of its condition of prelapsarian innocence, before it was corrupted by later, compromising practitioners. It also provides a drama of transparency and opacity more fully realized that that of the Pompidou Centre. In the latter case the reduction in the height of the building, the loss of the open ground floor, the considerably greater density of the completed steel structure than the one envisaged in the competition drawings and the direct correspondence of the structural form to that of the inner box all detract from the element of surprise in the building arising from different depths and perspectives. Much remains but the overall immediate external sense of regularity is considerably more powerful than originally intended. At Lloyd's, regularity is systematically concealed by the unpredictable shapes of the towers, the slanting of the central block in relation to the site and the variety of spaces left around the building. The elementary central plan can only be worked out, it is not immediately apparent. The result is a constant drama of movement in the perception of the building itself which is further reinforced by the dynamic rhythms of the staircases and the multiplicity of varying interactions between service and structural elements: here a stainless steel duct describes a single, uninterrupted line, there it seems laced tightly into concrete, steel and glass. On top of the service towers the blue maintenance cranes sit frankly as if peering downward, resolving the upward whirling of the towers below. 'Align all the cranes properly,' said Courtenay Blackmore gleefully, 'and they look like great, blue birds hanging over the City.' People, when they are added, are to be seen rising and falling in the external glass lifts and occasion-

ally glimpsed through the glass walls. Finally, of course, Lloyd's is a finished building without the unresolved sense of Beaubourg. That building could be extended infinitely, Lloyd's is closed and complete within its site.

The whole is an image of circulation, of movement and of change which, in itself, seems to be the point. It is pure activity which is being celebrated. In its individual manifest- ations activity is impermanent, indeed it is the essence of transience and mortality; in general, however, it is the only permanent thing we know. An apparent, ever-changing volatility within architecture, the most apparently enduring artistic medium of all, expresses just this contradiction. Rogers's staircases 'run' up his service towers, but really we know they do no such thing and they never will. Where the Pompidou Centre provided a frame for this continuous drama of human activity, Lloyd's is – to use a word of Venturi's – inflected towards it. Its form takes life from the life within and without. As such it expresses the movement rather than staging it and therefore represents an important movement in Rogers's style towards a more lyrical architecture.

Rogers's interpretation of all this in a historical context arises from his increasing sense of the city as a larger, single image of the same dynamic. Again, this can be seen as a reaction against powerful elements within modernism. The simplifying tendencies of modernist town planning ideas from Le Corbusier to the Smithsons can now be seen as the movement's most damaging legacy. It produced instant slums by over-designing housing in an attempt to realize abstractions. What, for example, could be sadder than the Smithsons writing of 'the new softly smiling face of our discipline'[6] and of the Georgian heritage in housing in 1973, one year after the completion of their monstrous Robin Hood Gardens estate in East London with its sinister scale and weird defensive layout?

Rogers views the city as the very embodiment of change and variation. In such a view imitation of the past is as absurd as the grand modernist plans to rip conurbations apart and

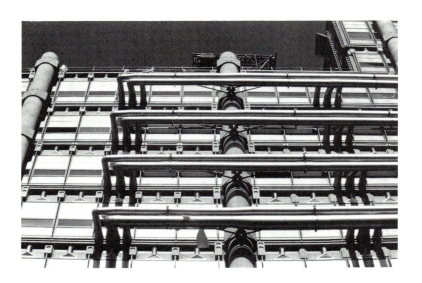

Aspects of the completed Lloyd's.
Illustrated London News

start again. New buildings are obliged to be modern in whatever way they see fit and only then can they provide a legitimate addition to the cityscape, adding to the depth of the urban experience by contrast and even contradiction.

In the case of Lloyd's this additive mania can be seen at its most fully developed. The building not only seems to shimmer and pulsate with life as it imposes its presence on nearby streets, it also changes radically even from distant perspectives. From Waterloo or Blackfriars bridges the dominant feature is the south window and the distance casts a silvery sheen over the whole structure producing an explicitly romantic waterside feel with the clearest references of all to the Crystal Palace. From Leadenhall Street only the tallest service tower is at first visible, projecting powerfully because of the leftward curve in the street. It seems menacing, partly because of its scale and partly because from here the depths of shadow within the structure have become dominant features. From the east an entire roofscape becomes visible with its service boxes, ducts, cranes and spiral service staircases. From here the building is at its most industrial, suggesting most explicitly the functional organization of parts of an industrial unit.

So Lloyd's does not suggest a single mood, it offers many. Similarly it evokes many metaphors – elements suggest entirely alien imagery as the cranes, for Blackmore, look like birds. Any one effect is provisional, to be modified by a change of position, of light or of the state of mind of the viewer. In that sense it is an uncontrolled building, offering any number of visual sensations without guidance or context. Certainly it can be fitted together in the mind in functional and structural terms providing the rational, cool, legible sense which is one part of what the architect had in mind. But that in itself becomes a difficult, shifting experience owing to the immense complexity which is on display. And, in any case, all the explanation in the world about replaceable elements, uninterrupted interior space and legible structure cannot fully answer the one unavoidable question which is: why does Lloyd's look precisely like that?

Rogers's justifications are attempts to answer that question for himself – to explain himself to himself. John Young once refused in a design meeting to draw one particular option they were considering saying: 'I'm not going to draw it, Richard, because I know you won't like it.' His detailed decisions are taken in an improvised, instinctive way which is disguised by the apparently seamless rationales always available for his buildings. 'Our language' is in reality a collection of images which for Rogers strike chords of harmony and completion. It is a web of apparent sense cast over a real void.

As such it would seem to represent the outer margin of subjectivity left to the artist after the collapse of first a transcendental synthesis and then a cultural one. Bereft of a catalogue of meanings he produces art as self-consistent as he can make it and in celebration of transience, process and the discontinuity of urban experience. For some artists similar choices have been born of pessimism and despair, for Rogers they are born of liberated delight. With Lloyd's he has attempted to rediscover his roots in the Renaissance as they were first explained to him on Nino's walks around Florence. The clarity of Brunelleschi is evoked and all the pure light of the new humanism which was to begin the long process of the destruction of the foundations of religion. From the rationalism of that tradition comes the certainty of the Lloyd's plan while from its humanism comes its exterior with its celebration of the perpetually unresolved, the eternal becoming, the provisional self.

Lloyd's is a great building produced by a man on a humanist tightrope. 'Our work is about giving order,' he has said, 'the problem about art is not finding more freedom, it is about finding obstacles . . . rules.'

7   Dreams of function

Winning the Lloyd's competition in April 1978 ensured that
Rogers would spend most of the rest of his life designing
buildings rather than teaching. It also kept his team together.
Richard Rogers & Partners only came into existence once the
divorce from Renzo Piano was complete, and that was not
until some months after the Lloyd's victory. As a result they
had not really stabilized in their new roles. There had been a
rapid contraction after the Pompidou Centre, combined with
a return to London and a long period of heart-searching.
Lloyd's meant the introspection had to stop. It was, for the
moment, the firm's only significant job and it rapidly expanded to devour everybody's time, expertise and stamina.
Roles for Goldschmied, Young, Davies and Rogers which had
been developing over the previous years now had to become
final – there would be no more support from powerful figures
like Piano or Foster. Rogers was now obliged to make the
personalities he had acquired for himself provide an alternative to the strong partners of the past. In a crucial sense this
meant he was on his own because the team was now quite
clearly his creation. They had been moulded by his shortcomings and his predilections. Where once Foster or Piano had
balanced his influence, creating their own personalities and
providing resistance and encouragement within the practice,
now Rogers was the one man at the top. Henceforth, the
name Richard Rogers would stand alone on the official RIBA
boards that decorate building sites, alone but for the '&
Partners' which follows. Much now depended on what was
meant by '&'.

The Lloyd's job provided one statement of confidence by a
client that he could do it. In spite of his misgivings, he had
fought furiously to win the competition, and he had happily
given guarantees that it would remain the practice's one

major project. The partnership was also convinced that the size of the practice should be controlled – thirty architects was regarded as the ideal size, making a total payroll of about forty-five when back-up staff are included. For perspective, both Pompidou and Lloyd's tied up about twenty architects for their entire duration. A speculative office block in New York, which Rogers took on in 1985, would involve two architects for eight months. There is a big difference between customized building and 'fast track' development.

It is thus hardly surprising that given the pressure of the need to make the practice stand alone, to build Lloyd's and to keep his firm within manageable proportions, his first response to an enquiry from Greycoat Estates in the early summer of 1979 was negative. He was still in the first flush of the Lloyd's design process and could not consider taking on anything substantial. He sent Goldschmied along to present an unconditional no to Greycoat's scheme for speculative office blocks on the South Bank of the Thames. Goldschmied, however, failed to convince the company and its lawyers. He came back to the office and told Rogers he would have to give them the definite brush-off. He too failed.

What, the developers had asked, would induce you to take on this scheme? Rogers had replied, on the assumption that it would be out of the question, that he would design the offices if Greycoat could somehow make the site run right down to the riverside. It was agreed and Rogers found himself with six weeks to produce a design for 1.2 million square feet of office space, 300,000 square feet of housing, 30,000 square feet of industrial space and an unknown number of shops, all within a 12.7-acre J-shaped site running from just behind the National Theatre to a point on the river just west of Blackfriars Bridge. This was the infamous Coin Street area over which some of the bitterest planning battles of recent years were to be fought.

Greycoat's problem was that it faced a public inquiry within weeks. The company already had a speculative office development designed for the part of the Coin Street area for which it held the freehold. But the public inquiry represented a major uncertainty and Greycoat's Stuart Lipton had called in a solicitor called Gary Hart to advise him. He in turn brought in the barrister, George Dobry, who said there was little chance of the rather low-quality existing scheme being accepted and advised Lipton to make improvements.

But time was desperately short and Dobry turned to Gor- don Graham to act as architectural middle man. Yet again Graham found himself dealing with discreet enquiries for a big client who did not want to say too much. Knowing little about the scheme involved, he suggested three practices, one of which was Richard Rogers & Partners. Lipton liked the idea so much that, by the time Rogers appeared, fully intending to turn him down, he was all too willing to accept his riverside condition.

Rogers could have had no idea of the scale of the problem in which he was to become involved. Certainly, he knew it was a massive scheme – he would need to speak to Lloyd's whose committee had stipulated that their building would take up most of Rogers's time – and he knew it had to be done quickly. But he had not realized the extraordinary strength of feeling which surrounds any development on the South Bank and which was to cast him in the unfamiliar role of servant to the capitalist property developers, an uncomfortable part for the creator of the Parisian People Place to play.

The South Bank's problems arise from the way London, uniquely among major cities, has allowed a river to divide it in two. From the wider perspective of Greater London, this has accentuated cultural differences between the south and the north. But the real disaster has been the effect on Central London. The South Bank became an industrialized river frontage, lined with warehouses and wharfs and obliged to face the groves and walkways of the North. As London de-industrialized, the contrast became more rather than less acute with the vacant, idle South Bank confronted by the teeming North.

After the war the Festival of Britain signalled official

awareness of the problem and the Royal Festival Hall marked the first step in the creation of a permanent South Bank arts complex. The arts as a service industry were part of the post-war welfare package that was to sweep away the abuses of the past. They were to be placed symbolically in the midst of the wasteland of the old world on the South Bank.

But the architecture compounded the errors of the past. It was not a question of the quality of individual buildings like the RFH, the Hayward Gallery and, latterly, the National Theatre, it was the way they all turned their façades to attract the northern middle classes and projected their rears to the south. Since they were also insensitively woven into the roads and walkways of the area, they became isolated, highly-specialized pavilions to which people scuttled to see an exhibition or a concert and from which they scuttled back home – usually to the north.

In addition, the big office development in the area – the Shell Centre – accentuated the difficulties by forcing its hard, impenetrable blocks rudely between Waterloo Station and the river. The walks provided through the centre from the station to the bridge and the arts complex only serve to underline the offhand nature of their conception.

Amid all this crushing development, houses still remained in the crowded area around Waterloo station and, not much further south, big local authority estates were springing up. The occupiers began to grow understandably sensitive about the obsession architects and developers seemed to have for putting walls between their homes and the river. The Shell Centre, in particular, caused irritation by failing to provide access to its basement sporting facilities as it had once promised. This sensitivity became so acute that Cedric Price, appointed by the Greater London Council to look at the whole area, claimed it was enough simply to walk about in a sheep-skin coat to be identified as one of the enemy.[1]

By 1979, the South Bank had become the site of a battle in the class war with all the crude distortion which that implies. The residents and the left wanted houses; the developers and the Tory government could only visualize offices. The issue centred on whether Coin Street was a local or national site. If it was local it should service local requirements for shops and houses – a suburban conception that assumed the area was not, in reality, a part of Central London. If it was national, the site was obliged to play a part in a larger theatre. It could not simply turn its back on the sweeping river frontages of the North Bank; it would be obliged, somehow, to relate to them.

Meanwhile, the anti-modern architecture movement was getting into its stride and the sculpted concrete pavilions of the South Bank were among its primary targets. From then onwards the capacity of living architects to solve anybody's problems anywhere was to be doubted seriously by large parts of the articulate middle class. An unholy alliance had been formed between the conservationist, anti-modernist right and the conservationist, anti-developer left.

Into this cauldron plunged Rogers: 'This is the last major opportunity to create a social magnet on the South Bank of the Thames and is also one of the last chances to link both sides of the river,'[2] he said as his Coin Street scheme was published, just before the inquiry started. He was to attempt to 'weave together the ghettos' by providing spaces for all the complex urban rituals, offering a panoramic, landscape quality and producing livable, workable offices.

The most unexpected element of the scheme was a new bridge across the Thames which provided the climax of a single pedestrian route from Waterloo Station through the centre of his development. Lipton had suffered no developer's qualms about the expense – the bridge's very presence would have added £1 or £2 per square foot to his office rentals, an indication of the sense of isolation intrinsic to life on the South Bank. The suspension bridge sprang from an island which Rogers hoped would take moorings and include a pier. The offices themselves hung either side of the walkway above rows of shops. At ground level something like 98 per cent of the space would be open to the public. Beside them, facing south, were the houses.

It was, inevitably, a rather crude, undetailed scheme at that stage, but it was nevertheless seen as the best solution on offer. Clearly Rogers was offering a good deal to the South Bank in the form of street life, even if the offices provided the *raison d'être* for the scheme. But the opposition was deeply entrenched. Perhaps because the ideas were underdeveloped,

Rogers's wire-mesh model could be too easily misunderstood. It left itself open to one damaging accusation. The Waterloo Action Group said it was a 'Berlin Wall' and thereby evoked the whole sad history of architecture on the South Bank. (It was a phrase that also revealed the power of the appropriate rhetoric in any debate about design. To point out that something looks like something else, usually unpleasant, is an appallingly potent weapon – one colour for the glass at Lloyd's had instantly been ruled out after somebody suggested it resembled horse piss.) Lambeth Council agreed. The Royal Fine Arts Commission was negative and even Sir Denys Lasdun, architect of the National Theatre, opposed it, using words that were to be printed on posters and plastered on walls in the area by the Action Group. The result was that Michael Heseltine, Secretary of State for the Environment, turned down the plan in July 1980 at the same time as he turned down the infamous 'Green Giant' office development on the South Bank at Vauxhall. 'As a generation,' said Heseltine, 'we shall be judged by the architecture we shall leave behind us.'[3]

But the rejection contained hints that a revised version of the same scheme might be considered and Greycoat decided to go for that, in spite of an attempt by Heseltine to nudge the company into running a competition. (It was perhaps as well for everybody concerned, not just Rogers, that Lipton resisted as Heseltine was to be behind the disastrous National Gallery competition.) Rogers went back to work and came up with less office space and more varied and obvious penetrations of the walls by existing roads – in fact, the principles of the design were scarcely changed at all. He elaborated more on the form of the walkway and produced dramatically detailed service towers which marched alongside a glazed atrium, rather like an elongated version of Lloyd's.

With rare and unintentional insight Liz du Parcq, Lambeth's planning chairman, commented on the new version: 'Greycoat's architects appear to have reduced the office bulk of their application, but they still seem hooked on features such as the pedestrian footbridge and the arcaded mall. These have a certain dream-like quality similar to the converted market hall in Covent Garden, but I am not sure they are practicable on this particular site.'[4] Such was the quality of thought within London's planners in the 1980s.

283

The Royal Fine Art Commission proved to have a wider imaginative range and to have had second thoughts: 'They now find this to be not only the bold and imaginative scheme they have always considered it to be, but also an appropriate one for the site in that it is no longer overbearing, yet without a doubt, metropolitan in scale. They also believe that it now carries with it a very good chance of bringing the South Bank to life,' wrote Sherban Cantacuzino.[5]

The whole Coin Street debate was duly replayed before another inspector. This time, the opposition to Greycoat had the added support of an extreme, left-wing GLC which had been elected just before the opening of the second inquiry. The political dimension was, as a result, sharpened.

And so, bizarrely, was the personal. The barrister opposing the scheme at the second inquiry was called Sears – he was the very same Sears who had once battered Rogers around the boxing ring at Kingswood House. Sears and Rogers acknowledged their old acquaintanceship but they never spoke of the boxing match.

In the event Heseltine was not simply going to endorse offices to irritate the left. He did not want the battle to go on for ever. Instead, he granted planning permission for both the local authority housing schemes and the Greycoat scheme. He assumed that the local authorities would simply not have the money and the offices would go ahead. He was wrong. The GLC had plenty of cash. Greycoat was asked how much it wanted for its land. With the office market in decline and continuing uncertainties about letting the development, the company saw a trouble-free way out. The land was sold to the GLC and in 1984 the Rogers scheme finally collapsed.

For the South Bank this will prove a tragedy. Local authority developments along the river have proved no more sensitive to its potential than those by government or commerce, and merely saying houses are good, offices bad, does not amount to an architectural programme. It will be a loss architecturally because it offered Rogers the opportunity of realizing his increasing sense of the importance of town planning on a huge scale. More than most architects he is difficult to analyse at the preliminary design stage because so much goes into the buildings during the assembly of working drawings and during the building process itself, but it is clear that his sense of the perpetually changing city and the need for a continuous variation of effect would have found a natural home in Coin Street. Its generosity of expression and range of incident are in even more direct contrast to its modern neighbours than Lloyd's is to the Commercial Union building. Furthermore, the punctuation of the South Bank skyline by the service towers – growing more dramatic with each new phase of the design process – would have reversed the tendency for every grand, visual gesture to be placed on the North Bank. Its obvious broad similarities to Lloyd's in terms of the plan of each element – the service towers, the atrium and so on – make it difficult to establish how far it would have represented a stylistic development. But it does seem clear that the more self-conscious modelling of the towers compared with the appearance of the Lloyd's towers at a similar stage indicate Rogers pushing his 'language' still further in the direction of planned expression and away from the happy accidents of function.

This is an important point, but it is a difficult one to extract from the complexities of the design process. There is no question that aesthetic choice has always played cat and mouse with functional considerations in Rogers's architecture, but

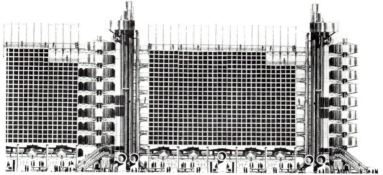

Above: The Coin Street scheme
Below: Detail of Coin Street showing the offices
and a service tower

in the past it often seemed that considerations of abstract
beauty have appeared at a later stage than at Coin Street.
This may seem inevitable in view of the length of time Coin
Street was actually on the drawing boards and in view of the
need to convince a planning inspector. But it is also clear that
Rogers's developing sense of history was leading him towards
a softer, more expressive, possibly more romantic, view of his
role. Much is revealed by the drawings of Coin Street from a
distance: they show its towers weaving in and out of the
South Bank's urban fabric, not dominating but perhaps commenting on the broken De Stijl-like forms of the National
Theatre, the plodding articulation of the London Weekend
Television tower and, most potently of all, on the incoherent
brutality of the Shell Centre. It is an elementary effect of
contrast which admits a degree of delicate complexity into
the over-simplified forms of the area. In so doing it could have
brought human scale to the South Bank by filling it with
incident, change and the insistent yet ambiguous metaphorical content which had appeared in his style at Lloyd's.

Most importantly, it had an expressive irregularity about
its skyline which was to speak ever more eloquently than the
'dumb boxes' of the past. Wittgenstein once mused: 'Phenomena akin to language in music or architecture: Significant
irregularity – in Gothic for instance.'[6]

But it was not to happen and Rogers was left only with a
sense of outrage and bitterness. He commented sadly that the
cost of the inquiries could have given Londoners five new
bridges over the Thames, while the final achievement of all
the political wrangling was for the left to buy out the right. It
was a process which had proved immensely painful – Rogers
and his assistants, Chris Wilkinson and John Sorcinelli, had
been subjected to dozens of all-night sessions perfecting his
evidence with Greycoat's lawyers. Dobry, his assistant John
Taylor, Hart and Gordon Graham seemed capable of working
without pause for days on end. At Team 4 Rogers had once
done the same, but now he was nearly twenty years older. He
found himself spending hours working on the very things at

which he was least competent, writing and public speaking. But he discovered a talent for surviving and often winning debating points during cross examination. It arose, presumably, from an old inability to recognize when he is beaten.

He had too to face scathing criticism of his role in bringing office development to the South Bank area. Dozens of times he was asked by campaigners, who had found the Pompidou Centre ideologically acceptable, why on earth he had taken on this job. Dozens of times he would reply that the Greycoat scheme offered the opportunity of deriving huge 'planning gains' from private developers, gains that left-wing local authorities, however ideologically purified, never seemed to achieve.

With this battle raging and Lloyd's beginning to attract interest, Rogers discovered he was becoming a public figure, something of a feat for an architect in Britain where awareness of the art is perhaps lower than in any Western country. But is was not a happy experience. With the massively expanded workload the practice had been forced to find new premises. John Young discovered some studios in Holland Park which the partners were unable to buy – the asking price was £250,000 – but which they managed to rent in partnership with PA Design Unit, another offshoot of Gordon Edge's company. They were the same studios used by Antonioni's fictional photographer played by David Hemmings in the film *Blow Up*. For the opening party – organized by Ruth and Young – they had hired a print of the film and, for some incomprehensible reason, had parked an American black-and-white police car outside. There were 350 guests, steel band and ice cream at midnight.

But Coin Street campaigners got wind of the affair and picketed the party. Ruth recalls staring out at the demonstration and the police car in front of the offices and feeling a chilly reminder of the scenes on American campuses in earlier years. Rogers characteristically agonized over the problem, and then invited some protesters to come in and dance as well as to argue their points. He was trying desperately not to play the role in which he was being cast. And he had, in a curious way, managed to strike up reasonable friendships with the protesters. The story made the newspapers, however, making anything other than role-playing almost impossible.

Other work was still flowing in. In 1978 three house designs had been completed, one for a house on Long Island for Ruth's parents and one for the American comedian, Steve Martin. The latter job had arisen via Ruth's brother, Michael Elias, who had written Martin's television show in America. The Rogerses stayed for a while with Martin in Aspen, Colorado. The Elias house on Long Island was obliged to cope with a site which was constantly being eroded by the sea, a problem which Rogers overcame by placing it on rails – this allowed it to be drawn away from the cliff edge over the years. The Martin house was an all-purpose design without a site. Martin wanted it to be as self-sufficient as possible in energy, hence its name, The Autonomous House. Rogers provided a windmill and solar panels all set in a delicate, spidery light-weight structure but, like the Elias House, it was never built. However, even in the early stages at which the projects stopped, it was clear that both suggested a desire to bring movement into building. Both had security problems as they would be left unoccupied for long periods so Rogers had introduced balconies which closed up like the petals of a flower turning the houses into sealed, impenetrable boxes. Finally, there had been a design for Michael Elias on the West Coast which was also never built.

But he was destined not to return to the domestic scale. The first building actually completed after the Pompidou Centre was to be the Fleetguard Manufacturing and Distribution Centre at Quimper in Brittany. For some purists – including Prouvé, the Pompidou Centre jurist – this was to be Rogers's most perfect building since Reliance Controls.

A very important aspect of this project was the client, for Fleetguard is a subsidiary of the American Cummins Engine Company which has a unique record of architectural patronage. This started in the late 1930s when the company commissioned Eliel Saarinen to build the First Christian Church in the company's home town of Columbus, Indiana. Then, in 1954, the company's foundation offered to pay the architectural fees for new local schools as long as the architects were chosen from one select list. Later, this programme was expanded to include all public buildings in the town. The result is a town full of architectural gems which, although they do not necessarily sit happily together, have certainly given the place a name. Practices involved include I. M. Pei, who built the library, Skidmore, Owings and Merrill, who designed the newspaper building, Venturi and Rauch, who produced a wittily bland fire station presumably as a comment on the self-consciousness of the whole enterprise, and Roche & Dinkeloo.

In addition, Cummins's own buildings are invariably designed by the best the company can find. In Britain this resulted in the factory at Darlington by Roche & Dinkeloo, which so impressed Rogers and Foster while they were designing Creek Vean and was to provide some of the inspiration for Reliance Controls, and a factory at Shotts in Lanarkshire designed by Ahrends, Burton and Koralek and completed in 1983.

'I don't like the phrase enlightened patron,' said the head of Cummins, J. Irwin Miller, 'because my reasoning is just that we are going to make more money doing it this way. So is the worker because he is going to be better paid. It is very expensive to be mediocre in this world.'[7]

For Quimper, Miller was advised to use Rogers by Kevin Roche. It was to be a simple industrial shed of just under 100,000 square feet to be built in fourteen months. It was, in many respects, a repeat of Reliance Controls, except that cost was not to be such a major restraining factor. Furthermore, the site was a substantially more important element – a medieval Breton town provided different demands from a Swindon industrial estate. Putting a shed in such a context was not easy and for some time Rogers worried that there seemed no way to soften its impact. The servicing demands meant that it would simply be too high and would thus rudely block the landscape.

The solution arose from a series of discussions with Peter Rice involved. Also on the team was Richard Soundy, an excellent architect to whom Rogers was later to offer a partnership (which he turned down in favour of setting up his own practice). The building was to be a tension structure. This meant that the structure and service elements would all be suspended from masts. It would provide for the skyline of the building a delicate network of vertical masts which seemed appropriate with the two rivers and the sea near by. These together with the diagonal tension members provide a more delicate alternative to a blank wall housing internal structure. The result is an extraordinarily confident building showing all the accumulated experience both of steel structure and of large multi-purpose industrial spaces. Locally it was greeted with some puzzlement. Nevertheless, a Quimper craftsman produced a hideous glazed ceramic plate with a painted image of the factory for the opening ceremony and the party was, as everybody involved noted, much better than the one that marked the opening of the Pompidou Centre. Michael Elias flew in from America, but Rogers almost missed it – he had been stuck for some time in the lift of his hotel.

The success of Fleetguard was to pave the way for what some, impervious to the appeal of the Pompidou Centre or Lloyd's, have come to regard as Rogers's best building – the Inmos factory. This was born in 1978 of the British government's sudden desire to catch up in the microprocessor race. Inmos was to be the start of a rapidly expanding new presence in the silicon-chip business. Ian Barron, the man appointed to achieve this impossible goal, wanted a flagship building which had the necessary air of demonstrable quality and confidence. As a factory, therefore, it was to have a clear expressive role over and above its demanding functional requirements. Or, to tighten this aesthetic knot a little further, its function had to be triumphantly expressed.

The design problems were immense. At first it was to be a

The Fleetguard factory at Quimper.
Ken Kirkwood

siteless building capable of being planted anywhere – this was partly because the site was as yet unknown and partly because there might be the opportunity to produce several factories to the same design. Secondly, it was to be expandable and thirdly, its production areas had to be kept cleaner than the average operating theatre. Silicon chips involve such a high number of functioning elements in such a small area that any impurity is fatal to their reliability. In spite of all this the design appeared as if pre-ordained.

A central corridor divided the 'clean' from the 'dirty' rooms, this then became the lower half of an H-section, the upper half of which accommodated external services placed on the roof for ease of access and replacement. It was this decision to place the services on the roof and in the centre which had unlocked the entire design process. Steel trusses spread like wings from this H to carry the glass envelopes of the building. Since the interiors were required to be column-free, the trusses had to be supported by tension members running downward from the tops of the H. These were not necessary to hold the building up, merely to prevent the trusses from deflecting. Technically, therefore, it is a 'tension-assisted' structure. Further tension members anchored the ends of the trusses.

This exquisitely simple solution appeared breathtakingly quickly with the aid of Tony Hunt, Rogers's engineer from Team 4 days. Hunt's approach contrasts sharply with that of Peter Rice. Whereas Rice would tend to consider a building strategically for a long period before committing himself to engineering solutions, Hunt would simply provide the best engineering options for strategies previously determined by the architects. At Inmos this worked because the design came together so quickly there was no strategic thinking left to do. The excellence of Hunt's detailed solutions can be judged by the way he set out to produce a pin-jointed structure in which no joint required more than one pin. (In the event only one required two.) The result is the gratifying sense of ease and completeness about every detail in the structure.

But immediately there was a politically-inspired delay of nine months. The building had finally been sited on top of a hill near Bristol but, after the delay, it was made smaller and resited in a valley in Gwent. Thanks to large-scale prefabrication of the elements, which allowed it to be constructed bay by bay, it was built in fifteen months. At the end of the process a large blue-and-silver technological butterfly sat enigmatically in a green Welsh field promoting aesthetic paroxysms of extraordinary violence amongst professionals and amateurs alike.

The first – amateur – reaction was from the Prince of Wales at the opening ceremony. The heir to the throne was at the stage where he was developing his ideas about architecture, ideas that were later to result in a notorious onslaught on the aesthetics of modernism. As he looked up at the steel lattices, the intestinal service ducts and the sweeping tension members he remarked to the architect: 'Well, Mr Rogers, it looks as though the engineers got their own way this time.' So the first confusion was announced – the building looked so aggressively functional that the Prince assumed the architects had contributed nothing.

For more sophisticated souls the problem was that the building was so evidently beautiful and yet it was impossible to pin down at what points entirely aesthetic decisions had been made. The engineering was as clean as it could be, but somehow even the services seemed to follow the general consistency with extraordinary obedience. Functionalism had seldom seemed so easy. Part of the problem with this is that functionalism as an aesthetic should suggest a degree of similarity between solutions to the same problems. But Rogers and his team – led by Michael Davies and Pierre Botschi – had arrived at something radically different for a function for which the number of precedents was proliferating daily. In California's Silicon Valley, in particular, highly simplified slick sheds had sprung up everywhere to accommodate the industry. These too had required a certain expressive confidence as they competed with each other in their images of efficiency and modernity – but they had tended to interpret this in a blank, bland, highly rationalized form which seemed to owe something to the Case-Book house tradition of Ellwood, Soriano and Eames. Mostly it can be seen as an expression of the industry's own mystique. The consumer, after all, cannot service a silicon chip any more than he is likely to understand it. It is a closed system which either works or is thrown away – only the priesthood of technologists understands it fully and it was appropriate that they should house themselves in blank, inscrutable boxes. In Britain, places like Milton Keynes were producing similarly smart, smooth industrial units in which the flatness of the façade was used to provide purely two-dimensional decorative effects.

The problem with such sheds and their residually high-tech imagery was that their flexibility only went half-way. Certainly their uninterrupted rectangular plans could be infinitely rearranged and logically any human activity can be enclosed in a shed as long as its dimensions are adequate. Unfortunately, the ever-increasing levels of service equipment required would always threaten to expand beyond the confines of almost any site. In placing the equipment on the roof where it could change and expand to the deflection limits of Hunt's steelwork, Rogers found a solution which both announced itself to the world and which worked. The result was to undermine the accumulated iconography of the silicon chip as a mysterious inhabitant of impenetrable black boxes by displaying the effort of its construction and the beauty of its operation. This was, in effect, the reversed, demystified side of the 1950s' fascination with slickly integrated technology as seen in American car design, flaunted in consumer advertising and embraced during the ICA colloquies of the period.

The sense that the building posed an aesthetic problem arose because its sheer visibility is overwhelming. It is not simply that the 'clean' versus 'dirty' antithesis is clearly expressed. It is rather that every truss and pin seems to speak of an inevitability in its design comparable to that of any old chunk of industrial plant. And yet it was all so evidently beautiful. Reyner Banham[7] compared this sense of inevitability to the effect of naval architecture, a comparison which evoked Le Corbusier's enthusiastic endorsements of the design of ocean liners.[8] The problem was that this all suggested a sort of replete functionalism at a time when the word seemed to have been hopelessly devalued or, at least, to have serious problems of respectability. Banham's synthesis concluded:

For we have seen enough of Functionalist architecture by now to know that, in spite of its seemingly temporary nature in an evolving technological culture, it can achieve not only the youthful beauty of promise but (if it gets to stand long enough) also the character of maturity as well. The ultimate test of Inmos as architectural art may well be: will it look as good as Gropius' Fagus factory or its 1911 contemporary, Graphic Controls in Buffalo, New York, when it has stood the same three-score-years-and-several, given the same degrees of appropriate maintenance?

To ask this is not to withhold judgment; Inmos looks good and appears to be delivering the promise of its good looks, at present. Rather it is to ask that it be judged ultimately in the full depth and rigour that are implicit in Functionalism in the grandest and noblest sense of the word.

The sleight of hand here is to raise functionalism – note the capital F in the extract – to the level of an absolute trailing clouds of moral imperatives. This is done in order to close the gap between the context of the beautiful and the context of the functional, a closure which makes it unnecessary to worry about the causal connection in the extreme functionalist position which says that if a thing is truly functional, it is *therefore* beautiful. If both are placed within the same transcendent, timeless context then the unfortunate relative, timebound connotations of function are overcome. Is Inmos a timeless piece of architecture or is it just a brilliant solution to a temporary problem?

The question may not, for the moment, be answerable, but the reason that it arises is important to this phase of Rogers's development. He is obliged to build amid the semantic fencing of late modernism which, in essence, is trying to gloss the language of early modernism as a means of providing a convincing sense of continuity. If, for example, functionalism can be sufficiently enhanced to take it beyond the discipline of the *Oxford English Dictionary*, then it may be developed coherently to justify a more plural repertoire than its original adherents ever envisaged. It may, in short, become vague enough to provide a 'language'.

The importance of this to architecture cannot be underestimated. The sense that a legible system of meaningful forms is essential to the art lies behind much of the reaction to the modern movement – most potently in Roger Scruton's defence of the classical.[9] Rogers repeatedly uses the word 'language' to describe his stylistic hallmarks and he does so as a way of making design decisions intelligible to himself as much as to anybody else. It is in this sense a personally chosen discipline – which is precisely why it is not a 'language', though it may be, in Wittgenstein's words, akin to language. Now it is clear that the basis of this discipline is function. Whatever the metaphorical impact of Inmos – its resemblance to a butterfly, the way it 'sits' in the field – it is all derived from the imagery of function. But so much additional work has been done on the imagery that to call it 'functionalist' is quite meaningless. Function may explain the use of a tension-assisted span – it prevents the roof members from deflecting and allows an uninterrupted interior space – but an ideology of function cannot show why the members should be so evidently designed to please. The obvious comparison would be with the detailing of a Gothic cathedral – function would explain the expression of structure, but it would not account for the crockets, finials and gargoyles with which the elements are encrusted.

The problem with Inmos is that it is too easy to like. First, it is in a green field site so the difficult problems of urban context with all their unhappy recent associations are removed. Secondly, it has an instantly identifiable overall form

Inmos. *Ken Kirkwood*

– the highest point at the centre slopes down the steelwork to the lowest points at the edge evoking, in an admittedly attenuated and unintentional way, the outline of a pediment. Thirdly, it provides the imagery of technology contained within this lucid structure rather than overflowing uncontrollably from its exterior. This all makes it an unusually appropriate testing ground for aesthetic controversy. It makes, as it were, the Rogers problem manifest in an unusually clear form. As such it is easy Rogers, elucidating rather than adding to his art.

Inmos was to have an offspring in the form of Patscenter, Princeton, a headquarters for the American end of the PA Technology group which Rogers had housed in Melbourn, Cambridgeshire. This was engineered by Rice instead of Hunt but, although it has a substantially simpler-looking structure, its overall concept is the same – a central corridor, two wings and a tension structure which also supported the services above the roof. Again, as at Inmos, there was a substantial element of showmanship involved. Goldschmied had pointed out to the client that the tension structure would be $170,000 more expensive than a standard shed but suggested they regard that sum as part of their advertising budget.

But in Princeton the head of the university's architecture school is Michael Graves. Graves is the arch post-modernist. He sprang from a New York-based group known politely as the New York Five and less politely as the Whites because of their addiction to the smooth, white planes of pre-war modernism. They were characterized by buildings which seemed austere and cerebral, yet often gratuitously complex. Explanations were provided by prose of surpassing opacity even by architectural standards. Graves, however, had moved decisively away from this monastic posture towards a decorative style involving a series of playful exercises with traditional elements like keystones or columns. To him Patscenter was 'just a slick aircraft hangar' and he would 'rather practise law than produce architecture like that'.[10] By the 1980s the various movements away from mainstream modernism had gone too far for any of them even to understand each other.

However, the 1980s also saw Richard Rogers & Partners entering an extraordinarily busy phase. By 1983 Rogers, Goldschmied and Young had decided to start turning away work as stability and affluence seemed to be staring them in the face. Holland Park was, by now, far too small and it was being shared with an expanding PA Design Unit. A new site was found by John Young, who spotted it while driving across Hammersmith Bridge. This was an unpromising-looking 2 acres east of the bridge on the north bank of the Thames. It was littered with industrial debris but there were some solid-looking Victorian warehouses of the kind the practice delighted in converting into studios. The whole area was illuminated by the reflected light from the vast expanse of the Thames visible at that point. It comes as a pleasant shock after the rows of anonymous terraces between Fulham Palace Road and the river.

In fact it had been the location of Duckhams's first oil refinery in 1931 – crude oil had been brought up the river by barge. The total site involved two simultaneous purchases for a total of £930,000 and it was bought, not by the partnership, but by Goldschmied, Rogers and Young as a group of individuals using fees accumulated over the years. There was no planning permission. Even with the increased workload it represented a massive leap in their respective financial commitments. Goldschmied was to come into his own as a developer architect on this project. Also, Ruth and Rogers had decided that they were at least ready to leave Belsize Grove. They had been searching for a house with the best possible views and light and as much horizontal space as could be achieved in Central London. They had found what they wanted in two neighbouring Victorian houses in St Leonard's Terrace, Chelsea.

The doubts that had characterized the period immediately after the completion of the Pompidou Centre had more or less evaporated. Lloyd's had made the continuance of the practice in London inevitable, at least until 1985, and the additional work that began to flow in suggested it would be a permanent state of affairs. At home, however, the family seemed to be shrinking. His three sons from his first marriage would soon all be old enough to be independent and Roo was no longer the baby that Rogers always seems to like having around the place.

But, for almost two years from 1981, Ruth had been seriously ill. For four months the cause remained undetected until, in the summer, a rare condition known as sarcoid was diagnosed by Nino. At the same time she had her eyes tested and was told by the optician that they were protruding slightly. She checked with Nino that all the tests she had just been through would have detected a thyroid abnormality and he assured her that they would have done. He also described the symptoms of an over-active thyroid gland.

Soon afterwards, during a trip to America, all the symptoms seemed to fall into place and Ruth found herself facing almost eighteen months of drug treatment on top of the months of tests and illness she had already suffered. She was, however, treated successfully, only to discover at the end of the process that she could have no more children. The whole episode provided Rogers with a sad counterpoint to the burgeoning success of the practice. He had feared the worst throughout the period before the final diagnosis and, even when those fears had been dispelled, the news that they could have no more children came as a blow.

It was a crisis for both of them – another child had been planned as a matter of course. Rogers's colleagues, friends and family were all slightly baffled – after the years of relative poverty and bringing up four sons, why did he not want to relax in affluence?

Unimpressed by such arguments, Rogers and Ruth decided to adopt but immediately found it would be impossible in England. The authorities pointed out that they were too old and already had children. But soon afterwards they met the American novelist Kurt Vonnegut and his wife who had successfully adopted via an agency in the United States. Ruth was still an American citizen so some of the bureaucratic problems should have been easy to eliminate.

The agency – known as the Golden Cradle – specialized in finding girls with unwanted pregnancies and then matching them with potential parents. In America the agency insists the adopters take the responsibility of looking after a pregnant girl while they are waiting for their own child. Clearly, this would not be the mother of the child they were to adopt but it did establish a high degree of reciprocal responsibility. (This condition would not be applicable, however, with an overseas adoption.) The Rogerses were promised a child and they sat back and waited. But a sudden change of policy at Golden Cradle meant the agency would no longer handle foreign adoptions. There was a series of frantic phone calls which resulted in a contact with another agency in Arizona. Again they waited, this time travelling to Turkey on a sailing holiday – it was the second year they had done so. They returned to learn that a seventeen-year-old Arizona girl was pregnant, and would they like the baby if it was a girl? It was due to be born in November. Ruth took the call and said they would. Rogers suggested they ring back and say they would take the baby whatever its sex.

They then embarked on the waiting process as if it was their own pregnancy. Rogers was at that time working on a potential project in Dallas and had to sit exams in the United States to be able to practise as an architect. That particular year the exams happened to take place in Arizona. It seemed too good to be true, and taking Roo out of school, the family travelled to Phoenix in November 1983. Ruth, meanwhile, had been engaged in an epic bureaucratic struggle with the British authorities to ensure they could bring the baby into the country.

The birth was late. They went sightseeing at the Grand Canyon and then travelled to Los Angeles to stay with Michael Elias. The baby still hadn't been born. Rogers had to return to London and Ruth went home to Woodstock and put

Roo into a local school. Her parents had been nervous about the adoption from the beginning and, amid that atmosphere of doubt, Ruth began to think the whole deal would simply never come off.

Finally, they were told the birth was to be induced and Rogers flew to New York. They stayed at the apartment of the architect, Norman Pfeiffer, and his wife, Patty, and it was there that they received the phone call telling them they had a son. There was another three days' wait – the period laid down by Arizona law during which the natural mother can change her mind – and they then flew to Philadelphia to receive the baby from the arms of a social worker in a hotel lobby. Even at this stage they were kept in suspense – it was a cold and snowy night and the social worker went at first to the wrong hotel. The child had dark hair, which has now turned bright blond, and they named him Bo. They lay for hours in their Philadelphia hotel bedroom with Bo in the same way they had once lain for days in Dr Vellay's Paris clinic with Roo.

Rogers's sense of family was restored. And, of course, Bo will presumably prove mercifully free of the learning difficulties that all Rogers's other children have inherited with varying degrees of severity. Ben, the eldest, did not learn to read until he was eight, although he was eventually to read politics, philosophy and economics at Oxford and is now doing postgraduate work in America at Columbia University. His parents were told that Zad would never be able to take 'O' Levels but he is now at Manchester University studying art history. Ab has proved the most severely dyslexic and his future remains unresolved, while Roo also suffers though seemingly substantially less.

Throughout Rogers's life it is difficult to separate the personal and the professional for work and family constantly flow together. In the middle of a family outing he will frequently be discovered in a corner, poring over piles of papers, having switched his concentration in an instant from a swirling mass of children, relatives, friends and passers-by. One

Rogers and Bo

At the Pont Neuf. *From left:* Ben, Rogers, Roo, Ab, Ruth and Zad

friend described coping with this fluid entourage as being like 'wrestling with spaghetti' but Rogers seems to have no difficulty. Indeed it is necessary to his peace of mind. Crowds of people arguing over the menu in a restaurant or making complex arrangements with each other are, to him, a state of rest.

For the children this has meant from the beginning that they have been swept up in the various complex processes and arrangements of his life. In their first years Ben, Zad and Ab were intimately if unconsciously involved in the struggles of Team 4 and later of Richard & Su Rogers. Obviously with the break-up of the marriage they became part of a new family, but they continued to receive his letters, telling long, elaborate tales about outer space, and to go on holidays with Rogers and Ruth. These were invariably precarious affairs. Often they would end up sleeping on beaches or in fields because of the shortage of cash. But, for the Rogerses, holidays were too central to their lives to allow lack of money to stop them from going abroad.

Yet, at the same time, they were conscious of being pushed academically. Rogers himself would often work between 6 a.m. and midday on holiday and he seemed to expect a similar intensity of dedication from his sons. Zad has commented that the family of John and Su is a typically English, relatively easygoing community in which success is desirable but not overwhelmingly important. The family of Rogers and Ruth, in contrast, is suffused with ambition, an American urge to 'go for it' and a certain severe acceptance of the need for hard work. Homework plays a constant part of family discussions.

In part, Rogers is evidently replaying Nino's role, though within the more freewheeling context provided by Ruth, for his own childhood has conditioned him to accept that nothing comes easily. His memories of academic failure, tutors, crammers and beatings have not made him anti-academic, they have merely convinced him that success involves a constant process of struggle. Work can never be left behind.

Roo and Bo, however, are growing up with a father who for them will appear consistently successful. The older sons are all used to ritual arguments with Rogers about whether or not his latest work represents a selling out of his socialism; the youngest will perhaps not see any such contradiction.

And their holidays are taken in greater comfort. These are now huge family rituals and often involve a constant stream of visitors dropping in wherever they happen to be. There are three major holidays at Christmas, Easter and in the summer, and these are interspersed with shorter breaks for Rogers and Ruth alone. Always some trip is being planned, always hundreds of people seem to be involved, always bags of papers and drawings are taken along as well.

But the euphoria of the end of 1983 with the practice booming, a new baby, and a new home to design evaporated rapidly during 1984. There had already been disappointments but the weight of continuing work had made these seem bearable. As Lloyd's moved into its later, less demanding phases, the disappointments began to outnumber the successes and, by the end of 1984, Rogers once again found himself facing the possibility of a massive shrinkage in the practice. It seemed like a complete replay of the collapse at the end of the Pompidou Centre project.

Perhaps the worst blow was Coin Street which finally ended its eventful run in 1984. That had involved the highest level of commitment from Rogers and the most agonizing about the role he had been obliged to play. And it had not only been his problem: several people in the office, sympathetic to the protesters' case, had refused to work on the project. But, perhaps the most saddening failure was the National Gallery.

London's National Gallery in Trafalgar Square is a weak, classical building designed by William Wilkins and completed in 1838. It is a sad climax to the square, which had been designed by Nash as a pause at the head of Whitehall on the ceremonial route from Buckingham Palace to St Paul's. Indeed the whole of Trafalgar Square represents a dispiriting spectacle. There is only one building of any quality at all – Gibbs's superb St Martin-in-the-Fields of 1726 – and, from a planning point of view, the square is a disaster as the central area is hopelessly isolated by a lethal roundabout of permanently congested roads. The National Gallery's plan involved developing an empty site at the north-west corner of the square with a new gallery financed by offices and shops.

In spite of the prevailing mediocrity of the architecture in the area and the relatively small size of the whole project – £25 million at 1983 prices – the competition was to attract more publicity than any other. Vast, catastrophically bad office blocks can shoot up in much more sensitive sites in the City and nobody will notice. But the combination of Trafalgar Square, a public building and an open competition seemed to awaken the British to architecture as never before.

As it was a competition for developers and architects, Rogers became involved at the invitation of a developer, Speyhawk. He was, in retrospect, a supremely logical choice. The problems of planning, circulation and attracting crowds were all ones he had proved capable of solving and, in view of the client, an architect with all Rogers's fine-art overtones might have seemed an obvious contender. All these factors began to dawn on Rogers as he was working on the design. He began to enjoy the task more than any he had previously done and to become more confident as time passed that he was a potential winner.

As usual, however, it had begun badly. The brief was atrociously prepared and bore all the signs of an inexperienced jury. Its most baffling element was the requirement that the gallery should be a basilica-like space. Frequent requests were put to the gallery and the jury for an elucidation of this term, but it soon became clear that they had no idea what it meant either. The only sensible explanation was that the client simply wanted a large space, although it was never clear why they should describe such a space with a term that, correctly used, means an aisled church with a clerestory. Furthermore, the brief contained hints that the new building should be appropriate to its context, although what that meant in the chaos of Trafalgar Square is difficult to establish. There are several contextual problems: Wilkins's façade is so flat that an addition in any style is going to project uncomfortably. A stronger composition would have been better able to bear an addition. The square itself is largely classical but devoid of any intelligible order which would suggest the outlines of a solution, and finally, the organization of the traffic meant the building would have to face on to an almost uncrossable road which divides it from the other obvious goal for pedestrians – the centre of the square itself with its pigeons, fountains and Nelson's Column.

However, the tentative nature of the brief allowed Rogers to develop one aspect of the problem from which, in the end, all his other solutions flowed. He became fascinated by the difficulties of the context. In the square itself it became obvious that a tower of some kind would strengthen the whole area by completing the triangle implied by the spire of St Martin's and Nelson's Column. But, on a wider scale, he came to realize that the site offered an opportunity – probably unique – for improving the environment of Central London. At the moment Trafalgar Square, Piccadilly Circus and Leicester Square stand isolated as discrete centres whose geographical relationship is largely unintelligible without some study. The first two are further removed from human understanding by the fact that they are used as traffic round-abouts while the third has been shabbily pedestrianized. By turning the National Galley site into a gateway he could at least start the process of linking the three by offering a visible route through from Leicester Square to Trafalgar Square. He would then add a pedestrian tunnel from under the site to Nelson, the pigeons and the fountains, completing a route in a way that had never occurred to the National Gallery's brief-writers. He had, once again, turned the brief on its head by removing the need for yet more offices in Trafalgar Square. The degree of pedestrianization in the Rogers proposal meant that shops could provide the commercial element instead.

Until the sense of this analysis became apparent, the design had been in danger of losing its way. Rogers had gone skiing, leaving the office to produce new drawings to meet this much more sophisticated town planning requirement. He was on the slopes when a man, clearly unable to ski, appeared over a hill, slithering wildly about on the snow and clutching a roll of drawings under his arm. It turned out to be Colin Mackenzie from the office dispatched to get his approval. The two of them spent the next few days working in the mornings and skiing in the afternoons and they succeeded in putting the scheme back on course.

Once it all made sense Rogers raced ahead producing the most elaborate and fully detailed model he had ever attempted at that stage of a project. He made it to the shortlist of seven which were chosen from the seventy-nine architect–developer groups who had submitted designs. The finalists went on display in the gallery on 23 August 1982. He studied the alternatives with mounting excitement. To his, perhaps prejudiced, eye they seemed uniformly weak with the prison-like Skidmore, Owings and Merrill entry striking him in particular as 'an absolute shocker' – Dada dismissed it as 'City baronial'. But the real point was that they all displayed an appalling lack of confidence. No exhibition could have summarized more succinctly the slough of despond into which modern architecture had sunk.

Furthermore, the press response – led by Deyan Sudjic in *The Sunday Times* – to the Rogers scheme suggested the crude conservationist line was not as deeply entrenched as Rogers had feared. But it was a leader in *The Times* that set the seal on his conviction that he had produced a winner.

There are seven designs. [said the leader] Two are of the hovercraft school of architecture, a modern improvement on lake–village principles of construction, the mass of the building hovering several metres above ground level, and care being taken to render its means of support invisible. Four designs are in the National Provincial style, their impeccable manners, indeed their old-world courtesy, proclaiming deference to Wilkins's familiar but not very distinguished gallery façade. And of course there is the boiler-room romance of Mr Richard Rogers, affectionately known as Sodu 82, thanks to the advocacy of Mr Owen Luder.

Luder, a champion of the modernist defence and president of the RIBA, had said on seeing Rogers's design: 'This is the architecture of a man who says, "Sod you! this is the way it's going to be!" '[11]

The leader went on:

Once the shock of its vocabulary wears off, its merits impinge upon the spectator. It alone among the designs rises to the opportunity. It is a monumental building. Trafalgar Square is a monumental space, though happily exempt from well-drilled regularity of the Baron Haussmann sort. It is enclosed by buildings of varying styles and varying quality. It does not therefore impose a preordained style on an infiller, but it does invite an essay in monumentalism.

In the north-east corner of the square is the spire of St Martin-in-the-Fields; central south is Nelson's pillar; Mr Rogers completes a triangle with a comparably conspicuous vertical accent. St Martin points to heaven, the pillar commemorates our greatest naval victory, Mr Rogers provides an aerial coffee-shop. The bathos is not altogether his fault; this is not an heroic or religious age.

It goes on to outline its planning advantages, raises questions about maintenance and comments that Rogers's 'eccentricity' is 'large in conception, bold in execution, a gesture of architectural confidence at a time of canonical uncertainty'.[12]

Rogers received additional support from a poll conducted by the gallery among the public who visited the exhibits. This poll had been conducted even though the architects had not been told about it at the brief stage – 10,000 of the 78,000 visitors voted. The Rogers scheme was the most popular but it also managed to be the most unpopular – the poll had asked visitors which scheme they hated most as well as which they preferred. Finally, he was shown a letter from Erno Goldfinger, the veteran architect who had worked with Perret and whose high-rise housing blocks in London are among the few that anybody actually likes, which said 'I don't know if

Above: National Gallery drawing
Below: The National Gallery model. *John Donat*

Luder was right as president to support Richard Rogers' plan for the extension of the N.G. but I must say that I consider that this project was the only one which was worthy of support.'

At the time of the interview Rogers was in Venice, having travelled there with his new friend Peter Palumbo on the first trip of the new Orient Express. He flew back and gave what he is convinced was one of his finest presentations to date with his assistant on the scheme, John Sorcinelli. He felt he won over the jury, yet something told him he would fail.

Sure enough, newspaper leaders, opinion polls and interviews were to matter little. The design by Ahrends, Burton and Koralek was chosen, although the jurors wanted extensive changes. When these emerged there was a howl of protest about the result which was joined by the Prince of Wales, who bafflingly, described Wilkins's dreadful façade as 'an old friend'. Finally, the National Gallery came upon enough money to build an extension without offices and shops and the whole process began again.

From beginning to end the competition had been a disgraceful shambles, the main achievement of which had been the rejection of the best entry and, potentially, of the planning gains it offered to London as a whole. Rogers was dismayed that these gains, so obvious to *The Times*, barely seem to have been mentioned among the jurors. It looked as though straightforward conservationist jitters had reacted to the overall styling – the Rogers 'language'. Stuart Lipton, his patron at Greycoat, thought the model had been too detailed. In his enthusiasm Rogers had provided an all-but finished building which said too much. It offered more scope for comment, and therefore rejection, than any of the others.

But at least the extent of the detailing does make it easier to read critically than most of Rogers's designs at the model stage. What emerges is a more complete and detailed realization of the street-level drama which had been envisaged for Coin Street. The walk from Leicester Square dips downward below ground level underneath the building to meet the entrance to the tunnel through to the centre of Trafalgar Square. This space is defined by the concrete structural columns supporting the gallery and the diagonal line of the offices. The office corners are curved to emphasize the flowing movement through the building, an interestingly significant irregularity which produces an 'expressionist' effect and reveals a significant development in his thinking. In essence, it implies a preparedness to take on a more sinuous and mobile view of the role of the building in defining urban space. Where the irregularity of the Lloyd's exterior is made to appear as an afterthought of function, the irregularity of the National Gallery emerges as a specific requirement in its own right.

The gallery, however, perched as a rectangular box above the whole structure stays with the clear, flexible solution of the Pompidou Centre. This may, in fact, have been a part of the problem, for the Pompidou Centre has long been criticized in fine art circles as a poor place to hang pictures. There are two aspects of this criticism: first, the massive steel trusses impinge too much on the total space of each floor, causing an unacceptable degree of visual clutter against which even the greatest paintings have trouble competing; secondly, the doctrine of flexibility means that paintings invariably have to be exhibited on movable panels giving an effect of impermanence which is inappropriate for the display of works of art. Rogers, however, maintains that the walls may be made to look as solid as anyone would wish. These objections have penetrated deep into the psyche of the international fine-art circuit and were raised in a correspondence in *The Times* arising from the National Gallery exhibition. François Lombard, Pompidou's head of the client programme, and Pontus Hultén, a former director of the Centre's museum, responded.

The Pompidou Centre is not just an art gallery, [they wrote] but a flexible multi-purpose cultural centre. The gallery, which comprises one fifth of the building is a great success and, contrary to Professor Broadbent's assertions, is most suitable for the hanging of both the permanent collection and temporary exhibitions. The separate internal walls and suspended ceilings were not afterthoughts but were part of the design concept to create appropriate scaled spaces for the different works of art.

The ratio of glass wall to floor is small compared to most contemporary buildings. This is principally due to the exceptional plan depth which allows a very acceptable level of energy consumption. Maintenance does not consume 50 per cent of the budget but, combined with energy consumption, it accounts for approximately 20 per cent of the budget.[13]

In the case of the National Gallery, however, Rogers's design would have gone some way to answering the criticisms, in so far as such an answer was possible or desirable. For a start, the brief did not give enough information to justify designing anything at the early stage other than a flexible open space – indeed the apparent conception of the meaning of 'basilica' suggested that that was precisely what was wanted. What he did, however, was to provide a highly ingenious system of top lighting and a flat floor with services underneath and a six-foot module size which would allow partitions to be erected anywhere. The partition system was not fixed, so that a convincing interior of any form from High Renaissance to rough-hewn rock could be created. The lighting system allowed daylight to be used like spotlights, with sliding shutters allowing precise regulation. It was, however, clearly not enough for the jury.

Overall, the important stylistic message from the National Gallery was the frankly decorative form to which it had adapted the 'language'. There was no central, inevitable requirement as there was at Lloyd's which would provide a reasoned programme for the kind of street-level variety for which he was aiming. There were, instead, far more subjective town planning considerations which had emerged in spite of, rather than because of, the brief. The result is a more relaxed, less assertive form than Lloyd's, similar in its frank use of landscape and skyline to Coin Street. Rogers's evident profound enjoyment of the whole project perhaps arose because of the freedom provided by the vague brief and its contrast with the precision of Lloyd's requirements. In sum, there is something about the National Gallery extension which looks suspiciously – and, in the event, sadly – like Rogers's most fully mature building.

Speyhawk, the developers, were pleased enough with the result to employ Rogers again to design an office development in the City on a site, coincidentally, immediately next door to Lloyd's. Unfortunately, if the National Gallery had been a fiasco which at least produced a good building, this project was to become a fiasco which produced first a good building and then a series of increasingly strange fantasies. The site, known as Whittington Avenue, fronts on to Leadenhall Street just west of Lloyd's. Everything looked promising: a good client, a corner site and the chance of building a companion to Lloyd's which would strengthen further the axis between the corner of the Bank of England and the main Lloyd's service tower. In addition, the building was not just to be a blank open area of office space but a mix of small and large areas which, Speyhawk reckoned, represented the best mix for the office market of the day. Overall, it was precisely the sort of complex urban problem which Rogers increasingly felt most qualified to solve.

In the initial phases Rogers came up with a block cut in two by a huge length of diagonal escalator which, on reaching the top corner, became a bridge which crossed to the roof of Lloyd's. Remembering Lipton's comments on the National Gallery model, however, he kept the total amount of information down to a minimum. It hardly mattered. A series of embarrassing meetings with a patronising City architects' department led by Stuart Murphy soon revealed that all that was wanted was some kind of pastiche of a Glasgow Victorian commercial façade of which the City's officers seemed to have grown inordinately fond. Specifically they wanted terracotta angels. Reasoning that since the design was deliberately vague in any case a vagueness which the City would like was just as easy as vagueness they wouldn't. Rogers had Laurie Abbott produce extraordinary drawings of strange, romantic cityscapes complete with angels, pediments and columns.

Their form was arbitrary and their style incomprehensible. They were complete red herrings, designed to pass the first planning hurdle at which point the Rogers team would start to try and recover lost ground. It was a somewhat wild strategy and, in any case, Whittington Avenue collapsed soon afterwards. It had become clear that the City was too deeply entrenched. So instead of taking the usual developer's route of sacking the architects, Speyhawk did the honourable thing and sold the site.

The list of disappointments grew longer. The BBC, impressed by the form of the Lloyd's competition, adopted the same format for their search for an architect to develop the site of the Langham Hotel – a vast Victorian pile just north of Oxford Circus. Once again Rogers was competing with Norman Foster – this time, however, Foster won. It was to be a shallow victory, however; the BBC later cancelled the development in favour of new buildings at White City.

In 1983 Rogers, Davies, Abbott and Ruth had sweated for three weeks in Dallas to produce a scheme for a huge, new shopping centre in Houston. It had arisen via an old family connection. Paulo, Ernesto's brother, had put them in touch with Stanley Marcus of the Dallas store, Nieman Marcus. The contact had initially held out the hope of building a Dallas Opera House but that job went to I. M. Pei. The shopping centre came next. A consortium of businessmen advised by Marcus had put together a plan for 4 million square feet of retailing space on a 100-acre site. Abbott, Davies and Rogers had produced the scheme in a three-week crash programme. It had been approved and then the consortium broke up.

Meanwhile, soon after the National Gallery, Rogers was fighting for the job of developing the site next to the Royal Opera House in Covent Garden. As with the National Gallery the ROH wanted to exploit its land to provide more room for itself and more finance. But, unlike the National Gallery, it had no wish to go through the charade of an open competition for finished buildings with all the attendant publicity. They went to the other extreme. The procedure adopted was low-

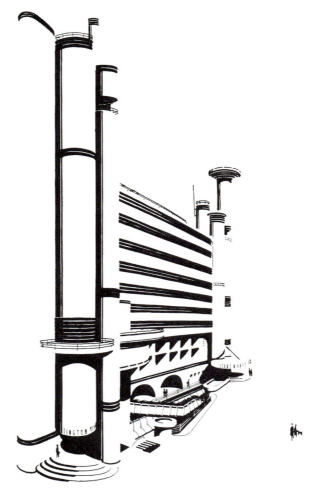

A Laurie Abbott drawing of Whittington Avenue

key and similar to Lloyd's and the BBC to the extent that architects were asked for submissions rather than designs. There was a painstaking process of seemingly endless interviews as the jury looked anxiously over their shoulders at the Trafalgar Square fiasco. The most notable feature of Rogers's submission was to startle everybody.

The Royal Opera House, an 1858 building designed by E. M. Barry, is a reasonable grand classical building which faces on to a back street. This anomaly seems to have arisen because of an English mistrust of the performing arts which made it impossible to house them in anything like the grandeur of, say, the Paris Opéra. Barry was able to get away with his giant six-columned Corinthian portico over a rusticated ground floor, but only by directing it into Bow Street rather than into the Covent Garden piazza. Next to it Barry built a cast-iron Floral Hall to sell flowers to opera goers.

Meanwhile to the rear is the Covent Garden piazza itself with its market buildings of 1830, whose conversion into shops had been completed by 1980. But, successful as the conservation and redevelopment of the Victorian Covent Garden has been, it has only revealed more clearly the huge architectural loss London once sustained. For, on the side of the piazza furthest from the Opera House, is Inigo Jones's St Paul's. Jones boasted of his design that it would be 'the handsomest barn in England', but it is a good deal more than that – it is unquestionably one of Britain's great buildings. Its simplicity and monumentality are executed with such precision that even the rather dull design of the market halls and their uninspired restoration seem to be enhanced by its presence. Jones, however, had originally been commissioned to redevelop the whole square in 1631 by the Earl of Bedford. He produced a severe series of Palladian façades along the north, west and east sides and an open area to the south. But the fruit and vegetable market moved in in 1671 and the respectable, civilized environment which Jones had intended rapidly deteriorated. Now nothing of Jones's original square – except for St Paul's – survives in exactly the form in which he designed it.

For Rogers, St Paul's is probably Britain's finest building and Jones her greatest architect. Furthermore, the Italian roots of Jones's design for the piazza obviously evoked ancestral and childhood memories. For the piazza side of the ROH development, therefore, he could think of nothing better than to restore the Jones arcades stone for stone with the aid of the entirely adequate archive material in the British Museum. As the buildings had only been a relatively thin slice, almost a façade and no more, running around the piazza, it allowed maximum use of the land behind. It was startling because of his popular reputation as the brutal 'sod you' modernist who sneered at the conservationists. In fact Rogers has always been in favour of exact reconstruction of suitably fine buildings – he did after all provide the setting for the Adam Room at Lloyd's and he had defended, in an argument with Ernesto, the reconstruction of the Ponte Santa Trinità in Florence, built in 1557 by Ammannati, after it had been blown up by the Germans. But the emphasis is on exact reconstruction, if necessary using the same tools to provide the same finish. What he does not like is building anew in a self-consciously historical style or in the form of pastiche.

The Jones restoration was to be the most precise element in the Rogers submission apart from some highly detailed breakdowns of the commercial side by Marco Goldschmied. Again remembering the dangers of being too precise, Rogers restricted the actual built detail to the minimum. On the Bow Street frontage in particular he indicated the vaguest, quietest masses ostensibly only to show scale but, in fact, also to suggest the practice was as capable of producing coolly restrained buildings as it was of filling the street with incident. Whether the quietness would have persisted to the end of the design process will never be known.

The submission resulted in Rogers making it on to a shortlist of two with Jeremy Dixon. The first interview was a disaster with the timing of each team member's contribution being hopelessly badly calculated. In addition they were obviously confronted with a jury of artistic types to whom their carefully worked-out business plan was a complete bore. Rogers persuaded the ROH to allow them to do a further presentation, which, to this day, he regards as the best they have ever done. But John Sainsbury rang him on behalf of the ROH. 'I'm sorry,' he said, 'I have some bad news for you.' Dixon had won.

A further disappointment was the delay – possibly not fatal – of a scheme for an office building in Seattle. Rogers had been invited to compete for this scheme by a local firm of architects called Boora. He had won this against competition from five American firms including the ubiquitous Skidmore, Owings and Merrill and Johnson & Burgee, the firm of the equally ubiquitous Philip Johnson who had been one of the key supporters of the Pompidou Centre. The shortlist of six had been chosen from a first list of forty architects by the client, the First United Methodist Church of Seattle. In August 1984, Rogers was selected to build what was intended to be a sixty-storey office block and church on the site of a turn-of-the-century classical building which was the existing church. It was to be a strictly commercial development with the same cost restrictions of every other speculative block in America and the same requirements for rapid completion. The only oddity was the client for whom Rogers, Abbott and Davies found themselves having to hold hands and bawl hymns at the top of their voices at a prayer meeting held to sanctify the process of designing the new building. We are not your clients, explained the pastor, the whole congregation is. Unfortunately one member of the congregation was less keen and he raised an objection to the demolition of the existing church. The City of Seattle agreed. It was, after all, just about the oldest object in the city. Rogers rushed out an alternative scheme which involved cantilevering the office block precariously over the old church but, for the moment, Seattle has gone quiet.

Meanwhile, a scheme for the Greater London Council to

convert the Round House in Camden Town into a black arts centre was to be thrown into limbo as the authority drew closer to abolition by the Conservative government. The team leader had worked in a joint venture with a black architect as part of the deal. Thus, at the end of 1984, twelve months after Rogers and Goldschmied had been turning away work, Lloyd's seemed to be all that was left.

The partnership had just moved into its new Hammersmith offices, having cleaned up the site. This process, at least, was going smoothly. For the end of the site nearest Hammersmith Bridge they had designed, and won planning permission for, a development of flats and they had sold the land on to a developer, retaining their role as architects. Elsewhere on the site they had built small studios and industrial units which had been let, and they were ready to start work converting one of the warehouse blocks as a permanent home for Richard Rogers & Partners. Botschi was in charge of the conversion. For the moment they had moved into another block. The whole scheme had been pushed ahead by new RIBA rules which allowed architectural partnerships to become incorporated. Rogers's practice had been the first in the country to take advantage and so he, Goldschmied, Young and Davies, who had become a partner in 1983, were now to be known by the new title of director. But the real value of the change meant that it allowed greater flexibility in the business of the practice and allowed them to raise finance to complete the redevelopment of the Duckhams site.

All of which would have been cold comfort if, as seemed likely, the practice was to be obliged to shrink from over forty architects to twelve. In principle, nobody objected to the idea of a smaller practice, but on the basis of selected work – not on the basis of no work.

There were, it was thought, two key marketing problems: first, the practice was assumed to be exclusive, and possibly, therefore, expensive; and, secondly, it seemed to have a single aggressive style which was out of step with the revivalist inclinations of most clients in the mid-1980s. The first arose from the buildings that had been constructed rather than from any policy of extravagance: Lloyd's was evidently a highly bespoke building with unique requirements and Inmos was a costly industrial shed because of its service elements. Seattle would have proved they could do large-scale office developments as cheaply as anybody else, and Rogers had taken on some small industrial units at Maidenhead for Speyhawk to make the point that they were still in the low-cost shed market that had once made his name at Reliance Controls. But nobody discussed doing anything about the second problem. Indeed, it is unlikely anyone could. Rogers could change his style with as much difficulty as he could his handwriting, while his dismay at most of the marketable alternatives on offer was such that he had no intention of doing so.

The pressure did not last long. In 1985 they found themselves suddenly flooded with small to medium-size projects including converting Billingsgate fish market in the City (to a securities trading floor for the American Citibank), a pump house in London's docklands which had arisen out of some strategic studies conducted by the practice, a factory for Linn Products in Glasgow, a private museum in Holland Park, the headquarters of the Wellcome company in Cobham, Surrey, an office development in New York partly to house the American end of the advertising agency Saatchi & Saatchi. The docklands studies involve the Royal Docks which account for half the total development area and could result in some of the biggest and most important Rogers projects of all. Wellcome unexpectedly echoes Creek Vean in that it is entirely covered with vegetation. The New York development, on Hudson Street, is an attempt to show that low-cost, rapidly built architecture need not be bad.

The office complement began to expand rather than contract: large numbers of smaller jobs require more architects than small numbers of large jobs. It means that as a business they are safe again, but they have remained well over their ideal complement of thirty architects. The ·figure is now hovering around forty and the current projects are of the

style of the mainstream work of a successful and stable practice. Something stranger is needed. As Goldschmied says, perhaps over-optimistically: 'Somewhere there is another
Lloyd's.' Rogers, however, has unquestionably survived all
the traumas of separation. His is the only name on the board
as it was in the early days of Lloyd's, but now it is clear why.

And there is one suitably strange job on the firm's books.   323
The City of Florence has asked the practice to look into ways
of creating 'a new pedestrian realm' along the banks of the
Arno where once Dada walked in an attempt to hurry the
birth of her son.

8   A smiling public man

How can we know the dancer from the dance? *Yeats*

'Mr Rogers has a mild manner and helpless air which belies his ability to hold his own.'[1]
'His firm is one of the leading exponents of the architecture of advanced technology.'[2]
'Rogers seems more like a television personality or the director of a successful advertising agency.'[3]
'Mr Richard Rogers, acknowledged as one of the outstanding architects of his generation ...'[4]
'Like his flat, his appearance still bears the strong imprint of student life.'[5]

The Rogerses' new home in Chelsea has been created from a pair of Grade II-listed Victorian stuccoed houses on a corner site not far from the King's Road. They had searched for two years for some way of creating large, horizontal spaces in London, a predominantly vertical city. On the St Leonard's Terrace side the house faces Burton's Court and, beyond, the Royal Hospital, which includes buildings by Wren, Hawksmoor, Vanbrugh and Soane. The other side is bounded by Royal Avenue, which is all that was built of William III's planned triumphal way from the Royal Hospital to Kensington Palace. The life of the King's Road is a short walk away down Royal Avenue – there the Chelsea Drugstore, the former hippy bazaar, has become a deeply upholstered coffee house and restaurant.

The Rogerses have converted the five-storey houses into two flats in the basement, one at ground-floor level, an open-plan area for Ruth and himself on the first and second floors and rooms for the children on the top floor. Entry to the main living area is across a small yard which Rogers has glazed over, using a network of dark grey steel. Steel bridges lead from the Royal Avenue entrance across this yard to different levels of the house. One of these leads up to the first floor which has been turned into one double-height room into which projects a large mezzanine. Because of the number of rooms that have been knocked into one, this is illuminated by twelve windows which look out towards Burton's Court. A single I-beam – painted with blue car-paint – rises through this space. One delicate bracket from this beam provides support at the centre of the mezzanine. Otherwise, although it clearly supports the ceiling, the beam has an arbitrary, sculptural quality. On the lower level is a kitchen and living area while on the mezzanine, which is reached by a single staircase running diagonally upward from the lower level, is their bedroom which can be enclosed by electric blinds lowered from the ceiling. A bathroom is placed to the rear of the mezzanine. A single well running from the basement to the top floor houses a steel spiral staircase which clatters and springs in use, and allows whatever children happen to be staying to race up to their area without passing through the main apartment. All the interiors are in white. The whole is to be filled with the Rogerses' increasingly large art collection which includes twelve of Andy Warhol's portraits of Mao Tse-tung as well as works by Susan Elias, Philip Guston and Reinhard Voigt.

A basement flat was to be occupied by a housekeeper/ babysitter often employed by the Rogerses to help Jan Hall. The ground-floor flat was to be occupied by Ruth's parents – Fred and Sylvia. The whole house has become an image of the densely inhabited tumult in which the perpetually gregarious Rogerses feel most at home. And yet it offers the tumult a stage set in which a drama of appearance and concealment can be enacted. Windows provide unexpected views, levels are ambiguous and yet blatantly theatrical.

It was not an easy job, in spite of the employment of Andrew Morris from the Rogers office as site architect and additional advice from John Young. While on the one hand Rogers was erecting £157 million worth of steel, glass and concrete in the City on time and within the budget, on the other he could barely manage to finish his own house. The glazing over the yard first ran into legal problems which threatened to destroy the whole scheme. However, a neighbour's complaint was eventually satisfied by a reduction in height of the total structure by one storey. Planning permission from the local authority came when the Rogers drawings were returned with the one condition scribbled on the edge: 'No exposed ducts.' The council officers knew exactly who the applicant was. The steelwork then caused problems – an ironic state of affairs since it had been designed by none other than Laurie Abbott, whose experience with several hundreds of millions of pounds worth of steel buildings did not prevent him from running into trouble with what Rogers insists is basically a big lean-to.

Noting that the building seemed to be encountering obstacles, an architect who lived near by in Chelsea wrote to Rogers thanking him for assisting in an argument with his wife. She had complained that he as an architect should be able to build their country house a little quicker. The scene of paralysis on the Rogers site enabled him to point out that not even the master of Pompidou and Lloyd's could make things run smoothly at home. He then offered his services as site architect and he added: 'P.S. Congratulations on the Gold Medal.'

Rogers was awarded the Royal Gold Medal for 1985 by the Queen on the recommendation of the RIBA. Two years earlier it had been won by Norman Foster. The Gold Medal is perhaps the single most important architectural award in the world. It is better known overseas than in England and it has been awarded to virtually every important modern architect. Rogers's citation read:

Alone among the internationally respected architects of the latter half of the 20th century Richard Rogers has brought to high technology an element of the Baroque, a richness and a popular touch.

There is a warmth and breadth of approach in his work which reflects his own personality. He is interested in people first and his buildings are firstly for people. 'People places' is one of his expressions and inevitably Centre Pompidou has become a peoples' place – the most visited and enjoyed building in Europe. His unsuccessful competition design for the National Gallery Extension was the only design which aimed to attract the crowds in Trafalgar Square, which linked the two. An attempt to seduce people into the building who would not normally visit galleries. An attempt to share more widely the pleasure of pictures by the appeal of an exciting and intriguing structure.

His new building for Lloyd's of London is a *tour de force* of structural ingenuity, constructional quality and a design of almost medieval richness of form in brilliantly expressed current technology. It will lead the heritage of the City of London into the 21st century with Richard Rogers a rightful heir to the traditions of Hawksmoor and Wren.

Peter Palumbo, who sponsored Rogers for the Gold Medal, said:

This truly individual architect, this great liberal democrat, this benevolent father – this demanding, vulnerable, exuberant and immensely generous personality – Richard, is known to me as a loyal and steadfast friend who has been by my side, totally supportive, dependable and unflinching, through a difficult period of my recent life. He is, quite simply, the nicest man I know.

Reyner Banham was co-sponsor:

In the Renaissance there were many buildings in the Doric Style, but only one Tempietto. Likewise, there have been many high-tech factories, but only one Inmos. More to the point than that, there have been many buildings by Richard Rogers and Partners, but only one Inmos. It is the high quality of the work that deserves the award, not the use of expressive duct-work or any other elements of style. One might even go so far as to say that the high quality of the work comes from a willingness to forget style when it is not appropriate, *not* to do what your admirers expect.

[Banham went on:] The work of Richard Rogers & Partners is functional, and it is their pride, as architects, that it should be so, but they are not so naive as to suppose that even Form, let alone

Beauty, follows Function. Form may not contradict function, but the step from Functionalism to Architecture has never been automatic. Instead of Louis Sullivan's inadequate formulation, let us go back to that of his much smarter predecessor, the sculptor Horatio Greenough, who said: ... and Beauty I take to be the promise of Function, made sensuously pleasing.

In the 1980s Rogers and Ruth became official public figures, staying with the Queen at Windsor Castle after a dinner party on 31 March 1981 at which, among the other guests, were the Chancellor of the Exchequer, the Roman Catholic archbishop of Liverpool, the Netherlands ambassador and the high commissioner for Guyana. Two of these 'Dine and Sleep' sessions are held each year. Once the guests for each were chosen from broadly the same professional area but, as Prince Philip pointed out to Rogers, this was generally disastrous as they were all obliged to talk shop. For the new mixed sessions, appropriate exhibits are arranged in the library as talking points after the meal, which consisted on this occasion of *quenelles de barbue* and *filet de bœuf* Wellington. Representing architecture, in honour of the Rogers presence, were some of the drawings of George III who had served an apprenticeship in the profession.

He began to move in government circles and generally 'represented' his profession. In fact, it was a process which had started some time before. The British had been slow to absorb the success of the Pompidou Centre but, as the scale and importance of Lloyd's became apparent, Rogers began to collect a string of 'honoraria' including a post on the RIBA council – accepted with extreme reluctance – and membership of the Royal Academy. The latter institution had not invited wives to his first dinner there, a state of affairs inconceivable to Rogers. In fact he had not even realized it was the case and had taken Ruth along as a matter of course. Once the mistake became clear, she had instantly decided to go home but Rogers turned stubborn, and, after a brief debate with a functionary in the lobby, they went in.

Most importantly, however, he joined the trustees of the

Tate Gallery in 1981. It is a position in which people customarily serve for seven years. Rogers had been formally invited by the Prime Minister and the trustees to join the board of nine members plus one National Gallery liaison member. He took the job, which involves about ten meetings a year, in the happy belief that it would be a way of forcing himself to meet people outside architecture and to take in influences from a wider sphere. Lord Hutchinson was chairman and Peter Palumbo the board's resident *enfant terrible*.

The work consisted largely of being shown pictures by the gallery's senior keepers and saying yes they would buy them or no they would not. In general, if there was money they would say yes, if not no. In addition, they were to oversee the strategy of the Tate.

The board consisted of a fairly amiable bunch of people attempting to do an impossible job. The buying power of the Tate in the modern art market had become minimal. Its government grant had effectively been halved over the past few years by the decline of the pound against the dollar. In addition the world market had become increasingly competitive as new, more aggressive institutions had begun to force up the prices of every passing fad. But, for the time being, the Tate had considerable laurels on which to rest in the form of a solid British collection and a reasonable international spread of modern art. There were also the Turners which were to be housed in the new extension – financed by the Clore family and designed by James Stirling – which was to be the main achievement of Lord Hutchinson's chairmanship.

After his first year Rogers became more active. He managed to have some spectacular tents – designed by Alan Stanton, one of the Chrysalis team who had worked on the Pompidou Centre – erected on the front lawn and the basement café was refurbished by Jeremy Dixon. Both were attempts to achieve what Rogers took to be the point – for the gallery to perform a greater public service and thereby to attract more visitors. But for every success there were half a dozen failures and Rogers began to feel as frustrated as he had when working for Middlesex County Council. Then his drawings had simply been consigned to some huge, locked chest, now his ideas were being indulged but resisted with perfect manners. In his irritation he became a mild agitator, attempting to subvert the civil service traditions which permeated the operations of the Tate.

But in 1984 the tensions within the system, hitherto glossed over by a certain muted willingness to play the game, broke the surface. Peter Palumbo had become the chairman-elect. He was known to be something of an agitator and to be in opposition to the policies and strategies of Alan Bowness, the Tate's director, but it was assumed his feelings would remain largely submerged in one of the many pools of reticence dotted about the Tate.

Instead, Palumbo spoke in an interview in *The Sunday Times*[6] of the 'dull ... turgid and unimaginative' Tate and attacked Bowness for buying fashionable work at high prices.

That he felt such things was unamazing; that he said them in public was not to be tolerated. Lord Hutchinson moved quickly to ensure that Palumbo would have to step down. The Rogerses had, since their trip together on the Orient Express, become close friends with Palumbo. They determined to find some way of saving the situation. Weekend meetings took place. The Rogers family, children and all, would be flown to Palumbo's Ascot home by helicopter for long discussions about the crisis. But Lord Hutchinson was adamant that a new chairman had to be found. He told Rogers that Palumbo had to 'do the honourable thing' in such solemn tones that, for a moment, he assumed nothing less than suicide was expected. The incident with the bren-gun at St John's had made him wary of the English upper class's ability suddenly to become bafflingly serious.

Technically Rogers was not available for the job of chairman as he was one of the four artist trustees, none of whom are customarily regarded as being in the running. Furthermore, he was already closely identified with Palumbo's view of things. Indeed, there had been an agreed strategy that until Palumbo became chairman Rogers would assist him by taking on the *enfant terrible* role in order to draw enemy fire and force through the required changes without compromising the future chairman. But in the midst of the fury of Hutchinson, who had been obliged to explain the whole embarrassing situation to the Prime Minister, and the disarray of the trustees, it began to seem that Rogers would make a logical chairman. After all, he shared the general discontent of the other trustees who had by and large sympathized with Palumbo, but he was not likely to make such an error of judgement. His first inclination was to turn it down on the basis that he did not have the time. But, eventually, he agreed.

His appointment was to mark a significant swing in the policy of the Tate and, ultimately, to turn into a task which, Rogers feels, is as important as the building at Beaubourg or Lloyd's. Lord Hutchinson had believed that the excessively aggressive raising of private money would let the government off the hook as far as funding was concerned and was therefore tactically unsound. Rogers, however, took the view that the Tate was sinking fast and it would be madness simply to wait and hope for a lifebelt from the state. Furthermore, he did not accept that the chairman's job was to be a low-key mandarin whose primary responsibility was to keep everyone calm and to ensure that he left things more or less as he found them. This is a fairly standard, if unacknowledged, civil service point of view. But it was not one that Rogers felt either temperamentally able to adopt or that was appropriate as the Tate slipped ever further behind in the modern art world.

So, at a meeting of the trustees at the Bear Hotel in Woodstock, he outlined a fifteen-point programme for development of the Tate, all the elements of which he insisted were necessary – he wanted, at all costs, to avoid any horse-trading. The first move was to set up a foundation chaired by Palumbo which was to start raising private money with an initial target of £50 million in ten years. At the time of writing Rogers was searching for a director of this foundation and finding himself deluged with an extraordinary number of willing but inappropriate retired generals and ambassadors. Other moves included a complete reorganization of the interior and the gardens, as well as the construction of a Tate pier on the Thames. He was beginning to conclude that the beliefs which had carried him through in architecture would carry him through at the Tate – and that meant a similarly active approach to the building's users and what few passers-by there happened to be on that windswept part of Millbank. It also meant subverting the usual civil-service reticence by buying the keepers the occasional beer.

Ironically, however, the Stirling extension turned out to be one of the things effectively working against his policy. Much as he has always admired Stirling's work at the Architectural Association since the late 1950s, he felt this building closed the gallery off still further from the river and did not signal its connection to the east with Westminster.

The reason the Tate has taken on such immense significance for Rogers is that he feels he knows what had to be done and that he is the man to do it. He has been visiting the gallery for years and has always regarded it unquestioningly as one of the most important places in London so he is appalled both at the possibility of its decline and at the apathy with which this possibility is often greeted. When Prince Charles paid an official visit to the gallery he mentioned in his speech that it was his first visit. Rogers naturally assumed he meant first 'official' visit, but was horrified to discover that it really was his first visit of any kind. Confronting the deeply ingrained philistinism of the British ruling classes has been a sobering experience for Rogers.

His goal at the Tate is to ensure its viability by raising private money without jeopardizing public funds and by making the whole gallery as active as possible. Such ambitions may seem self-evidently desirable but they seem to have been ignored by the administrations of the past. The very entrance to the gallery puts off the visitor who is confronted by a long, empty axis culminating in two broom cupboards and a pair of exit doors.

What should be happening, believes Rogers, is what happens at the Pompidou Centre where a variety of activities overlap, changing and affecting each other and drawing the visitor in with the hope of surprise and excitement. Against this, he feels, an architectural rethinking of the building, should be able to provide quiet, contemplative spaces.

The Tate has become an official role for Rogers, placing him on the mysterious list of the great and the good. This is periodically consulted by faceless officials in Whitehall who wish to fill one of the various honorary posts which are dotted about the British system like paint splashes. By implication this means he is no longer 'controversial', he has become one of the modern-art Establishment as respectable as the English modernists he once met through Marcus Brumwell – in fact, Ben Nicholson is a fellow Tate trustee. Jan Hall, the faithful nanny, noted during 1985 how the dinner guests at Belsize Grove seemed to be increasingly titled and noticeably wealthier – even, indeed, recognizable!

This public role is, ironically, providing Rogers with the opportunity to fulfil some of his original ambitions in architecture, for, initially, he had not conceived of himself as the designer of big, showpiece buildings. Instead he viewed architecture in the broadest possible terms as an improver of life, a sustainer of culture. He has found he can approach the Tate problem in the way he has developed of analysing a brief – determining goals, and then achieving them by capsizing the expectations of others. This fits his own perception of himself as, first and foremost, a generalist, a taker of the strategic view. It also coincides with his growing awareness of town planning – most obviously in the Royal Docks and the National Gallery, but also in Florence and in a recently developed obsession with London. He is now convinced that London, a fragmented, ill-planned city, could be transformed relatively cheaply by the development of a few simple routes which would weave the city together. The National Gallery scheme offered this opportunity with three central squares, but it could also be done by connecting the numerous commons south of the river or by providing straight routes from Waterloo through the West End up towards Hampstead.

It is all, of course, based on Italy – on the life in the streets and squares of Florence or Venice. They remain his ideals of urban life and urban life remains his image of the supreme peak of civilization. Almost fifty years after he first suffered the shock of moving from a bright Florence to a grey Bayswater, he is now trying to unite the two. Nino's dream of England has become Rogers's dream of Italy in London.

It was the Tate which introduced him to the extraordinary figure of Peter Palumbo. Apart from his activities at the Tate, Palumbo is also a quite obsessive lover of modern architecture. He owns Mies van der Rohe's Farnsworth House in the United States and his one abiding ambition for more than twenty years had been to build one of Mies's last designs – an office block in the City of London. To this end he had steadily accumulated almost all the necessary freeholds on the site which was to be known as Mansion House Square. He had fought his way through every planning stage only to find by the 1980s that the tide of taste had turned against him. Both the Greater London Council and the City of London had decided Mies's scheme was inappropriate for the City and conservationists had mobilized to stop Palumbo in what came to be regarded as the great setpiece battle of the styles – the 1984 Mansion House Square public inquiry.

Rogers appeared for Palumbo to deliver a massive forty-page testament to his faith in modern architecture which was to inspire the remark from Stirling: 'Good God, Richard, I didn't know you were an intellectual.' Ruth and Rogers spent four months with lawyers preparing the evidence, a task comparable to the three years' work they jointly put in on the Academy Editions monograph on his work published in 1985. It may also be regarded as a rehearsal for the book they have always intended to write together: *Sex, Food and Architecture*. Indeed these joint efforts with Ruth represented the climax of Rogers's lifelong attempts to remove any discon-

Rogers with Peter Palumbo at the Mansion
House Square inquiry

tinuity between his personal and professional lives. In particular, the introduction to the monograph and the house in Chelsea were entirely the result of the two of them working in partnership – and both, in their way, represent a definitive version of Rogers's view of himself, ideally balanced and ideally explained.

Rogers's proof of evidence in favour of Palumbo's scheme is an extraordinary document which reveals both his painstakingly systematic method of conducting an argument, developed from the days of Coin Street and as a discipline to contain his enduring problems with language, and his determination to order architectural history into a continuing narrative. At one point, for example, he lists three great architects from each succeeding century:

20th century: Le Corbusier, Mies van der Rohe,
   Frank Lloyd Wright.
19th century: Sullivan, Richardson and Labrouste.
18th century: Ledoux, Hawksmoor and Nash.
17th century: Borromini, Bernini and Wren.
16th century: Michelangelo, Sangallo and Palladio.
15th century: Brunelleschi, Alberti and Bramante.

In the following paragraph he adds: 'What could be stronger proof of Mies' position in history than the inclusion of his name amongst this list of great men?' He goes on to assert Mies's place in the classical tradition from ancient architecture through Palladio, Schinkel, Ledoux and Dance, commenting: 'The designs of these architects, extraordinary and consistent as they are, provided an inspiration for the architects of the modern age who were horrified by the chaos of 19th century eclecticism and sought to express their solutions to architectural problems in the clear language of their classical forebears.'

The evidence is a document produced by a man no longer on the outside either in the sense of being the persistent under-achiever at school or the young, committed, avant-garde artist-as-outsider. It is the testament of a man almost aggressively on the inside – of the Great Tradition, of enlightened patronage, of a rediscovered and still intact humanist continuity. Nevertheless, its assertive rather than reasoned tone suggests an insecurity and, from behind the carefully assembled lists and points, one can detect the faint but distinct sound of Rogers still trying to account for Rogers for the benefit of Rogers.

Early in 1985 another move was made to draw him deeper into the role of public figure when London University asked him to become head of the Bartlett School of Architecture. The reasoning was clear enough. The Bartlett has suffered badly in recent years from its low profile – the AA, in particular, having attracted most attention as the breeding ground of new architecture. Having Rogers would announce to the architectural world that it was back at the leading edge of new building design. In fact the move seemed to make so much sense to the university authorities that they offered him two jobs in one: the Bartlett professorship of architecture and the headship of the Bartlett School. This increased the total salary they could offer and they provided further incentives by removing most of the administrative load usually involved. Much emphasis was laid on their insistence that he continue in practice and on the success of a former head of the Bartlett, Llewellyn Davies, in combining design work with an educational role.

Ruth was against the idea, convinced as ever that her husband was destined to design buildings rather than to teach others. Dada and Nino, however, were enthusiastically in favour. They both shared Continental memories of all distinguished architects having academic posts. In addition, Nino was keen on the certainty of pension entitlement. But finally he turned it down – work, after all, was picking up rapidly just as he was considering the offer.

'I have given much thought as to how I could organize my life,' Rogers wrote to Sir James Lighthill, provost of London University, 'in order to both practice and teach. I have also discussed the situation with my partners. Unfortunately I have had to conclude there is no way at this stage of my career that I could undertake such a challenging position without my office or the University suffering under the strain.'

Rogers was also to resist a move to make him president of the RIBA, the supreme representative of the profession in Britain. The manoeuvring took place behind the scenes and Rogers responded by recommending that Sir Denys Lasdun be chosen.

He did, however, take up the short-term post of Eero Saarinen professor of architectural design at Yale for an academic year ending in 1985. He had been nominated by Kevin Roche, the inheritor of the Saarinen practice, who had financed the establishment of the post. He took the job while work was slack but it ran into the hectic early months of 1985. The effect was to turn him even further against the academic life as he shuttled back and forth between London and New Haven. He also found himself obliged occasionally to stay without Ruth at the New Haven Hotel. Being alone in hotel rooms remains one of the enduring horrors of his life. He stood this torture for two days and then moved in with friends, a lifeline to which he can always cling.

It is this relationship which has laid the foundation of the persona that is Rogers today. Ruth's relaxation, openness and seeming lack of inhibition startled him out of his habitual acceptance of a gulf between an official life and a private one. This discontinuity evidently had its roots in the contradictions between his failures at school and his success in the world outside. He was encouraged to adopt the role of an outlaw, flowing uncontrollably like water around problems set by an unjustly disciplined world. This produced an innocent bravado and it validated his need to lean on others, whether to copy their exam papers or to teach them to draw his ideas.

At Epsom and the AA the outlaw role continued to be a useful posture. His academic achievements, for most of the time, remained minimal and he could lapse into his Continental, subversive, outsider role – his range of reference seeming to suggest that he was above and beyond the pedantry of his tutors.

But architecture suddenly began to undermine the whole façade. He became successful, acknowledged to have a rare talent beneath the bad drawing and hesitant articulation. At Yale he remained a dissident but by then it was from a position of strength: he now really thought he could prove the authorities wrong rather than simply pretending he could. But it remained an act of faith and the catastrophic practical problems of erecting Murray Mews renewed the sense that success at anything visible, official and approved could never be his. Success came, none the less, at Creek Vean and Reliance Controls, strengthening his confidence but all the time with the nagging sense that he could only do it with Norman Foster. The possibility of being found out remained.

After the break-up of Team 4 he found himself in limbo, unable to produce clear reasons for pursuing any particular course – the Spender house could so easily have been a tame brick vernacular building and everything afterwards a routine improvisation on the familiar forms of the past.

Meanwhile, he was conducting clandestine affairs, accustomed by the many personalities of his past to dividing his mind in two between Su and his family and the girls with whom he slept. He and Ruth suddenly glimpsed the possibility that such divisions were no longer necessary for either of them.

This new ease in his personal life was not at first matched by a similar relaxation in his professional life. The Pompidou Centre unquestionably gave him an international architectural presence – but again it had been done with a powerful equal, Renzo Piano. Piano, like Foster, was his own man, competent and confident, and he provided expertise which Rogers knew he could never have.

Finally, with Lloyd's and the increasing evidence of its success, Rogers balanced the personal and professional equation. He discovered he had assembled a team, almost without knowing it, which could replace the strong equal partner

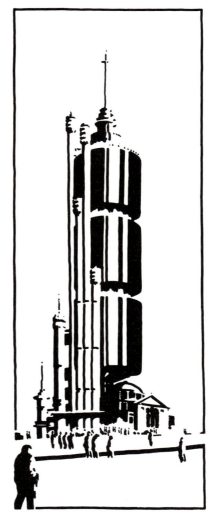

341

Sketch proposal produced in 1984
for the development by the First
United Methodist Church in Seattle

with an array of determined and loyal specialists. His office organization is now a precisely worked-out image of his idea, the Ideal Gang. The partners – or, as they are now, directors – are paid on a salary scale based on multiples of the payment to the lowest paid full-time architect. This leaves a profit at the end of the year which is not simply absorbed by the directors. After providing for taxes, pensions and staff bonuses, the residue of profit is allocated between reserves and charitable trusts. The completion of the Hammersmith development will allow the firm to recover something of the atmosphere of Hampstead – an informal amalgam of work and family life.

Outside work, if there is such a place for Rogers, the Gang has widened to take in a close group of intimates. Two very close friends were met during the building at Beaubourg – Thomas Cottle, an American psychologist, and Ronald Dworkin, professor of jurisprudence at Oxford. With all of them Rogers will have his strange, mobile conversations which occasionally harden whenever he feels a preciously held belief is being challenged. He will tense up, talk falteringly but seriously. He will seem for the moment to be holding an opinion with muscular tension, and the old, precious God of Nino's will seems to surface once again.

So the Rogers world is growing into the image of Rogers. He has found it can be made to suit what he is. Just as a defrocked priest had once said it didn't matter how you hit the ball as long as it gets there, so now he discovered that his way of doing things could work. He could be Richard Rogers, the public man, simply by being Roj to his heart's content. With this came the emphasis on history and the Great Tradition, the new insider image and the whole aura of the fifty-two-year-old, smiling public man. As if in symbolic endorsement of this new stability and sense of place, he has even grown in recent years to know his brother Peter, a site engineer who now works closely with Stuart Lipton. Previously he had seemed no more than an acquaintance.

Meanwhile, the great, tumbling, chaotic party that is his

family life functions better than ever. There are the ambitious and frequent holidays and huge meals into which the boys' girlfriends, acquaintances and contacts are drawn as if hypnotized. With his extended family Rogers has achieved a rare accommodation. He is helplessly attached to all his children, but there are subtle differences in the relationships. They disagree violently but, as Ben says, 'I do not recall ever having heard Richard admit that he was wrong in an argument about anything other than a straight issue of fact.' Yet they retain an extraordinary closeness and degree of mutual understanding. His ambitions for them are unlimited.

In every respect it has become a life in which Rogers can function – and Ruth was the catalyst which allowed him to create it.

It was no mistake that, in his Gold Medal speech, he thanked his parents; he thanked Foster and Piano for teaching him about architecture; and he thanked Ruth Rogers for teaching him about life. He should have said *my* life.

But that is only part of the history, the public, the narrative part. The part that obeys no such order is the part that actually produces the buildings. All the scene setting of the biography – private, public or cultural – can only show a context, not a cause. And yet there is something in the style of the scenery that casts clear light on the real action. There is, for example, the continuing ambiguity of Rogers's relationship with others. Superficially he seems to depend on them, to rely on them for solutions to problems he cannot solve. He is usually the first to suggest calling in a specialist and he has a kind of awestruck, uncomprehending respect for professionalism in any field – an obvious legacy of Nino. Even of the Queen, after his night at Windsor Castle, the clearest memory he could evoke was the sense that , 'She's a pro.' But a closer look reveals he is only calling in the 'pros' to do his bidding. What that is may not be clear but, from their advice and their thoughts, he derives what he wants.

For Rogers is a man who realizes himself in others. In them he seems to detect and recognize elements of himself which he can then use. In a sense he only seems sure of his own existence through others – in the loneliness of a hotel room he may fear the eclipse of himself in the sheer absence of response. Even objects, familiar in their usage, are of no help as they remain, of necessity, unfamiliar in their connotations as they are untouched by those he knows. Only the transient context of the familiarity of another's life and home can compensate. When Ruth is away he goes home to his parents.

It is understandable, therefore, that the public rationales for his art which he most encourages are those which lay stress on its gregariousness and its accessibility. It is understandable that he should seek large-scale political justifications for his design decisions. All such applied meanings – postrationalizations, he would call them – have the apparent effect of submerging the one personality in the many in feigned modesty. They thus provide a wider version of the teamwork of his own office with all its democratic, populist overtones.

But the emphasis of all these easy meanings is quite wrong. Rogers is not losing himself in the crowd, he is finding himself there. The unusual element in his case is the apparent absence of introspection, a habit normally assumed to be a prerequisite of the creative life. But Rogers conducts his introspection through others. His inner voice is the constant chatter of the world, continually creating him, and from which he distills a sense of what he wants, needs or is obliged to do.

This is as well, for the ideologies and the talk of 'people places' in themslves would provide no art. Indeed, they are so flexible in their implications that they could equally well justify building Lloyd's in the shape of Mickey Mouse, exactly as Le Corbusier's early writings could perfectly well have justified building the Villa Savoye with a Corinthian colonnade. For the nets of words that are repeatedly thrown over architecture repeatedly fail to trap their victim. Certainly they are capable of crippling our perception of the art just as calling Coin Street the Berlin Wall could blind many to the 'significant irregularity' of its profile. But always so much –

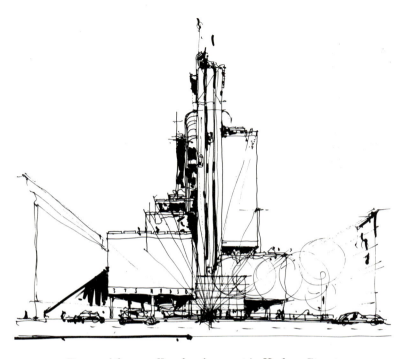

Proposal for an office development in Hudson Street,
New York, 1985

indeed everything worthwhile – escapes. It is not that architecture defies language, rather that it is too closely allied. Mere style, of course, is nothing like language but the whole slippery process of design with its elusive amalgam of whim and the customer's requirements does share something of language's perpetually provisional syntheses of the need to be heard by others and the need to hear oneself. So in architecture considerations of function for ever dance teasingly around considerations of art.

Writing of his art last year[7] Rogers quoted Wittgenstein: 'Architecture immortalizes and glorifies something. Hence there can be no architecture where there is nothing to glorify.'[8] In typically optimistic style Rogers was ignoring the more chilling possibilities implied by the second sentence, but equally, Wittgenstein omitted the *obligation* to glorify. Rogers found in the process of architecture, a process akin to language, a way of talking his way into an imagery that implied for him a wholeness and harmony frequently denied him by his experience of the world. It also provided him with the most unequivocal of arts – the most enormous, the most literal way of externalizing and glorifying that sense of wholeness. Having found that process he was obliged to pursue it because there seemed to be no other. The fact that, like every other modern artist, he was obliged to build upon private fictions and then, like many other modern architects, to provide public justifications, does not detract from the uncompromising manner in which he first created and then pursued his course.

His discovery of a way of producing self-sustaining, self-consistent buildings as whole, as confident and as fine as the Pompidou Centre, Lloyd's and the National Gallery is a great achievement, comparable perhaps, in its suave, risk-taking quality, to his winning of the title of the Epsom Gang's champion freefaller, able to fall through trees slowed only by the lightest taps on the branches as they passed.

It is an achievement made the more extraordinary by the way those buildings flowed through the elements of his life, changed but not defined by Ruth and Su, Dada and Nino, George and Peter, Micky and Julie, Georgie and Wendy, Rudolph and Chermayeff, Foster and Piano, Young and Goldschmied, Davies and Abbott, Ben and Zad, Ab and Roo, Bo and Jan ... tension and compression, steel and glass, kisses and smacks.

Notes

1 A better world . . .

[1] Roger Marvell (who was quoting Waugh in this article) in the *New Statesman and Nation*, vol. XXXI, no. 776, p. 7, 5 January 1946.
[2] V.S. Pritchett in the *New Statesman and Nation*, vol. XXIX, no. 724, p. 11, 6 January 1945.
[3] Cyril Connolly in *Horizon*, vol. XII, no. 69, p. 149, September 1945.
[4] Anthony Jackson, *The Politics of Architecture: a history of modern architecture in Britain*, p. 161, The Architectural Press, 1970.
[5] Lionel Esher, *A Broken Wave: the rebuilding of Britain 1940–1980*, p. 60, Allen Lane, 1981.

2 . . . And how to build it

[1] Frank Lloyd Wright, *The Natural House*, p. 13, Pitman, 1971.
[2] Le Corbusier, *Towards a New Architecture*, p. 289, translated by Frederick Etchells, John Rodker, 1927.
[3] Adolf Loos, *Ornament and Crime*, published as *Ornament und verbrechen* in Vienna in 1908.
[4] Maxwell Fry, *Art in a Machine Age*, p. 159 and p. 20, Methuen, 1969.
[5] Sigfried Giedion, *Space, Time and Architecture*. The third, enlarged, edition appeared in 1954.
[6] Nikolaus Pevsner, *An Outline of European Architecture* first appeared in 1943.
[7] I use historicism in, I believe, the correct sense. In architectural circles it has come to mean merely references to past styles. Here I take it to mean the belief in history as a potentially comprehensible plot whose determining factors can be scientifically isolated. The first definition is perhaps better expressed by such terms as revivalism, pastiche or eclecticism. The second suggests a precise, deterministic view of history as facts to be understood and accepted.
[8] *Towards a New Architecture*, p. 21.
[9] Reyner Banham, *Theory and Design in the First Machine Age*, Architectural Press, 1960.
[10] Evelyn Waugh, *Decline and Fall*, p. 120, Penguin, 1975.
[11] *Horizon*, vol. XII, no. 67, p. 12, July 1945.
[12] Sigfried Giedion, *Space, Time and Architecture*, p. 311, Geoffrey Cumberlege/Oxford University Press, 1954.
[13] Nikolaus Pevsner, *An Outline of European Architecture*, p. 16, Pelican, 1982.
[14] *James Stirling: Buildings and Projects 1950–74*, p. 14, Thames and Hudson, 1975.
[15] *Building*, vol. CCXXXVIII, no. 18, 2 May 1980.
[16] Reyner Banham, *The New Brutalism: ethic or aesthetic?* The Architectural Press, 1966.
[17] Banham, p. 11.
[18] Banham, p. 11.
[19] Alison and Peter Smithson: *Without Rhetoric: An Architectural Aesthetic 1955–1972*, p. 2, Latimer New Dimensions, 1973.

[20] Quoted in *Gabo*, p. 151, with introductions by Herbert Read and Leslie Martin, Lund Humphries, 1957.
[21] *The Times*, 5 April 1958.
[22] Quoted in Sherban Cantacuzino: *Howell, Killick, Partridge & Amis*, p. 10, Lund Humphries, 1981.
[23] John Summerson: *The Case for a Theory of Modern Architecture*, RIBA Journal, vol. 64, no. 8, pp. 307–313, June 1957.
[24] For this material on the Maison de Verre I am indebted to the article by Kenneth Frampton in the *Yale Architectural Journal Perspecta 12*, pp. 77–128, 1969.
[25] Le Corbusier, *Towards a New Architecture*.
[26] Quoted in *Contemporary Architects*, edited by Muriel Emanuel, Macmillan, 1980.
[27] Quoted in *Contemporary Architects*.

3 'Ciao, vecchio!'

[1] Frank Lloyd Wright, *The Natural House*, pp. 89 and 91, Pitman, 1971.
[2] Ibid.
[3] Originally published as *Modern Californian Homes* in 1962 and subsequently as *Case Study Homes*, Hennessey & Ingalls, 1977.
[4] *Financial Times*, 30 November 1967.
[5] *Circle*, edited by J.L. Martin, Ben Nicholson and Naum Gabo. Faber & Faber, 1937.

4 Steel cuckoo

[1] Leonardo Benevolo, *History of Modern Architecture Vol. one: The Tradition of Modern Architecture*, p. 256, Routledge & Kegan Paul, 1971.
[2] Quoted in Benevolo, p. 256.
[3] Sigfried Giedion: *Space, Time and Architecture*, p. 253, Geoffrey Cumberlege/Oxford University Press, 1954.
[4] Le Corbusier, *Towards a New Architecture*, p. 2.
[5] In an interview with the author.
[6] Robert Venturi, *Complexity and Contradiction in Architecture*, p. 48, Museum of Modern Art, New York, 1966.
[7] Quoted in Reyner Banham, *Theory and Design in the First Machine Age*, pp. 128–130, The Architectural Press, 1960.
[8] Richard Hamilton, *Collected Words*, Thames & Hudson, 1983.
[9] Peter Cook, 'In Memoriam Archigram', in *Daidolos*, no. 4, pp. 54–58, 15 June 1982.

5 Dead albatross

[1] *New York Times*, 30 January 1977.
[2] *Newsweek*, 2 January 1978.
[3] First published in *Architectural Design* vol. 147, no. 2, 1977. Republished in Alan Colquhoun, *Essays in Architectural Criticism: Modern Architecture and Historical Change*, The MIT Press, 1981.
[4] Roland Barthes, *Mythologies*, Hill and Wang, New York, 1982.
[5] Ludwig Wittgenstein, *Culture and Value* translated by Peter Winch, p.42e, Basil Blackwell, 1980.

6 Dat ain't building ...

[1] Clive Aslet, 'Will the Bell Toll for Lloyd's?', *Country Life*, p. 231, 25 January 1979.

[2] Letter from F. Fielden to E.G. Chandler, City Architect and Planning Officer, 21 March 1979.
[3] *Financial Times*, 7 March 1980.
[4] *Richard Rogers*, Architectural Press, 1985.
[5] *Architectural Review*, vol. CLXIX, no. 101, pp. 265–282, May 1981.
[6] Peter and Alison Smithson, *Without Rhetoric: An Architectural Aesthetic 1955–1972*, p. 36, Latimer New Dimensions, 1972.

7 Dreams of function

[1] Bryan Appleyard, 'Waterloo Wasteland', *The Times* 23 May 1983.
[2] 'Bright Future for the South Bank', *Architects Journal*, August 1979.
[3] *Building*, vol. 239, no. 7149, p. 13, 25 July 1980.
[4] *Building*, vol. 240, no. 7172, p. 12, 9 January 1981.
[5] Letter from Sherban Cantacuzino, secretary of the Royal Fine Art Commission, to Richard Rogers, 17 December 1980.
[6] *Architectural Review*, no. 1020, p. 21, February 1982.
[7] Reyner Banham, 'Art and Necessity', *Architectural Review* vol. CLXXII, no. 1030, p. 34, December 1982.
[8] Le Corbusier, *Towards a New Architecture*, p. 100.
[9] Roger Scruton, *The Aesthetics of Architecture*, Methuen, 1979.
[10] Michael Graves has made this quip on several occasions – this time in conversation with the author.
[11] Quoted in Martin Pawley, 'Rogers and high-tech heart', *The Guardian*, 5 February 1985.
[12] *The Times*, 9 September 1982.
[13] Letter in *The Times*, 11 October 1982.

8 A smiling public man

[1] *The Sunday Times*, 8 July 1974.
[2] *Financial Times*, 6 February 1985.
[3] *Observer*, profile, 10 February 1985.
[4] *Daily Telegraph*, 19 September 1979.
[5] *Guardian*, 30 April 1985.
[6] *The Sunday Times Colour Magazine*, 29 April 1984.
[7] *Richard Rogers*, p. 8, Architectural Press, 1985.
[8] Ludwig Wittgenstein: *Culture and Value*, translated by Peter Winch, p. 69e, Basil Blackwell, 1980.

Index Page numbers in *italic* refer to illustrations

Abbott, Carl, *100*, 98–101
Abbott, Laurie, 110, 116–17, 119, 196–9, 218, 228, 248, *263*, 315–16, *317*, 320, 327
Ahrends, Burton & Koralek, 124, 289, 312
Aillaud, 163
Alsop, Will, 182
Amery, Colin, 250
Amsterdam, Stock Exchange, 69
Appleby, Sally, 110, *184*, 186
Aram Hospital, 153, *155*
Archigram, 181, 183–5
Architectural Association, 65, 72–88, 109
Archizoom, 48
Arup, Ove, and Partners, 154, 165, 195, 202, 214, 215–16, 240, 241, 252–3
Arup Associates, 237, 238, 241, 250
Aslet, Clive, 244
Attenborough, Richard, 154
Ayer, A. J., 68

Baltart, Victor, 171–2
Banfi, Gianluigi, 54, 55
Banham, Reyner, 77, 78, 86, 295, 328–9
Barker, Tom, 211
Barron, Ian, 290
Barry, E. M., 318
Barthes, Roland, 224
Bartolini, Carlo, 48
Bartolini, Dario, 48
Basildon, housing, 227–8
Bassett, Charlie, 102
Bauhaus, 62, 63, 170
BBC, 316
BBPR, 55

Behrens, Peter, 61
Belgiojoso, Ludovico, 54
Benevolo, Leonardo, 82
Berlage, 63, 69
Big John, 48–9
Bijvoet, Bernard, 89
Bing, Judy, 195
Binney, Marcus, 244–5
Black, Misha, 134, 152
Blackmore, Courtenay, 241, 249–50, 251, 252, 258–9, 260, 265, 270
Bland, Ken, 108–9
Boora, 320
Bordaz, Robert, 163, 186, 190, 214–15, 216, *217*
Botschi, Pierre, 147, 293, 321
Boulez, Pierre, 216–18, *217*
Bovis, 251–8
Bowness, Alan, 331
BPR, 55
Branch, Michael, 31–2, 34, 36–7, 39, 51, 53, 56, 71, 101, 106, 111, 118
Breuer, Marcel, 170
Brown, Neave, 110
Brumwell, Marcus, 79–82, *83*, *90*, 101, 111, 123, 134, 188–9, 334
Brumwell, Rene, 80, *83*
Brumwell, Su, *see* Rogers, Su
Buchanan, Peter, 269
Bunshaft, Gordon, 102, 174, 246

California University, 231
Camden Town:
  Murray Mews, 110, 111, 112–13, 115–16
  Round House, 321

Campaign for Nuclear Disarmament (CND), 84
Camus, Albert, 68
Cantacuzino, Sherban, 283
Casabella, 55
Casson, Hugh, 135
Castelli, Leo, 19
Chareau, Pierre, 89
Charles, Prince of Wales, 293, 312, 333
Cheam, 46
Cheeseman, Georgie (later Georgie Wolton), 66, 69–71, 74, 76, 78–9, 91, 103, 106, 107, 148
Cheeseman, Mr, 71, 82, 237
Cheeseman, Wendy (later Wendy Foster), 66, 71, 79, 103, 107, *108*, 110, 126, 133, 135, 235
Chelsea Football Club, 154, 202
Chermayeff, Serge, 96, 124, 228
Chrysalis, 199–200, 330
CIAM, 54, 69, 78, 87
Cobham, Wellcome, 322
Collins, Canon, 84
Colquhoun, Alan, 86, 92, 222–4
Connolly, Cyril, 47
constructivism, 80–1, 177, 182
Cook, Peter, 185
Cooper, Sir Edwin, 235, 244–5
Cornell University, 151
Cottle, Thomas, 342
Coulsdon, 107–8, 123–4, *125*
Craig, Sterling, 85
Creek Vean, 81, 111, 112,

115, 116–19, *120, 121, 125*, 130, 340
Crown Estates, 228
Cummins Engine
  Company, 288–9

Dallas, 316
Dalsace, Madame, 89
Darlington, Cummins
  Engineering, 117
Davies, Llewellyn, 338
Davies, Michael, 199,
  216, 251, *263*, 277,
  293, 316, 320, 321
Dawson, Chris, 199
Design Research Unit
  (DRU), 81, 134–52
Deutscher Werkbund, 61
Dine, Jim, 264
Dinkeloo, John, 117, 289
Dixon, Jeremy, 319–20,
  330
Dobry, George, 279, 286
Domus, 55
Donat, John, 123
Downs Lodge, 35
du Parcq, Liz, 283
Duchamp, Marcel, 182
Dugdale, Tony, 199
Dupont House, 142–3
Dutert, 176, 181
Dworkin, Ronald, 342

Eames, Charles, 127
Eames, Ray, 127
Ede, James Chuter, 40–1
Ede, Lillian, 40
Edge, Gordon, 227, 287
Einstein, Albert, 61
Elias, Fred, 151, 192,
  326
Elias, Michael, 192, 231,
  288, 290, 301
Elias, Ruth, *see* Rogers,
  Ruth
Elias, Susan, 191, 192
Elias, Sylvia, 326
Elizabeth II, Queen, 329,
  343
Ellwood, Craig, 98, 127
Entenza, John, 127
Epsom College of Art,
  65–71

Evans, Eldred, 74, 98,
  124
Evans & Gailey, 124

Festival of Britain, 46–8,
  81, 279–80
Findlay, Ian, 236, 241
Flack, Peter, *184*, 186
Flanagan, Barry, 265
Fleetguard, 288–90, *291*
Fletcher and Stuart, 132
Florence, 17, 18, 19, 323
Foot, Michael, 84
Foster, Norman, 81, 93,
  97–101, *100*, 103–33,
  108, 135, 147, 228–30,
  269, 316, 327, 340
Foster, Wendy, *see*
  Cheeseman, Wendy
Foster Associates, 105,
  230, 236, 238, 248
Franchini, Gianfranco,
  154–7, 165, 186, 190
Francis, Sir Frank, 163
Franklin, Owen, 111, 113
Freud, Ernst, 101, 111
Fry, Maxwell, 60
Fuller, Buckminster,
  105, 130, 131, 212
functionalism, 293–6,
  328–9
futurism, 63, 178–80, 182

Gabo, Miriam, 94
Gabo, Naum, 80–1, 94,
  111, 134, 177
Gairinger, Ermengarde
  'Dada', *see* Rogers,
  Ermengarde
Gairinger, Carla, *44*
Gairinger, Eugenio, 48
Gairinger, Lida, 48
Gairinger, Ricardo, 20,
  44
Garnier, Tony, 61, 62
Gasson, Barry, 153
Giedion, Sigfried, 60–1,
  69, 72, 76, 86–7, 101,
  173
Giscard d'Estaing,
  Valéry, 166, 215–16,
  218, 219

Glasgow:
  Burrell Collection, 153
  Linn Products, 322
Gleeson, 257
Godalming, 25
Golden Cradle, 301
Goldfinger, Erno, 310
Goldschmied, Andrea,
  186
Goldschmied, Marco,
  147, 156, *184*, 186,
  199, 226, 235, 240–1,
  251, 266, 277, 298,
  299, 319, 321
Gollins, Melvin and
  Ward, 246
Gowan, James, 74
Graham, Gordon, 236–7,
  241, 244, 264, 279, 286
Graves, Michael, 298
Greater London Council
  (GLC), 280, 283–4,
  320–1
Green, Sir Peter, 241,
  249, 257–8
Greycoat Estates,
  278–86
Gropius, Walter, 59, 62,
  170
Grut, Lennart, 211

Hall, Jan, 126, 150, 152,
  191, 326, 334
Hamilton, Richard, 76,
  181, 182
Hampstead, 91, 106, 342
Happold, Ted, 154, 159,
  186, 190
Harris, John, 260
Hart, Gary, 279, 286
Henderson, Nigel, 76
Henrion, 91, 104, 123
Heseltine, Michael, 282,
  283
Heysham, Sir Terence,
  235
Houston, 316
Howell, Bill, 85, 86
Hultén, Pontus, 265, 313
Hunstanton, 77, 78, 126
Hunt, Anthony, 110,
  129–30, 142, 292

Hutchinson, Lord, 330, 331–2

Inmos, 290–8, *297*
Institute of Contemporary Arts (ICA), 76–7, 78
Ipswich, Willis Faber building, 228, 248
IRCAM, 216–18, *217*
Iveson, Lalla, 153

Jaffé, Michael, *122*, 123
Jencks, Charles, 225
Jiricna, Eva, 259, 260–4
Johnson, Philip, 97–8, 163–4, 165, 186, 192, 320
Johnson & Burgee, 320
Jones, Inigo, 318–19
Jones, Sir Horace, 249
Jordan, Robert Furneaux, 73

Kahn, Louis, 93, 96, 97, 106
Kaplicky, Jan, *184*
Killick, John, 85, 86, 92, 114
Kingswood House School, 26–30, 31, 35
Kite, the, 147
Kramer, Hilton, 221
Krupp, 214–15, 218, 257

Laclotte, Michel, 163
Lambeth Council, 282, 283
Lasdun, Sir Denys, 282, 339
Le Corbusier, 59, 60, 61, 62, 63, 69, 77, 78, 79, 124, 170, 174, 177
Legnano, Sun Treatment Centre, 55
Leicester University, 78, 88
Lewis, Whitfield, 91
Lichtenstein, Roy, 182
Liebaers, Herman, 163
Lipton, Stuart, 279, 281
Lissitzsky, El, 69, 177
Littlewood, Joan, 182

Lombard, François, 62, 313
London:
  Aybrook Street, 143–4
  Billingsgate fish market, 322
  Coin Street scheme, 278–87, *285*, 306
  Commercial Union building, 246–8
  Covent Garden, 318–19
  Crystal Palace, 172–3, 274
  Festival Hall, 81, 280
  Golden Lane, 77, 88
  Langham Hotel, 316
  Lloyd's building, 235–75, *247*, *254–5*, *272–3*
  Mansion House Square, 335–8
  Millbank Riverside scheme, 228, *232–3*
  National Gallery, 164, 282, 306–15, *311*
  Robin Hood Gardens, 271
  Royal Opera House development, 316–20
  St Pancras Station, 62, 171
  Shell Centre, 280, 286
  South Bank, 278–86
  Trafalgar Square, 306–15
  Whittington Avenue, 315–16, *317*
London County Council (LCC), 77, 85
London University, Bartlett School of Architecture, 338–9
Long Island, 288
Loos, Adolf, 59, 61, 269
Loste, Sebastian, 162
Luder, Owen, 310
Lynn, Jack, 77–8
Lyons, Eric, 124

McCoy, Esther, 127
Mackenzie, Colin, 309

Maillart, Robert, 174
Malevich, Kasimir, 177
Mandrot, Hélène de, 69
Manni, Eugenie, 16
Marcus, Stanley, 316
MARS (Modern Architectural Research group), 87, 134
Marschner, Bud, 195
Marta, *52*, 53–4
Martin, Sir Leslie, 134
Martin, Steve, 288
Melbourn, Patscentre, 227, *229*
Menzies, Stuart, 80
Middlesex County Council, 91–2
Mies van der Rohe, Ludwig, 59, 63–4, 77, 101, 106, 170–1, 174–5, 335–6
Miller, J. Irwin, 289
Miller, John, 86, 152, 186, 188
Miller, Peter, 261
modernism, 59–65, 86–7, 169–70
Moholy-Nagy, Laszlo, 170
Mollard, Claude, 222, 224
Mondrian, Piet, 81, 119
Montgomery, Field Marshal, 38
Morris, Andrew, 326
Morris, Hugh, 75
Morris, William, 77
Moser, Karl, 69
Murphy, Stuart, 315
Mussolini, Benito, 15, 16, 54–5

National Service, 49, 50–7
Neoprene, 117
New Brutalism, 77, 78
New Empiricism, 77
New Humanism, 77
New York:
  Hudson Street, 322, *345*
  Lever House, 102
New York Five, 298

Newton, Eric, 72
Nicholson, Ben, 80, 134, 334
Niemeyer, Oscar, 163, 186
Norwich, Sainsbury Centre, 228

Ollins, Wolff, 154
Otto, Frei, 202

PA Design Unit, 287, 299
PA Technology, 227
Pacific Palisades, Eames house, 127
Palumbo, Peter, *304*, 312, 328, 330, 331–3, 335–7
Paolozzi, Eduardo, 76
Paris:
 Les Halles, 161–2, 172, 215, 216
 Maison de Verre, 89, 180–1, 192
 Pompidou Centre, 86, 154–7, 159–219, *167*, *168*, *187*, *198*, *201*, *203*, *204–10*, 221–6, 229, 242, 313–14
Parker, Peter, 128
Pattrick, Michael, 74–5, 84–5, 88
Paxton, Joseph, 172–3, 176
Peacock, Frank, 107, 110, 116–17, 126
Pei, I. M., 237, 238, 289, 316
Pelham, David, 152, 191
Peressuti, Enrico, 54, 73
Perret, Auguste, 61, 62
Perriand, Charlotte, 79
Pettifer, Brian, 251–2, 257
Pettifer, Sheila, 251
Pevsner, Antoine, 80–1
Pevsner, Nikolaus, 60, 72
Pfeiffer, Norman, 302
Philip, Prince, 329
Piano, Renzo, 145, *184*, *213*, *217*, 251, 277, 340

Lloyd's building, 240
Pompidou Centre, 154–219
Piano & Rice, 228
Piano & Rogers, 145–7, 153–219, 228, 235–51
Picon, Gaetan, 163
Pompidou, Georges, 159, 160–3, 190, 215, 221
pop art, 76–7
Popper, Karl, 182
Portsmouth, IBM offices, 228
post-modernism, 225
Powell & Moya, 47
La Pratellina, 15
Price, Cedric, 182–3, 280
Princeton, Patscenter, 298
Pritchett, V. S., 45
Prix de Rome, 92
Prouvé, Jean, 164, 189, 288

Quimper, Brittany, Fleetguard, 288–90, *291*

Radlett, 123
Read, Herbert, 82, 89
Read, Sophie, 82, 115
Regent Street Polytechnic, 133
RIBA, 235–6, 321, 329, 339
Rice, Nemone, 211
Rice, Peter, 186–8, 202–12, 240, 252, 290, 292
Richard & Su Rogers, 135–45, 226
Richard Rogers & Partners, 105–6, 251, 277
Richmond Park, 88
Rietveld, Gerrit, 69
Roche, Kevin, 117, 227, 230, 289, 339
Roche & Dinkeloo, 289
Roehampton, 77, 85
Rogers, Ab (RR's son), *146*, 147, 302–3, *304*
Rogers, Ben (RR's son),

114, 126, *146*, 192, 302–3, *304*, 343
Rogers, Bo (RR's adopted son), 300–6, *303*
Rogers, Ermengarde 'Dada' (RR's mother), 17–34, *21*, *24*, 39, 41–5, 66, 68, 69, 75–6, 141, 150, 185, 338
Rogers, Ernesto (RR's cousin), 16, 18, 42, 45, 46, 54–6, 65, 73, 78, 88, 180, 267
Rogers, Giorgio (RR's uncle), 22, 30, 34
Rogers, Lina (RR's grandmother), 30, *43*
Rogers, Marcello (RR's grandfather), 16, 22, 30, *43*, 46
Rogers, Nino, *see* Rogers, William Nino
Rogers, Paulo (RR's cousin), 316
Rogers, Peter (RR's brother), 33
Rogers, Richard
 architecture:
  at the Architectural Association, 65, 72–88
  awarded Royal Gold Medal, 327–8
  decides to take up, 56–7
  education, 59, 65–88
  factories, 126–32, 226–7, 288–98
  first experience of, 47–8
  gains experience of, 85
  housing, 110–14, 135–43, 227–8, 288
  and interior design, 261–5
  Lloyd's building 235–75
  manifestos, 138–41
  National Gallery, 306–15

partnership, 277–8, 342
Pompidou Centre, 154–7, 159–219, 242
public inquiries, 123, 278–9
steel buildings, 126–32, 138, 200–15, 246, 327
studies in the United States, 93–103
stylistic confusion, 88
teaching work, 133, 151, 338–9
Team 4, 105–33, 135
use of concrete, 253–7
works for DRU, 134–52
works for Middlesex County Council, 91–2
see also individual projects
character:
75, 92–3, 339–47
academic ability, 29–30, 31, 32, 34–5, 36, 46, 88
appearance, 66, 79
clumsiness, 18
courage, 31–2
depressions, 31, 132, 218–19
dyslexia, 31, 51, 302
European sensibility, 45
gregariousness, 31
intelligence, 32
relations with women, 71, 72, 91, 147, 340
early life:
birth, 15
parents' influence on, 19
cultural influences, 19, 39, 42, 45–6
and his mother's family, 20, 44

and his uncle Giorgio, 22
health, 20
moves to England, 22–5
nursery schools, 23, 25
learns English, 23
at boarding school, 26–30
persecution, 28–9, 38–9
the Gang, 32–3, 36–7, 39
discovers girls, 33–4, 39
goes to a crammer, 34–5
St John's School, 35–6, 46
influence of his parents, 75–6
and the Army Cadet Corps, 37–8
family debates, 39–40
political development, 39–40
travels to Italy, 42–6, 49
imprisoned in Venice, 49–50
National Service, 48, 50–6
decides to take up architecture, 56–7
private life:
adopts Bo, 300–2
affair with Ruth, 147–52
becomes a public figure, 287, 329–34
break-up of marriage with Su, 147–51
Chelsea home, 325–7
considers settling in America, 231, 235
exhaustion, 230–1
family life, 299–306, 343

and Georgie Cheeseman, 69–71, 70, 78–9
home life in Paris, 191–5
interest in reading, 39, 75
marries Su, 91
marries Ruth, 192
sport, 35, 36
travel and holidays, 71–2, 151, 153, 301, 305, 306
as a trustee of the Tate, 330–5
work with Ruth, 335–6
Rogers, Roo (RR's son), 192, 193, 231, 239, 300, 301–2, 304, 306
Rogers, Ruth (RR's second wife), 71, 163, 197, 231, 250, 287, 299, 304, 316
background, 147–8
meeting and affair with RR, 147–52
work for Penguin, 152, 191
in Paris, 191–5
RR marries, 192
and paintings for the Lloyd's building, 264–5
illness, 300
adopts Bo, 300–2
work with RR, 335–7
influence on RR, 343–4
Rogers, Su (RR's first wife), 83, 90, 95, 184, 305
family background, 79–82
first meets RR, 79
increasing interest in architecture, 85–6
at LSE, 86, 89–91
marriage, 91
visits the United States, 92–103
and Team 4, 103, 107, 133

first son, 114
family life, 126
work for DRU, 134,
  143
break-up of marriage,
  147, 150–1, 188
and the Pompidou
  Centre, 155, 159,
  186, 188
relations with RR, 188
Rogers, William, (RR's
  great-grandfather),
  15–16
Rogers, William Nino
  (RR's father), 16–34,
  39–40, 41, 42, 46,
  68–9, 75, 141, 275,
  300, 338
Rogers, Zad (RR's son),
  124, 146, 302–3, 304
Royal Fine Arts
  Commission, 249–50,
  282, 283
Rudolph, Paul, 94–6
Russell, Bertrand, 68, 84

Saarinen, Eero, 96, 102,
  106
Saarinen, Eliel, 289
Sainsbury, John, 320
St John's School, 35–6,
  37–9, 46
Sandberg, Willi, 164, 200
Sant'Elia, Antonio,
  178–80
Sartre, Jean-Paul, 68
Schindler, Mrs, 102
Schindler, Rudolf, 102
Scruton, Roger, 296
Scully, Vincent, 97, 102
Sears, 29, 283
Seattle, 320, 322, 341
Serete, 237, 238
Sheppard, Peter, 135
Skidmore, Owings and
  Merrill (SOM), 102,
  289, 309, 320
Smith, Ivor, 77
Smithson, Alison, 76–7,
  78, 126, 271
Smithson, Peter, 76–7,
  78, 86, 87–8, 96, 126,
  271

Sorcinelli, John, 286, 312
Soriano, Raphael, 127
Soundy, Richard, 290
Span, 124
Spender, Humphrey,
  135, 141
Speyhawk, 307, 315–16,
  322
Stam, 69
Stanton, Alan, 199–200,
  247, 330
Stevens, Mark, 222
Stirling, James, 72, 74,
  77, 78, 88–9, 92, 98,
  123, 128, 192, 330,
  333, 335
Sudjic, Deyan, 309
Sullivan, Louis, 59, 61,
  174
Summerson, Sir John,
  86–7, 177
Sutcliffe, Mark, 115
Sutton, school, 126
Swindon, Reliance
  Controls, 126–32,
  136–7, 229, 269, 289,
  340

Tadworth, Universal Oil
  Products, 226–7
Tange, Kenzo, 211
Tate Gallery, 330–5
Tatlin, Vladimir, 177
Taylor, Brian, 66
Taylor, John, 286
Team 4, 81, 103–33, 135
Terry, Quinlan, 267
Texas Gas, 102
Tinguely, Jean, 264–5
Tonks, Henry, 38
La Tourette, 79
Tree, Julie, 33–4, 40, 57,
  69
Trieste, 16–20, 51, 54, 72
Tubbs, Ralph, 47
Tuskegee Institute, 94–6

Ulting, Spender house,
  135–42
Universal Oil Products,
  143, 226–7
Utzon, Jorn, 163

Varnadoe, Kirk, 237
Vellay, Dr, 192
Venice, 49–50
Ventris, Betty, 114
Ventris, Michael, 114
Venturi, Robert, 165,
  175–6
Venturi and Rauch, 289
Vonnegut, Kurt, 300

Warhol, Andy, 182
Waterloo Action Group,
  282
Wates, 107, 123–4, 125
Waugh, Evelyn, 64
Webb Zarafa Menkes
  Housden, 237, 238
Westcott, Deer Leap, 82
Wilkins, William, 306,
  308, 312
Wilkinson, Chris, 286
Wimbledon, house for
  RR's parents, 140,
  141–2
Wittgenstein, Ludwig,
  224, 286, 296, 346
Wittkower, Rudolf, 72
Wolton, David, 103, 148
Wolton, Georgie, see
  Cheeseman, Georgie
Wright, Frank Lloyd,
  59, 61, 63, 98–101,
  106, 117–18, 119, 123,
  127–8, 261

Yale University, 93–102,
  99, 100, 241, 339
Young, John, 109, 113,
  127, 135, 141, 142,
  143, 147, 149, 184,
  226, 235, 263, 277,
  299, 321, 327, 387
  Pompidou Centre, 157,
  185–6, 190, 199, 219
  Lloyd's building, 240,
  241, 251, 253–4,
  257–9, 260, 261,
  274–5

Zip-up House, 82, 143,
  144, 149
Zunz, Jack, 240